Closing the Gap Behind Him . . .

Finally they weren't more than twenty yards apart. They were coming up on a bridge. The Ford pulled a little ahead. The driver took a quick glance at Austen as he went by. Austen recognized the type: he had seen a lot of them in certain bars, talking to the little old Chinese gentlemen who ran the contraband weapons traffic over the border into Cambodia. 'Nam had been full of them. They flew planes or acted as bodyguards or taught the tribesmen up in the Laotian mountains how to use a mortar piece. They were the scariest people in the world.

Suddenly, the red tail lights on the Ford lit up. Austen slammed on the brakes, bracing himself against the wheel as he waited for the impact.

BAM!

But it was more like a small explosion than the tearing of metal. Austen's car began to turn into a skid. God, if he could just keep it on the road . . . All he could do was keep hold of the wheel and pray. The Ford was gone as if it had disappeared. He could see the bridge coming at him . . .

THE
PRESIDENT'S
MAN

NICHOLAS
GUILD

PUBLISHED BY POCKET BOOKS NEW YORK

POCKET BOOKS, a division of Simon & Schuster, Inc.
1230 Avenue of the Americas, New York, N.Y. 10020

Copyright © 1982 by Nicholas Guild

Published by arrangement with St. Martin's Press
Library of Congress Catalog Card Number: 81-16690

ISBN: 0-671-46008-0

First Pocket Books printing August, 1983

10 9 8 7 6 5 4 3 2 1

POCKET and colophon are registered trademarks
of Simon & Schuster, Inc.

Printed in the U.S.A.

THIS BOOK IS FOR MY FRIEND,
TOM E. HUFF,
FOR ALL THE RIGHT REASONS.

Prologue

Dancing with the Devil

I

He had been very careful.

There wasn't any choice. Yesterday afternoon, while buying a few sheets of brown paper and a box of mailing labels from the nice lady at the drugstore, he had happened to notice a couple of goons in a dark blue Chevy, slowing down for a look. They had already made one try and now, apparently, they were out in force; if they spotted him again they weren't going to be at all shy about how they behaved, and it would be just too damn bad for the innocent bystanders. So he had been careful.

He had the package in his coat pocket; it wasn't much larger than a man's billfold, so nobody would spot it. They didn't know about the package. They didn't know what they wanted, except to kill him as quickly as they could and then hope that their problems would go away on their own. But it didn't matter whether they killed him or not—except maybe to him—because once Austen had his final clinching piece of the puzzle, then they could kill anybody they felt like and it wouldn't do them any good.

Except that Austen was in DC, all those thousands of miles away.

He had thought about it all night, worked it all out for himself because it was impossible to sleep—it was hard even to close his eyes. He had just lain there, on his back on the loadbed of a truck some farmer had left parked overnight behind a tiny, dilapidated adobe house—his girlfriend's, apparently; at a quarter to two in the morning he could still hear her high-pitched laughter.

His original idea had been to wait until the post office opened, but that wasn't going to work. Lover Boy would want to be on his merry way well before eight-thirty in the morning. Even your ordinary corner letterbox might not be enough, not if the wrong parties saw you dropping something inside—after all, not everybody believed in the sanctity of the mails.

Once it was done, well, he would just have to try and make a run for it. Maybe he could hotwire a car and find someplace to get himself lost. Maybe somehow he could get down to Sacramento and then catch a plane . . .

But first he had to get rid of the package. Then he could feel at perfect liberty to worry about saving his neck.

There was a bank across the street from his motel; he would settle for that. It had one of those twenty-four-hour card-operated gizmos where you could get a hundred dollars out or deposit your dividend checks anytime you felt like it, and, like most of them, it had a mail slot. Bank buildings were possessed of alarms—they weren't going to try breaking in on the off-chance that he might have left something behind for the postal service.

On the theory that there was no point in risking getting picked up as a vagrant, he waited until five-thirty before he crept out of the truck and started on his way. The sidewalks, of course, were perfectly deserted, and his footfalls seemed to smack down on the pavement with appalling violence. Once or twice a car came swishing by, but he was on the lookout and always managed to dodge out of sight well before the headlights could reach him. When he could, he kept to the alleyways, away from the streetlamps.

It took him better than a half-hour to reach the rear wall of the bank building. The mail slot was right beside the front entrance. The bank was a corner building, and you couldn't have slipped a playing card between it and the liquor store next door. There was nothing for it but to go around by the street side.

Every step of the way he felt indecently exposed. There was a little border of lawn next to the curb; he tried walking on that for a few paces, hoping it would be quieter, but then he thought it just made him more conspicuous and went back to the sidewalk. At the corner the yellow traffic light was blinking—proceed with caution, as if he needed reminding. There didn't seem to be a soul about, but somehow he had never been so scared in his life.

When he reached the corner he almost ran to the mail slot, his hand in his pocket the whole way, gripping the slender little package. As silently as he could, he pushed back the metal cover and shot the package inside. Then he stepped over to the huge stainless-steel grid marked "All-Day, All-Night Banking" and, just for protective coloration, pretended to punch in a number.

Now he was on his own. The bloody thing was off his hands, and he had nothing to look out for except his own precious hide.

He heard the tires squeal behind him and caught himself turning to look. But there was no time for that, no time at all—it didn't help him any to see the red smear of the traffic light reflecting on the front bumper, and the rear window rolling down. But he ran anyway and didn't look back again. It was too late for that, too late for anything, and he didn't want to have to watch it coming.

The wind was blowing due east. Even at the northwest entrance to the White House Frank Austen could feel the damp cold from the Potomac, more than a mile away, as he stepped out of his limousine. He whispered a word of thanks to the Marine sergeant who opened the door for him, smiling as the guy almost twisted his arm out of its socket saluting, and allowed himself a moment to straighten his legs.

He disliked being driven; he had never adjusted very well to being a Washington mandarin, and it made him feel restless. The trip from Langley felt as if it had taken forever instead of slightly less than a quarter of an hour. He was too young to be spending his life on the back seat of a car; that sort of thing was for the dark side of forty, so by rights he should have been safe for three whole months.

The weather had held off all week, but this was the coldest day he could remember so early in November. God—that wind! Standing against it, his hands jammed into the pockets of his black overcoat, he made a tall slender figure, a stranger in any landscape. His lean, ascetic, not-quite-brutal face would never have betrayed him, but one of Frank Austen's best-kept secrets was that he hated cold weather.

He could feel the tightness gathering around his eyes, eyes that even now seemed to laugh at the joke, and he knew that in another few minutes his sinuses would be killing him.

Well, the secret would stay kept—he might be miserable, but he had been blessed in that respect. Fortunately, considering the line of work he had fallen into, he wasn't the type to wear his heart on his sleeve. Life was a joker; he had learned that a long time ago.

"I'll buzz you when I'm ready, Jimmie," he said, bending down for a word with his driver. Jimmie thrust his square blond head through the car window and nodded grimly, just as if he had received an order to pull out the .45 Colt automatic he kept clipped to the underside of the dashboard and use it to punch a nice, symmetrical hole through the Marine, whom he kept glancing at with apparent suspicion. Jimmie was young and took things very seriously. "Pick up Mr. Timmler at the airport and bring him with you. I expect I'll be about an hour and a half—and, Jimmie, check your mail while you're about it."

The limousine crept stealthily off, around the corner of the building and out of sight, and Frank Austen turned to look at the concrete steps that led up under a blue canvas awning to the business entrance to the West Wing.

The huge double doors were as familiar to him as the weary expression he saw every morning in the mirror. They were the back way to power, the only real way, the way you came when it was no part of your object to be chased across the lawn by a crowd of television reporters hungry for a celebrity to put on the six o'clock news. They were the way you came when your business was with the president of the United States and no one else, and in the nearly four years that he had served this particular president they had never lost their power to make him have to wipe his hands dry. He braced himself and marched up the stairs like a man ascending the scaffold.

Even before the guard at the cloakroom had disappeared with his coat, he discovered that Howard Diederich was upon him, the lines of his charcoal-gray suit standing out crisply within the doorframe. He hadn't heard Howard approach, but that was the way with the man—he had the happy knack of simply appearing, smiling his suave, I'm-in-perfect-control-of-the-situation smile, and holding out his hand for you to shake. When you took it, it responded with no discernible pressure; the fingers were lifeless in your grasp.

No one observing these two men together—the ironic courtliness of the one matched against the clipped and gloomy self-restraint of the other—could have avoided the conclusion that they detested one another. Nevertheless, certain necessary fictions had to be maintained. Frank Austen forced himself to look a shade friendlier. "Morning, Howard," he said, glancing furtively at the wall clock to make sure there were at least a few minutes left before noon. "You stay up all night watching the returns?"

"Yes—it was a great triumph." The chief of staff, conscious of himself as the principal architect of that triumph, smoothed his pale gray silk necktie with the flat of his hand and smiled again. It was a peculiarly sly, feline smile. "Most of the West, the entire Northeast, even Ohio. Almost a grand slam. We stayed up until nearly three, but it was all over but the counting long before that. The president is unquestionably the most popular man in the western hemisphere this morning."

What was that, a threat? Under the circumstances it was undoubtedly just that. Howard Diederich, the politician's politician, the confidant and first minister to our newly anointed king, was flexing his muscles ever so slightly. *We* hadn't meant the Herr and the Frau and all the little Diederichs—Howard's children were all grown up, and his ex-wife, about whom Austen had heard only rumors, had been happily married to a swimming pool contractor in Phoenix, Arizona for the last eleven years. No, *we* had been none other than Diederich and his lord and master, sitting in their shirtsleeves in the Oval Office, hunched in front of the television set while they passed the Crackerjacks back and forth and watched John Chancellor hand them another four-year option on the world.

And if *we* wanted your ass, the implication was—even yours, Frank Austen—that meant that *we* could have it.

But it was a peculiar kind of triumph, tasting of self-mockery and the most bitter of wisdoms. Somehow, by some inflection that Austen had never been able quite to pin down, Howard always managed to pronounce the words *the president* as if they were the answer to some private joke.

"Well, then, I should find him in a good mood." Austen arranged the muscles of his face into one of his carelessly unreadable smiles. "Maybe I should grab my chance and hit him up for a raise."

They exchanged a few breathless, unpleasant syllables of laughter, and then Howard—gently, as if the operation required the greatest possible tact—took the director of Central Intelligence by the arm and escorted him down a short corridor and into the office that belonged to the president's appointments secretary, who rose from behind his desk to grasp each of them in a fierce handshake.

It was an interesting moment. Jerry Gorman was one of Howard's little discoveries; taken on as an advance man during the first campaign, he had made enough of an impression to find himself, at the ripe old age of twenty-eight, only a thin walnut door from the holy of holies. That suited Howard, because whatever Jerry found out at his little listening post he told Howard. It also suited Frank Austen, because, as it happened, Jerry was one of his snitches too.

The interesting question was whether Howard knew.

"The son of a bitch," Jerry had whispered one night, resting his head against a grape arbor in the garden of a house rented by the secretary of defense while waiting for his own out in Colorado to sell—it was only the third month of the new administration. "That son of a bitch, he'd have me fitted for a studded collar if he could get one the right size from General Services. That smug bastard."

Jerry hadn't been enjoying himself that evening. When you're an appointments secretary you get invited to all the right parties, but nobody is much interested in talking to you. So he usually found himself with a lot of free time to drink too much and nurse the bruises that were collecting on his ego.

On this particular night, while he waited in the dark for the cool freshness of the April breezes to work their cure, while he stared down at the secretary's grass, lacquered almost black in the thick yellow light of the ornamental gas lamps, Jerry had unburdened his heart to the director of Central Intelligence, who he knew, even as early as those days, was Howard Diederich's principal adversary. He was just drunk enough to be that careless.

Frank Austen had listened, and the next morning he had set in motion some cautious inquiries about Jerry Gorman's relationship with life. You moved slowly in these matters, since there were no guarantees that you weren't being fed a plant, but by the first anniversary of Inauguration Day—a little private party the chief threw for his old stagers—the director could look across the room to where Jerry seemed to be measuring a wastepaper basket to throw up in and know, as well as it was possible to know anything in such a case, that he had that nice boy in his pocket. Revenge and ambition, they were wonderful things, solid and dependable. The only constants in an unsettled world.

But, of course, Howard Diederich knew all about revenge and ambition and—who could say?—might just conceivably know about Jerry Gorman as well. Anything was possible.

Austen squinted nervously at his watch and then at the door that led to the Oval Office. It was still about a minute and a quarter shy of noon, but the president had a well-known obsession with punctuality and it wouldn't have been at all out of character for him to be sitting behind his desk at that precise moment, counting off the seconds on the Seiko quartz watch he reset twice a month against an electronic time signal down in the code room. When Simon Faircliff said, "Come by around twelve and we'll have lunch," *around* was a term of enormous precision.

"Is he in?" Austen asked, turning to Jerry. But Jerry never had a chance to answer, because suddenly the door opened and there *he* was, in a pair of light gray trousers, wearing a cardigan over his white shirt. He grinned as if by the most consummate stealth he had caught all three of them in some ludicrous act, and his eyes settled on the director of Central Intelligence.

"Frank—it's wonderful to see you." He held out his hand, and Frank Austen paced off the eight or ten feet that allowed him to take it.

It was like approaching an idol. Simon Faircliff was a man of considerable physical presence—six three and built on a large scale; he reminded you of a wall. And there was more to it than that. The guy radiated power the way some women do sex appeal. It was like having a light directed into your eyes; he was simply dazzling.

Without so much as a glance at the other two men, the president threw his huge arm across Frank Austen's shoulders like a net, dragging him captive into the next room. When they had crossed the threshold, he pushed the door closed behind him with the flat of his free hand, and they were alone.

"Let's have a look at you, boy," he growled with proprietary affection. "Come over here and sit down. We've got a little time to visit before lunch—you feel like a drink? What'd you think of the returns last night? Wasn't that something? Wasn't that more fun than a damned peep show?"

The president dropped into his oversize padded leather desk chair, bracing his foot up on the edge of the desk as if he were about to push himself away and go rolling back into one of the four ceiling-high windows that stood like sentinels in the curve of the rear wall. It was an attitude Frank Austen had watched him assume often enough over the dozen or so years he had worked for him; it was the Simon Faircliff equivalent of the crouch that precedes the spring. It meant, in that gestured code that communicates what words are so often meant merely to obscure, that his lordship was feeling aggressive.

Austen just smiled, nodding his head behind his folded hands, like a parish priest listening to the plans for the Easter pageant. "I switched it off as soon as CBS gave you the election. Even that much made me feel guilty—the CIA isn't supposed to be interested in partisan politics."

Simon Faircliff threw back his head and laughed at his director's exquisite joke, crowing like a rooster—more in exaltation than anything else, because it hadn't been that funny.

The few seconds in which the president indulged his ecstasy provided a peculiar privacy. Frank Austen found himself, for all practical purposes, alone in the room, and he allowed his gaze to drift across the vast desk—really more of a library table with a few file drawers built under one side—that had ascended with its owner through a succession of House and Senate offices to the absolute focus of government. In another four years, so the plan went, it would be moved again, to the seaside house near Fort Ross in California, and from there, in another fifteen or twenty, to its final resting place in the inevitable Faircliff Memorial Library.

Certainly it didn't look like a museum piece; Faircliff, to his credit, had always cared little for the trappings of power. There were no miniature American flags in marble holders, no bronze medallions encased in plastic, none of that. Just a couple of telephones, a pencil holder, a copy of that morning's *Post*, three disorderly piles of pale blue briefing books, and a color photograph in a stand-up frame of a pretty, blond, eighteen-year-old Vassar freshman, smiling her mystified smile as if wondering what all the fuss was about.

"How is she, Frank?"

The director of Central Intelligence glanced up into the president's face and smiled—their eyes had come inescapably to rest on the same object, almost making her a third. "She's fine, Simon. She sends her love."

"Like shit she does." The sentence was punctuated with a single muted explosion of something that bore only the remotest resemblance to laughter. "I haven't even seen her in over a year—you two live right over the river in Alexandria, and she and I haven't laid eyes on each other more than half a dozen times since I took office. Like shit she sends her love."

Faircliff lapsed into a moody silence; the lined unhappiness of his face reminded you that he really was, after all, sixty-three years old. He stared blindly from under his light brown eyebrows, not expecting a reply, listening to some inner voice telling him, again and again, that nothing in this life is an unqualified pleasure.

"Over forty-seven million people voted for me yesterday," he continued quietly, almost to himself. "I swept the party to the largest congressional majority since Johnson; there probably isn't a more loved man in America at this precise moment; and my own kid can't stand the sight of me. Why the hell does she hate me so much, Frank? What's the big grievance? God, if anybody knows, you ought to."

Austen only shook his head—there was nothing else he could do, really. The truth would serve no one. The truth, in this case, was the last thing anyone would ever wish to hear. "I don't have any idea, Simon." He smiled wanly, shrugging his shoulders. "She doesn't exactly take me into her confidence either, not anymore."

"No, I suppose not."

Then Faircliff smiled his magic election-day smile, and Austen followed his line of sight to a small door that had opened at the other end of the office and turned around to see a solemn-faced black man in a white mess jacket standing there. It was time for lunch.

They followed the melancholy figure into a small dining room, not much larger than one of the staff offices honeycombing that part of the building, where places had been set for them at the near corner of a table covered with a heavily starched white cloth. There was already a Bloody Mary waiting in the center of one of the plates; Austen sat down in front of the other and ordered a glass of ginger ale, just to be companionable.

At first, the conversation tended to be halting and was conducted in murmurs. They talked over all the harmless topics of Washington life—the election results, the probable identity of the Senate minority leader's new mistress, the prospects for any Supreme Court justices doing the decent thing and dropping dead. All the while it was fairly obvious to the trained observer that, even as Faircliff was describing with delicious comic elaboration his opponent's concession statement, he was holding something in. He never glanced at the waiter, who moved back and forth from his serving cart to the table as anonymously as any machine, but he was clearly impatient.

At last, when they were alone with their stuffed pork chops (the president was now officially abandoning his campaign-trail diet), Faircliff cut off a small piece, tasted it, and, without registering any reaction, put his fork down and turned to his director of Central Intelligence exactly as if the meal were over.

"In seven or eight months, I want you to move over to State, Frank. I can't do it now without making it look like some sort of post-election purge, but Harry Towers wants to step down anyway; his wife's sick and he's eager to move her back to Michigan, where she can be near their children. You can name your own successor at Langley, someone you can keep under your thumb after you've made the jump, but I want you to start the briefings as soon as you can—I don't suppose those lounge lizards know much that you don't, but get on it early. Maybe we can make it six months."

"Mr. President, I don't—"

"Piss on it, Frank," he said sharply, brushing the objection aside with an impatient sweep of his hand. "I want you at State, and State is where you go. It'll look better—the public's never really trusted the CIA."

In an instant he seemed to lose interest in everything except what was on the table in front of him. With wonderful deliberation, he cracked open the hard roll that had rested on its own little plate just above his napkin, tearing off a fragment and smearing it with butter. It was an astonishing performance; you might have supposed you were in the presence of some saintly, patient archaeologist scraping away the dust of millennia from a Hittite amulet.

"Simon, what the hell are you talking about?"

"What do you think, stupid?" Faircliff queried slyly, treating Austen to a curious sideways grin. "I've got responsibilities, haven't I? I've got to think of the welfare of the country. We won big last night, kiddo—a rising tide raised all the boats, and those good party stalwarts who won with us, from the Senate right on down to the dogcatcher in Mankato, they all owe us, and they know it. All that loyalty and love, we can't let it go to waste, now can we? I'm going to be the one to settle the destiny of this nation, and I'll decide on my own successor. The people have seen to that. You just wait—when gradually it begins to dawn on everybody that you're the heir apparent, they'll fall all over themselves to smooth the way for you. Just you watch, boy—I'm going to raise you to glory. I'm going to make you the next president of the United States."

Two hours later, when he emerged again into the gloomy midafternoon sunlight, the first thing Frank Austen noticed was the black immensity of his limousine, which was waiting for him just beyond the shadow of the blue awning that was still flapping sulkily over his head. Another Marine, this time a corporal, held the rear door open for him as he slipped inside, where he shared the seat with the slight, gray, wistfully smiling form of his deputy director, George Timmler.

"Did it come yet, Jimmie?"

The blond head shook back and forth without turning around. "No, sir."

"Then take us back to Langley," he snapped, touching a button that raised a smoked glass screen behind the driver's seat, sealing the two compartments off from one another. George, whose hands were folded together in his lap, turned ever so slightly in the direction of his master, simultaneously raising his eyebrows perhaps a sixteenth of an inch.

"You're looking peevish today," he said evenly. "What did the great man want?"

"You won't like it."

"All right."

The limousine started up; you couldn't really hear the

engine, only feel a slight vibration that came up through the soles of your shoes; and the Marine corporal saluted. George Timmler looked straight ahead, as if the subject of Austen's meeting had been dismissed from his mind. Perhaps it had—George had been on a plane from Los Angeles since the very crack of dawn; perhaps his mind was simply numb.

"I've been nominated to be the crown prince. We go by easy stages, first Foggy Bottom, then the White House. He loves me like a son, so I get to inherit the family business."

George continued to stare through the glass partition at the dim outline of Jimmie's head, as if not a word had registered, and then, very slowly, his lips pursed out, and he emitted a low whistle.

"I told you you wouldn't like it."

"The question is, do *you* like it? What are you going to do, take him at his word? I wouldn't blame you a bit."

"Wouldn't you?" Austen allowed himself a pained smile. "I know you've never quite approved of me, George—no, save yourself the trouble. Personal considerations aside, you've never really thought of me as a certified Company man and you've been right. I've always been Simon Faircliff's man, just another slimy opportunist. Slimier than most, probably. But not that slimy, George. Not quite slimy enough to go for this number."

George reached over and patted him lightly on the knee with a bony, fragile-looking hand. "I've always thought you were one of the nicer slimy opportunists. You see Howard Diederich's fine hand in this, I take it."

Austen nodded. "It's got his fingerprints all over it."

"But you didn't tell him flat out that you weren't buying."

"No. No, if I did anything like that the cat would really be out of the bag."

"Then you think Diederich suspects already?"

The expression on Austen's face revealed nothing whatsoever. Inside, he could feel his heart dissolving into a cold trickle that seemed to be collecting somewhere down around his bowels, but he tried to keep any of that from registering.

"He's no fool, you know—that's what all this has been about. He's trying to buy us off before it's too late."

II

When Michael Starkman was shot down in front of the Oroville Bank and Trust, it happened that only two people, across the street at the International House of Pancakes, witnessed the murder. Six-fifteen was usually a little early for the breakfast trade. At that hour, as a general rule, there were just a few early risers from the motel next door, so the police had only the waitress who was working the tables along the front window and a farm implements salesman up from Los Angeles . The salesman had just sat down and hadn't even had his coffee yet, a fact that seemed to weigh extraordinarily heavily with him, and the waitress, even three-quarters of an hour after the fact, still couldn't quite be made to understand what had taken place.

Actually, neither of them had had more than a quick glimpse; they had merely heard the screech of tires and looked up to see a man collapsing on the sidewalk. The assailants might have been creatures from Mars for all they knew, and they couldn't agree on a description of the car. Really, they hadn't seen anything much, except a guy bleeding all over the curbstone through the hole where his lower jaw had been.

Officer Wagnells took it all down very carefully anyway. Oroville didn't get a murder more than once every two or three years, and now there were two real corkers within twenty-four hours of each other, both involving strangers, so he was conscious of the need for more than routine thoroughness as he listened to the thin, quavering voice of the dealer in thresher blades and automatic seed drills:

"He just seemed to come apart—just spun around, his arms flying and pieces of him going off every which way. There was so much blood in the air you would have thought they gunned him down with a paint sprayer."

At this point the waitress, who had been softly whimpering the whole time, found it necessary to hide behind her dishtowel. She was a solid enough looking haystack blonde in her mid-forties, but apparently this sort of thing was just too much for her, and she trembled like tomato aspic. Officer Wagnells couldn't blame her in the least.

"Miss," the salesman went on, his voice low and apologetic as he turned away from the policeman who was sitting across the table from him, making heavy penciled notes in the pages of a tiny memo book. "I think I'll just pass on the blueberry waffles, if you don't mind."

Outside, with his memo book stuffed into the pocket of his shirt, Wagnells could see that almost nothing had happened since he had arrived from headquarters. The county forensics man, who was still picking slugs out of the stucco wall, was the only person in sight who seemed to have any clear idea of what he should be doing. It wasn't at all the sort of thing anyone was used to. The body still lay exactly where it had fallen, covered with a tarpaulin.

Wagnells, whose wife, for the best reasons in the world, was always hounding him to go on a diet, squatted down awkwardly next to one corner of the tarp and picked it up for another look. He had been with the police for twenty-eight years, and not since his stint with the paratroopers, when he had done an eighteen-month tour of duty in Korea, had he ever seen a gunshot victim to compare with this one. He had to keep convincing himself that it was real—that it was even possible.

"Jesus Christ," he whispered to himself. A shadow fell across the sidewalk next to him, and he looked up into the disapproving eyes of his duty sergeant, who seemed to be regarding the corpse with something like resentment. Wagnells shook his head and looked down again. "What'd they use on the poor bastard, do you suppose? Get a load o' that—it looks like somebody's been tryin' to dig holes in his face with an axe."

"Cover him up again, Charlie. We don't want to frighten the tourists. You find out anything useful inside?"

Charlie Wagnells stood up and hooked a thumb over his heavy woven-leather utility belt, still shaking his head. "Nah. They didn't see nothin'. Maybe somebody oughta talk to 'em again when they settle down some, but I don't think we're gonna get anything we can use from those two."

The two men stared down at the lumpy but recognizably human outline covered by the pale tan tarpaulin.

"Any idea who he is yet?"

"Not a clue." The sergeant, a thin, dissatisfied-looking man, kept plucking at the sleeve of his heavy leather jacket with a hand that reminded you unpleasantly of a hairy, agile spider. "He doesn't have a thing on him, not even a set of car keys. There's plenty of money in his wallet but nothing else; looks like the guy didn't believe in credit cards."

"Look at this."

They turned to the county forensics man standing a little behind Officer Wagnells. In the palm of his hand were nestled eight or ten twisted little pieces of dully shining metal.

"About nine millimeter, I figure—they must've drilled the points. No wonder his head's nearly torn off."

The sergeant picked up one of the fragments of lead and held it up in front of his eye for a closer inspection. With every passing second his sense of personal affliction seemed to grow. "A nine-millimeter submachine gun using hollow-point bullets. This ain't no jealous husband we got on our hands."

The men from the coroner's office began the work of transferring the corpse to a body bag and then into the back of their wagon. They left behind a sizeable pool of blood that overran the patch of grass along the curb and trickled into the street; the fire department would have to send someone out to hose that away if they didn't want the dogs getting at it. The sergeant gave the forensics man back his tiny piece of evidence and touched Charlie Wagnells on the arm.

"First that guy in the elevator at the Ramada Inn, and now this," he said, his voice almost toneless. "Let's go back to the office; there's nothing more we can do hanging around here."

As they walked toward their squad car, the sergeant jammed his hands into the pockets of his leather jacket, and his gaze hunted morosely over the pavement. During the ride he was silent, staring at the few inches of carpeted car mat between his shoes. They eased into their parking space beside the rear entrance, and Officer Wagnells twisted around on his bulging waist and viewed his superior with perplexed concern.

"What's the matter, Sarge? You worried that it might take us a while to nail these guys?"

"Charlie, we ain't gonna nail anybody." He smiled grimly and continued his close inspection of the floorboards. "We're just a couple of small-town hick policemen, and we ain't gonna get anywhere near an arrest. These guys were real pros—they're probably a hundred miles away by now and still moving. I just keep wondering what made it worth their while to come all the way up here. I just keep wondering who our John Doe was and what he could have done to make anybody that mad at him."

Two months after his marriage, Frank Austen had purchased a house in Alexandria. In those days he was only a senatorial aide, drawing a salary that hovered just below eighteen thousand a year, but money hadn't been a problem. The late Mrs. Faircliff, whom Austen had never met, had belonged to a cadet branch of one of the old California railroad families, and the Austens had found themselves able to manage quite comfortably with a three-bedroom colonial that backed onto the Potomac River. Dorothy Austen suffered from allergies, and a doctor had told her husband that being close to the water would be good for her, although she continued to spend about seven months of the year being forced to choose between, on the one hand, runny eyes and a constant buzzing sound in her head and, on the other, something like narcolepsy brought on by the antihistamines. The two extra bedrooms were supposed to have filled up with the children they were going to have, but that had been another disappointed expectation.

Nevertheless, the house had a flagstone terrace overlooking a lawn that sloped down to the river's edge, and on nice evenings you could sit out there with a drink in your hand and listen to the waves lapping against the shore line after the occasional speedboat went tearing by. And when the evenings weren't so nice you could sit in your study behind the big picture window and watch the naked tree limbs, like the gnarled, arthritic fingers of old women, as they answered with a kind of palsied spasm to the irregular wind. Frank Austen spent a great deal of his time in his study when he was home, much of it staring out through the picture window as he nursed a ginger ale and considered the complexities of public and private life and the difficulties, sometimes, of distinguishing between the two.

He was alone at the moment. If he had ventured onto the minstrel's gallery at the top of the stairway to the second floor and dropped a quarter down to the tiled floor of the entranceway, the whole house would have tinkled like a bell. His wife was gone.

They slept in separate rooms, so she wouldn't disturb him

if she happened to return late; it was an arrangement he had grown so used to that he hardly resented it anymore. Besides, there were times when the perfect privacy afforded by his failed marriage had its compensations, when the public business virtually demanded it.

Espionage was not a profession that allowed you to take work home from the office. Most of the files in the vaults at Langley couldn't be removed from the premises, not even by the director himself, and everyone was discouraged from leaving the wadded-up first-drafts of reports and memos in their study wastepaper baskets, where they would be carted out with the trash and, doubtless, retrieved and read by whoever the poor slob was in the Russian embassy whose duties included pawing his way through official Washington's garbage. So you worked within the semisecurity of the CIA compound, and that way you didn't have to worry about whether your cleaning woman or the wife of your bosom or your ten-year-old son qualified as an acceptable security risk. It made life simpler.

But there were always exceptions. As everybody knew, Frank Austen was not merely, or even most importantly, the director of Central Intelligence; he was also Simon Faircliff's son-in-law and, in contravention of the Agency's charter and even of normal administrative lines of command, a founding member of the Faircliff cabal, one of the inner voices to which the president always listened before making any significant political decision. Austen was the president's fair-haired boy. He was trusted, so the story went, with things that lay well outside his official province. There was always work that was too sensitive even for Langley.

Thus it was that once a month a team of Company specialists came by the three-bedroom colonial to sweep it for listening devices, and the telephone in Austen's study was equipped with a government-issue scrambler. He even had a wall safe, but he had never been stupid enough to leave anything there; nothing was ever committed to paper long enough to require storage.

The remaining contents of the study were prosaic enough: a small table supporting a heavy glass ashtray that had never seen service; a couple of chairs, one of them a thronelike affair of oak veneer and Naugahide—J. C. Penny Imperial, according to Dottie Austen, who had actually bought the thing at one of the tonier department stores in Chevy Chase; a bookcase filled with the eighteenth- and nineteenth-century novels that had been Austen's principal recreation ever since college; and, on the inlaid leather desktop, a framed photograph identical to the one on the desk in the Oval Office. Written in the corner, just above the signature, was *"Facilis descensus averno"*—easy is the descent into Hell. A wedding present, Dottie's only half-joking suggestion for the family motto. Perhaps, after all, they should have had it inscribed in letters of fire over the front door.

So while her husband sat alone in the study of their empty house, watching the pale green telephone on his desk as if he expected it to explode, he was not entirely without companionship. Dottie was there with him, repeating over and over again the warning with which she had begun their married life: easy is the descent into Hell.

Of course, she was always issuing warnings. It was part of her style. "Daddy called this morning," she had said only the evening before. They sat on opposite sides of a circular glass kitchen table, over a pair of Chinese TV dinners and a bottle of rather good German white wine; it was uncharacteristically cozy and intimate, the way it had been that whole last year of his bachelorhood, when Dottie used to smuggle herself up to his three-room apartment for beer and pizza and heavy breathing. But that had all been a long time ago. It was difficult now to believe it had ever happened.

He didn't say anything. He merely looked attentive and waited. It was an old and settled grudge between those two, and he had learned from experience how much he had to lose from seeming to take sides.

"He wanted to talk about you, naturally. We started out with the routine about how he missed his baby girl and just wanted to hear the sweet sound of my voice, but he got around to the other fast enough. It seems you're to be the new secretary of state, so what's the problem?"

She leaned forward on her elbows, resting her head on the backs of her hands, and her large, lustrous brown eyes grew even larger, giving her pixyish face a faintly mocking expression. In the old days it might have been a come-on, but now it was simply a challenge for him to sally forth and do battle yet once more for his sworn liege, the wicked king Simon. That was why she hated him, because he had pledged his faith not only to her but to her father as well, and it seemed that the two loyalties could never be reconciled.

"I'm a spy, not a diplomat," he said finally, picking up the pale green wine bottle and making something of a show of seeing whether there was enough left for another couple of glasses. There was. Apparently the period of truce was over, or perhaps he had misunderstood from the beginning and it had never really begun. In either case, he was weary in advance.

"But it's not just that, is it?" She picked up her glass, holding it delicately around the rim with just the tips of her thumb and first finger, and peered inside as if she expected to see her reflection in the wine. Then she set the glass down again and seemed to forget all about it; it was one of those little actions that appear to have some sort of meaning and don't, that are only something to do when, for the moment, you don't want to mean anything.

She glanced up at her husband suddenly, giving the impression that she had momentarily forgotten he was there in the room with her, and smiled. It wasn't a very encouraging smile. "He wants something more, doesn't he. And you don't want to give it to him. That must be a novel experience for you both."

"He wants me to succeed him. State will give me better visibility with the voters while the party figures out that I'm the one Simon wants them to nominate next time. There—I thought that would surprise you."

Neither of them spoke for a moment. In fact, neither of them even moved; they might both have been listening for some faint sound from the outside. And then, very gradually, by a process that didn't seem to involve discernible change, Dottie's face grew rigid with contempt.

"I doubt if he thinks that much of you. It must be one of his practical jokes; he just doesn't think you're either that smart or that tough."

"I'd agree with him—and with you. I'm not either one. But that's what he says he wants." Austen shrugged his shoulders and took a sip of the wine. He seemed hardly to taste it at all.

"And you'll do it, won't you. You'll stall, but you'll go through with it just the same. Even to this you won't say no."

In his study, alone in the house, Austen shook his head and smiled at the photograph of his wife, the way he hadn't been able to when she was really there in front of him. "This time, baby," he murmured, "this time it'll be no."

He had forgotten to put a coaster under his ginger ale, and beads of condensation were running down the sides of the glass onto his leather desktop. It would make a ring and the cleaning lady would be furious. He smiled and took out his handkerchief to wipe up the water.

He was almost ready to put in the call himself when, finally, the telephone registered a muffled buzzing sound. He picked up the receiver and put it to his ear but didn't speak.

"Frank? Is that you, Frank?"

"It's me, George—how did they turn out?" He shifted uncomfortably in his chair and looked out through the picture window at the leafless trees that stood along the river's edge, frighteningly aware that he had just reached the absolute turning point in his life, and perhaps in the life of the whole nation.

"Perfect," came the reply. "This clinches it. We could even prove our case in a court of law, God forbid."

"It'll never come to that. It can't be allowed to come to that. Put the stuff in deep storage and tell Mike to come home. We'll have to give him a medal or buy him lunch or something. He's done good work."

There was one of those unpleasant pauses, about a second and a half in which you know you have said something terribly wrong, and Austen found himself actually holding his breath.

"Mike isn't coming home," George said slowly, almost as if the words were being extorted from him one at a time. "I got the word an hour ago from one of our people in Justice. The Oroville police sent in a request for fingerprint identification this morning; no details, just a John Doe murder victim. The switch was made, and they'll get the card on one of those Mafia apes that dropped out of sight last year. I guess they must have zapped him right after he made his drop."

"Yeah."

But you didn't sit around and chat about your fallen comrades—it was against the etiquette of the profession—and certainly not over the phone. Even with the scrambler, the conversation was supposed to be as unspecific as possible, so they observed about five seconds of respectful silence before George asked for his instructions.

"Bury the stuff good," the director found himself saying. "You know the drill—assume they'll have you by the balls within the hour. I'll know where to look. Good night, George."

He replaced the receiver on its cradle and sank back into his chair, suddenly very sorry for everybody. Sorry for Mike, who was dead out in California. Sorry for George, whose special protégé Mike had been. Sorry for the whole fucking rest of the world. Sorry, in fact, for everyone except himself. In his case, it would turn out to be nothing more than simple justice.

His wife, staring at him from her brass and walnut frame, caught his eye and seemed to direct him to the warning she had left out in plain sight for him. *Facilis descensus averno*. Well, she had been right about that—the road down had been easy enough.

Part One

The Road Down

I

It had all started twelve years ago with a plane ride.

In those days the air fare from San Francisco to Los Angeles was $21.90, or just about one-fifth of all the money Frank Austen had left in this wide world after paying his next two weeks' room rent, but there was what looked like a pretty fair shot at a job with one of the better-connected Wilshire Boulevard law firms if he could just get his ass down there by four o'clock that afternoon. At least, they had made it sound like a pretty fair shot.

Austen had shaved, showered, gotten his one and only suit back from the dry cleaners, driven himself over to the airport from his third-floor Berkeley walk-up, and picked up his ticket all within about an hour and three quarters. His flight left at two minutes after twelve—lots of time.

So instead of standing in some snack-bar line for a wilted, overpriced sweet roll and a paper cup of watered orange juice, he had found himself a seat in the passenger lounge, where, after the compulsory but hopeless effort to interest himself in the book on courtroom procedure he had brought along for window dressing, he resigned himself to the only topic that seemed capable of commanding his attention at all anymore, the bleakness of his prospects. It was like a litany of desperation: has our boy Frank made a mess of his young life? Yes indeed, he certainly has.

Six months out of the army and, if this afternoon fell

through, he had his nose right up against the wall. He couldn't seem to get it together; he had already failed the bar exam twice, once the month before he had been drafted and now again, six weeks ago. To be honest, he had never been a particularly distinguished student of jurisprudence. Things had come to such a pass that he had begun to consider whether he ought to reenlist. The army had been sort of fun—at least there he had known where he was.

Probably because he hadn't passed his bar exam, his application for posting to the inspector general's office had been ignored, and he found himself a second lieutenant in the military police, assigned to counterintelligence. Maybe they had known something he hadn't, because it was like a very sophisticated game of cops and robbers, and he learned quickly enough that he had a certain flair for it. He spent a little over two years in Saigon, setting up wiretaps on visiting congressmen and cutting deals for information with the Chinese opium traders who crossed back and forth over the border into Cambodia exactly as if the Vietcong didn't exist. When he was ready to be sent home, it took him a full two weeks to introduce his successor to his network of snitches. While it lasted, it was a rich, full life.

But it was a long stretch to lie fallow. He had taken the more important volumes of his law library with him when he was shipped overseas, but somehow there never seemed to be much time—the truth was, perhaps, that he hadn't wanted there to be time—and he discovered, while packing up his footlocker the night after his noisy farewell dinner at Madam Nang's frowsy little brothel just off the Street of the Red Flowers, that the bindings were rotted through and infested with little insects that fell to the floor in showers like fine dust if you hit the covers against the edge of a table. He ended up wrapping the whole bunch of them in a plastic garbage bag and leaving them in the back alley with the melon rinds and the empty catsup bottles.

As he sat by himself in the PSA flight lounge, he was the victim of very mixed feelings indeed. Officially, he wanted this slot at Barton & Cambiner so bad he could taste it; it would be just what he needed to pull his act into shape. There was, however, a part of him that dreaded this final wedding to prosperous, impregnable respectability.

But the dark powers always seem to provide us with the means for surrendering to our lesser selves. In this case their instrument was Pete Freestone. Apparently it had to be that way, because suddenly there Pete was, as if he had been implied in the dawning of creation, dressed in an appalling kelly-green sport coat, smiling and waving a pudgy hand at Austen from in front of the cigarette machine. That they should just happen to run into each other on that particular morning, that they should find themselves booked on the same flight to Los Angeles, was something that Austen had long since given up ascribing to the time and chance that happeneth to us all.

Poor Pete. He was one of the nicest guys in the world, about as earnest and unsinister a person as it was possible to imagine. They had known each other ever since college when, one dark night in the middle of exam week, this fat kid from the *Daily Californian* had come around to Austen's dorm room to interview him for an article on student reaction to the free speech movement and the attendant riots, about which, of course, Austen cared less than nothing. They had talked until after two in the morning—about everything but the free speech movement, as it turned out.

In those days Pete, like everybody else, had worn his hair almost to the shoulders, and he had made quite a picture, sitting there on the foot of the bed, his eyes seeming to bulge out of his round face, carrying on the conversation with his whole body and sweeping that great mane of lank brown hair out of his face every few seconds the way someone might open a pair of curtains.

They met again in Saigon, where Pete was a staff correspondent first for *U.S. News & World Report* and then for the *Los Angeles Times*. There the relationship had broadened—and so, predictably, had Pete.

When it had happened to be in both their interests, they would sometimes trade scraps of information, and they learned, in the process, that within certain reasonable limits they could trust each other. A wary respect developed between the squeaky-clean reporter with the double chins and the angular MP whose work was carried on without much reference to the law. It was the sympathy of opposites.

And now here he was. Like a genie out of a bottle.

Austen waved back and, after the obligatory shoulder slapping was over, arranged to have their seating assignments together on the flight down.

"You still with the *Times?*"

"Yeah." Pete Freestone smiled and made a gesture of comic resignation. "They've got me on local politics—I think the idea is I'm supposed to decompress slowly after 'Nam. I got sick of Thieu's press conferences, but mostly I got sick of the food, I think. I left about a month after you did. You still with the army?"

Austen shook his head. "Believe it or not, I'm on my way to get interviewed for a job with a law firm."

"I don't believe it."

"Neither do I."

The plane began boarding, and Pete, in his preoccupied, roundabout way, got on a rather rambling story about what he had been doing up in San Francisco.

"I can hardly credit the guy," he was saying as the stewardess wheeled by with her stainless-steel water wagon and he ordered himself a drink—probably just for the sake of the little tin of peanuts that came with it. Austen settled for a complimentary ginger ale. "He's up to his eyebrows in this thing and so far, except for me, nobody seems to have noticed. He's on the ballot for the primary next month—unopposed, I might add, except for some horse's ass of an L.A. city councilman no one's every heard of—and there's every chance in the world, what with the way they love the man down in Orange County, he might even be able to beat Simon Faircliff. Who knows?—with a little luck, instead of sending a great man to the Senate next November, California might just elect its first full-fledged labor racketeer. Wouldn't that be nice?"

"Is Simon Faircliff a great man, then?" Austen smiled. It had been an axiom in Saigon that politicians were Yahoos, a kind of degenerate subspecies that smelled bad and liked to throw dirt. If you were a cop, or even a reporter, you were supposed to have figured out a long time ago that there were no heroes in the world.

Pete didn't even look embarrassed.

"Yes," he said, nodding his head the way someone does in assenting to a self-evident proposition. "Yes, I think it's safe to say that Simon Faircliff is a great man; at least, he might develop into one if he ever gets the chance. He's done a good job in Congress, and he seems to think there might be one or two things in the world more important than just hanging onto his office. Yes, he's like a breath of fresh air. You—"

"All right. Okay." Austen raised his hands in surrender. "Congressman Faircliff is a regular prince, and his opponent is a fink and a gangster. Fine. So if you know all this, why don't you blow the whistle on the little creep? I thought that was what newspapers were for."

Freestone pressed himself back into his seat and stared sullenly at the vodka and tonic on the little fold-down tray in front of him.

"That's the part I like best. I know it all, but I can't prove a word of it. My paper tells me it doesn't particularly want to get sued. I even know, at least I'm pretty sure, that there's to be a meet sometime in the next two weeks where he'll be with the man himself, but what am I supposed to do—follow him around in my tinny little blue Volkswagen until he slaps a court order on me to leave him alone? My paper won't provide the manpower for a full-scale, twenty-four-hour-a-day blanket over the guy—we wouldn't even know how to do a thing like that without getting caught—and I can't tell them exactly where or when. So probably, unless I get ridiculously lucky, he'll slip through and I might as well have never known about it in the first place. You sure you're out of the cloak-and-dagger business, Frankie?"

They laughed—it was a big joke—and Austen nodded and said yes, he was sure. "Besides," he went on, "we're in the States now. All that kind of thing's illegal over here. I mean, actually against the law, like precious little ever was in Saigon. I could go to jail. So could you."

"Yeah. I suppose so. Hey, is that the ground down there? God, I hate landings—they're the worst part."

But the plane didn't crash, and they separated in front of the terminal building. Somebody was there to pick up Freestone; Austen thought he would have time enough to wait for a bus instead of shelling out for the cab fare, so they promised each other they would get together again sometime or other.

The long ride up Crenshaw Boulevard, once he got away from the sound of the planes overhead, was a kind of ordeal by concentration. By some quirk he was almost the only person on the bus as it lumbered along past the pizza parlors and the karate studios and the used-car lots; each time it wheezed to a stop the doors would open to let in a gasp of stale, hot air smelling of asphalt, but no one ever seemed to get on or off. It was possible to imagine the journey would be endless, and Austen was not above hoping that it would be. He was suffering through an agony of dread.

"Mr. Dunstable can't see you now; your appointment isn't until four o'clock." The receptionist peered at him from behind her desk, exactly as if she were some sort of mechanical device.

"I know. I'll just wait if you don't mind."

He perched himself on a loveseat covered with what looked like blue burlap and, just for appearances, picked up a magazine from the coffee table in front of him. He was going to be good as gold.

An hour later he was back on the street; the interview had lasted exactly seventeen minutes. They had already decided on their candidate, if he was any judge, and it obviously wasn't Frank Austen.

You have terminal cancer, my boy. The harelip can never be repaired, all your underwear got shrunk at the laundry, and your best girl has run away to Norman, Oklahoma with a three-legged Bible salesman. He couldn't imagine why he was so fucking surprised.

He should have known from the first moment, when he first entered the room and Mr. Dunstable didn't come out from behind his desk to shake hands. He got a nod and a "Good afternoon, Mr. Austen," and that was it. In fact, the man hardly looked at him, confining himself instead to alternately making little penciled checkmarks on the front of a manila folder and tapping the eraser against his desktop. He simply wanted to get rid of him as soon as he decently could. It wasn't something he even bothered to disguise.

"Your difficulties with passing the bar . . ." Tap, tap, tap went the eraser head.

"Well, ah, I think you could say it was a matter of timing. In the first instance I just wanted a crack at it before I got drafted, and in the second I had gotten so far away from all that . . . The army didn't leave me much chance for . . ."

"And your precise duties at that time were—"

"Classified." Austen smiled, perhaps a little thinly. "I'm sorry, but I can't discuss any of that. All that's classified."

Mr. Dunstable frowned, making a few more checkmarks on the folder, and pursed his lips as if in the presence of some palpable falsehood. Or maybe he just didn't like being told that something was none of his business.

And so it went.

"Well, certainly we'll be in contact as soon as we feel we have a suitable opening," he had said, standing up and extending his right hand like an object offered for measurement. The human touch at last—perhaps it was meant to be some sort of consolation prize.

Austen had no idea how far he had walked along Wilshire Boulevard before the sight of a cement and wood-slat bench next to a bus stop reminded him of how tired he was. According to his watch it was nearly quarter to six, and he couldn't remember having eaten anything the night before. There was a Zim's directly across the street.

A hamburger and a large glass of iced tea didn't make him any cheerier. He felt restored, but not to favor with the world. "As soon as we feel we have a suitable opening." Who did he think he was kidding, the prick?

All right. If they wanted to play hardball they might discover that that sort of thing was very much in Frank Austen's line. After paying his tab, he went back to the public telephone and put in a call to the *Los Angeles Times*. Pete Freestone was out, probably gone for the day, but when he showed up for work the next morning he would find the message.

II

"You see the situation?"

They were sitting on Pete Freestone's sofa with the newspaper clipping file spread out in front of them on the coffee table, where it competed for space with empty beer cans and a couple of bowls of potato chips. Pete had very definite ideas about keeping your strength up for the ordeal.

Yes, in outline it was clear enough what had happened. It seemed that the current attorney general for the state of California, a man named Edward Tilson, had once, some years before entering public life, committed the unpardonable blunder of accepting a favor from one Giancarlo Salvarini. The precise nature of this favor would probably never be discovered, but since Mr. Salvarini had begun life as a coat holder for Albert Anastasia and had only decided to test the promise of the West after that gentleman's assassination in a barber's chair in 1957, the possibilities were endless.

"He's a real dinosaur," Pete assured his friend, his fingers disappearing into the potato chips. "He goes around on crutches because somebody blew half his spine away in a gang war back in the late forties. He's the genuine article—a real old-fashioned crime czar."

Austen nodded and continued studying the faces in the news photos. He could see how it might have happened. Perhaps at the time Mr. Tilson hadn't considered the matter very serious, just some trivial emergency for which you procured the services of the nearest professional thug, but if so he had been mistaken. Giancarlo Salvarini looked like someone who had learned very early the advantages of keeping a tight hold, and doubtless over time, favor had followed favor. Somehow you never got to pay these things back; link was forged upon link until the weight of the chain made itself felt.

Yes, indeed, we all knew what that was like. Austen closed his eyes for a moment to concentrate on the throbbing that seemed to center just behind them. It had been a long day. He had never made it back to Berkeley; he had picked a motel out of the phone book—the one that happened to be closest to the restaurant from which he was calling—and had left the number with the girl at the *Times*. Twenty minutes after he checked in, Freestone was on the line, and they had been at it ever since. It was only quarter after eight in the evening, but he felt as if he hadn't seen a bed in days.

But enough of that—it was Salvarini he had to think about now. You were dealing with an empire. Salvarini's interests were nothing if not extensive—he was rumored to have a hand in everything from the cocaine trade to the recording industry—but the particular piece of business that had led him to the brink of a grand jury indictment was a reasonably small-change operation, nothing more than a sideline.

By that not-very-mysterious process by means of which the strong tend to absorb the weak, Salvarini had found himself in possession, two or three years previously, of what amounted to an underground railroad through which illegal Mexican labor was provided to some of the lettuce ranches and vineyards in the central part of the state. And, needless to say, Salvarini's organization collected a brokerage fee at both ends of the transaction.

But perhaps the scheme hadn't appealed to the artist in him, or perhaps he hadn't had any faith that there was ever going to be any real money in it. Certainly there had never been any particular shortage of desperate, exploitable wetbacks around, so the growers weren't without sources of their own, and, God knew, Salvarini's ideas of an acceptable margin of profit were anything but modest. In any case, he turned the management of the thing over to one of his lieutenants and, apparently, forgot all about it.

He must have forgotten about it, because it came as enough of a shock to him when twenty-three Mexicans from one of his consignments were found wandering around half-dead in the middle of the Anza-Borrega Desert, and it came as quite a shock to everybody when the authorities were led back to where the bodies of another twelve were strewn out over the sand like pieces of driftwood on a beach. The survivors, when they were feeling up to it again, proved understandably spiteful and talkative. The chain of incrimination led very quickly up to Salvarini's lieutenant, who, in turn, offered to testify against the boss in exchange for immunity from prosecution. It was all very uncomfortable.

And it was from this difficulty that Salvarini expected Edward Tilson to rescue him.

"Awkward, isn't it." Pete Freestone lifted up an empty beer can that was beginning to leave a damp circle over the newspaper account of Tilson's announcement for the Senate and, apparently not knowing what else to do with it, set it down on the floor. "The grand jury convenes again in two weeks, and the only chance Salvarini's got is to have it all quashed right there. We're talking about a big fall here. We've got twelve dead Mexicans, which means, in addition to the racketeering charges, they could tack on an additional twleve counts of felony murder. And with somebody like Salvarini, either they leave him alone or they throw the book at him. Tilson wants to settle for nailing the lieutenant, who's already said enough to put himself on death row, but he's under heavy pressure from his staff. They want to go for the brass ring, and a couple of them are ready to resign and make no end of a public stink if their boss chickens out. Remember, he's only a month away from the primary, and he's *supposed* to be a lead-pipe cinch—he doesn't need this."

"So Salvarini will want to be reminding him whom he's

supposed to be more afraid of. Or is that putting it too crudely?"

Pete gave a little astonished laugh and shook his head. "My friend, it's a bit difficult to put things too crudely where this particular *Siciliano* is concerned. He learned his trade in a rough school; I wouldn't want to be Tilson for the next two weeks."

"How did you put all this together?"

Pete grinned—he was such a clever boy. "I was doing background interviews on the campaign—you know the sort of stuff; what a saint the great man is to work for—and I had a couple of quick drinks with a guy in the organized crime section who wanted to know why the AG was being so very kind to Giancarlo Salvarini. It really bothered him. He didn't have any answers and neither did I, and it didn't seem very likely that Tilson would be terribly illuminating. So about three weeks ago I was up in San Francisco for an exclusive with Simon Faircliff, and on a hunch I went to see whether his wife would have anything to say about it."

He saw the puzzled expression on Austen's face and smiled, getting up to disappear into the little kitchenette for another couple of beers.

"Tilson's wife, stupid—Faircliff's wife died about three years ago." His voice sounded hollow behind the refrigerator door. "Mrs. Tilson was very forthcoming. It seems that Edward's moved out on her and wants a divorce as soon as the election's over; he's got himself a girlfriend about half his age, and the wife isn't real pleased about it.

"Anyway, the wife knew about the Salvarini connection. Not much—she seemed to think the Don might have helped her husband cover up some old hometown scandal. But she knew enough to bring everything else into focus. Can you imagine anybody being that dumb, letting his wife in on a secret like that and then walking out on her a month before announcing for the Senate?" Pete reappeared in the doorway, laughing softly to himself.

"She was ripe to spill her guts," he went on, offering a can of Hamms. "I just happened to be the first person who asked her. We must have talked for about two hours, right there in her front parlor, over cookies and tea. She told me everything she could think of that would make Mr. T look bad, but the Salvarini thing was the best, hands down. She really hates her old man, wants to see him go down in flames. She's a sweetheart."

Austen took the beer can that was offered to him and held it against his head for a moment. It was lovely and cool and made him feel almost human again.

"What makes you think Salvarini will want to make his pitch himself?" he asked wearily. "Why shouldn't he just send one of his goons, or a tame lawyer? Why take the risk?"

Freestone shook his head. "No, he'll come himself. The risks are all the other way." He smiled and held up his hands, palms out, as if he were stating the most obvious proposition in the world. He was a nice guy, but it was clear that he was having a lot of fun with Messrs. Tilson and Salvarini. "Figure it from his point of view. Tilson's a prize; maybe he's going to be a United States senator in six or seven months. If you had a handle on a deal like that, how many people would you tell about it? Salvarini's a very jealous man, not the least little bit trusting. And besides, he likes the feel of your face under his shoe. I met him once; it was about a year before I got posted to 'Nam, and he was having some IRS troubles and I happened to see him at a Lakers game and decided, what the hell, I'd give him a try. Jesus, I thought he was going to come right out of his box after me and beat my fool head in with one of those crutches of his. He's an animal—he'll enjoy scaring the shit out of Tilson."

"How much time have we got?"

"It's hard to say. Two weeks until the grand jury sits— that's the bottom line. Any time before then."

"And you're sure the big reunion hasn't already taken place?"

"Reasonably sure. My police contacts tell me that Salvarini hasn't left Los Angeles in the last ten weeks, not since before this whole business blew up, and Tilson's been up north campaigning, I think largely to be out of Salvarini's reach. Anyway, his staff's still working up the brief, so he hasn't told them to be good and crawl back into their cages yet. Maybe he's still making up his mind."

Suddenly there didn't seem to be a great deal more to say. They had cut their deal: Pete would bankroll the operation, and Austen would set it up—and, just by the way, take the rap if he got caught—in exchange for one copy of the physical evidence and forty-eight hours' grace before Pete filed his story. Pete had no desire to know what Austen wanted with those forty-eight hours; he was satisfied as long as his precious scoop wasn't blown.

Austen cocked his head to one side and pulled back his sleeve to have a look at the time. "Come on, then, my plane leaves in an hour."

"You sure you'll have enough money?"

"No fear." He touched the place where his wallet now bulged under his jacket. "The fellow's a friend of mine from *La Guerre;* he's letting us have his special veterans' rates."

The "special veterans' rates" turned out to be twelve hundred fifty dollars for about as much eavesdropping equipment as could be conveniently fitted into a child's lunchbox.

"And I want the receiver and the headset back, Frank." Arnie Schwab, to emphasize his point, held up the first and middle fingers of his right hand like a bishop displaying a crucifix. "Two grand they cost new. I want 'em back, Frank. The rest of the stuff, I can understand that it might be a little inconvenient, but because it's you I'll refund twenty bucks an ear on what you don't use."

Then his hand dropped flat to the little circular wooden table at which they were sitting, almost the only two people in what had to be one of the dingiest bars south of Market Street. Arnie, with his coarse black hair sticking out over the neckband of his green tee shirt and his eyes glittering darkly in his meaty face, looked like he belonged there. He also looked like he expected you to kiss his hand for the enormous favor he was doing you, but that was where appearances were misleading. Anyone who took Arnie Schwab's first offer was a doorknob.

"I'll give you nine hundred for the whole package, and I'll want two back for the receiver. I'll also give you long odds you stole every wire of it out of the back of a supply truck in Saigon." Austen smiled and Arnie started forward in his chair, apparently stung to the bone with indignation.

"Sure I did, what did you think? I could've gotten five years for it—aren't the risks I take worth something? Eleven hundred, and one-fifty back for the receiver, and that's my last offer."

"An even thousand, and one seventy-five back."

"Done."

Afterward Austen walked back down the dark street to where his car was parked, scared to death every minute that some clown would come rushing out of the shadows and try to mug him, and drove back to his apartment in Berkeley. He had come straight into San Francisco from the airport, and his plane back to Los Angeles left at quarter to three in the morning.

So there was no time for even a couple of hours of sleep; the best he could do was take two aspirin and a cold shower. He packed his suitcase with enough to last him a week—at last report, there were still such things as laundromats in LA—and looked around him, at the Michelin calendar pinned to his closet door and the open copy of *Humphry Clinker* lying print-side down on the chair in front of his desk, and wondered whether he would ever get home, or whether these were items he would be getting out of storage someday, when he had finished his stretch in the Los Angeles county jail. He didn't know; the sort of thing he was contemplating might be worth five years too.

The attorney general is entitled to police protection. In addition to a bodyguard, this protection consists of a uniformed officer on duty in front of his apartment door. The attorney general was not due back in town until the next afternoon, so the guy at the door would be the only problem.

Actually, it was no problem at all—in fact, it was dead simple. Austen went downtown and bought himself a tan work shirt and trousers, along with a pair of black rubber boots, a paper surgeon's mask, and a pump can shaped like a fire extinguisher and filled with some particularly nasty-smelling "insecticide," and he was your complete exterminator man. He even had one of those machine-stitched cloth nametags for his shirt pocket. He was a "Phil."

Tilson's bachelor pad wasn't in nearly so grand a building as you might have expected. His estranged wife had the house in San Francisco, the one he had bought with his share from one of the most successful law partnerships in California, and for appearance's sake his girlfriend had her own place about three-quarters of a mile away. Besides, most of his time in recent months had been spent either in Sacramento or on the campaign trail, so why should he burden himself with a palace? There was no doorman; Austen would have been interested to learn what the poor slob was paying out to Mrs. Tilson in support.

There wasn't any trouble about picking the lock downstairs; in the army he had learned to do that kind of thing so fast that to the casual observer it looked like he was simply letting himself in with a key. The lobby was barely large enough to fall down in; he turned a corner and found he had a choice—the elevator or the stairs. He took the elevator.

"This Tilson's place?" he asked, glancing quickly at a slip of paper he had taken from his shirt pocket for just that purpose (it was the receipt for his pump can). The policeman, who was holding his hands together behind his back, looked at him blankly.

"You got a key? The owner says he wants the bugs smoked out before the guy comes back—I guess nobody's home."

"I have to come with you," the policeman announced, holding up the key. His tone was apologetic. "It's a rule. I could lose my job."

"Sure."

He started in the kitchen, spraying along the baseboards and coughing every once in a while behind his paper mask for dramatic effect. The compound in his pump can was a concentrated version of something the Vietnamese used for keeping the ticks off their cattle and was every bit as pungent as advertised. The cattle had never seemed to mind, but it wasn't very long before the attorney general's sentry service took out a handkerchief and began wiping his eyes.

"Is that stuff safe to breathe?" he asked after a couple of minutes. He was already standing in the kitchen doorway, as far away as he could decently manage without actually leaving Austen alone in the room.

"Not if you're a cockroach." Austen looked over his shoulder and grinned at him, readjusting his mask with his free hand. "I suppose so; it makes some people throw up, though. It's somethin' new."

"Well, I'll just . . ." The rest of it was lost in his retreat. He went back outside to the hallway and resumed his post, leaving the front door open about half an inch, apparently as a salve to his professional conscience.

Well, what the hell. The plan was a veritable success. Austen drew a pair of thin plastic gloves out of his back pocket and slipped them on. If he was a nice quiet boy and didn't do anything to make his friend at the door nervous, he figured he had about five minutes. Plenty of time.

A quick check of the premises established that there were exactly three telephones: one in the bedroom, one in the kitchen, and one in what seemed to be Tilson's office. In each case, Austen unscrewed the earpiece from the receiver, knocked out the little speaker, and inserted a tiny microphone transmitter about the size and shape of a dime. The little darlings had adhesive backs and would stick to the inside of the hollow plastic shells forever. Everything was back together again in about twenty-five seconds. There were also three larger bugs, like poker chips, that went in the bedroom, up under the metal frame of the bed where the cleaning woman would never find it in the course of her dusting, and under the desk in the office, and against the back of one of the ornamental fireplace logs in the living room—one could only hope that Tilson wouldn't fall prey to an unaccountable urge to toast marshmallows anytime that summer.

The hard part was the amplifier. By themselves, the ears would only transmit over fifty or sixty yards, fine if you happened to be next door, but a trifle impractical otherwise. The amplifier would pick them up and boost the signal enough to allow for nice clear reception at up to three miles, but it was about the size of a cigarette case. He pried it out of the inside cuff of his boot and looked around the living room for a good spot.

He thought about inside the TV set, but settled on the bookcase. He picked out a copy of *The Collected Short Stories of Henry James*—obviously a gift and showing no signs of ever having been read—cut the centers out of pages 82 through 203 with a razor knife he had brought along against just such an emergency, and inserted the amplifier into the cavity, letting about two inches of wire antenna come out through the back of the volume.

"I turned on the air-conditioning in there—that ought to carry off the smell in about three hours. You might just duck in and switch it off before you go home."

The policeman nodded and smiled and waved farewell as Austen stepped into the elevator and disappeared, his heart pounding like a hammer. He couldn't understand why burglars weren't found dead of cardiac arrest more often.

The girlfriend's apartment was easier. There was only one

phone—in the bedroom, naturally enough—and a single microphone in the living room seemed plenty. They had agreed that the girlfriend was an outside chance; unless he was a perfect shit, Tilson wasn't likely to involve his little sweetie with a number like Salvarini.

"So that's it?" Pete Freestone asked as they waited for a couple of meatloaf specials at a diner just off Olympic Boulevard. For a moment Austen only stared at him; he was keeping his head propped up with his hands and, now that the adrenaline had stopped pumping so hard, was in serious danger of falling asleep.

"No, that's not it. Now we've got to rent a motel room within easy range of both amplifiers, and then you and I have to stand watch over the receiver for as long as it takes until Tilson gets his summons."

"But everything's wired."

Austen only shook his head, smiling unpleasantly. "Not quite, pal. As soon as our boy gets back from his travels, I've got to figure out a way to bug his car."

III

Tilson was very cooperative about that. He was so eager after all those weeks out wowing the electorate that he didn't even bother about going home first; he called his lady love directly from the airport.

Austen saw the little red light start up on his receiver, which meant that somebody's phone was ringing, put on his headset, pressed down the "record" button on the portable tape recorder, and made a note of the time. He hadn't expected anything to happen for at least another hour; he had even let Pete go off to Chicken Delight to fetch them something to eat, taking the car with him.

The conversation only took about forty-five seconds, and he thought he might just drop dead from a stroke before he heard a key in the motel room door and saw Pete enter, balancing a couple of paper cups of Coca-Cola on top of a two-gallon drum of fried chicken.

"Dinner's going to have to be delayed," he announced calmly. "The attorney general flew in horny. If we step on it maybe we can still make the distance before he does."

Pete set his burden down on the television set and simply stood there, as if not quite certain what he should do next. His eyes kept drifting over to the chicken, with all the longing of lost opportunity.

"Do I need to explain? This'll be the perfect chance to wire his car, but I've got to know what it looks like first." He unplugged the receiver from its wall socket and slipped it into a TWA flight bag with the tape recorder. "Come on, come on—starting now one of us has got to be hooked up to this gizmo every minute."

Eleven minutes later, in the underground garage of the lady's apartment building, his legs were just beginning to go to sleep as he crouched behind a gigantic black Lincoln Continental when something a little smaller, like a Jaguar Mark IV, pulled smoothly into a space near the door to the lobby. There was nothing like practice.

Like anyone else in the state who had watched the local news anytime in the past three months, Austen knew Edward Tilson by sight. He looked older standing under the light by the lobby door while he sorted through his keys for the right one; his hair seemed a little thinner and his craggy, hawklike face a little puffier around the throat. But it was him. Austen waited until he was inside and the door had snapped shut behind him before he stood up, his knees crackling like dry wood in a fire, and felt in his pocket for the microphone.

Two and a half minutes later he was outside on the street. He got about forty yards before Freestone's Volkswagen pulled up alongside him.

"How did it go?"

"Easy." He pulled the door shut and allowed himself to sink back against the upholstery. "Tilson was in such a tearing hurry that he didn't even bother to lock the goddam car door. He must imagine that girlfriend of his is really terrific stuff. I thought the fires were supposed to bank a little after fifty."

"I don't know. Maybe divorce does that to some guys. Where did you hide the mike?"

"Up under the dash." Austen stared out the window, his face a weary, resigned mask, as if he had just forsaken the last illusions of his youth. "I imagine by now the chicken's probably stone cold."

*   *   *

It was, and all the ice in the paper cups had melted, rendering the Coca-Cola about as tasty as rain water. But they would eat things a lot viler over the next five days while they waited in their motel room, taking the headset in four-hour shifts. Except when the maid came to do the room and they drove the Volkswagen in huge circles around West Hollywood so the receiver, which had an adapter plug for the cigarette lighter, wouldn't run the battery down, they almost never went outside. Doubtless the management had begun entertaining some very unflattering conjectures about what they could be up to, locked away together hour after hour in that little room, but Pete Freestone had paid a week in advance and Los Angeles is a city celebrated for its tolerance.

Austen spent most of the time reading about Simon Faircliff in the newspapers. The *Times* hated him—no wonder they weren't so wild about having Pete pull the rug from under Edward Tilson—but the *San Francisco Chronicle* had arrived at the conclusion that he was Moses, come to lead us out of the wilderness. And it wasn't all just hype, either; the man clearly had something to him.

Once they happened to catch him on the eleven o'clock news. It was just a thirty- or forty-second clip; the congressman was delivering a speech in Berkeley, and the crowd, which seemed to be mainly kids from the university, kept breaking in on him with applause after every sentence. They loved it. The war was still an active proposition, even if everyone knew that at least our part in it would be over within another couple of months, and probably three-quarters of Faircliff's listeners still had draft cards to burn.

And then some clown with a Fu Manchu moustache and his hands stuffed into the pockets of an army fatigue jacket pulled a little away from the mob and asked whether the congressman would favor abolishing the selective service, and the crowd cheered like they already knew the answer—hell, Faircliff was a California liberal and had first made a name for himself by attempting to get the state Bar Association to come out against the war.

"No," he announced calmly. Everyone was so stunned that you could actually hear the wind blowing across the grass behind him. "There is such a thing as the legitimate use of force; if you don't believe me, just ask Ho Chi Minh. I fought in World War II, and I've never learned to be ashamed of that. When this war is over, we will still need an army. We have real enemies in the world, nations that constitute real threats to our freedom, even our existence. It just so happens that North Vietnam isn't among them."

And then the camera froze on Faircliff's face. He looked exactly like a lion, like he didn't give a damn how the voters felt.

Well, doubtless that sort of thing probably played pretty well with the Veterans of Foreign Wars, but they weren't going to line up behind him anyway—their hearts belonged to Edward Tilson. And, doubtless, sitting in a motel room somewhere with his campaign staff, Faircliff might be forgiven for wishing the question had never come up. But it had, and he had answered it, possibly without thinking first and foremost about what the answer was going to cost him.

It was only a moment on the television screen, something fitted between the sports report and a human interest piece about some old fart with the world's largest collection of tin ashtrays, but it made you understand why Pete Freestone professed such admiration for the congressman from San Francisco.

But you couldn't read newspapers endlessly, and for the rest their watch was rather like the experience of combat— long stretches of boredom punctuated by moments of breathless excitement. Every time Tilson's phone rang, you felt your heart right there between your teeth.

Tilson used the phone a lot. Most of the calls were just routine, but some of them were interesting in various ways. Together they were a paradigm of the human condition, a rough study of the texture of one man's life. Tilson was clearly not a man built to the heroic scale. The attorney general had a wife and a girlfriend and a lot of other problems; he was up against it.

"The poor bastard," Pete would murmur, listening at the headphones while he made machinelike progress through a bag of cheese puffs. "The poor pathetic bastard."

Of course, it wasn't all Lux Radio Theater. There was a lot of hard, usable information, the sort of thing that, had they not themselves been waiting around for the length of rope with which they planned to hang him, would have been worth something to someone.

For instance, they heard it direct from the lips of Tilson's own campaign manager that he had a man in the Faircliff

organization, somebody named "Curtis," who was sufficiently well placed to have access to the minutes of staff
meetings, and even to the congressman's personal appointments lists.

And they also learned of the almost irresistible pressure
Tilson was feeling over the Salvarini matter, that he was
almost more afraid of his own subordinates than he was of
the unlovable Mr. Salvarini. In fact, the troops had just
about served notice that if the case were not allowed to
move ahead they would see to it that enough dust was kicked
up to keep Edward Tilson out of office—any office—for as
long as the memory of man. They meant business, apparently. They could smell blood.

But it was the private drama that was most affecting.
Austen had always known that Pete Freestone was a soft
touch for the sufferings of humanity. In Saigon Pete had
been a perfect maniac for war orphans and the withered-up
old women who used to flood in from the Delta after every
post-monsoon offensive, but Austen had never imagined that
the personal problems of a well-nourished politician would
have evoked such sympathetic interest.

"That woman is a bitch," Pete would mutter, playing back
a tape of Mrs. Tilson's most recent conversation with her
guilt-ridden husband. He was always playing them back;
once he woke Austen out of a sound sleep for a rebroadcast
of one of her more outstandingly nasty performances. *What
will you do if you lose, Edward?* she purred. *What will that
adolescent clinging vine of yours think if in six months
you're nothing but a middle-aged lawyer? How will you deal
with that, Edward? She thinks you're such a great man now.
Whatever will you do then?* So perhaps it was no miracle that
he was so desperately smitten with his young lady, who
really was young and sounded like an amiable enough simpleton.

And so it stood. What way the lover and the public servant
and the possessor of a compromising secret would finally
jump was an open question, probably to no one more than to
himself.

For five days Frank Austen and Pete Freestone listened.
They ate cold pizza and drank warm soda and waited for the
game to start while they learned what the stakes would be.
They listened while Tilson carried on his public and private
negotiations over the telephone, and they listened while he

sat alone in his one-bedroom apartment watching Johnny
Carson.

"Can we be sure Salvarini will call him at home?" Pete
would ask when he was oppressed by thoughts of how much
money he was laying out and what his boss would say if he
came back from his unexplained absence without a story.
"Maybe we've figured it wrong. Maybe he'll send the guy a
letter or something. Maybe they've already made contact."

"Salvarini won't put anything in writing because he's not
that stupid, and if he wants to talk he'll call Tilson at home.
You can't imagine he'd call him at the office, can you? But
beyond that there aren't any guarantees. Relax. Take a nap.
Go out and get me a bottle of ginger ale if you're feeling
restless. But shut up."

On the fifth night, at a little after four forty-five in the
morning, an hour after Austen had gone to bed imagining he
wouldn't be able to stand another day of this nonsense, the
telephone in Tilson's apartment rang. The voice on the other
end of the line was thick and gravelly; from the first syllable
it was impossible to believe it could belong to anyone except
Giancarlo Salvarini.

Rise and shine, bright boy. You know who it is.

"Frank, wake up. For God's sake, Frank, wake up."

There was this terrific racket, which turned out to be Pete
Freestone's knuckle thumping away on the top of his skull.
He opened his eyes, but not before he felt himself being
pulled out of bed by the sleeve of his pajamas.

"Wake up—he's made the call."

"I'm up."

For an instant he imagined that Salvarini and Tilson must
be in the motel bathroom together, because why else was
everybody whispering? And then he began to take his bear-
ings and saw, in a flash of panic, that with all the excitement
Pete had forgotten to turn on the tape deck, and he almost
broke his leg stumbling over a chair to get to the "record"
button. He thought he must have set the world's indoor
speed record for twelve and a half feet from flat on your
back.

*. . . you think? I was just bein' nice? You cheap slob, you
figure a way. One hour—the end of Elvida Street, off the
Coldwater Canyon Road. You be there.*

They played it back twice, the whole quarter of a minute
of it—even down to the click when the connection was

broken—and Austen found Elvida Street on their Standard Oil Company map of Los Angeles.

"If we push it a little, we can get there in twenty minutes," he said, shoving his legs into his trousers as he tried to remember what else people generally wore in public.

Actually, they made it in a little under sixteen.

Assuming that his first consideration was privacy, Salvarini had picked his spot with care. Elvida Street ran the length of a housing development that was still under construction; beyond the pavement the ground fell away quickly into the canyon, a desolate landscape of raw ground and scrub.

Austen found a place to park about half a mile away and well out of sight. They walked back, carrying their equipment with them, and set up on the second floor of an unfinished three-bedroom structure in which the walls were only half up on the side that faced the street. They could lie there on the floor, in what would someday be the master bedroom, and make their tape recordings and take their photographs and be perfectly invisible. The distance was about two hundred yards—they didn't dare risk anything closer—but Pete had a telephoto lens on his camera, and, once the sun came up, they would even have the light behind them.

At seventeen minutes before six, Tilson's car came to a stop against the railings at the very end of the turnaround. He got out and closed the door behind him, and they saw that he was wearing a tan raincoat, although there wasn't a hint of a cloud and the temperature was already up into the middle seventies. He kept his hands in his pockets and waited, staring down at the asphalt.

"We're in luck," Austen murmured, as much to himself as to Pete. "He's left his window halfway open—if they don't go wandering off, we'll be able to get every word."

Six minutes later a black Mercedes pulled up beside Tilson's Jaguar, and Salvarini himself opened the door, handed his dead legs through the opening, and rose up behind his shining aluminum crutches. Tilson hardly even looked at him.

Salvarini was a huge man, an impression somehow enhanced by the ponderous slowness with which he dragged himself forward, seeming to hate the very ground because he couldn't get over it any faster. He wore a shiny black sharkskin suit and, except for the absence of a hat to cover the bald spot that sat like a target in his tarnished gray hair, looked every inch the successful hoodlum.

Austen became aware of a faint clicking sound beside him and saw that Pete had begun snapping his pictures. He turned on the tape recorder, pressing one cup of the handset against his ear so he wouldn't have to wear the stupid thing. Their subjects might as well have been performing on a sound stage.

It was then that he began to entertain a vague and unpleasant suspicion. He reached over and touched Freestone on the arm, and for a moment the clicking stopped.

"Whatever happens," he said calmly, "whatever you see, don't make a sound, and don't stop shooting. Get every frame of it."

Pete nodded, seeming a little uncertain about what he was agreeing to, and then turned back to his camera, and the clicking resumed.

. . . s'pose I care if it costs you your ass? You're bought and paid for, Tilson. You're just so much dead meat if I get pissed and decide to carve you up, you little shit. I want it dropped, and I don't give a fuck how bad it smells for you— you smell pretty bad already. How you think the voters're gonna feel when they hear about that little jam of yours back in 'sixty? Huh? It was at once a ludicrous and tragic performance. Salvarini was really enjoying himself, like a sick little boy with a new white mouse to torture. His voice was rising higher and higher in a kind of ecstasy of frustrated savagery.

And all the while Tilson said nothing. Most of the time he kept his eyes turned to the ground, only looking up now and then, giving the impression that he was trying to settle with himself how much more he could stand. It was an endurance contest, and he bore it with his hands pressed into the pockets of his raincoat as if he were hanging on for dear life.

You stupid bastard, Austen thought to himself as he listened to the rising tide of Salvarini's obscene and violent eloquence. You big stupid bull, you shouldn't ever have come here alone.

And then all at once it happened. Salvarini never stopped yelling; he might not even have noticed when Tilson began slowly bringing his right hand out of his raincoat pocket. If he saw anything, even a flash of light off the gun barrel, he never had a chance to let anyone know about it.

They were just tiny figures down on the road, like dolls. And yet the shot Austen heard through his earphone sounded like the announcement of Armageddon.

"Get it all, Pete," he whispered, and the click, click, click of the camera shutter went on with hardly a pause.

Salvarini was pitched backward by the impact of the bullet. At that distance it was impossible to tell where he had been hit, but he spun around in a half-turn as he fell and landed across the railing that marked the edge of the canyon and the end of the road. It was obvious that he was dead, even before he started to go down. Tilson didn't have to fire a second shot.

He simply stood there for a moment, still pointing the gun at the spot where Salvarini had been standing, and then, when Austen had almost begun to wonder whether he had lost the power of independent movement, he returned the gun to his raincoat pocket. He took his time, as if the action marked some definite conclusion, like the actor's final line before the curtain rings down.

Immediately afterward he was all business. He rushed forward and pushed Salvarini's body over the railing, pulling him up by the leg and letting him slip down behind until he disappeared from sight down the landfall, throwing the crutches after him. Then he went back to his car, got in, backed up to turn around, and drove away.

Pete started to get up, but Austen threw his arm across his back and held him down. "Not yet. Let him get safely away. Remember, he's the johnnie with the gun."

Afterward they went down and had a look. The bullet had made a neat hole through the left lapel of Salvarini's suitcoat; there was hardly any blood, but his eyes were open and the expression on his face was still twisted with rage. Obviously he never knew what hit him.

"I wonder whether Tilson thinks he got away with it," Pete said as he stepped backward a few yards to snap a picture of the body.

"Why shouldn't he? If any of Salvarini's people know whom he came up here to meet, they won't tell anyone. They'll want to see whether there isn't some way they can use it. Besides, who would believe them? The interesting question would be whether or not Tilson cares."

They climbed back up to the road. Salvarini had rolled about twenty feet before he got hung up on a clump of bushes, and it was dusty work.

"What happens now?"

"You mean to us?" Austen shrugged and bent down to brush some dirt from his trouser leg. "Nothing much. We go back to town, you get your pictures developed, and I find someplace to copy the tapes. Then we pretend we've never heard of each other. On Monday morning, you call your editor and he calls the cops. Tilson's going to be very surprised when you run all this on the front page."

Four hours later Austen was on a plane to San Francisco, with twenty-eight nine-by-eleven black-and-white photographs and three cassettes of tape in a large manila envelope he carried balanced across his knees. He wasn't going to let it out of his sight until he was ready to deliver it to its destination.

The plan had come into his mind as a completed thing, settled down to the most trivial detail, even before he had left his message with the switchboard operator at the *Times*. He had kept the telephone number of Simon Faircliff's local congressional offices on a slip of paper in his wallet and had been following the candidate's movements through the newspapers. Austen would track him down if he had to go after him with bloodhounds.

But like so much else in this whole peculiar business, it was destined to be much easier than that. Where the gods wish us to damn ourselves, they strew our path with rose petals. All Austen had to do, once he had retrieved his suitcase from the luggage carousels, was put a dime in the pay phone and call.

"Faircliff for senator." It was a deliciously feminine voice. Austen allowed himself a deep breath and braced himself against the glass wall of the phone booth.

"I'd like to speak to the congressman. It's very important."

"I'm sorry, Congressman Faircliff is unavailable at the moment. If you'd care to leave a message, stating the nature of your business and leaving your name and number, I'm sure he'll get back to you as soon as he's free."

"My business is with the congressman only. It's very

important. Please tell him that if I can have fifteen seconds of his time he'll find it rewarding."

He could hear the murmur of something like an argument in the background, and he closed his eyes and whispered the secular version of a prayer. He discovered that he had to remind himself to breathe. Probably about a quarter of a minute elapsed, but it felt much, much longer.

The voice he heard next was masculine, deep and musical, and familiar to him from the evening news. "All right, this is Faircliff. You've got your fifteen seconds."

"Congressman, nine days ago, at a meeting of your senior staff, the vote was six to four that you should publicly disassociate yourself from your earlier support of the Property Tax Reform Bill. You decided not to follow the recommendation. The decision was also made not to endorse the likely Democratic presidential nominee until after the Miami convention—are you still listening?"

"Where did you find that out?" Faircliff asked quietly. You might have thought it was of only the remotest interest to him; you had to admire the man's cool.

"Have you got a man on your staff named 'Curtis'?"

"Yes—Paul Curtis. He's on my fund-raising staff. He's engaged to my secretary."

"Then your secretary hasn't been very discreet." He paused for a moment, discovered that the receiver was getting slippery in his hand, and transferred it to the other while he took a couple of deep gulps of air. "But Paul Curtis is just small change; you can have him as a token of my good faith. The rest you don't get over the phone, but I promise you're going to hang on my every word."

"What do you want, Mr. . . . ."

"Austen, Frank Austen. I want half an hour of your time, and it has to be today. It isn't going to cost you a cent."

"All right, Mr. Austen. Can you be here in an hour?"

He could be there in an hour, but just barely. The city was jammed, he couldn't find a place to park, and then he had to walk five blocks up Powell Street, which was as steep as the Matterhorn. But he made it and was shown into Faircliff's office immediately.

He hadn't realized how huge the man was. Faircliff stood up from his desk to offer him a hand and blocked out the wall behind him.

"What is it you have to tell me, young man?" The tone

was delicately poised somewhere between an invitation and a threat. Austen sat down on a small leather-covered chair, exactly as if it were wired to twenty-two hundred volts and provided with leg cuffs.

"You expect to run against Edward Tilson after the primaries. You won't. Tilson's going to self-destruct; until this morning he was a creature of Giancarlo Salvarini—I'm sure you've heard the name—and about six hours ago he liberated himself from that embarrassment by shooting Salvarini through the heart." He tossed the manila envelope onto Faircliff's desk. "Take a look at the photographs. Get a cassette player and listen to the tapes. It's all there, and Monday afternoon it'll be on page one of the *Los Angeles Times*. You can forget all about Mr. Tilson."

Faircliff said nothing. For a long moment he was motionless and silent, like a stone idol; the impression of weight and gravity was enormous. Then, very slowly, he placed his hand over the envelope and slid it toward himself across the desk. His eyes never left Austen's face.

With each photograph the lines around his eyes and mouth seemed to deepen. Finally he put all the photos back inside the envelope, turning down the flap and closing the clasp with great care. "My God," he whispered, apparently only to the back of his hand. "He's destroyed himself. The poor bastard."

Yet again Austen experienced a certain surge of admiration for the man. To his credit, what seemed to impress him first was the pure tragedy of the thing.

"I don't think I need to hear the tapes," Faircliff said quietly. He had that trick of seeming to be soft-spoken, although anyone could have heard him from anywhere in the room. He looked up at Austen again, and his face hardened. "I think you'd better tell me how you're involved in this. This isn't some prank, you know—Edward Tilson, as far as I'm aware, was always a decent man. I think you'd better tell me what you've done to him."

"I haven't done anything to him; he's done it to himself. Let's just say that I arranged to be a witness. Tilson's going to blow up, and all I'm doing is allowing that bomb to go off of its own accord. You won't be involved, and neither will I."

"What is it you want from me, young man?"

"I want a job, congressman." Austen allowed himself the

luxury of a deep breath and a look at Faircliff's face. What he saw wasn't terribly encouraging; the man seemed to be chiseled out of granite.

"I deliver this to you for nothing," he went on, bracing himself for the final effort. "Consider it a small sample of the sort of thing I'm capable of getting done. I think you're an ambitious man, congressman—I think you have a right to be. I admire you a great deal more than I'd ever be able to make convincing just at this moment; I think you may be just what this country needs. But we can't all be star gazers, and if you're really going as far in the world as doubtless you're planning to, you're going to need somebody at your elbow who knows that the other side of the moon is dark."

IV

Edward Tilson never came to trial. The last person known to have seen him alive was his mistress. He stopped by her apartment for a few minutes that Saturday morning to explain that something had come up quite suddenly and that he would have to be out of town for a few days; if she noticed anything peculiar in his manner she never mentioned it to anyone. Late Monday night, within a few hours after the police issued their warrant for his arrest, he was found shot to death in his car on Interstate 40, about fifteen miles from the Arizona border. The presumption was suicide; it was impossible to determine whether he had seen that day's paper or heard any news broadcasts on the radio.

Simon Faircliff went back to Washington that autumn as the newly elected senator from California, and Frank Austen went with him, which was very much to his satisfaction.

It would be many years before he learned to think about his role in the destruction of Edward Tilson with anything like discomfort. That was something reserved for a later period, after he had ceased to marvel at his luck and the brilliance of the life that had suddenly been offered to him. During this first several months in Washington, however, he was too busy to be anything except completely happy. He was Simon Faircliff's bright-eyed boy, and the senator was introducing him to the unrivaled pleasures of power.

The first thing Faircliff did was assign him to spend his

evenings studying for the California bar exam. "You're going to be a senatorial aide," he said. "It's important, for me and for you, that you have a certain standing."

So while Faircliff breezed through the campaign, Austen spent his days learning about constituencies and how to run an office staff and his nights boning up on the civil code. Now that he could pursue the thing with relative peace of mind—and now that it no longer really seemed to matter very much—he found he could manage without any great difficulty. In January he flew back from Washington to sit the exam, and when the results were published several weeks later, he found he had finished in the top quarter. He was a lawyer now, and he was Simon Faircliff's hatchet man, and it was all the biggest joke in the world.

For the rest, he reorganized and ran the senator's offices and kept the lobbyists at bay. He worked up the option analyses and wrote the speeches; Faircliff was great on delivery and very good when he was speaking off the cuff, but if he sat down with a pencil and a yellow legal pad and tried to come up with something on his own for the League of Women Voters or the opening of a new post office in Stockton, it came out sounding like a cross between a legal brief and the *Book of Revelation*.

Austen was the tailor-made assistant, always there and always ready, and the senator was properly appreciative. But what he appreciated even more was that share of Austen's duties that was conducted after business hours. The senator's new boy had discovered fairly quickly that Washington wasn't so very different from Saigon and had started laying down his pipelines. Like Saigon, Washington was filled with rootless, frightened women; just out of college or fresh from the rice paddies, it didn't appear to make much difference—they all seemed to wear their clothes too tight and they all seemed to need something to hold on to. So his love life was very well stocked and, while he lay on his side in all those darkened bedrooms, things kept being whispered into his ear. And if once in a while a few hundred dollars disappeared from petty cash because some typist over in the minority whip's office had to have a favor, nobody was going to ask any embarrassing questions about it.

It was like a food-chain: you caught the flies to fatten up the spiders, and you fed the spiders to the birds and the birds to the cats. If you worked on the principle that it was always necessary to get more than you gave, you did all right. You made friends with a reporter you had met at a party in some girl's apartment and you heard all about how some new giant transport plane the army had contracted for was running way over budget; the senator could use information like that, so you told your new friend about how the secretary of defense, who was a Republican anyway, was very worried about his son's business dealings with a Nicaraguan company owned by the dictator. The reporter went away happy, and the contact tended to extend itself more or less forever. The same principle could be applied to diplomats, civil service workers, even other senatorial aides. It constituted the one real difference between the only two cities in which Austen had ever found proper scope for his talents—where Saigon ran on money, Washington ran on gossip.

All the gossip that came Austen's way ended up in the briefing papers Senator Faircliff read with his crescent roll and his coffee first thing in the morning, making him the envy of Capitol Hill, where he cut his own deals, and making Austen, at eighteen thousand dollars a year, the most underpaid man in the Senate office building.

"I hear Morrison offered you twenty-five if you'd walk across the aisle and be chief dog-robber for him, Frank—why didn't you take it?"

"You're going to wind up president and he isn't. When you get there, you can appoint me to the Supreme Court for services rendered."

It was all a big joke.

From the very first he had never even considered the possibility of working for anyone except Simon Faircliff. They both knew that, and they knew that it had almost nothing to do with personal ambitions. Austen was that happy person who had discovered for himself the loyalty of a lifetime; he understood his man through to the bone, knew all his little quirks and personal vanities, and didn't give a damn. Simon Faircliff was at once his personal property and his hero on earth. Don Quixote had found his Sancho Panza and vice versa.

So it was a reasonably tranquil and contented Frank Austen who strolled across the grass in his employer's backyard in the third year of his tenure as the gray eminence behind the throne. The chief was giving a garden party, with no reporters invited, for once, and the chairman of the Federal Securities and Exchange Commission, who had gotten pretty thoroughly sossled on piña coladas earlier in the afternoon, had just been pushed into the swimming pool for having annoyed somebody's husband. He was being helped out by a lobbyist from ITT, and a waiter hired for the occasion had just come rushing from the house with a towel. Austen, who had reasons of his own for not loving the chairman, was wondering how the old fart would enjoy arriving home in his sodden Dacron suit to find Jack Anderson sitting on his doorstep, asking whether he had any statement. All that would have been necessary was to walk into the senator's bedroom and pick up the phone, but this after all was a private party and there were dangers to making people too afraid of you. Just this once, he would let it ride.

Simon Faircliff was what passed for an honest politician, but he had been married to a very wealthy woman and could therefore, as the saying goes, afford to be honest. The backyard of his house covered about an acre and a quarter of very choice Chevy Chase real estate, and there were something like two hundred people standing on it, most of them clustered in little knots around the swimming pool and within convenient reach of the bar.

These tended to be rather staid affairs and, as a consequence, none of the ten or twelve unattached young women who had been invited largely for window dressing had as yet pulled off her clothes to go skinny dipping or decided to do a strip-tease at the end of the diving board. Probably no one was getting his rocks off in the bathhouse, and, aside from the one incident with the SEC Chairman, there hadn't been anything even approaching a fistfight.

Over near the ceramic birdbath, slightly away from everybody else, Faircliff was standing with a drink in his hand, talking with a particularly handsome couple, both in their mid-forties. The man looked like a college athlete who had simply gone a little gray, and on top of the good looks he had the perfect assurance of manner that constitutes political star quality. He was also smart enough to thrill the fuzzy-haired intellectuals and was the darling of the right-of-center moderates. He was Clayton Burgess, who, barring the unforeseen, would doubtless end up with the GOP presidential nomination in another five years. The guy was also squeaky-clean, but Austen had lately started a file on him, just in case.

Impressive as Senator Burgess was, Simon appeared to be concentrating most of his attention on Mrs. Burgess. This wasn't very difficult to understand; she was a beautiful woman, slim and elegant, with masses of black hair, and Simon had a very discriminating eye for that kind of beauty. Austen watched the conversation with faint uneasiness. He decided he had better mention to his number one that it would be better if he weren't quite so obviously appreciative.

"You look like you're measuring Clayton Burgess for a shroud," said a voice behind his right shoulder. He turned around to see a small blond woman in her early twenties, pretty in an interesting way, with large, intelligent eyes in the sort of face that would probably always look disarmingly young. He smiled, genuinely pleased, as if someone had just given him something.

"How can you say so? Senator Burgess is Lohengrin—everybody knows that." The smile stayed on his lips, perhaps tightening just a shade as he observed the odd, speculative way she was looking at him.

"You're Frank Austen," she said at last, as if something had suddenly recalled the fact to her mind.

"I know—I've known for years." He turned away. There wasn't time in this life for groupies, even the ones who looked like they might know how to touch a nerve. He had almost forgotten her by the time she spoke again.

"What are you going to do to Burgess anyway?" She was even closer now, almost pressing against him with a kind of aggrieved intimacy. "Are you going to spread stories about how he seduces little boys, or will you settle for just sending in an anonymous tip to the IRS and then feeding him raw to one of your tame sharks at the *Post?* Which is it to be, Mr. Austen—hmmm?"

All at once, he found, he was deeply stirred; and he couldn't have said why, because the lady was talking a lot of dreadful rubbish. Nevertheless, one's glands did not always obey the commands of logic.

"Why do I get the feeling that you don't like me?"

"Oh, I like you fine, Mr. Austen. It's your employer I have a certain amount of trouble with."

"But not enough to keep you away from his parties." He

smiled, but it was obvious the dart hadn't gone home. "And you're very high on Clayton Burgess?"

"I've known him since I was sixteen. There isn't a better man in Congress, and that includes your illustrious Senator Faircliff."

It was said with such conviction that he had to stop smiling. Besides, there was nothing funny about the way her tanned arms looked against the pale blue silk of her sleeveless cocktail dress. "And what would you know about my illustrious Senator Faircliff?"

"Why, Mr. Austen, I'm surprised at you," she warbled mockingly, tilting her head a little to one side so that her cap of yellow hair bounced enticingly. "I thought you would have recognized me from that awful picture he keeps on his desk. I'm the prodigal Dottie."

"I see. Well, you'll have to forgive me; it isn't a very good likeness."

"No, it isn't. Now I'm sorry; have I embarrassed you?"

He shook his head, aware that she was guying him.

"Well, I wouldn't want you to go around worrying that you'd gotten in wrong with the boss's daughter."

"Don't let it bother you, sweetie," he murmured, showing his teeth in a nice ratty grin. "I don't have to worry about where I stand with the senator, and besides, they haven't exactly caught me with my hand up your dress, so we can both relax."

After that, somehow, he managed to get away from her. The sun was just beginning to set over the back trellis, and he was looking around for his host so he could say goodnight, when he saw him shaking hands with the Burgesses by the little garden path that led around the other side of the house to the circular driveway in the front. When they were gone, Faircliff turned back toward the pool, and his faithful retainer intercepted him about halfway to the bar.

"Your tongue's hanging out, Senator."

Faircliff's head snapped around in a little start, and then he smiled wanly and put his hand on Austen's shoulder. "Jesus, Frank, was I that obvious? I don't know, I must be getting old. I'm even thinking maybe I should get married again."

"Fine. Great. But not to that one; she's already got a husband. The voters won't love you if you break up America's happiest couple."

"Maybe you're right." He let his hand slide lovingly down Austen's arm, in that way politicians have, and then suddenly slapped him on the shoulder blade. It was just a playful blow, but Austen found it advisable to take a sudden deep breath. "Say, did you meet my little girl?"

"Yes, I met your little girl. What's she doing here? I thought she was back in California, living with your draconian sister-in-law."

The senator laughed, and his aide, just as a precaution, dodged out of range.

"You don't miss much, do you, Frank?" He laughed again, this time a little more quietly, and looked down at the toes of his Gucci loafers, which still glowed like obsidian. "Well, I talked her into coming out here for a few months. I don't know, maybe she'll like it and stay. Maybe she'll get a job here. I'd like that. I've hardly seen her at all since her mother died."

Austen didn't say anything. He simply stared into the glare off the swimming pool and wondered whether his employer was getting restive and whether that would be likely to create problems. Leching the competition's old lady, kids, talk of marriage—he didn't know. Maybe he should hunt around for some nice juicy forty-year-old widow for him; maybe that would settle him down. After all, perhaps he was lonely. He'd been on his own for six years now, and at his age you probably got tired of sport fucking sooner. Maybe having the daughter around would do the trick, too, provided she was a good girl and didn't bring them all to grief one way or another.

"You want me to stick around and help pour the drunks into their roadsters?"

"No, Frank. You go on home. The party's just about over."

On the drive back into DC he tried not to think about anything at all. He just wanted to look out for the cops and the lunatics and get home in one piece; he wanted to spend the rest of the night in front of the television set, eating his Dinner-in-a-Pouch turkey slices and watching the Annette Funicello Film Festival like the rest of the human race. But there wasn't a chance in hell of his doing either one. That was another big difference—in Saigon you could switch it off once in a while, but Washington turned you into a perpetual intriguer.

He tried to remember whether he still had any chocolate ripple ice cream at home and, deciding that the chances were not very good, turned into the parking lot of a Quik-Way grocery store.

It always gave him a peculiar sensation to enter these places, as if in a well-ordered world his mother would still be doing all the shopping for him and his father at the Safeway on Belburn Avenue, just as she had all through the years of his childhood. On some purely inconsequential level, he still equated his paychecks with the fifteen-dollar-a-month allowance he had received in high school, and the whole business of dividing them up into rent and car payments and money for clothes and food and newspaper subscriptions inevitably struck him as unreal and slightly pretentious, as if he were laying claim to an adult dignity and self-sufficiency to which he had no more right at thirty than he had had at fourteen. He picked up a couple of frozen pizzas and a can of creamed corn and stood in line behind a pair of teenage girls who were buying movie magazines, reading the headlines of the *National Enquirer*—"Doctors Reveal New Super Diet," "Peter Sellers' Shocking Childhood"—and wondering whether anything ever again would make any sense at all.

Well, doubtless this too was just a phase he was going through. Tomorrow would be Sunday, and on Monday morning he would go to work to discover that some boob in the House was calling for an investigation of congressional travel expenses. There was something he would be able to feel the reality of.

In the line of little covered parking spaces that passed for a garage to his apartment building, he noticed an unfamiliar tan Kharmen Ghia, the driver of which went unrecognized for several seconds before he pulled in next to her.

"You were very rude to me," Dottie Faircliff announced as she leaned out over her door. "But I've decided to give you a chance to make it up."

"And how do I do that, take you up to my apartment and jump on your bones?"

"Well, you might feed me first."

She looked very beautiful with her large eyes and her fluffy blond hair, and the nicest part of all was that she wasn't being the least little bit coy. If she had been anyone except Simon Faircliff's daughter, he would have found himself wondering what it was she was hoping to buy with her delicious young body. He found himself wondering that anyway.

"Then isn't it lucky I just bought an extra pizza."

"Yes, isn't it. Today seems to be your lucky day."

V

Whether Simon Faircliff had any idea that summer and autumn that his little girl was spending a good share of her off hours in Frank Austen's bed was a matter of conjecture. Dottie had decided to stay in Washington at least for the time being, and perhaps—if he knew why—her father regarded her continued residence with him as just another instance of a difficulty his superlatively competent aide had been able to smooth away. But in any case, no word on the subject ever passed between the two men.

Dottie, of course, hadn't a doubt in the world. "Sure he knows," she told Austen once. She had gone into the kitchen, stark naked, oblivious to the open window, to make herself a cup of Sanka.

"For a while there he was having me followed, and then I stopped seeing the same little brown Volvo in my rearview mirror all the time, so I guess the man must have told Daddy it was only you, and Daddy probably breathed a sigh of relief and paid him off. With you, at least, he knows he isn't going to have anybody coming down on him for blackmail or anything, and beyond that I don't imagine he cares. After all, I'm twenty-three."

"Wonderful." Austen dropped a bathrobe over her shoulders and went back into the bedroom to finish dressing.

He wished he could put so happy a construction on the matter, but he knew Faircliff well enough to be reasonably sure that if he was keeping his mouth shut it was only because, perhaps right then, he didn't feel there was much of anything he could do. He could fire Austen, of course, but that wouldn't change anything; Austen would simply put in a couple of phone calls around town to kick off the bidding and come up before the end of the afternoon with a five-thousand-dollar-a-year hike in salary, which would hardly be much of a move toward ending the affair. But now or later, if he didn't appreciate Austen's screwing his daughter, he would find a way of letting him know about it.

Faircliff was no prig—he was as free and easy as the next guy about the weaknesses of the flesh—but some men aren't entirely rational on the subject of their own daughters. Austen knew Faircliff probably as well as anybody, but the domestic side of his character was a closed book to him.

And Dottie? Well, it was always a nice question what she really believed or wanted. Maybe she was just out to get to the old man through his trusted lieutenant, to sow a little dissension just for the pure pleasure of doing mischief. That was perfectly possible; Austen didn't really have any idea how, at bottom, she felt about him, and her relationship with her father was certainly composed of enough conflicting elements of hatred and love, defiance and desire for reconciliation, to push her to almost anything.

And there it was. Faircliff was Austen's career, his life's work, the way another man's might be spreading the gospel in the jungles of Lower Borneo, and Austen had discovered, much to his own surprise, that he was in love with Dottie. They were the two people he cared about most in the world, and they were in some sort of obscure feud that he couldn't possibly hope to understand but that certainly, one way or another, was going to number him among its victims.

In fact, he couldn't be sure that it hadn't already. From about the middle of September on—it wasn't the sort of thing he could date with much precision, since he couldn't even be sure it was actually happening—a peculiar kind of reserve had crept into his relationship with Simon. Nothing appeared to have changed; his was still the first voice the senator would hear in all matters great and small, and every week they still had lunch together out of brown paper bags in Simon's office. It was more a matter of tone than of substance, and, since it coincided with the introduction of a new face in the Faircliff organization, it might not have had anything to do with Dottie at all.

Simon had waited until the last possible moment, on the plane back to Washington just before the end of the summer recess, to tell him. "I fired Marty Eilberg," he said quite suddenly, while he was staring out his window and probably wondering whether the wing wasn't about to drop off. Flying was the one thing the senator seemed genuinely afraid of; he usually spent the twenty-four hours before embarkation popping tranquilizers like jelly beans. "He's a lousy analyst. He probably would have cost us the election last time if you hadn't happened along. I phoned him and gave him the word last night. The son-of-a-bitch told me I could take my job and stick it; how do you like that?"

"You want me to start scouting the talent pools?" Austen asked, not terribly surprised or grieved by the loss of Marty Eilberg, who was a jerk and a screw-up and who had once gotten falling-down drunk at a reception for the new junior senator from California. When he then had to be driven home, Eilberg had thrown up all over the rear seat of Austen's car. Austen did, however, wish that Simon would consult him about these matters first; like all courtiers, he disliked surprises.

Faircliff only shook his head. "No. In fact, that's the only reason I let the little piss-ant go so suddenly; I got a chance to hire somebody I've been looking at for years."

He turned from the window, glanced around him nervously, smiled, and flagged down the stewardess to order a vodka gimlet—his third that flight, and they were only over Kansas. Austen, who had long ago learned that his employer was least to be trusted when he was most glib, experienced a sinking feeling that he was reasonably sure had nothing to do with the altitude.

"Who is he?"

"Oh, a fellow who helped me a lot when I ran for Congress the first time," he answered, just a little too airily. "He went into advertising—he's a vice president with Bate & Palmer down in Los Angeles—but he's made his pile and wants to join up. His name's Howard Diederich."

The stewardess came back with the vodka gimlet and asked whether they were ready to be served dinner yet, and Austen nodded. You could have either Chateaubriand with scalloped potatoes or chicken Kiev with rice; it was always either Chateaubriand with scalloped potatoes or chicken Kiev with rice. They took the steak, having learned from experience that the chicken tasted like so much buttered whoopie-cushion.

For a long time they ate in perfect silence. The overhead cabin lights went off, and they shared a small bottle of dreadful New York State red wine. The subject of Faircliff's new acquisition seemed to have been dropped.

"When he comes, I'll want him to take over day-to-day management of the office." It was the first word Faircliff had spoken in nearly an hour. "I want you to start moving over more into policy formation and running that network of closet-skulkers of yours. You've been spreading yourself too thin for a long time now, Frank, and we have to think of the future. We've got an election coming up before you know it."

"That's three years away. If you've hired this new boy to replace me as well, why don't you just say so?"

They regarded each other in the dim pinkish light from the overhead console with an approximately equal sharing of surprise and resentment, although after the first moment you would have thought the surprise was all the senator's portion.

"I'm amazed at you, Frank," he said quietly, like a man whose feelings have been deeply wounded. "I thought you had more faith in my regard for you than that. I'd thought of this more as a sort of promotion, getting you out of the cheap-shit stuff and more involved with what's important— and is going to get more important." He paused and looked slightly away, as if peering into some indistinct, impalpable future. "I need advisors, Frank, not people to sharpen the pencils. I want you to start getting yourself ready for when we make our big play. I would have thought you'd have understood that."

Well, he could always manage a good speech; it was like turning on the hot water tap with him. He could always get you just where you lived, the bastard. Austen found that he had been suitably humbled, and in that peculiar way that belongs only to the masters, in which he felt valued and loved at the same time.

"All right, okay. I'm sorry. But I work for nobody but you, Simon." He clenched his fist and set it down quietly on the armrest between them. "You put this guy over my head, and I walk. It's as simple as that."

Faircliff smiled, since he had won, and then turned a little away and snagged the stewardess again—probably to order another vodka gimlet. "Sure, Frank," he said, without really looking at him. "I understand that. You'll never have any other boss but me; I wouldn't have it any other way."

And that seemed to settle the matter. They got in at Dulles airport at about eleven o'clock that night and, as arranged, someone was there from the office to pick them up. Austen was dropped off at his apartment first, since it was on the way to Chevy Chase, and when he went into his bedroom to unpack his suitcase he found Dottie sitting up in bed in a pair of his pajamas, reading one of his Fanny Burney novels.

"How can you stand this tripe?" she asked, as if inquiring into a miracle. "It's all about dippy little girls falling in love."

He hadn't been expecting to see her until the next evening, and the sudden sound of her voice managed to startle the hell out of him.

Howard Diederich was supposed to arrive at the end of the month, but in the meantime there was enough to keep everybody occupied. For one thing, Marty Eilberg spent most of his first full week of unemployment trying to get Austen on the phone. He was sorry he had told the senator to shove it; it was strictly something that had happened in the heat of the moment, and he needed some help getting another job. Austen gave instructions to the switchboard girl that he was going to be either in conference or on another line or dead until Marty took the hint and left him alone, but he had underestimated the man's tenacity.

On his second Monday after returning from California, he looked up from the egg salad sandwich he was having for lunch in the employee's cafeteria of the Senate office building, and there was our boy—dark, skinny, and mournful in a wrinkled black raincoat, standing in front of his table.

"Leave me alone, Marty," he said wearily. "I don't owe you a fucking thing, and I'm not using up any favors to put you back on the federal payroll."

Marty simply pulled out the chair on the other side of the table and sat down, cradling his head on his hands. His huge knuckles, sticking out like so many fragile porcelain knobs, were somehow both obscene and pitiful, like an infirmity uncovered to cheat you of your sympathy. Austen found himself unable to overcome a feeling of shame; still, he would have liked to be able to kick the fellow in the shin.

"I know, Frank," Marty answered, sighing audibly. "I'm not asking for the world; I just wish you'd try to get Faircliff to write a better letter for me. I'm sick of politics. I'd like to see if I couldn't get back into investment services, and a good letter would help."

"What did he say, just that you hadn't been caught with your hand in the till?"

Marty nodded.

"You know as well as I do there's not much chance of his turning the other cheek. You know how he is."

"I know, Frank. But he might if you asked him." The wheedling eagerness in his voice was almost physically painful. Austen pushed his sandwich away, wondering why he couldn't just tell the obnoxious little creep to fuck off.

"All right, but don't come near me again. If I get it I'll mail it to you—just leave me the hell alone."

"Thanks, Frank," Marty exploded, exactly as if he had been keeping the two words under pressure. "I'll never forget this, pal. I owe you one." He sprang out of his chair, and it was all Austen could do to avoid having his hand clasped in abject gratitude. And then, quite suddenly, he was gone.

Fortunately, the senator was off touring some stupid water project in South Carolina and wouldn't be back until Wednesday, so Austen could wait until then to think about the problems of the unemployed and to devote himself to what he considered the really interesting question of what they were all supposed to make of this Diederich person.

It was a puzzle you could really get lost in: what makes a man throw over a successful career telling lies about under-arm deodorants to sign on for sixteen thousand a year as a political operative and general office factotum with Simon Faircliff? You don't buy a lot of Havana cigars for sixteen thousand a year. Hell, it was two less than Austen himself was drawing; he had seen the cheat sheets with his own eyes.

A year or so before a big election, he could understand it. Bate & Palmer would give their boy a leave of absence to work his little miracle and he would be back in his corporate suite the first Wednesday in November. But Diederich was chucking the whole thing, and in the name of what? Even the next run for the Senate was three years off. It just didn't figure.

"All I know is that my mother couldn't stand the sight of him," Dottie murmured, almost through her teeth. She had

spent the whole evening, from about six-fifteen on, rolled up
in nothing but a percale bedsheet; everything had been
absolutely tremendous until Austen mentioned Howard
Diederich.

"When Daddy decided to give up his law practice and run
for the House, he was just there, like a genie out of a bottle.
She never wanted Daddy to run. Do you want some Sanka?"

He shook his head and watched her swing her legs over
the edge of the bed and feel for her tiny silk slippers, the only
personal articles she ever left in his apartment. Except for
the short hair, she might have been a Roman matron strolling
out to the kitchen in her permanent-press toga. For a moment he lay next to where it was still possible to feel the
warmth of her body on the crumpled blanket, and then, on
an impulse, not really sure what he had in mind, he slipped
into his bathrobe and followed her.

"Why are you so down on him all the time?"

"Daddy?" She looked over her shoulder at him as she
filled up his teapot with cold water. "Why should you care?"

"Take my word for it."

She stood there, her back to him as the water ran, not
moving, but he could sense a certain rigidness coming over
her. It was as if she were nerving herself up for something.

"All right, if you must know. Mommy didn't want him to
run, and then, not even a year after the election, she died."
She turned around, keeping her back to the sink. The hand
that held the teapot was trembling slightly, but that might
have been because the teapot was heavy.

"I was at school most of the time; I didn't see them much,
but I know she was terribly unhappy. And not simply
because she didn't like Washington or anything like that—it
was as if the whole world had come to an end for her. Even
when we were all back in California together, sometimes
she'd just start to cry, for no reason at all. And then she
died. They said it was a stroke, but I don't believe that. He
just broke her heart. He as good as murdered her."

"Don't you think that's quite a bit to lay on him? Were
you there when it happened?"

She shook her head, smiling a sad cynical smile. "No, I
wasn't there, but neither were you. What's the matter,
Frank? Don't you think your hero would be capable of
driving his wife to her grave?"

"I think he'd be capable of just about anything, but so

what? She might really have had a stroke, you know—just a piece of plaque pulling loose from the inside of an artery, the sort of thing you get from eating too many plates of *gâteau d'abricot à l'orange*. Politicians' wives get depressed and go to pieces all the time—it's something of an occupational hazard—and the two might not have had a thing to do with each other."

"Maybe not. But, once again, why should you care?"

They stood looking at each other like enemies, almost the whole length of the kitchen between them, and then Dottie set the teapot down on the counter and folded her arms together in front of her, seeming to lose track of everything in some absorbing unhappiness. He came toward her and took her in his arms, forcing her to feel his body against hers, to notice that he was there in the room with her and would insist on being heard when he gave his answer.

"Because we've got to tell him about us. It sounds dreadfully corny, I realize, but I love you and I'm tired of this hole-and-corner stuff. I want to get married—will you marry me, Dottie?"

She raised her eyes to his face, and there were tears in them. But she was clinging to him now as if for dear life; her hands slipped inside his robe until they were almost all the way around his back.

"You have a lousy sense of timing, Mr. Austen." Her voice was no more than a whisper.

"That's not an answer. Would you like me to repeat the question?"

"No." She shook her head, and then she smiled at him in a way that made him melt inside. "No—yes. Yes, I'll marry you, if it's what you want."

"It's what I want. Don't be dense—of course it's what I want."

"Then love me, Frank. Right now, right here, make love to me, Frank. If you want me, then take me."

"Kitchen floors are bad for the back," he said, taking her face in his hands. "Not to mention the knees and the elbows."

But he could see she was serious, that she meant every word of it and wasn't hearing a thing he said. She was pulling him down like a weight; her bedsheet already had slipped from her shoulders, and he let the two of them sink together. She opened her legs for him and wrapped them around his waist as he came inside, sobbing into his ear, whether on account of passion or from some mysterious grief of her own it was impossible to know.

VI

Simon Faircliff was back in his office Thursday morning, but before Austen could find the right moment to talk to him about Dottie a few other things got in the way.

First there was the matter of Marty Eilberg's letter, which had top billing in the folder of papers Austen slid across the boss's desk at the beginning of their regular nine-fifteen routine-business meeting. Faircliff opened the folder, adjusted the glasses that he would gladly have perished before owning to in public, read about a line and a half of the closely written single-spaced page, and looked up with an expression of calm astonishment, his eyebrows disappearing into his hairline.

"This is a letter of recommendation for Marty Eilberg," he announced, the way someone else might have informed you that one of the buttons on your coat sleeve was missing. "It makes him sound like a cross between Bismarck and Albert Schweitzer. What can you have been thinking of, Frank?"

He pushed it aside and went on to what was underneath, which happened to be a memo on the proposed new campaign-spending law and must therefore have been much more engrossing, because he hardly noticed when Austen rose a few inches out of his chair and deftly replaced the Eilberg letter.

"Be big-hearted and sign it. You won't even have to lie—as you can see, I've already done all the lying for you. Give the guy a break, Simon, and get his ass off my front stoop before the landlady starts entertaining an idea that I've sublet the doormat."

Both the senator's hands were resting palm-down on the desktop, with the fingers widely spread, which wasn't usually a very promising sign, and then, quite without warning, he smiled one of his resigned, how-could-I-possibly-refuse-you-anything smiles and reached for his pen.

"All right, just to show I don't bear any ill will." He

handed the sheet back with a kind of subdued flourish, and then his eyes returned to the spending-law memo. "I want you to take the train up to New York today," he said after a little pause, but without seeming to have any attention for anything except what he was reading. "Stay overnight; make it look like you're out on a razzle, if anyone should happen to be interested."

Oh Simon, you suave dog, what is it you've just bought yourself with Marty Eilberg's pathetic little hide? Austen tried to conceal his admiration in the presence of all this smooth duplicity. So Simon wanted a little errand run for him—you wondered what it could possibly be about that he would feel the necessity of trading for it.

"Sure. What do I do when I get there?"

"Just meet a man in a bar," Faircliff answered, finally glancing up from his absorbing sheet of paper and putting it away without, apparently, having noticed that the memo was continued on the other side. He smiled again, as if conscious of being involved in an absurdity. "I honestly don't have the faintest idea what it's about," he went on. "But how bad can it be? All you're doing is picking up a package and bringing it home."

Austen went back to his apartment to pack a suitcase and write Dottie a little note that he pinned with a thumbtack to the bedroom door; it would be awkward to phone since, at that hour of the morning, he wouldn't get anyone except the senator's manservant, who kept an inventory of all calls. He toyed with the idea of taking along the Baretta automatic that had been lying at the back of a drawer ever since his return from the army, but it finally seemed a trifle melodramatic under the circumstances. After all, he wasn't about to burn anybody down in the lobby of the Essex House just to protect some anonymous supporter's clandestine contribution to the office entertainment fund.

He was lucky with his train connections and was in Pennsylvania Station by one-twelve that afternoon. His appointment wasn't until nine o'clock that night, so he checked into his hotel, hung his good suit up in the closet so the wrinkles would have a chance to fall out, washed his face, and took a taxi to Bloomingdale's, which turned out to be only about five blocks away, to see whether he couldn't find something nice to take back to Dottie.

At half-past eight he was occupying a table not much larger than a manhole cover in a place on Seventh Avenue called the Peppermint Shack. He had eaten a very lovely, very filling, and quite indecently expensive meal at a French restaurant on Fifty-third Street—what the hell, it was on the office credit card, and he was supposed to be giving a creditable imitation of a gentleman on the town—but he was beginning to wonder whether perhaps all that food hadn't been something of a mistake.

The big attraction at the Peppermint Shack was a line of skinny little Puerto Rican girls who danced naked on a narrow stage that ran almost the whole length of the room, and who allowed nice men to tuck five-dollar bills all any which way into their G-strings. The lady behind the bar wore a transparent, mint-green babydoll nightie, but except for purposes of business hardly anyone noticed that she was there. The only thing you seemed to be able to buy was beer, which tasted like cow piss, gave you gas, and cost, with the tip, about twelve dollars per seven-ounce bottle, and if you didn't get a refill at frequent enough intervals to suit them the waitresses, who dressed like members of a motorcycle gang, would start telling you in a very loud voice that you'd better get the fuck out and make room for the paying customers. Austen had been inside a thousand dives very like it in Saigon, except that perhaps none of them had been quite so stridently unpleasant.

Its merits as a place of assignation, however, were obvious. It was as dark as the inside of a cow's stomach—God knows, you wouldn't have wanted to find out what strange substances were making the floor so sticky under your shoes—and you couldn't have asked for a more private atmosphere: the men were only interested in the girls, and the girls were only interested in collecting money.

By quarter to nine, Austen was into his fourth beer and had already been compelled to face the horrors of the men's room twice. The dancers, between their performances on the stage, would drift around among the tables, smiling luridly and trying to catch your eye so you would invite them to sit down for a drink—several such interesting conversations were taking place in various dark corners; you had the impression these people had known each other simply forever—but after a few tries the poor little drabs got the message and left him alone.

The man he was waiting for would stand by the bar; there would be a copy of *Newsweek* in his jacket pocket, folded in half lengthwise so you could see the first four letters of the word, and he would answer to the name of "Bernard." It was all very much like a bad movie—even Faircliff had been embarrassed—but apparently Bernard was insisting. It wouldn't do to keep things simple and have the guy ring us up at our hotel; no, we had to pretend the whole world was interested in our every move.

And at three minutes to nine there he was, a plumpish, balding man in a charcoal-gray suit that looked as if it had probably been hand-tailored for him on Saville Row. This was no messenger boy. Austen decided he would give him a little time before he got up from his table and made contact; it would be entertaining to see how the guy behaved himself.

Not very well, actually—at least, not by the standards Austen had learned to apply in Vietnam. This was an amateur. His hand kept sneaking down to caress the edges of his magazine, as if he worried that it might somehow have fallen out, and he was sweating; it was a cool night outside, and, although the place was kept reasonably warm (doubtless so the entertainment wouldn't come down with goosepimples), our friend had found it necessary to wipe his face twice in the space of about a minute and a half. He was scared. This wasn't the sort of thing he did regularly.

Nobody else seemed to notice, however. Probably this was the way half the clowns who came in here looked, middle-aged corporate types in a perfect terror they might be seen by somebody from their tennis club.

"How are you, Bernard?" Austen had been standing right behind him, and he was afraid for a second the guy was going to have a seizure. He put a hand on Bernard's shoulder, the way you might steady a plank of wood to keep it from falling over. "You mustn't be such a bundle of nerves, Bernard; somebody might think you weren't having a good time."

The barmaid came up to them, her huge doughlike breasts swaying from side to side behind their little curtain of mint-green gossamer, and treated them to a look of bored inquiry. Austen smiled, lifting into view the beer glass he had been farsighted enough to bring along with him from his table, but the other man merely gaped, as if he couldn't imagine what she wanted.

"Order a beer, Bernard. It's how they make their living here."

Bernard nodded mechanically and reached inside his jacket for his wallet, and the barmaid went away, to return in about fifteen seconds with a glass and a very wet brown bottle, both of which she held up delicately with first finger and thumb as if displaying a couple of prize trout. Obviously a keen judge of human psychology, she short-changed him two dollars, and he stuffed the money into his pocket without noticing.

Austen decided to keep the pressure up. He was curious; he didn't like it when people involved him in things he was supposed to take on faith, and he didn't have anything to lose by pushing just a little.

"You've got something for me? Or perhaps we're just here to drink in the atmosphere." He waved his hand casually, seeming to take in the whole dismal scene, and grinned. "Perhaps you'd like me to tell my principal that you've thought better of it and he should just forget the whole thing."

It seemed to work. Bernard's hand dove for cover in his trouser pocket and came out as a clenched fist; when he opened it there was a small key with a red plastic handle, the number 437 embossed over it in white, lying in his palm. He stared at it stupidly for a moment, giving the impression he would have liked to remember where he had seen it before. Austen reached over and picked it up.

"Grand Central Station—and tell Diederich that this pays all the bills, that this ends it and I want to be left alone."

Austen was sure he was bluffing and decided he would try his hand at that himself. His grin widened, and he put the key out of sight in his pocket. "You have an open-ended account, pal. You'll be hearing from us again."

It seemed to be a terrible moment for Bernard. The man looked absolutely appalled; his eyes grew wide, and he appeared to be trying to swallow but without success. Then he jammed his hands into his jacket pockets and swept past and out into the night.

"Your friend didn't finish his beer." It was the barmaid. Austen turned around to see her smiling loosely at him, as if they were sharing a joke. He smiled back, perhaps not very nicely.

"No, he didn't. But he didn't miss much, did he."

He didn't wait around for a reply.

Outside he took a deep breath of the sweet cold air. It was lovely after the Peppermint Shack, with its hazy atmosphere of sweat and spilled beer; it was even quiet. He walked down toward Fifty-sixth Street, feeling as if he had stepped into a meadow in Wisconsin. He didn't catch sight of Bernard again until he turned the corner.

It didn't amount to more than a guess and an impulse. Something about the way the man had hit the door suggested he would turn to the left, and Austen had decided to follow him. What the hell; he was still curious, and he didn't have anything better to do. Besides, it was beginning to be sort of like the old days. The luggage locker in Grand Central Station could jolly well wait for a couple of hours.

He didn't really suppose he could keep it up for very long—Bernard would probably flag down a cab in a couple of minutes and disappear forever—but that wasn't the way it worked out. Bernard just walked in a straight line without looking to the right or the left, as if his object were less to get somewhere than simply to pull himself together. After about half a block he took the *Newsweek* from his pocket and threw it angrily into a trash can, but for the rest he kept going doggedly on; his hands hanging limply down at his sides and his head bent. Austen kept to the other side of the street and gave him as much lead as he dared.

At Fifth Avenue, his man stepped off the curb against the light and nearly got clipped by a bright red Datsun that swerved and sounded its horn and scurried off like an insect. This seemed to bring him to his senses, and he was a different person by the time he made it over to the East Side. He cut left and started toward the park, traveling more slowly now, paying attention in a normal way to his surroundings.

Still he didn't give any sign that he was tired of walking. Maybe he lived somewhere around here and was on his way home. People did live in midtown Manhattan, a few of them, the ones who could afford it, and this guy didn't look like any socialist, with his pink, well-shaved face and his British suit. Could be he was a native of the place.

Austen kept along behind, feeling like Exhibit Number One as he passed in front of the huge lit windows of the Doubleday bookstore, but his quarry gave no indication that he suspected anyone was following him. At Fifty-ninth

Street they turned east again—yes, this was a man on his way home.

Home turned out to be a brownstone between Madison and Park. Bernard let himself in with a key, and a few seconds later windows on the first and third floors went dark, so apparently the building hadn't been cut up into flats. Bernard had the whole place to himself; he wasn't poor. Austen waited for about three minutes and then crossed over to read the house number, which appeared on the iron paling that closed off the basement entrance, and the name on a brass plate just below the doorbell.

Storey—Mr. Storey of number sixty-seven. Fine. Now we knew whom we were dealing with. He managed to get a taxi at Park and gave directions for Grand Central.

The package turned out to be just that, an oblong box, about three inches by five by two, wrapped up in brown paper. There was no writing on the outside, it didn't rattle, and probably it didn't weigh more than two or three ounces. Austen took a dollar bill out of his wallet and measured it against the top—too small. If there was any money inside there couldn't be very much. Beyond that, it could be anything. Diamonds, microfilm, a bomb, somebody's middle finger, a chocolate eclair, anything at all.

After mature consideration, he decided against unwrapping it for a look inside. You never knew—it could be wired somehow, or there might be some elaborate and unobvious code worked into the wrapping itself. He was curious, but not that curious. After all, giving him the sack might be the least terrible thing Simon would think of to punish such a breach of confidence; they seemed to be playing by different rules lately.

He dragged the telephone book out of the drawer under his hotel room night table and looked for a Storey with that address. There wasn't one, which only proved the guy had an unlisted number. It wasn't chic to be in the phone book. But anybody with the money to support a Manhattan town-house was very likely to be of some significance in the world. Tomorrow morning, before his train left, he would drop by the Forty-second Street library and take a peek into *Who's Who*. In this country, millionaires weren't suffered to live anonymous lives; somebody had to have heard of Mr. Storey.

"Tell Diederich that this pays all the bills . . ." And Diederich, the story went, was still out in California, waiting for the moving van to pull up behind his apartment. He hadn't even warmed his new office chair yet, and already gilt-edged city slickers were dropping by the body shops to deliver mysterious packages for him.

Austen changed into his pajamas and went into the bathroom to wash his face. This floor of the hotel showed all the symptoms of having been redecorated recently. The walls were a brilliant, rather synthetic-looking peach, and everywhere you looked there were mirrors—in the bathroom you had the feeling of being at the center of a crowd. He looked around at all the other Frank Austens who were busy drying their hands and wondered whether perhaps he shouldn't take a vote.

"What do you say, fellas?" he murmured to the walls. "Does it smell all right to you?"

Apparently not.

VII

STOREY, CHESTER ARNOLD, banker; b. Weatherford, Tex., Apr. 9, 1921; s. Walter and Ida (Taylor) S.; B.S., Harvard, 1946; Ph.D., Columbia, 1948; m. Beatrice Patricia Howland, Aug. 5, 1950 (div.); children—Anita Hancock, Joyce Bennett; m. Susan Aldrich Lind, Jan. 23, 1968 (div.). With Inland Sec. and Trust, 1948-55, 2d v.p., Cent. Manhattan Bank, 1955-58, v.p., 1958-61, sr. v.p., 1961-65, pres., chmn. bd., 1965—; also dir. Stillman Fund, 1967—, trustee Farleigh Univ., 1970—. Served from lt. (j.g.) to lt. comdr. USN, 1942-45. Recipient Navy Cross, 1944. Mem. Internat. Exec. Service Corps, Am. Philos. Soc., Phi Beta Kappa, Sigma Alpha Epsilon. Republican. Episcopalian. Clubs: Harvard, Knickerbocker. Home: 67 E 61st St. New York City NY 10021. Office: 388 Park Ave. New York City NY 10022.

Certainly the least anyone could say about Howard Diederich was that he employed very high-class bagmen. Even on the train back to Washington Austen had a reasonable amount of trouble believing that someone had actually stepped out of the pages of *Fortune* and into a place like the Peppermint Shack for the purpose of handing over to him a package about half the size of a brick.

The senator was nowhere around the office, which was hardly surprising—Congress seemed to think that the weekend began immediately after lunch on Friday—so he deposited the package in the safe to which only he and Faircliff had the combination, per standard operating procedure. Then he went back to his own little cubicle and made a phone call.

Forty minutes later he was seated in a small fish restaurant not half a mile from the University of Maryland. Austen hadn't had lunch yet, and the place was particularly well known for its softshell crab. Had he been consulting his stomach alone, however, he probably would have picked somewhere closer to Washington, or perhaps might even have contented himself with a peanut-butter sandwich in the privacy of his own apartment. He was there because he knew that in such a place, and at such an hour, he could be reasonably sure of not running into anybody he knew.

The waiter had just brought him his clam chowder when Marty Eilberg came through the door. Austen thrust up a hand to attract his attention.

"Sit down, Marty," he said, smiling and making a sign to the waiter to bring another menu. "I've got your letter in my pocket, and all your problems in life are solved. How does New York grab you? You want to go to work for Central Manhattan Bank? Sit down and have some chowder—it's freezing outside."

Marty didn't so much sit as kind of wither into his chair. For several seconds he was simply an object on the other side of the table, unconscious of the waiter's repeated attempts to put the menu into his hands, apparently unaware of anything except the three words that finally became his first intelligible response.

"Central Manhattan Bank?"

"You want a drink, Marty? Waiter, bring the man a scotch and water and some of that clam chowder."

"Central Manhattan Bank?"

"That's right." Frank Austen held up the bread basket, shaking it once or twice, the way you might a rattle if you were trying to attract the attention of a child, and after a few seconds Marty Eilberg took a roll and set it down on the checkered tablecloth next to his place setting; it would be something like a quarter of an hour before he touched it again.

"You ever heard of Chester Storey? He runs the joint. He's a great friend and admirer of Simon's, and he'll probably take you on his personal staff if you play your cards right when you show him that letter."

The waiter came back with the chowder and a drink—it looked like something connected with the whiskey family, but God only knew—and Marty took a long swallow. After that he was his old self again.

"Is that all I have to do, just ask for the job?" His eyes narrowed as if he suspected some sort of trap, which wasn't so unreasonable of him. Austen smiled and nodded and broke open a roll, scattering pieces of crust here and there around his soup bowl.

"Simon doesn't know a thing about this," he said, letting the smile die. "After I leave here, I won't either. A little finesse is what's called for—and a good memory. I want you to remember that it was me who put this in your way, Marty. I'm not interested in your gratitude, but it may happen one of these days that I'll want you to do a little something for me, and I'll want to hear from you from time to time, just to know how things are working out and how you're hitting it off with Storey. I'll expect you to bear that in mind for a long time."

After that, the meal went off very well. Marty got it through his head that he was to suggest, merely suggest, that Simon Faircliff had been the one to advise him about applying to Central Manhattan, and that he might do well to make a glancing mention, at some point or another, of Howard Diederich. He wasn't to suggest anything there; the magic of the name would have more potency if it were allowed to remain undiluted by any inferences that could possibly be checked. And he was supposed to keep Austen advised at all times of his home address and his telephone numbers, there and at work. He was to avoid any contact with Austen's office; he could use the mails and write to him at his apartment. He digested all that and a great deal of lobster tail besides, and he left the restaurant a happy man.

Austen's feelings were a little more complicated. It didn't make him feel any better to be on to something, since whatever it was could only be dangerous to himself or to Simon Faircliff—or both. It had occurred to him that Faircliff might know very little more than he did himself, that this all might be Diederich's scam and that the boss man might need to be protected from his new lieutenant. It had also occurred to him that that might be nothing more than the way he wanted to read it. He was the head boy now; he wasn't interested in having any rivals. The wish might be father to the thought. Well, he would have to see.

The following Monday morning he finally saw Howard Diederich. That was a beginning. Senator Faircliff practically met Austen at the front door. "Come on, Frank," he said, wrapping Austen's shoulder in one hand as they stood by the coat closet. "Howard got in last night. I want you to meet him."

The introduction was simple enough. Diederich was in his office, fishing objects out of one of the three packing cases that had come for him the Wednesday before. He straightened up when the two men filed through his door and shook hands. His sleeves were rolled up almost to the elbows, and Austen noticed that the man's forearms were as thick as telephone poles. Clearly he wasn't as tame as he looked.

For the rest, he was a compact, self-possessed-looking man of about average height, very tidy in his dark gray trousers and his sleeveless charcoal sweater. In fact, everything about him suggested a certain grayness, as if he had been conceived entirely in monochrome. His eyes and his hair were black, but of a black that reminded you of heavily tarnished silver. And a smile kept struggling to express itself at the corners of his mouth, as if he were faintly amused at the impression he knew he must be creating. All in all, there was something very formidable about him. Austen didn't like him any better than he had expected to.

Faircliff seemed simply to withdraw to a safe distance, like a man watching a couple of dogs square off for a fight, a man who hasn't yet made up his mind which way to place his wager.

"I hope you've found a nice place to live."

"Oh, yes. I've taken an apartment in the Watergate; it's very comfortable."

"Spent much time in Washington before?"

"No, not really. I lived in New York for a few years when I was younger, but somehow I never got down to Washington."

"Oh, really? Well, you won't find this as lively as New York; Washington's just kind of an overgrown company town."

"Yes, I've heard that . . ."

It was similar to a thousand other conversations Frank Austen and everybody else in the world had every day. After the fifteen or twenty minutes mandated by common politeness, and after offering and being thanked for offering to do anything he could to help the new kid in the schoolyard find his way to the bathroom, Austen went back to his own office with the uncomfortable conviction that everything was up for grabs now, and that Simon would be watching, probably thinking it was all funny as hell, to see who came down with what.

These symptoms, needless to say, had not gone unobserved. The senator from California was sufficiently disturbed by them that, as soon as he could get away from his Sunday golf game with the vice president and a couple of wealthy constituents, he drove over to pay a late afternoon call on his new senior aide, whom he found in his apartment, assembling the cabinetwork for an intimidating complex stereo system. The two men sat down together at opposite ends of a sofa that looked as if it would probably have to be cleaned after its journey from one coast to the other, and Howard Diederich listened with the collected gravity of a priest hearing confession.

"I just don't know, Howard." Fairchild shrugged his massive shoulders as he leaned more heavily against the arm of the sofa. "I wonder whether I didn't make a mistake by sending him up to New York. Maybe I should have gone myself."

Howard Diederich shook his head. "No, you did the right thing. The less you concern yourself with that side of things the better; we simply can't afford to have you compromised at this stage. Besides, I checked the package and it hadn't been tampered with, so what could he either know or suspect that can be of the slightest danger to us now?"

"Nothing."

"Then what are you worried about?"

"You don't know him," Faircliff announced, apparently to the neutral tan of the carpet. "He's very clever; I could tell you stories . . . I don't know what games you've been up to, and I don't want to know, but if Frank ever gets it into his head . . . he's just not the type to let go very easily, is all."

"I thought you liked him. I thought you said he was so very capable and loyal and would be of such use. Have you changed your mind?"

"I do like him. If I could have had a son . . ." Faircliff got up, simply because he couldn't bear being still another moment, and went over to look at the disassembled pieces of Howard Diederich's record turntable, laid out in some incomprehensible order on the floor.

Diederich simply smiled. He appeared not to have moved a muscle anytime within the last week, but he smiled. "You're going to have to get used to it, Simon. In five years you'll be president of the United States; that's the plan. And you'll have to deal with all kinds of very clever people who won't be in on our various little secrets—a whole government full of them. We've got to use people, Simon. We simply won't have any choice."

He was quiet again, as motionless as an idol. The effect was somehow very calming, and Faircliff resumed his seat, leaning back into the sofa cushions and closing his eyes, like a man accepting defeat. "Then what do we do about Frank?" he asked, his voice almost without expression, as if the subject had ceased to interest him.

"Didn't you tell me he was sleeping with Dottie?"

It was an unexpected question. Faircliff seemed to come back to life with a jolt; he twisted around to face Diederich, and his whole attitude suggested a certain belligerence, a willingness to take offense. "What of it?"

"It seems a simple enough solution." Diederich cocked his head a little to one side, his immobility shading off imperceptibly into the faint irony that seemed somehow the essence of the man. "It's something I learned a long time ago: personal loyalty is nothing unless it is supported by self-interest. You say that Frank Austen is loyal to you, and now

you seem to want to qualify that, implying that there might
be limits. Very well—tie him closer. Give him something to
lose. Let him marry Dottie."

His smile emerged again, like a thing almost exhausted by
the labor of being born. "Certainly it should provide him
with something else with which to occupy his mind."

And that was how, quite unexpectedly one day, Frank
Austen found that the issue of his future had been settled for
him. He simply discovered that he was faced with two facts.
The first of these was that Diederich, after the initial week or
so, seemed to retreat into the middle distance, that his own
position with their boss had suddenly become even stronger.

The other was not so much a fact as an event. He arrived
back at his apartment one evening, about a week after he
had figured out that he was once more head boy, and found
Dottie sitting in the armchair in his living room, her feet
curled up under her and her arms held close to her body, as if
she was anxious to take up as little space as possible.

"Daddy and I have come to an understanding," she said.
In the artificial light of the only lamp she had thought to turn
on, her brown eyes took on a darkness, almost a lifelessness,
like those of a figure carved out of black marble. "It seems
that our getting married is to be the price of your rise in the
world. He didn't put it in so many words, but he plans to
come down very hard on you if we don't."

Austen set his briefcase to rest on a table. Otherwise, he
hardly moved.

"It's not something I have to be flogged into doing—you
know that, Dottie. We've talked about it before."

"It's not you he's worried about. He seems perfectly sure
you'll jump just the right way; it's me he thinks he's got to
bring into line."

It was odd how she appeared visibly to sag at that moment. Austen came over and knelt beside her chair, covering
her hands with his own.

"How long have you been sitting here, Dottie?" he asked,
but she only looked at him—almost through him—as if
surprised and saddened by the stupidity of such a question.

"Will you tell me something, Frank? I'll marry you anyway—I don't think we really need anything but the truth—
but will you tell me? If I asked you to quit, without giving

any reasons, if I just asked you to chuck it and go to work for somebody else, would you do that for me, Frank?"

He shook his head. She seemed to have a right to the truth. "Not without a reason, sweetheart. I can't believe that would do us any good."

"No, perhaps not."

Part Two

**The Bread
of Secrecy**

I

"It's not very complicated, Simon. If you want the nomination, you've got to win the Senate big next time. If we want the presidency, we've got to take California like San Juan Hill."

Such was the gospel according to Frank Austen, delivered over lunch in the senator's Washington offices about six weeks after Austen had returned from a brief honeymoon in Bermuda. The senator agreed.

"Fine, Frank," he said, stirring a packet of artificial sweetener into his coffee; he was going through one of his more-or-less regular phases of being very concerned about his weight. "You see to it, okay? I want you to run that show." He smiled, and Austen suddenly realized that he had just condemned himself to spending the next two years of his life aboard transcontinental planes.

But it wasn't such a bad time. Dottie would drive out and pick him up at the airport—he discovered that it made a difference, having someone to come home to—and sometimes, when he had to be gone for more than a few weeks, she would go with him and stay at her aunt's in Pacific Grove, where they could see each other at least once in a while. The aunt was very fond of Dottie and always kept her room for her, where, if you left the window open at night, you could listen to the waves breaking.

They were in California for their second anniversary, and

Austen drove up from Los Angeles to San Francisco and they spent the week-end at the Mark Hopkins and had dinner on the big night at a Japanese restaurant called Mingei-Ya, because Dottie was absolutely wacko about sitting around on the floor and eating raw fish and something called O-Mitsutaki.

"My feet are asleep."

"That's perfectly ridiculous. People all over Asia sit around like this all the time without their feet going to sleep."

"Nevertheless . . ." He tried to move and managed to bang his toes against a table leg. "Oh God! Now it's awake with a vengeance."

And then she started to laugh. "Poor Frank—I'm sorry, but if you could see the expression on your face . . . I really am sorry. Here, have some more bean curd. You poor darling.

"Will you still love me if I want to eat with a knife and fork tomorrow night?"

"Yes, baby, I promise I'll still love you—even then."

When she didn't come along, he would bring her home pineapples and boxes of See's chocolate truffles and loaves of sourdough French bread, all the things she missed, carried in plastic shopping bags and balanced on his knees between San Francisco and Washington.

In San Francisco, Austen rented a little two-bedroom apartment, simply because he was there often enough to make it cheaper than staying in hotels, and sometimes Dottie would phone him at odd hours of the morning and they would talk for ten or fifteen minutes and then say goodnight, and Austen would roll over in bed and go back to sleep.

He wondered sometimes, with a certain amusement, whether perhaps, she wasn't checking up on him, but she needn't have worried. Probably, if asked, he would have described himself as a very happily married man. And if he stayed away from other women, it wasn't because he was worried about getting caught—if the idea had occurred to him, he would have thought it was ludicrous—but from a kind of emotional fastidiousness. Other women weren't Dottie, and therefore he didn't really seem to want them.

So together or apart Mr. and Mrs. Austen lived in peace. They had even managed, somehow, to sustain a truce for the time being about his work for her father. About her father, period. He might have been leaving the house every morning to go stand around the bus terminal soliciting dimes.

Nevertheless, the business of getting Simon Faircliff reelected went on with relentless efficiency. By January of that political season the shape of things had become clear, and Austen, having assembled the mechanism, went back to Washington to submit his analysis and make his recommendations. On his second night in town, he picked up Howard Diederich at the Watergate and together they drove over to Chevy Chase to sit in Faircliff's living room and settle the shape of the campaign.

"Okay, Frank," Faircliff began, handing him a glass from the portable bar his manservant had set up before being sent off to the movies. "You've got your goddamned ginger ale, so lay it out for us."

Austen held up the fingers of one hand, wiggling them in the air like the characters in a puppet show. "It comes down to this," he said quietly. "My snitches tell me that we've got a good possiblity of up to four serious contenders for the Republican nomination—the more the merrier, but I think four is the most we can reasonably hope for. Two of them have already announced; Turnbill has got his committee in place, so we can count on him unless something really drastic happens to make him chicken out at the last moment, and Harry Arnott wants to but probably requires a nudge to get him to take the risk."

"Who the hell is Harry Arnott?" Faircliff asked, his face wrinkling in distaste. "Do we know him?"

"He's an asemblyman from Orange County, and he's got delusions of grandeur. You know the type—a little to the right of Genghis Khan—but he has a certain following among the bomb-shelter set. He's not insignificant and can be counted on to call everybody a lot of lousy names. He should be encouraged."

Howard Diederich raised a finger and smiled faintly. He was sitting on one end of the sofa, his right foot hooked in behind the opposite knee, like a marble statue of patience. "So what do you propose?" he asked, his voice barely audible.

"I propose that we feed the fires of discord." Austen allowed his eyebrows the privilege of arching slightly. "I propose we make all the trouble we can for Boothe and Warnke, since it's short odds one of them will be running against us in the fall. God, I wish somebody would just tell Congressman Boothe to go away and leave us alone; it would give me hives to have to go up against that smoothie. I propose we nourish Turnbill and Arnott and hope they all four of them have a lot of fun this spring and summer and come out of it with no end of battle scars and bad temper. I've got pipelines into all of them, so I can maybe steer things to some degree, but it'll also take money."

"I'll see to it you have all the money you need, Frank, starting as soon as you like." Diederich smiled again as he spoke, and the two men shared a silent moment of understanding, a kind of treaty between enemies. Then Austen smiled too, raising his glass of ginger ale in salute.

"Howard, one of these dark nights I'm going to have to ask you where you come up with all those envelopes full of hundred-dollar bills."

"I've never heard any complaints from—"

"We can worry about that later," Faircliff broke in, shooting Austen a pointed glance. "Go on, Frank. You've set the dogfight going among the opposition, and I suppose they're more or less guaranteed to cut themselves to pieces before either Warnke or Boothe gets nominated. Just by the by, which do you think it will be?"

"Boothe." Austen made a sour face. "Sorry, chief, but that's what it looks like."

"Well, you never know . . ." Howard Diederich sighed wearily, which, with him, could have been interpreted to mean anything at all.

"And then what happens?"

"And then . . ." Austen took a sip of his ginger ale and paused; it was his little surprise, something he had been saving; and he watched the changes in Simon's face with a good measure of personal satisfaction. "And then you run unopposed."

"But what about Hannah—I thought . . ."

"No." Austen set down his glass on the coffee table, shaking his head with a kind of playful gravity. "No, I had lunch with the governor last week and explained the facts of life to him—it's about time somebody did. It seems he's been having quite a time for himself with his secretary, and last month, at the Western Governor's Conference in Hawaii, somebody put a tape recorder under his bed. The conversation gets a little muddled in places, but my impression is that the lady performs certain services for him that aren't available at home. I don't really suppose, these days, that the voters would care, but his wife would. Mrs. Hannah, I'm told, is something of a holy terror, and besides she's the one who's got the money."

Faircliff brought the flat of his hand down to his leg with a smack. He was ready to laugh out loud, except that he was too startled to make a sound. "Frank, where the hell did . . . Jesus."

"Simple. The secretary came to me, all of her own free will and with the tape reel in her handbag, a very foxy lady with a score to settle." A glance passed between Austen and his father-in-law. No, Simon, I haven't got anything going on the side, not with this one or any other. So you can stop pretending to worry about the domestic happiness of your little girl.

"I guess she doesn't like him or something—apparently, he doesn't appreciate her spiritual qualities." He picked up his ginger ale, held it absent-mindedly for a moment, and then set it down again, making a face. The charm had gone out of everything.

"Anyway, I gave Hannah a copy of the tape over dessert and told him to take it somewhere he wouldn't be disturbed and see how he liked it. He phoned the next morning and pledged his unqualified support."

For perhaps as long as a full minute, the three of them maintained a morose silence, rather as if they had all witnessed something shameful and were waiting for the impression to pass a little so they wouldn't have to mention it. Then the senator rose and went over to the bar and mixed himself another light scotch and water. He glanced at the others, raising his eyebrows in inquiry, but Diederich shook his head—he had barely touched his drink—and Austen was too preoccupied to notice.

"Anything else?" Faircliff asked, sitting down again. When there was no answer, he looked more directly at his son-in-law and frowned. "Frank, anything else you want to say? Any other little messages from home?"

"Just one." Austen shifted uncomfortably in his seat, wondering why all of a sudden he felt so damn mean.

"I think it would be very helpful," he said slowly, as if

weighing each syllable, one at a time, "if you would get off this foreign policy jag of yours. The war's over, Simon—people don't want to hear about Southeast Asia. We've got double-digit inflation and bad unemployment, especially down around Los Angeles, where they've lost all those aerospace contracts lately. People want to hear about that; they want a little sympathy and a sense that you're as pissed off about their problems as they are. They don't care a tinker's damn about Indochina, and all you've talked about for the past six months is some little slant-eyed military dictator."

Faircliff had listened without apparent emotion, but that didn't mean anything. When he lapsed into those motionless, impenetrable silences, he became as unpredictable as a cobra. But finally he shrugged his shoulders, stretching the corners of his mouth into a thin, irritated smile. "It's important, Frank. This U Ba Sein is headed for a fall, and if we're not careful he'll take us down with him. It has got to be discussed."

"It can wait, Simon; it can wait until after the election. Hell, half the people I talked to had never even heard of Kyauktada." Austen leaned forward, resting his elbows on his knees, and his voice took on an almost pleading quality. "I know it's important, boss. But so's your reelection. All I'm asking you to do is to make a few less speeches about the yellow peril and a few more about the price of groceries. Okay?"

"Okay, Frank." The senator nodded and smiled a little more warmly, as if he were indulging the whim of a child.

All the while, Howard Diederich had been staring vacantly at the bricks in the fireplace, slowly smoothing down the fabric of his trouser cuff. He waited until he had managed, in that mysterious way of his, to draw all attention to himself, and then he turned to Austen.

"Then I take it," he began in a languid, toneless voice, "that if we follow your recommendations we can regard reelection as a given; the only question will be the size of the victory. I'd be interested to have Frank's thinking on what kind of showing we'll need to have a respectable chance two years from now."

"Fifty-five percent." Austen allowed himself to grin. "Fifty-five percent has a nice substantial feel to it, especially for a liberal Democrat running from California. Simon could be nominated for God on fifty-five percent."

So that was what they ran for. And that was why Frank Austen spent the next several months lashing the party barons into line like so many galley slaves. The labor leaders and the county commissioners and the ethnics and the state assemblymen, they all thought they had you over a barrel because you had an election coming up, and they all had to be reminded about where the bodies were buried. It was a little ritual, like a rite of passage, and Austen, because it wouldn't do for the senator to soil his hands, got to wield the ceremonial knife.

"Hiya, Frank."

It was eleven o'clock, Tuesday, the twenty-first of February, so this was Steve Rankovic, president and ruling spirit of the Federal Transportation Workers' Union, come up from Los Angeles for the day to throw his weight around and glamorize the premises with his blue-and-green plaid leisure suit. He was a real treat; he shook your hand and grinned, showing all his teeth, like a debauchee being introduced to a schoolgirl.

"Now you tell the senator that I want this containerized cargo bill passed," he went on, dropping your hand and throwing himself back into a chair. "You tell him to remember that I got thirty-six thousand guys, all dues-payin' members, and we got a quarter of a million in our political education fund, and we got . . ."

"You haven't got shit, pal." Frank Austen didn't even smile. "And just because I like you so much, I'm not even going to tell the senator that you were here. He wouldn't appreciate it, you know; he doesn't react too well to being crowded."

He sank back in his chair and, after a few seconds, picked up a pencil that was lying on the desk in front of him, clutching it like a scepter.

"What's the matter with you, Rankovic? Haven't you seen the new Field poll? The senator doesn't need you—he's going to take this election in a walk, and if you don't quit fucking around like this, after November he's not even going to be able to remember your name."

In the end, the union contributed seventy-five thousand

dollars and the services of a hundred and twenty campaign volunteers, and Austen didn't even offer to take their president out for lunch. The poor bastard left the Powell Street offices cringing like a whipped dog.

The midday rainstorm had just abated, and the packed brown earth around the monastery at Pwin Soo, just outside the capital, swam with muddy little rivulets that in time would find their way to the Great River, and from thence to the delta, and finally to the green sea beyond. So, U Ba Sein had heard often enough from his brother, does the soul of the virtuous man journey at last to the mercy of Buddha.

The president for life, who wore a moustache after the Western fashion, along with the uniform of a field marshall, ordered his car to stop directly in front of the ornate entrance to the main temple, where he knew he would find Ko Yeik at this hour, still at his prayers. He looked out the window and frowned at the mud, wishing his brother the abbot were a little less traditional in his views and would order his fellow monks to cover in asphalt at least so much of their road as stretched to the gatehouse—he was wearing new boots, imported for him from Italy.

Still, one's last surviving male relative, and especially so holy a man as Ko Yeik, deserved the attention of an occasional visit. In fact, as U Ba Sein was fond of telling anyone who would listen, he counted these interviews with the abbot as among the chief consolations of his busy, careworn life. And this was true. His brother was too much of a simpleton to care about intriguing, and thus his conversation, full as it was with pious nonsense, allowed the president for life an opportunity to rest his suspicions.

The driver came around and opened the car door for him, saluting smartly, and U Ba Sein stepped out into the mud, which rose as high as his instep.

He smiled, showing teeth stained to the color of fresh blood with betel juice, adjusted his military cap so that the braided visor shaded his eyes, and looked around him. There was a column of jeeps both behind and before his own shining black Citroën limousine, and his bodyguards all carried the lastest and most sophisticated of the automatic rifles sent from the United States. Their sullen, brutal faces gave him an enormous feeling of satisfaction.

In the twenty-three years since he and a cadre of other

middle-level army officers—all safely dead now, victims, within the first eighteen months, of his own assassination squads—had taken power by overthrowing the old, leftward-leaning monarch with the blessing of the American CIA, he had never lost sight of the fact that the loyalty of the junior officers and the rank and file among the soldiers was his key to survival and power. The king, to his sorrow, had put his faith in divine right and the general staff, and these had brought him to the dungeon where he had finally been drowned in a bucket that had served as the prisoners' latrine.

The army had the best of everything, the best women, the best food, the best of anyone who was fool enough to bring a complaint against them, and they were properly appreciative. He could do anything—he was safe from anyone—so long as they remained so.

His brother, of course, took a different view.

But his brother, immediately upon the death of his wife, had retired from the world. Grief had been the excuse, grief and the accompanying estrangement from all mortal joys, but actually it had been weakness. Ko Yeik's wife had been his senior by over seven years, and U Ba Sein could hardly credit anyone, even his brother, with being fool enough to shed many tears over the loss of such. His own European wife and his Kyauktadan mistress did well enough between them, but to abandon life for a woman struck him as not only foolish but indecent. It was a symptom of almost Western effeminacy.

He entered the gloomy temple and strutted across the stone floor until he stood just behind a thin figure kneeling in a saffron-colored monk's robe, through which the knobs of the spine were clearly visible. The monk rose, still facing the statue of Buddha, a Knobby triangle of gold leaf at the back of the altar.

"So you come once more, my brother."

U Ba Sein smiled again. "You knew who it was?"

Ko Yeik turned around. His shaved head seemed to have been carved from sandstone, and there was no smile on his lips, which were thin as parchment and perfectly straight. "I do not often hear the sound of boots within these walls."

"No? Should I have come with my feet bare, and perhaps shaved my head as well?"

"It would be better so."

The president for life looked from his brother's face to that of the Buddha behind him, and his eyes narrowed uncomfortably as he noted the resemblance.

"I am building a pagoda, Ko Yeik," he said, drawing himself up straight. He was a short, thickset man, and his brother, to his vast annoyance, was much the taller. "My agents buy fish to set free in the Great River. *I* will not enter the next life as a mud rat."

Ko Yeik merely closed his eyes for a moment.

With one accord, the two men left the altar, pacing quietly across the stone floor. U Ba Sein, unconsciously perhaps, tried to muffle the sound of his boot heels.

"You have many sins upon you. You will be obliged to build many pagodas, and life is short, brother."

U Ba Sein laughed quietly as he contemplated the abbot's unmanly anxiety—if it was that. Was he not the head of a mighty army? Was he not president for life? Did he not have the backing of the government in America?

"Do you fear for my safety, Ko Yeik?" he asked, letting his eyebrows arch and wondering, not for the first time, whether perhaps his brother did not harbor a certain tenderness for the old days—perhaps even for the monarchy.

"I fear for your soul. I doubt much you would find happiness as a mud rat, yet even so . . . ."

Beside the main temple was a garden, completely enclosed, with a stone cloister around the other three sides but open to the sky. The gravel pathways were still wet with rain.

"May I offer you tea, brother?" The abbot smiled, raising his hand to a novice, who immediately bowed from the waist and disappeared. "Many hands are raised against you, brother. Is it not so? The Lord Buddha teaches that the only safety is in virtue."

"Your concern is excessive," the president for life snapped. Perhaps it had been a mistake to come. "Except yourself, perhaps, no one is without enemies, but I am safe enough."

"You misinterpret me, brother."

They stood together silently, watching a huge, brightly colored carp that swam in the pool at the garden's center, just as if those few yards of water were the wide world and it their absolute and unquestioned sovereign.

When, after a few minutes, the novice had not returned

with their tea, the abbot turned to look for him. Instead he saw two men, dressed in the saffron robes of the monastery. They looked frightened. He did not recognize either of them.

"I am sorry for you, brother," he said quietly, his voice calm and sad and barely audible. "It seems your good works have come too late."

It was three-forty in the morning on the first Sunday in April when the telephone on Austen's night table started ringing like a fire alarm. He got his hand on the receiver in time to keep it from going off again and waking Dottie, who in the darkness was visible merely as a series of lumps under their blanket, and once it was safely off the hook he took his time about sitting up and swinging his legs over the side of the bed. Fortunately, he was still too sleepy even to be annoyed. "Yeah—who is it?"

"It's Gus Paulson," came the answer, as bright as a dime. "Remember me? I just got off work twenty minutes ago, and the first thing I did was hunt up a safe phone to call you from."

It took a while, but, yes, he did remember. Gus Paulson worked in the crisis room over at State, apparently on the graveyard shift, God damn him to hell. He was one of those young men in a hurry who did favors for people; probably Austen was the second or third person he had called that night. He wanted to rise in the world, did Gus; he didn't want to spend the rest of his life manning a teletype.

"I appreciate it. Now, what's happened? Are we at war or what?"

"No, man." Austen could hear the laughter at the other end of the line, and he looked at the dull red numbers of his digital alarm clock and considered how much he hated people who could find anything funny at three forty-two A.M.

"No, we're fine. It's your boss's pal, everybody's favorite gook generalissimo. Somebody got to him while he was visiting his brother in a Buddhist monastery. Reports are that both of them ended up looking like pieces of Swiss cheese."

"Who, U Ba Sein?" Austen was fully awake now and feeling around frantically, trying to find his bedroom slippers with his toes. "Is he dead? Is it confirmed?"

"Oh, he's maggot meat for sure. It happened about three

hours ago, and the country's in a perfect turmoil. They don't know if the Tien Pok is behind it, or maybe his own people—they don't know shit. The assassins were killed instantly by the little bandit's bodyguards, and it looks like the generals are going to fight it out among themselves about who gets to be the next strongman. It's hit the fan, pal."

"Thanks, Gus. I'll remember you when we rule the universe."

He put the receiver back in its cradle, and for several seconds he just sat there on the edge of the bed, trying to figure out what it could mean. U Ba Sein was dead. Kyauktada was up for grabs, the whole country. Nobody knew whether the Tien Pok guerrillas were communists or not, although they got most of their military support from Russia, and sure as hell they had no love for the American imperialists who had been propping up that corrupt, sadistic old brigand for the past quarter of a century. A little military dictatorship carved out of the base of the Malayan peninsula, perhaps a quarter of a minute of automatic-weapons fire and half a dozen dead bodies later, and suddenly we've got the biggest diplomatic crisis since the end of the Vietnam War.

Well, it wasn't exactly as if Faircliff hadn't warned them.

"What's the matter, Frank? Who phoned?"

He turned around to see that Dottie was awake enough to have rolled over—but that wasn't really very awake. He smiled at her, perfectly aware that it was too dark for her to be able to see him, and touched her hair with the tips of his fingers where it nestled on her pillow.

"Everything's fine, precious. I'm just going into my study to make a couple of phone calls."

II

For the next five days, until a series of radio broadcasts from the capital made it pretty clear that the Tien Pok was now in control, news out of Kyauktada was fragmentary at best. The first really clear account came from the American ambassador, after he was unceremoniously expelled and driven over the border into Burma by order of the new Council of National Reconciliation.

Apparently the generalissimo's army simply disintegrated into a number of warring factions, and the Tien Pok was able to annihilate some of them and come to some sort of murky Oriental understanding with the others. Within the week they had constituted themselves as the only government with any popular support at all and had been immediately recognized by both Moscow and Peking. And suddenly it looked as if that whole corner of the Southeast Asian peninsula might be teetering on the brink of a communist takeover.

There was near-pandemonium in Washington. There was talk that the secretary of state might be forced to resign, and the Senate Foreign Relations Committee, of which Simon Faircliff was one of the more visible members, was charged with conducting a full-scale review of the situation, complete with public hearings.

All this had been foreseen, and the strategy for turning it all to the best advantage had been worked out in detail on that first Sunday night in April while Frank Austen sat in the study of his darkened house in Alexandria and talked to his father-in-law over the telephone.

"It's a mess, Frank. It's a real can of worms." The senator, like everyone else in the Western hemisphere, had been sound asleep, so it was difficult to tell whether he was genuinely depressed by the news or merely groggy. "This whole thing could have been avoided if they'd only listened."

"That's right, chief—and that's what you've got to keep saying, over and over. So let's not be shy; let's give it to them with both barrels."

"You're a cynical son-of-a-bitch, Frank."

"I know chief. That's what you pay me for. Go back to bed."

For the next six weeks, the senator from California was almost never absent from the evening news, and day after day the American public could watch the spectacle of President Brubaker's most senior foreign policy advisors being admonished that, after all, it wasn't as if nobody had told them this would happen. All at once Simon Faircliff seemed to have inherited the mantle of Jeremiah; it was enough to make you weep that the presidential primaries were still two years away.

From the very beginning Frank Austen found himself a

very popular man. While Senator Faircliff was sequestered away in Washington, apparently saving the republic, all the local California press were painfully eager to interview his campaign coordinator and principal aide.

One of the privileged newspapermen was, naturally, Pete Freestone, who had risen in the world and was now a senior political writer for the *San Francisco Chronicle*. In fact, on the afternoon of the second telecast of the Senate Kyauktada hearings, they had a date for lunch at a Chinese restaurant in the Cannery.

Out of sentiment, and to prove he was a native, Austen took the cable car over Russian Hill, jumping on the rear at Jackson Street and thus avoiding the ticket taker, who never got back that far. It was a tradition, like the running of the bulls at Pamplona; only the tourists paid. He skirted the edge of Fisherman's Wharf, wondering as he watched the steam rising out of the lobster pots whether perhaps they shouldn't have settled on Bernstein's Fish Grotto No. 9 instead. It was a beautiful day—the fog had burned off hours ago—and the place was crawling with people in shorts and palm-frond hats you could buy anywhere from street vendors for two-fifty a throw.

Maybe Shang Yuen had been a better idea.

He was a little early, which was fine. He was supposed to be back at the office by three-thirty for a budget meeting, and he wanted a chance to duck into the gourmet shop on the first floor to pick up a couple of things for Dottie—he was going back to Washington the day after next, and she did look forward to her Care packages.

Across the street in a parking lot there seemed to be some sort of gathering of about a hundred fifty people, and some guy up on a vegetable crate was talking through a little portable public-address system. Austen experienced a certain unpleasant twinge when he recognized one of Ted Boothe's advance men as the speaker. The crowd continued to swell until, after about ten minutes, there were perhaps five hundred people jammed together like a swarm of bees; then a black Lincoln came around a corner and pulled up by the sidewalk and out stepped the congressman himself, as if on cue. There was a little round of polite applause as he made his way to the podium and took the microphone.

Austen had heard the speech before, often enough so that about half the time he could fill in the tag lines. But the performance was a technical triumph he found endlessly fascinating. This was somebody who had charisma gushing out of him like water from a ruptured fire hydrant. He was simply good at it.

Ted Boothe would be the GOP candidate; the hunch was hardened into a certainty over the weeks. It wasn't a question of anyone's political philosophy; Boothe was your typical upper-middle-class moderate-to-conservative type. He was so damn much a class act, so much the good-looking, youngish, honest prep-school athlete turned corporation lawyer sort that everyone just wanted to love him and trust him. The Republican fight had been every bit as nasty as anyone could have hoped, but very little of all that mud had stuck to Boothe. He would win the nomination and he would be damned dangerous.

There was no way he could beat Simon Faircliff, especially after this Kyauktada thing, but he could make it close. He could cut down the margin of victory enough to make things very awkward when Faircliff declared for the presidency. He could dim the luster, and that they didn't need.

Austen turned around when he felt a hand on his arm; it was Pete, smiling in amusement.

"He's not going to be struck by lightning," Pete said, still smiling as he shaded his eyes and looked up at the skyline. "Too nice a day—there isn't a cloud anywhere. Come on, rest your killer instinct for a while. Let's have lunch."

The restaurant wasn't crowded, so they got a table over by the window and had a view of almost the whole waterfront area. But neither of them was there to admire the scenery. Over drinks it was, no, the senator didn't really care whom the Republicans nominated, since he expected to stand on his record and trust to the good sense of the voters. Over the crackling rice soup it was, no, the senator hadn't really had time to think about the presidency; although he wasn't foreclosing any options, he had been much too busy running for reelection and, incidentally, trying to bring some coherence to American foreign policy after this Asian disaster. Austen didn't have any illusions about being believed; the moves on both sides were dictated by an etiquette no less complicated and strict than that which prevailed at the court of the Manchus, and doubtless it was better so. If your job required you to lie to your friends, at least this way there was no question of deception.

About halfway through the pressed duck and the sweet-and-sour fish, without a word, they declared an armistice—sort of. They could speak their minds, within limits, and there would be nothing for quotation.

"How's it going with you and Diederich?" Pete asked over his third bowl of rice (he hadn't gotten any skinnier over the last five years). "I hear all kinds of rumors. He was a real tiger in the ad business; a lot of people were glad to see the back of him. How about it, Frank—you boys hitting it off?"

A smiling Chinese waiter in a red jacket came up and asked them in that gracious, noiseless way Chinese waiters have, whether everything was fine, whether there was anything they needed. Austen smiled back and shook his head—no, everything was perfect and they were packed to the eyeballs, thank you very much—and the waiter slipped away like a ghost.

"Howard minds the store in Washington and takes care of the money." He put down his chopsticks and tried to shake the cramp out of his hand, wondering what anatomical advantage Orientals had with the damn things and how he was ever going to manage if, once Faircliff was president, he were sent to China as ambassador. "He stays out of my bailiwick, and I stay out of his. We get along fine."

"Okay. Just wondering."

When the waiter came back to start clearing away the dishes, Austen began to get restless. He hated to sit around at the table after a meal; his tail always began to ache. But Pete decided he had to try the coconut ice cream, so they stayed for dessert. Austen didn't find the idea of coconut ice cream even slightly tempting, but with careful handling his fortune cookie could be made to last almost forever.

When finally they were finished it was, astonishingly, only two-fifteen. Pete decided he would tag along to the gourmet shop and watch Austen buy big flat loaves of peasant bread and hundred-count boxes of teabags. It wasn't very long before he got a shopping basket himself and started stripping the place of candied fruits, tins of date pudding, wine splits, imported English trifle mix, and every other sort of trash you could imagine.

"These places are my downfall," he said as they waited in the checkout line; his tab, in the end, came to around thirty-six dollars. Austen smiled.

"Every place is your downfall."

"I'll bet your senator loves this Kyauktada thing. I watched him on TV yesterday afternoon; he was terrific, like he'd been practicing for months. If it keeps up past the summer, he should be unbeatable in November."

"It wouldn't hurt."

"Hey, Frank." Freestone put his hand on Austen's sleeve, his face suddenly very smooth and serious, the way it used to be in college when he talked about the grape boycott or, sometimes, the war. "Frank, how could he have known? I've been down in the morgue, going over his old interviews, and it's like he looked into his crystal ball and saw somebody was going to put a bullet in U Ba Sein's ear before the year was out."

Austen just laughed and took a couple of mint patties out of a plastic container next to the cash register while the girl was figuring his change. "He keeps a pack of tarot cards in his desk. Here, you want one of these?"

The grip on his arm only tightened. "Don't shit me, pal. You remember what we did together once? Faircliff must have known—did you tell him, Frank?"

It was an odd moment, standing there in the enclosed patio next to the escalators, people streaming around them as if they were just a couple of blocks of wood. Austen experienced something of a shock when he realized that Freestone was absolutely serious.

"He couldn't possibly have known, Pete," he said slowly. "What are you talking about? He couldn't possibly have *known*."

Austen spent almost the whole of the last month before the primaries in Washington. He almost managed sometimes to forget about the election for a while; the senator, on his advice, was concentrating on the Asian hearings and leaving the political spotlight to the Republicans so everyone back home could watch them undisturbed while they tore each other to pieces. Besides, the senator needed help prepping. They spent hours together examining staff reports and the thousands of pages of testimony that had accumulated by then. It was awesome, a kind of dry run for what it would be like if they ever really did make it to the White House.

But eventually it was necessary to go back. He wanted to be in California for at least the last week before the vote. He

wasn't worried about the nomination—there weren't any
challengers—but he just wanted to be there to keep a rein on
his own people, lest the opposition tempt somebody into
doing something stupid. So he packed his bag and booked
two seats aboard United, and Dottie phoned her aunt and
told her to expect some visitors. He figured it was a kind of
semivacation; all he had to do, really, was be vaguely
around, so he would probably be able to spend about half his
time in Pacific Grove helping Dottie collect pieces of driftwood. He needed a rest.

The only big event was the statehouse reception, where he
had to wear a black tie and try to keep Governor Hannah
from drooling on his shoes in front of the civilians. All the
party grandees were there—plus selected members of the
press—and you were supposed to strut around and act
confidently modest about how well everybody was going to
do in the primaries, which were four days later. Needless to
say, Dottie had categorically refused to attend.

By ten o'clock Austen was catatonic with boredom. He
hated these huge parties, and the state politicians and their
wives put him to sleep. It would have been insupportable if
Pete Freestone hadn't been there; they kept bumping into
each other, more or less at random, like a couple of Ping-
Pong balls in a college physics experiment.

Pete was planning to leave in about another half-hour and
drive straight down to San Francisco; he was trying to talk
Austen into coming with him, and Austen was weakening
fast when a waiter came up and murmured something into
Pete's ear about a telephone call.

"It's the night desk." He shrugged his shoulders, allowing
the gesture to extend itself all the way up into his face until it
hit his eyebrows. "They probably want to know whether
they can put the paper to bed or whether I've caught
anybody dancing naked in the fishpond. I'll only be a second."

He was gone a little longer than that. Austen got another
ginger ale and considered whether perhaps he really
shouldn't just pick up his bag at the motel and drive back
that night with Pete. It was a settled issue with him by the
time he saw Pete coming back through the potted palms that
were supposed to camouflage the short corridor leading to
the powder rooms and the broom closet with five telephones
that had been turned over to the press. He was thinking

about sandy beaches and tidepools in the lava rocks and big tangled patches of seaweed thrown up by the waves, and then he saw the expression on Pete's face and forgot all about them.

"What the hell happened? Did Los Angeles crack off and start drifting away with the current? What is it?"

Pete just took a swallow of something that looked like it went down hard. It was several seconds before he could bring himself to say anything.

"Ted Boothe was killed in a car crash three hours ago."

III

The next morning's newspapers carried all the details. It seemed the congressman and his wife had been on their way to a fund-raising dinner from their home in Pacific Palisades when something went wrong with the steering linkage on their Cadillac Eldorado and they went over a hundred-fifty-foot embankment, rolling and burning every inch of the way. It would require an autopsy to establish whether the Boothes had been killed by the impact or the fire, since it had been some time before the highway patrol could get a crew down to the crash site, and the bodies weren't in the best possible condition. There was no suspicion of foul play. It was simply a terrible accident, one of these grotesque, meaningless catastrophes that overtake people sometimes, reminding us all that we are merely mortal.

Howard Diederich sat in the lobby of the Huntington Sheraton Hotel in South Pasadena, a copy of the *Los Angeles Times* spread out over his knees. He read through the article on the accident twice and then turned to a piece on the editorial page, in which the consequences of Ted Boothe's death on the race for the Republican senatorial nomination were anxiously discussed—the *Times* had endorsed Boothe—and he carefully refolded the paper, set it down on the end table next to his chair, and went out to the front entrance to order his rented car.

He had to be fairly cautious in Los Angeles; he had lived there for years, and there was always the chance that he might run into someone who would recognize him. But Los Angeles, after all, was big. People hardly looked at you, and there were enough little districts and suburbs shading off into one another that you could take your pick of protective colorations. And besides, he was a native; he could always account for what had brought him there on any given day, so it wouldn't matter so much even if he did get spotted. In the end he settled on Eagle Rock, a depressing triangle of laundromats, lawnmower repair shops, supermarkets, and one-family stucco houses with brown front yards the size of postage stamps, wedged in between Pasadena and Glendale. It seemed unlikely that anything would bring his rich and powerful friends from Bate & Palmer to such a place.

Tucked into the waistband of his trousers he carried a little six-shot .45 automatic, chosen for its small size and intimidating caliber and concealed inside the metal frame of his suitcase so that airport security wouldn't catch it if they X-rayed his luggage. He hadn't gone armed since World War II, and it made him feel ridiculous and strangely exhilarated at the same time. He wondered whether he wasn't beginning to get carried away by the pure melodrama of the thing.

There was a decrepit A & W Rootbeer stand on York Boulevard; you sat out back on picnic tables—that was one nice thing about Los Angeles, it hardly ever rained—and there was a men's room to afford a moment of privacy. Diederich had remembered the place from an earlier occasion; he drove past just to make sure it was still there and then stopped in at a pharmacy to place his call. He would pick the time and the place; and he was in no frame of mind to start trusting anyone.

Twenty minutes later a dark blue Plymouth crept into the parking lot and came to a stop in one of the rear slots. The man who climbed out was perhaps as much as an inch less than average height and obviously very solid under his light tan suit; he had thinning black hair and a straight black moustache, and his eyes were little more than slits. One had the impression that he was a tough, resourceful, dangerous man, and that that was precisely the impression he wanted to convey. Diederich happened to know he was forty-seven years old.

He came and sat down across from Diederich at one of the picnic tables. There was a white paper bag between them, and Diederich opened it up and took out something wrapped in a piece of waxed paper.

"Here," he said quietly. "Have a hamburger; we're supposed to look like we've come here to eat." The other man unwrapped the thing and peered at it through his narrow eyes as if it constituted an affront to his personal dignity. Apparently he couldn't bring himself to taste it, because it continued to lay untouched in front of him.

"The papers have Mr. Boothe listed as an accident—is there any reason to imagine they might have to change their minds?"

"No." The man smiled slightly, which had the curious effect of making him look as if something were hurting him somewhere. His voice sounded unnaturally harsh, almost like the grating of coarse sandpaper. "The device that caused the steering to lock was a tiny plastic thing that would have burned up in the fire. I crowded him a little around a turn and he went right over. No witnesses."

Diederich appeared not to have been listening. For several seconds he merely stared off into a corner of the parking lot, and then all at once his attention seemed to snap back into place. Under cover of the table, his right hand now held the .45 automatic, and it was pointed directly at the other man's belt buckle. He was perfectly prepared to fire; he had once read an extremely detailed dossier on this particular maniac, and he absolutely wasn't going to start fooling around with him.

"That's fine," he said, his face empty of expression. "You've done very well; I hope we can continue to work together. But before we get down to terms, you and I are going into the men's room back there and I'm going to satisfy myself that you aren't wired—no, do the smart thing and keep your hands up where I can see them. I'd hate to have to kill you just now."

The other man didn't attempt to move. His name was Yates, and he had soldiered as a mercenary in the civil war in Zaïre. Before that he had been a pilot with Air American in Laos for the CIA and had been wounded in the neck after being shot down near the Cambodian border, which was what had paralyzed one of his vocal cords and given the peculiar pained quality to his smile.

"How do you know I wasn't wired the first time?" Yates asked as he heard the lavatory door swing shut behind them. Without being told, he leaned against the far wall, his hands up over his head and his feet wide apart.

"Because the first time was in an airport." Diederich ran

his free hand slowly and carefully over the man's whole body, going through his pockets, feeling for any rectangular object, or perhaps a wire. "If you'd had anything on you then, you would have tripped a metal detector. Besides, you hadn't killed anyone yet, so you might not have felt the necessity of retaining a little life insurance of your own."

There was nothing, not even a pack of cigarettes. Yates was clean, which was reassuring. "Now perhaps we can go back outside." Diederich pocketed the automatic and opened the door for him. "I hope you don't resent a reasonable precaution."

"Would you care?"

"No."

"I rather thought not."

What happened next was as predictable as the movements of a ballet. Diederich had figured on something of the sort, and he was ready when Yates suddenly lurched toward him, twisting from the waist as he attempted to drive a fist into his solar plexus. Diederich managed to parry the strike—it surprised him a little that he should still remember how after all these years—and just allowed the flow to carry him on from there, hooking a foot in behind Yates's knee to take him even more off balance and, as the other man started to fall, catching him in the side of the head with his elbow. It was all he could do, while Yates lay face down on the lavatory floor, hovering somewhere between consciousness and oblivion, to restrain himself from finishing the job. A single sharp, snapping blow to the base of the skull and—

But he caught himself in time. He still needed Yates; he forced himself to remember that this wasn't some sort of training exercise but the real thing, and he needed Yates alive and functioning.

It wasn't going to hurt, however, if the stupid thug learned who was in charge. It was a lesson worth impressing.

Yates was bleeding a little through his nose, so he pulled him up into a sitting position—he might have broken the damn thing, and it wouldn't do to have him strangle in his own gore. Then he stepped away and waited.

It was perhaps a minute and a half before Yates came around. A kind of shudder passed over him and he groaned, even before he opened his eyes; he must have been hurting in a dozen places at once. But all the fight seemed to have gone out of him—he wouldn't be any more trouble.

"You came to me very highly recommended, Mr. Yates, but that was a stupid thing to do," Diederich said evenly, a dim smile pulling at one corner of his mouth. "I can't imagine what you expected to accomplish."

"I don't like . . ." And then a twinge seemed to pass through the side of his face, and he put his hand up to cover his cheekbone. "Ah, forget it. You're right—it was stupid. It won't happen again."

The smile was allowed to come to some faint semblance of life. "No, I'm sure it won't. Now—shall we go back and finish our delicious lunch?"

While Yates wiped the blood from his upper lip and checked in the bathroom mirror for damage, Diederich went outside alone. Surprisingly, it was still only the middle of the afternoon; somehow he had expected that hours had passed, that it would be the dead of night. When he touched his hamburger, he was astonished to find that it was still warm.

And he was hungry. The discovery came to him with all the force of revelation; probably it was nothing more than nerves. By the time Yates came back out, Diederich had finished everything, even the french fried potatoes, which looked and tasted as if they had been carved from bamboo.

"Are you ready to hear my proposition now?"

Yates came down heavily on his bench seat, and his narrow eyes rounded in surprise. It was like watching a snake dazzled by a strong light.

"Do you still have one?" he asked.

Diederich nodded. "I hope neither of us is unreasonable enough to hold a grudge. A moment of temper . . . well, perhaps you were right to resent it—perhaps I was a trifle cavalier." He indulged in another of his wintry, almost imperceptible smiles. "After all, we're soldiers on the same side. We have the same enemy."

"So what is it you want me to do?" Yates was leaning forward on his elbows, visibly more relaxed. The moment of danger had passed, it seemed.

"I want you to recruit an army." He was silent for a moment. He wiped his fingers on one of the thin paper napkins provided by the management and waited for what he had said to sink in—Yates's reactions were important. And Yates liked the idea.

"An army?"

"Well, perhaps not an army. Let's say a platoon. And why

not? You've fought the communists all over the world; why not fight them here as well, where it might be made to matter? Find a dozen or so of the right kind of men . . . specialists. You'll know where to look. We want the sort who will do their work and not be inclined to probe too deeply into what it means. As I said, you'll know where to look."

"And what am I supposed to do with this—this army?"

"We'll think of things." The faint, ironic smile was allowed to broaden into something almost like a grin. "There'll be plenty of money, so get the very best. And the world is full of men like Congressman Boothe. We'll manage to keep you occupied."

IV

On the night of November second, while Simon Faircliff was in San Francisco waiting for the moment of his triumphant appearance before the frenzied, joyful riot of his supporters in the ballroom of the Saint Francis Hotel, Frank Austen was alone in Aunt Nina's bedroom in Pacific Grove, watching the election returns on television. The strategy he had mapped out so many months before was an overpowering success; almost without drawing a deep breath, they had captured 59 percent of the vote.

No one was surprised, although the margin of victory was a full two points higher than the Field poll had predicted only the week before, but everyone knew they were watching the emergence of the Democratic front-runner, the anointing of the standard bearer, the real beginning of the next presidential campaign. The crowds at the Saint Francis knew it; they were wild, drunk with exultation. In a way it was fearful, as if they could think of nothing beyond this moment of almost pagan joy—as if they didn't want to.

Austen watched it all from a safe distance, not knowing what to think or feel. He had worked his guts out toward no other end. The senator was well on his way. The Kyauktada hearings had made him a national figure, almost a national idol, and now he had walked over the opposition like they weren't even there. Barring the unforeseen—and Austen had the unaccountably uncomfortable feeling that now even the unforeseen would somehow be tailored to Simon Faircliff's advantage—the way to the nomination would be like a ticker-tape parade. Faircliff would just ride by, and the crowds would stand along the sidewalks and cheer. It would be as simple as that.

At ten o'clock Austen decided that Aunt Nina would probably want her bedroom back to go to sleep in, so he turned off the set and went out into the kitchen, where that lady and his wife were seated at the breakfast table, drinking coffee and talking in murmurs.

"Did you see enough?" Dottie asked, perhaps only a little maliciously.

"Yes, plenty." He smiled weakly and pushed his way through the door to the veranda and then down the steps to the beach. He wanted to be alone for a while. He simply didn't want to talk to anybody.

Most of the neighboring houses, of which there weren't very many to begin with, were only weekend places, and apparently their owners were back in the city earning the money to keep them up, because all of them were dark. Once you stepped out of the penumbra of light from Aunt Nina's kitchen window, you might as well have been alone on a deserted island. Here and there a line of waves might catch an obscure glimmer from somewhere, enough to impart to them a kind of satanic luster. He could hear the waves hissing up on the sand, and he could hear his own footfalls, but for the rest the world seemed empty.

He would have the week off. He was due back in Washington on the tenth, but until then he was just supposed to take it easy and repair the damage from the campaign. Senator Faircliff knew what he owed to Frank Austen, and he was very grateful. A week in the sun—the fruits of victory.

He sat down facing the ocean and tried to see whether he could make out the line of the horizon. He wasn't sure.

"I brought you out your sweater." Dottie was directly behind him; he hadn't heard her coming, hadn't expected her, but he discovered he wasn't in the least surprised. She dropped his heavy brown cardigan over his shoulders and crouched down beside him. "It's nearly winter—you must be cold."

"I hadn't noticed but, yes, I suppose I am." It made him feel better to have her there with him, and he put his arm around her and forgot all about looking for the horizon. It didn't seem so important now.

"You're still thinking about Ted Boothe, aren't you."

"Ted Boothe was an accident. Pete and I went over every inch of that together and came up with exactly nothing. The police checked the wreckage. It was either mechanical failure or else maybe Boothe had had one too many and misjudged the turn. There's no evidence of anything else."

"But you're really not satisfied with that," she murmured, covering his forearm with her hand where he held her. "You don't really think it was an accident at all."

"It was an accident."

The wind must have picked up, because suddenly he really was cold. In Washington it would be raining like hell and in the forties, but out here you just put on a sweater if you happened to go out for a walk in the middle of the night. Somehow, all at once, he missed Washington. He would have liked to be lying in their bed at home, falling asleep and listening to the rain as it dropped softly on the roof.

It was odd how one could sense changes in the emotional atmosphere; without a word being said or a muscle moved, in the time it takes to draw in a breath, he knew somehow that Dottie had ceased to be simply his wife, sitting beside him on a stretch of moonless California sand, and had become that other thing she was from time to time, in the bad periods when their marriage seemed curiously beside the point, when she was just Simon's child—or, more accurately, Simon's dead wife's daughter, a sort of reversed Electra.

"But doesn't it at least give you a certain sense of *déjà vu?*" she asked calmly, as if they had been discussing the most neutral subject in the world. "Doesn't it ever strike you as odd how unlucky Daddy's political opponents have always been?"

"People who lose always think they've been unlucky."

Even in the darkness he could see that she was smiling at him contemptuously, as if he were being deliberately stupid. And perhaps she wasn't so very far off the mark, he thought to himself; he knew very well what she had meant.

"The first time he ever ran," she went on, just exactly as though he had never spoken, "the very first time, when nobody thought he had a chance in hell of beating an incumbent, Brian Chabot, the esteemed congressman from the Fifth District, suddenly found himself fighting a tax fraud indictment. It cost him the election, and he ended up spending eighteen months in prison. And then there was Edward Tilson—but of course you know all about that, don't you, Frank—and now Ted Boothe. One supposes that Chabot should consider himself lucky; at least he's still alive."

"I never laid a finger on Edward Tilson, Dottie; he didn't require anybody's help to ruin himself. And Simon didn't have a thing to do with it, didn't even know it was going on until it was all over."

"No? No, of course not. 'Simon' always comes out of everything smelling of soap, doesn't he."

Austen restrained himself from pointing out the obvious— that it was just possible Simon Faircliff always retained the appearance of innocence precisely because he hadn't done anything wrong. Presently all this might pass and they would be back where they had started.

"And then there's always the small matter of my mother. You can't say he didn't have anything to do with that."

"Come on, Dottie," he said quietly, bringing his hand up to rest on her shoulder. "You make it all sound like something out of a Sax Rohmer novel—are we back to that? What do you think he did, manufacture a blood clot? Even if he could, do you really think he would have?"

Dottie shrugged, seeming to brush him away with the motion. "Sometimes."

"Look, sweetheart, he isn't Fu Manchu. He isn't . . ."

And suddenly he felt the absurdity of the thing. As if Simon Faircliff, who was a decent and respected man, needed to be defended like that. And it made him feel somehow strangely threatened, as if he had been teetering hazardously close to the crumbling edge of his own reason.

And just as suddenly he understood that it was Dottie who was at hazard. Dottie, who now sat with her hands folded together in her lap, not quite withdrawn but no longer touching him. Dottie, who was able to say, in the most reasonable voice in the world, "Are you really so sure he isn't just exactly that?"

Parents and children.

It was a relationship with which Frank Austen could claim

very little recent experience. His mother, whom he had loved as much as young men generally loved their mothers, had died of cancer while he was still in law school, and his father was a pleasant enough man who tended his vegetable garden down in Anaheim and took very little interest in anything else. He corresponded with his son at irregular intervals—mostly about how the tomatoes were doing—and they saw each other for a couple of days perhaps once every eighteen or twenty months. A comfortable indifference existed between them.

For about half a minute he considered broaching the subject to Simon, but there wouldn't have been any point. Simon had probably always been rather casual about being a parent—after all, that was one of the things you had wives for—and his experience at the other end was even more meager than Austen's, since both his parents had been killed in an automobile accident in 1938, during his first term in college.

"They went off one of those crummy little wooden bridges they have up there—they were on a fishing trip; the goddamned thing didn't even have a guardrail—and either the fall knocked them both cold or they panicked and couldn't get the doors open in time, because they both drowned. In seven feet of quiet water, people who had been swimming in mountain rivers ever since they were babies. You'd hardly think it was possible." He had told Austen the story, in more or less the same words probably half a dozen times. It touched him so little, apparently, that it had become the sort of anecdote that was trotted out after dinner as simply a curious episode, like something he might have read about years ago in *Field and Stream*. No, there was no point in discussing Dottie's problem with Simon.

So the following Thursday, after cooking up an excuse to explain his absence, Austen did what was dictated by character and professional training and drove up to San Francisco to drop in on Pete Freestone at the offices of the *Chronicle*.

"Let me see your morgue file on Faircliff and I'll buy you dinner," he said, hoping Pete wouldn't ask him why. What was he supposed to answer with, the truth?

I think my wife is in the process of slipping her cable. She seems to be under the impression that her old man, the respected senator from California, goes around murdering people, and I just want to make sure of my ground before I start calling in the witch doctors. That would have gone over big with the boys in the city room.

"Sure." Pete smiled so wide his cheeks almost succeeded in closing his eyes. "You're not getting together a new campaign bio already, are you? Such an eager beaver!"

"Yeah, something like that."

And then they could both laugh, because it was such an enormous joke, and Pete clapped him on the shoulder and took him downstairs to a huge basement room that was nothing but filing cabinets with a couple of microfilm scanners set up in a corner. He opened a drawer, took out three small cardboard boxes with *Faircliff* printed in heavy black lettering on the top flap and held together with a rubber band, and tossed them to Austen.

"You know how to use one of these monsters?" he asked, pointing to the scanners. Austen nodded. "Good. Well, I'll be up in my office when you get bored. Frascati's sound good to you? I've developed this thing lately about fettuccini."

"Sure, terrific." Austen smiled tensely, wishing his friend Pete, whom he loved like a brother, would get the hell out of there and leave him alone with all those yards and yards of microfilm. "I'll only be about an hour."

As soon as the door was closed, he took the spool out of the box marked *One: 1937–1968* and clipped it on the left-hand spindle and threaded the film through the guides and onto the empty spool on the right-hand spindle. The thing was really childishly simple to operate; you just flipped on the light and turned the two little hand cranks that drove the film until whatever it was you were looking for was projected against the screen.

Austen might have been trying to disarm a bomb. By the time he was ready to start grinding through to page 1, he had to wipe his hands dry. They left huge dark stains on his trouser legs—he was scared, he realized with something like surprise—although of what, he couldn't have said. And he didn't even know what he was looking for.

The first page was simply a little eight-line squib about how the Oroville Badgers—presumably the high school football team—had won the state championship. The date was November 28, 1937, and the team captain and quarterback was Simon Faircliff.

Odd that he had never known Simon to take any interest in football.

The next clipping was a little longer: *"February 20, 1944— CALIFORNIA MAN RECEIVES SILVER STAR. Marine First Lieutenant Simon Faircliff of Oroville was decorated today by Major-General Holland M. ("Howling Man") Smith for conspicuous gallantry during the recent action at Tarawa Island. Also honored were . . ."*

There was nothing more until September 15, 1950, and that was only a place in the list of those passing the California bar exam—Faircliff had finished third in the whole state after graduation from Stanford Law in June, where he had come after completing the senior year at Yale that the war had interrupted.

"One goddam semester," Austen had heard him say often enough. "I come out of the Marines, I'm a captain, and I'm twenty-five years old. And I've got to go all the way back to New Haven for one goddam semester. I can't get my degree until I pass the course in probability and induction. Well— maybe it was just as well."

And then the following year, the wedding.

It was a big affair, splashed all over the front page of the society section, because the bride and her family were charter members of the old San Francisco aristocracy, dating back to the days when D. E. Chambers had stood with Hopkins and Stanford and Charles Crocker as one of the great capitalist barons of the gilded age.

Miss Mildred Louise Chambers, if you could judge anything at all from a twenty-seven-year-old newspaper photo, looked to be a wistfully pretty little creature, so maybe Simon's motives hadn't been totally mercenary. The first thing that struck Austen was how much the new Mrs. Faircliff reminded him of Dottie, and the second thing was how odd it was that he had never seen her face anywhere before.

Dottie just wasn't the picture type. She didn't carry around any snapshots in her wallet; her affection for people simply didn't take that particular turn. Austen had had to browbeat her for weeks to get a copy of her college yearbook photo for the desk in his study. And besides, she had still been in her teens when her mother died, well before the age at which people normally thought of collecting big studio portraits of their parents. So with Dottie it was perfectly understandable.

But Simon was a regular trophy hunter. He practiced a certain austerity in his Senate offices, but the wall of his den at home was solid with framed certificates and photographs of Senator Faircliff with everybody from the chairman of the San Francisco Chamber of Commerce to the president of the United States. That wall constituted a kind of informal history of his public and private life.

Except that there was no Mrs. Faircliff.

Austen simply couldn't account for the fact that he had never noticed so obvious an omission before. Of course, there could be all kinds of reasons for that. Maybe he had never really cared for the lady, or maybe he had cared for her a great deal and simply didn't like to be reminded of what he had lost. In any case, since Simon wasn't very likely to unburden himself on such a subject any time soon, Austen figured he would just have to learn to live with that particular ambiguity.

So hello, Mrs. Faircliff—and what will we ever know about what it is that seems to torment your unhappy daughter?

The rest of the spool simply reviewed Simon Faircliff's rise through his profession. The antitrust suit against American Petroleum was a textbook case; the brief was a work of genius that Austen had read about in law school. The Lyle perjury trial, *Montclair vs. Liddel,* the Peruggi investigation—that had been a lark, the young corporate lawyer's personal crusade against one of the biggest chemical companies in the nation, years before "ecology" was anything more than a piece of jargon among biologists. And the speech against the war Simon had made when they elected him vice-president of the California Bar Association; more than anything, probably, that had been what had propelled him into politics. Austen knew it all. The public record had become his bible, his source of solace, that to which he could return in moments of doubt—and who was so inhumanly perfect as to be above doubt?—when he needed to remind himself that, if sometimes he had to do something a little raw, at least it was in the service of a great man.

That was what Pete had called him, all those years ago. A great man, provided he ever got the chance. Well, Austen had seen to that chance, time and again, and he would go on seeing to it. And the right hand would go on not knowing what the left hand did.

The second spool began with the announcement for the House of Representatives. Austen ran through all that as quickly as he could, until he came to what he suddenly discovered he had been looking for all along—the obituary notice on Mrs. Faircliff.

January 15, 1970—FAIRCLIFF, Mildred Louise . . . Beloved wife and mother . . . After a short illness . . . No flowers, by request.

On the next page, a grainy photo of Simon, with Dottie on his arm—her face was in shadow and it could have been anybody, but he assumed it had to be Dottie at that age—coming down the steps of the front entrance of the Washington Square Methodist Church.

So at that moment, at least, as they walked away from the funeral together, she couldn't have formed the idea yet that her father had been cruel to her mother, that he was anything except . . . Except, well, her father. All that must have come later.

But from where? That was the interesting question.

He arrived back in Pacific Grove about one-fifteen the following afternoon, blessedly too late for lunch, which usually consisted of the ladies' latest experiment in vegetarian cuisine—zucchini casseroles, that sort of thing. He pulled into the carport, wondering who had taken the Rover, and found his answer when he saw Aunt Nina down on her hands and knees along the flower border, pulling out slender wisps of rye grass with the swift, darting precision of a bird hunting for insects.

"Dottie's gone into town," she announced without looking up. He had the impression she was addressing herself not so much to him as to his shadow, which slanted across the grass like a dark thumbprint, stopping just beside her. "She's got it into her head we're all going to have a cookout on the beach tonight, and she went to pick up some crabs and sweet corn."

All that was visible of Aunt Nina was the rear view of a pair of extremely faded jeans, rolled up to about mid-calf, and the crepe soles of her heavy, mud-stained gardening shoes. That, and the rim of the floppy straw hat she always wore outside because her nose had a tendency to begin peeling like an onion if she got too much sun. In her mid-sixties, she was an American Gothic with a six-figure income and a sense of humor, the sort of woman who had read Thoreau early in life and had never recovered.

The widow of a pleasantly alcoholic painter who had drunk himself to death in 1955, just too soon to witness the sudden flowering of his reputation—or to cash in on the warehouse full of watercolors he left behind—she had lived her whole adult life in the beach house at Pacific Grove, chasing the seagulls out of her vegetable garden and conducting long and passionate arguments about modern poetry and radical politics and the proper management of one's diet with the down-at-heel bohemians who regularly trooped through the place in search of comfortable sofas and free food, and from among whom she had chosen the painter as the one love of her life. To him, through the thousand provocations of their ramshackle marriage, and even through her endless bereavement, she had been entirely faithful, maintaining a cranky, unadvertised celibacy. With the exception of her immediate neighbors, everyone liked her tremendously.

Austen liked her too, which was why, when he sat down on the wide wooden steps that led up to the front veranda, he wasn't sure whether he shouldn't simply forget the whole thing and take a walk on the beach.

"Tell me about Dottie's mother," he said finally, his voice hardly more than a murmur. Aunt Nina looked up from her weeding and frowned; her severe, birdlike face creased around the mouth and eyes.

"Tell you what? She liked peppermint-stick ice cream, she thought *Ladies' Home Journal* was the gospel according to St. Matthew, and she'd get hysterical if she didn't get to the beauty parlor twice a week."

"That isn't quite what I meant." He smiled thinly, shrugging his shoulders. "How did she get along with her husband? Were she and Dottie particularly close? That sort of thing."

Sitting back on her heels like a Chinese coolie, Aunt Nina lifted off her straw hat and fanned herself with it meditatively, giving the impression she was trying to decide whether or not she should become angry.

"What are you after, Frank?" she asked finally, her eyes

narrowing. She still hadn't made up her mind, apparently. "Is all this something that man you work for has cooked up?"

"*That man* isn't an ogre, Nina—he's a United States senator. And no, he hasn't cooked up a thing. I just want to know for myself. I've got a certain stake in all this, and I just want to understand. What happened when Dottie's mother died?"

"Dottie was in school back in Massachusetts when Mildred took sick. It didn't take but about a day and a half for my little sister to die, and it was all over by the time Dottie got home."

"That isn't quite what I asked."

It had all at once turned rather cold. The bushes that maintained a precarious existence along the edges of the sandstone cliffs were beginning to tug slightly at the landward wind, and out over the ocean ominous-looking clouds had started to pile up. It was possible they wouldn't be having a cookout on the beach after all. And Aunt Nina, the last of her tribe, continued to crouch there beside her flowerbed, hugging her shoulders in response to some inner drop in temperature.

Quite unexpectedly, her eyes filled up with tears. "You can think what you like," she began, lowering her gaze as she seemed to retreat for safety into herself. "I suppose I never should have said anything—I should have carried it with me to my grave. But I saw her face before she died, my baby sister, and she was so afraid."

"She'd had a massive stroke. From what I understand, she'd only just barely survived that one; who the hell wouldn't be afraid?"

Aunt Nina stood up and began brushing the dirt from her knees with the tips of her fingers. When she spoke again, she had returned to her usual crisp, unemotional self. "Look, Frank. I nursed a husband and both my parents through their last illnesses, and I knew my sister Mildred. She wasn't the wisest woman in the world, but she was no coward. I've seen the fear of death often enough to know what that's like, and Mildred wasn't afraid of dying. Not just of dying."

"Of what, then?"

"I don't know. She wasn't able to speak a word, so she couldn't tell me, could she? It's possible she didn't even know herself. But she still had just strength enough left in one hand to hold onto mine, and she didn't want to let go. I could see it in her eyes—she didn't want me to leave her alone."

"Wasn't her husband there?"

Aunt Nina stared down at the ground, her face rigid, like Cassandra in old age.

"Yes, he was there. Him and his henchman, the one with ice water in his veins."

"Diederich? Diederich was at the hospital?"

"Yes. Mildred had always hated him. I think she was more afraid of him . . . I can't explain it, really—it was just a feeling. He never came near her room—at least, not any time while I was there—but it was as if she could feel him prowling around through the corridors.

"And then I did leave her. Only to make the arrangements for Dottie to come back home, just for an hour. And when I returned, Mildred was dead."

V

On the last weekend before its never-to-be-sufficiently-damned presidential primary, New Hampshire was trying to shake itself loose from the aftermath of a blizzard. In Manchester the sidewalks were piled six and seven feet high with crusted, filth-streaked snow, and when you ventured off the curb you usually found yourself well over your ankles in what seemed to turn into slush the instant it came in contact with any object warmer than fifteen degrees above zero.

Frank Austen had spent the better part of the last year commuting back and forth from Washington on an almost weekly basis, and he had discovered that, innocent California boy that he was, New England was not the place for him. Ever since October, the whole state had been freezing cold, and for that alone he had learned to loathe it with a peculiar intimacy.

But it was a good political state. Starting from absolute scratch, he had built up a very solid organization of people who had worked for *la causa* all the way back to the days of Eugene McCarthy, and for the most part they knew what they were doing. Some of them were so good he had already put them on the payroll and, when it became obvious they had this one locked away, shipped them down to Massachusetts for the next big round. Faircliff had hired himself a first-class campaign manager once things got rolling, and now that the backers could smell victory there was more money coming in than they knew what to do with.

That final Sunday, at least for types like Austen, was the season for cutting one's post-primary deals—provided you could get away from the working press long enough. Reporters were about one to the square yard, and by now all of them knew Austen and all the other principal players by sight, so if you showed up in the lobby of Howard Johnson's when your man was staying at the Fireside Inn they would be all over you, wanting to know whose throat you had come to cut.

"I'm just partial to their French toast, boys; after all, it's seven-thirty in the morning." And you would grin and wave, and they would follow you up in the elevator anyway. There just wasn't any trust left in the world.

So you had your meetings in laundromats and the men's rooms of restaurants and the backs of taxis, anywhere you could snatch a few moments of privacy. Frank Austen and Verne Hardcastle had theirs in the parking structure behind the Holiday Inn.

It didn't take long. Hardcastle knew he would come in a distant third, and he was almost out of money anyway. He just wanted to get something for himself before he went back to El Paso and braced for the uphill fight to keep his House seat.

"It isn't over yet," he said, shifting his weight from one foot to the other. He didn't like the cold either. "Harry Kramer could still take it away from your man if I threw my support that way. It isn't over yet."

"It's over for you, Congressman."

"Look, all I want is some help back in Texas. Faircliff could afford to be a little generous—a couple of lousy campaign appearances."

"And maybe, if you don't happen to make it, a nice soft job in the administration until your federal pension matures? You weren't by any chance thinking of that, were you, Congressman?"

Hardcastle smiled that cunning good-ol'-boy smile that perhaps worked wonders for him west of the Pecos, but seemed to grate like sandpaper on the sensibilities of the good people of New England.

"Wouldn't hurt, sport. Wouldn't hurt one bit."

"Fine. You make your announcement on Wednesday. I suppose I can guarantee the appearances—and maybe a little extra something for the war chest—but I don't know about the job. That'll be up to Simon. It might help if it comes out sounding right when you throw in the sponge." The same sort of conversation was taking place all over town.

But Hardcastle wasn't even the main item of interest that morning. Austen had nearly forgotten him and was busy thinking about the meeting he would have that afternoon with Clayton Burgess up in Berlin when, as he turned the corner of the stairway and started out through the automobile entrance on his way back to his hotel, he was nearly run down by a light gray Mercedes with New York license plates. There was a loud screech of rubber on concrete, and the car just missed clipping him as he walked past. He was so startled that he almost reached out to steady himself against the right fender.

And when he looked up, who should be behind the wheel, staring at him like a man who had just seen his name written in blood across the bedroom wall, but the noted financier and frequenter of strip joints, the eminent deliverer of parcels.

"Chester Storey."

He could hear the words forming in his mind, although he hadn't the faintest idea whether or not he had actually spoken them out loud. For just a split second the two men simply gaped at each other through the windshield of the Mercedes. It was obvious that for both of them recognition had been instantaneous, for all it had been five years since the last and only time they had met. Austen, of course, didn't have any idea how he looked, but Storey's mouth actually dropped open.

And then the split second was over, and the car lurched past him and was up the ramp and out of sight. It was really tearing—over and over, each time more faintly than the last, Austen could hear the tires squealing around one corner after another. The man was scared to death, apparently, and couldn't think of anything except getting free. If anybody was up there trying to get to his car and happened to get in the way before Storey made it to the roof, it was going to be too damn bad.

Austen walked the five blocks back to the lot where he had left his rented Buick, wondering at this strange reemergence and trying to figure whether there wasn't some way he could find out what it might mean.

But except in the broadest outline, there wasn't a chance of that. Obviously the man had been summoned—he wouldn't have come up to Manchester just for the thrill of it—and Howard Diederich, who was occupying a room next to Faircliff's at the Sheraton Wayfarer in Bedford, tended to be pretty tight with his little secrets.

Berlin, New Hampshire, resting in the northern extremity of the state, was hardly a garden spot. After the picture postcard charm of the White Mountains, you came down into this sooty little industrial smear, the approaches to which were guarded by huge factory smokestacks as thick as stockade posts against the dingy winter sky.

It was an early Sunday afternoon, so the factories had the forlorn look of ruined, forgotten antiquity. The downtown too was almost deserted; one had the feeling that people here, when they weren't working in the dark satanic mills, hardly existed at all.

Austen found his hotel without any trouble. A room had been reserved there for him under the name of Davenant, and he was to wait in it until Clayton Burgess came down from his own room on the seventh floor and rang the buzzer. It had all been arranged in advance, a little subterfuge to have a few quiet words without the two of them appearing the next day as an item in the *New York Times*. It was simply part of the inherent inconvenience of political life.

He carried a suitcase, mostly because he didn't want to attract attention by checking in without one, and as soon as he had put it on a rack and hung up his overcoat and his jacket in the closet he stretched out on one of the twin beds, cradled his head in his left elbow, and tried to fall asleep. It was no use—he was too tired. And his stomach was beginning to give him trouble, which was hardly a paralyzing surprise. Too many peanut butter sandwiches and too much tea. It was a wonder he wasn't dead from malnutrition.

At quarter to two he was awakened with a start by the buzz of the doorbell. For an instant, while sleep and consciousness were still mixed up together, he thought he was being electrocuted—what else could that awful zapping noise be?—and then he remembered and rolled over to the edge of the bed to get up and open the door.

"My God, Frank—you look like the sole survivor."

"Don't be snide, Senator; we can't all campaign out of our backyard. Come on in and pull up a beanbag."

The distinguished senator from Connecticut, looking, as always, extremely distinguished indeed, stepped over the doorframe and allowed Austen to lock up behind him. He at least didn't seem like a fugitive from the press, but then he probably could have robbed a candy store and made it into something resembling an imperial procession. It was a question of style.

At forty-eight, Burgess still possessed the grace and appearance of a much younger man; nothing but the little tufts of gray that had collected here and there around his temples and a certain natural gravity saved him from being referred to as "boyish" in the Washington social columns. He was the only man Austen had ever known who could have worn a blue blazer and a yachting cap without looking like a horse's ass, though he never had, so far as anyone knew. Beside him, even Simon looked like a peasant.

Burgess took his seat on one of the hotel's ugly little wood-frame chairs and smiled, making you feel like his kid brother. "How's Dottie?" he asked, deftly tugging his trouser legs as he crossed one over the other. "I haven't seen her in an age."

"Neither have I. By the time I get Simon into the White House, she'll probably have forgotten my name."

Burgess laughed politely. You had the uncomfortable feeling that nothing but good manners kept him from pointing out that you weren't going to get Simon into the White House. And then the polite smile that went with the polite laughter disappeared, and he became politely serious. It was time to talk business.

"Simon wants a truce," Austen began, leaning forward from the corner of the bed where he was sitting and resting his elbows on his knees. He figured he would do the man the courtesy of dispensing with the fancy footwork. Burgess, after all, was one of the grownups. "We agree to tone down the hostilities until, say, after Illinois. By then both of you will have shaken off the weak sisters, but in the meantime all this sharpshooting in the newspapers isn't getting anybody anywhere. After all, you and Simon aren't going to be running against each other for another five months."

"Don't tell me Simon's worried; the polls show he could go as high as forty percent on Tuesday."

"Simon worries about nothing. I do it for him."

They weren't more than six or seven feet apart, and Austen was beginning to feel uneasy. More and more lately, it occurred to him that he was brokering for the presidency of the United States, for the greatest concentration of power that could be put into a single individual's hands, and it was beginning to weigh on him. They weren't fucking around anymore. He let his hand dangle between his knees, as if someone had cut the nerves, and looked up into Burgess's face with a weary smile.

"Look, Senator, you're a fine man. Simon's a fine man. Either one of you would make a terrific president—the great American public, the lucky jerks, will probably have in front of them the best choice they've ever had. It doesn't need to get nasty. Besides, neither one of you is very good at going for the jugular. But Simon's got me, and I'm the biggest son-of-a-bitch in the business."

"Come on, Frank." The senator laughed—apparently he knew better. "I always thought of you as a nice guy. Hell, I'd offer you half again what Faircliff pays you if I thought you'd take it. How long have I known you? Four years? Five? You're not anything like the bad ass you like to think; you shouldn't say things like that about yourself, or somebody might believe you."

"I'm a politician, Senator. I make my living by the badness of my character. But you and Simon are something else, something better. For practical reasons—and for the sake of the country—I just think it would be nice if we kept it that way. Oh, I'm not saying the occasional swipe isn't okay. The voters expect it and it's good for the circulation. But if you concentrate on your Republican brethren, I'll keep Simon on a leash. See if I don't."

Burgess rose out of his chair and put his hand on Austen's shoulder. It was a friendly gesture, and indication of the man's refinement of feeling. "I always liked you, Frank, and I'll think about it. Say, listen—why don't you come up to my room in a couple of hours and you, me, and a couple of the boys can have some dinner. Room service. Nobody's going to put it in the papers."

"Sorry, Senator." Austen smiled and shook his head as he too rose to his feet. He tried not to show it, but he felt enormously honored. "Hotel waiters sell that kind of thing, and tomorrow you'd read the *New York Times* and find out all about how the front runners are ganging up to squeeze out the competition. Ask me again after November, when the smoke's had a chance to clear."

"When you've whipped my ass?"

It was a joke, and they laughed together.

"Believe me, Senator, I wish you both could win."

His original plan had been to drive back to Manchester as soon as his meeting with Burgess was finished—even stopping somewhere along the way for dinner, he probably could have made the distance by early the same evening—but Austen was absolutely at the end of his tether. As soon as he had closed the door on his visitor, he sat down again on the corner of the bed and simply went blank for about three quarters of an hour. It could have been longer—it could have been three-thirty in the goddamn morning for all he would have been able to tell the difference in those first few seconds after he came out of his trance—but all he knew was that his mind had simply gone numb for a while, and that nothing like that had ever happened to him before.

It was obvious he was in no condition to drive, so he placed a long-distance call to the campaign headquarters in Bedford, left a message that there were a couple of loose ends that would keep him in Berlin until the morning—the fuzzier the lie the better, he figured—and walked across the street to a coffee shop for a chiliburger and a chocolate malted. After that he went back to his hotel room an slept straight through until seven the next morning.

The road was still icy in places from the blizzard a few days before, so it was a good idea to be careful. Fortunately traffic was thin. It was actually a kind of restful pleasure; the necessities of driving didn't allow you to think about anything else, so you got a little vacation from the part of yourself that found it necessary to worry about the future and the past. On this highway threading through the New Hampshire mountains, there was only now.

He was just coming down the grade from Whaleback Mountain when he noticed the pale green Ford that was keeping a discreet two hundred yards behind him.

It wasn't anything he was worried about—after all, Interstate 93 was just about it in terms of significant roadway. Except that this guy never seemed to gain on you and never seemed to fall behind. You'd lose him going around a turn and then, sure enough, there he would be in your rearview mirror again. It was as if he were pacing himself against just you.

The only other time in his life Austen had ever been followed was by a pimp in Saigon. The pimp had some idea that he was entitled to restitution for one of his whores whom Austen had arranged to have introduced to an ARVN general, who subsequently made her his mistress, but Saigon could be a very scary place, where every day nice American soldier-boys ended up in alleyways with their guts leaking out through their fingers. In the end it had been necessary to take a couple of MP sergeants and call on the pimp at the bar he used as a headquarters to invite him to reconsider his position, and after that the matter had been tactfully dropped.

They had hit a flat stretch by the time the Ford started to close the gap. He didn't come roaring up, but it was clear after a couple of miles that follow-the-leader time was over. A hundred fifty yards, a hundred twenty, a hundred ten. He knew what he was doing.

Still, Austen wasn't going to worry about it; he hardly gave it a thought. After all, it was a great big divided highway. There was plenty of room for everybody. Maybe the guy was just bored and wanted to play tag. To hell with him. Austen got over into the right-hand lane.

Finally they weren't more than twenty yards apart. The Ford kept the inside lane. They were coming up on a bridge—you could just see it in the distance, a couple of low silver arches in the morning sunlight—and the Ford pulled a little ahead. There was only the driver, and he took a quick glance at Austen as he went by.

So much for the reporter theory. Two can look as cheaply as one, and this was nobody Austen had ever seen at any of the dozens of press briefings he had attended since the struggle for the minds and hearts of New Hampshire had begun back in the last millennium. He would have remembered.

This joker, if you could judge by appearances, looked like he was in another line of work altogether. Austen recognized the type; he had seen a lot of them lounging around in the air terminals or leaning up against the rail in certain bars, talking in low tones to the little old Chinese gentlemen who ran the contraband weapons traffic over the border into Cambodia, where the Khmer Rouge paid off in raw opium. 'Nam had been full of them.

Generally they started out as soldiers, fighting in somebody's war somewhere, and when their hitch was over they changed out of their uniforms and just stayed on. They worked for whoever had the folding money; they flew planes or acted as bodyguards or taught the tribesmen up in the Laotian mountains how to use a mortar piece. They were the scariest people in the world.

This one had the tight, hard face of someone in constant physical pain; his eyes weren't much more than just a pair of horizontal creases. And the impression of immobility was somehow intensified by the straight black moustache that went aross his upper lip as if it had been branded on.

And then he pulled away, leaving Austen to study the back of his head and draw what conclusions he could from that.

The bridge was probably less than a quarter of a mile away—the shoulder of the road was beginning to slope off more and more—when the Ford pulled directly in front of Austen.

Suddenly, just before they would have made the bridge, the red tail lights on the Ford lit up and Austen saw they were going to collide if he didn't do something. He slammed on the brakes, bracing himself against the wheel as he waited for the impact.

BAM!

But it was more like a small explosion than the tearing of metal. Austen's car began to turn into a skid. All at once he was fighting to keep control, and he wasn't winning. God, if he could just keep it on the road—he was going all over the place.

Austen tried to aim for the first bridge support, hoping for a glancing blow that wouldn't kill him outright and would get him inside and onto the bridge itself, where the guardrail might keep him from dropping over the side like a stone.

All he could really do was keep hold of the wheel and pray. The Ford was gone as if it had disappeared. He could see the bridge coming at him. He could see . . .

Afterward, when he woke up—whenever that was—he couldn't remember the impact. Everything else was perfectly clear, but the shock, the noise, had gotten lost somewhere. For the first few seconds all he knew was that he hurt practically everywhere; then, when he tried to move, he discovered that his left arm wasn't working. He couldn't even move it.

He was lying on the floor, most of him on the passenger's side, and he could taste blood. A little investigation revealed the cause—there was a cut on his forehead that felt like it was probably all the way down to the bone, and he was practically covered in the stuff. He had to blink several times, very hard, to get his right eye open.

But what the hell—he was alive.

Slowly, with the pain in his arm hardly allowing him to breathe, he managed to get up onto the seat and have a look outside. The car was on the bridge all right, smack in the middle and blocking off both lanes in that direction. There weren't any other cars in sight—he didn't have a line of traffic backed up behind him—so he couldn't have been out more than a couple of seconds. He took a handkerchief out of the pocket of his trousers and put it to his head, nervously wondering where else he was injured. That was about as far as he cared to take the inquiry just at that point, thank you very much. If he could stay conscious and keep from collapsing back down on the seat like a rag doll, he would be delighted.

Pretty soon there was another car—a blue Pinto, thank God—coming from the other direction. It went past, turned around, and came back to pull up behind him. Austen watched in the rearview mirror without much interest as the man got out, slammed the door behind him, and cautiously walked up to the car as if he expected it to burst into flames within the next second.

"You all right, mister?" he asked, looking in through the broken side window.

Softly, because his ribs were beginning to bother him, but nonetheless quite audibly, Austen began to laugh.

The man in the blue Pinto, whose name was something like "Furbrick," drove him into a little town, the name of which he never did find out, about five miles down the road. The state police dispatched a tow truck to pick up his car, and the local doctor, who had his offices on the second floor over the Panhandle bar and steak house, sewed up his head and assured him that all he had done to his arm was dislocate it at the shoulder. By two o'clock in the afternoon, with his arm in a sling, he was able to hobble over to the garage at the Chevron station across the street and see about his car. He had rented it in Manchester and it was fully insured, which from the look of things was probably just as well.

"Yer tire blew." The mechanic grinned with the joy of absolute conviction. He was a tall, cadaverous-looking individual with hands that were completely blackened with axle grease, and the biggest elbows Austen had ever seen on anybody. "You got lucky, mister. People die all the time from stuff like that."

Sure enough, on the left front tire there was a piece gone right out of the whitewall, about two inches by three and almost perfectly rectangular. Austen put his finger into the hole and felt around on the inside, although precisely what he was looking for he couldn't have said.

"What would do something like that?" he asked. The mechanic only shrugged, as if it hardly mattered.

"Couldn't say, mister. Maybe jes' a defect—they don't make 'em like they used to."

"Right."

No factory defect ever made such a nice neat hole as that, but a little patch of plastic explosive would. Put one on the inside of the tire, with a small radio-controlled detonator, and every trace would be blown right out when the tire exploded. Austen remembered how the light green Ford had climbed in front of him and then hit the brakes, forcing him to do the same, and how it had shot away immediately afterward. The son-of-a-bitch had been trying to kill him.

"What d'you want me to do with the car, mister?" The mechanic smiled once more; he was safely back in the world of the practical. "It's gonna take some work to get this baby rollin' again."

"I don't know. I'll call the rental company—it's their headache."

*　　*　　*

Fortunately, there was bus service to Manchester, so after Austen had phoned Penny-Pincher Rent-a-Car and explained that a defect in one of their tires had nearly left him at the bottom of the Pemigawasset River Gorge, he caught the three-seventeen south.

All the rest of the way down Interstate 93, there wasn't a thing in the world to do but think. He tried to imagine what he could have done lately to make anyone, anyone in the wide world, want to kill him. True, there were several dozen professional Democratic politicians, loyal to other candidates, who might bear him some ill will—after all, his man was going to wipe the plate clean tomorrow—but generally people like that didn't think in terms of anything so subtle as a plastic bomb on the inside of your tire. And there was no one else—no jealous husbands, no stiffed bookies, no one. No one except, perhaps, Chester Storey.

Of course, it could have been simply a coincidence. What, really, could old Chester have to be so nervous about? Anyway, he didn't want it to be Chester Storey. Chester Storey, whatever the hell else he was, was strictly a family scandal, the private business of the Faircliff-for-president cabal and no one, absolutely no one, else—and we do not want to go looking for things with which to tarnish the candidate's halo. Whatever this stupid business was ultimately about, it had to be kept away from Faircliff.

Still, that might not be so easy. Even if you forgot all about motive, you were still stuck with the problem of opportunity. The guy had planned it, followed him up to Berlin, rigged his car, and then followed him back so he could do his little trick. Ergo, somebody had known right where to look for him.

And who would be able to know a thing like that? When Austen had phoned back to Bedford to tell them he wouldn't be returning that night, how would the message have been routed? Who generally took care of that kind of routine business? Who else but Howard Diederich?

And now some guy with a face you could probably strike matches on had tried to tumble him off the road. To roll and burn, just like the late Congressman Boothe.

"But you don't really think Ted Boothe was an accident. Like my mother was an accident? You're not satisfied with that, are you?"

No, he wasn't. He had never come right out with it, not

even to himself, simply because it sounded so goddamned dumb. And because Dottie hadn't believed in accidents either, and he hadn't wanted to set that pot boiling again. And the result had been a gradual, almost imperceptible estrangement. There seemed fewer and fewer moments when her father's shadow didn't fall between them. And now they hardly ever even saw one another. They hardly ever . . .

And it wasn't just that he was busy with the campaign. It was that, too, but not the way anyone else might have expected. It wasn't just that he was away all the time, but that he was away trying to make Simon Faircliff, her father, the Simon Faircliff who kept a man like Howard Diederich as his familiar, into the president of the United States—that was what she couldn't bring herself to forgive him for.

When he got into Manchester, he was exhausted. Perhaps it was his being troubled in his mind, or perhaps it was nothing more than the constant little adjustments he had had to make to protect his arm and the bruises on his ribcage as the bus jolted along; it had been rather like having to stand at attention during the whole one and a half hours. He had had a long and eventful day, so he indulged himself in the luxury of a taxi ride out to the hotel in Bedford.

He asked at the desk whether Senator Faircliff was in, and the clerk smiled and nodded and said, yes, the senator had been in since at least four that afternoon; he knew because the girl at the switchboard had been kept very busy. He looked as if he were ready to laugh discreetly at this little shared joke—we all understood the idiosyncrasies of these famous politicians, now didn't we?—but Austen wasn't in the mood. The clerk's smile withered up like a daisy in the Sahara.

Faircliff's room—his suite, actually; the bedroom was next door—was 426 and, as usual when he was home, the door was open. When Austen walked in there were five people sitting around on the sofa and the two armchairs. There was Faircliff, of course, and Diederich, naturally, and then there was some kid named Gorman, who seemed to belong to Howard. Then there was Percy Grube, the New Hampshire chairman, and somebody Austen had seen once or twice but whose name he couldn't remember—he had something to do with voter registration.

Faircliff was perched at the far end of the sofa where he

could watch the door, and when he saw Austen he suddenly rose about halfway out of his seat, exactly as if the burlap upholstery had all at once been turned up to about five hundred degrees.

"Jesus, Frank—what *happened* to you?"

"Nothing. I had an accident with the car. I'm fine."

Faircliff came over to him and brought him to the unoccupied end of the sofa, as if he were helping an invalided old woman into her wheelchair. Austen sat down and smiled, and everyone shook their heads and looked worried and inquired whether there was anything he wanted—like maybe a doctor, or perhaps just a bourbon and water to dull the pain. None was more insistent than Faircliff, whose face, when he wasn't trying to persuade his son-in-law that he really ought to check into a hospital, was set in a grim, worried, resentful mask, as if he were just beginning to figure something out.

But in that first moment, that half-second or so before they had fallen into the roles the situation demanded of them, they had all betrayed themselves. And now Austen had his answer.

Because Howard Diederich had been startled enough to have forgotten for just an instant that he was always supposed to be as smooth as a dish of cream, and the first thing he had let show on his face was less surprise than disappointment.

The son-of-a-bitch had known.

VI

In one of the unfurnished rooms on the seventh floor of the Palmer House, Frank Austen leaned against a wall and waited. Downstairs, and in hotel rooms scattered all over Chicago, people were lying around in an abject stupor, watching the results come in from the Illinois primary and looking forward to their first straight six hours of sleep in three weeks. For the moment their work was finished, Austen reflected sourly. But he was still up here, far away from the bowls of pretzels and the comfortable sofas and the sweetness of victory; he was still waiting for Julius Danzig to show up so they could negotiate Harry Kramer's surrender.

At seventeen minutes after eight the door swung noise-lessly open and Danzig stepped inside. He was a big, solidly built man, nearly six foot three and bulging out of his pearl-gray suit; his curly black hair was falling into his dark face, and he looked like he hadn't had much sleep lately either.

"Were you followed?" Austen asked. The question was merely for form's sake. Danzig shook his head.

"What do you want, Frank?" The impatience in his voice was nothing more than fatigue; the two men were on friendly terms, and both of them understood that, as professionals, they were supposed to be immune from the rancor of the campaign. After all, they weren't children.

"I want to know Kramer's price for a nice, heartwarming show of party unity tomorrow morning."

"Come on, Frank." Danzig made an impatient little gesture. "All this is a trifle premature, isn't it?"

"Not really. The early returns have Faircliff with sixty-three percent—"

"Right—the *early* returns. That's just the Chicago vote. You know as well as I do that you'll lose downstate."

"Yes, but not by enough to pull us below fifty-six percent, and we're beating your brains out in the rest of the country."

For a long moment they simply scowled at each other. They both were familiar with the arithmetic. It was just that the habits of rivalry die hard.

"It wasn't a very elevating campaign, was it?" Danzig said finally, dropping his gaze to the floor, where he seemed to regard the paper walkways laid down for the painters with considerable personal resentment. "You guys didn't pull many punches."

"Spare me, Juley—we weren't any nastier than you or anybody else. We were just more skillful. Now, tell me, what does Kramer want?"

"The vice presidency."

"Not a chance."

"Then we'll fight you right down to the wire."

Austen smiled, both because he knew Juley Danzig was bluffing—and knew that Danzig knew that he knew—and because it was the right time to be accommodating.

"Come on, pal," he said softly, almost caressingly. "You know they can't stand each other. Your man can have anything he likes—so long as it's outside of Washington, D.C."

"Yeah, well . . . I'll see." Danzig shrugged, as if the problem no longer interested him. But they both knew what he meant. There was a question of pride to be considered; the governor would wait until, say, Saturday to climb on the bandwagon. Everybody needed time to lick their wounds.

"What about you, Juley?" Austen smiled again, trying to keep it from sounding like he was handing out alms. "We can always use quality people, and you'd be wasted down there in Pensacola, hustling newspaper space for the orange growers. Why don't you come in with us and help rule the world."

But Julian Danzig merely shook his head. "No thanks, Frank. I've had my brush with the big time, and I just don't seem to have the stomach for it."

And that was how it ended. They didn't have much left to say to each other, and after a few more minutes Danzig went upstairs, presumably to tell his employer the bad news, and Austen was left alone to consider the fact that the last obstacle between Simon Faircliff and the Democratic presidential nomination had now been removed. There was nothing left except the triumphal march. And it had all been so much easier than he had ever expected.

But he found that his accomplishment—and it was very largely *his* accomplishment—was peculiarly beside the point. All he really cared about just at that moment was going back downstairs and getting some sleep. Maybe by the next morning, if he were lucky, he would have stopped asking himself, over and over again, just where along the line he had stopped liking Frank Austen.

But the next day, once again, he was back on the road.

The Faircliff campaign was no longer working out of a couple of hotel rooms. Within the limits of the federal election laws, they had all the money they knew what to do with. After the convention in Miami there would be a new ceiling and a whole new budget, but theoretically they were still in the nominating phase and there was plenty of cash lying around to make the California effort, where Faircliff would now be alone on the ballot, into an unprecedented show of strength.

Austen had sold the idea that California and the West were going to be the keys to the November election, so he wanted to use the last round of primaries as the real start of the fall campaign. He wanted to make a strong impression early so that the Republican nominee—officially the name was still to be filled in, but he knew in his heart of hearts it was going to be Clayton Burgess—would come to regard any serious assault on Simon Faircliff's home turf as an exercise in futility. After all, what you had you had.

So he set up shop on the second floor of an office building on Market Street, within walking distance of the old senatorial offices on Powell, and he went to work. He had a budget of about a million and a quarter and all the staff he could ask for, and he flew back and forth to Los Angeles sometimes as often as three times a week. He was in the big leagues now; it was almost as if they had their hands on the government already.

All he had to do was stay alive to enjoy it.

An hour after he had gotten back to Manchester all those weeks ago, as soon as he could get Howard Diederich alone without being too terribly obvious about it, he had made a great show of confiding his suspicions.

"I think the guy was trying to nail me, Howard. You should have seen the hole in my tire—it was such a perfect rectangle it looked like someone had cut it out with a knife."

Diederich had sat on the edge of the sofa in Austen's room, looking as gray and immovable as ever, one of his enigmatic half-smiles playing over his face. You might have supposed he was listening to someone describing the action of a movie.

"Frank, why would anyone want to kill you?" he said finally, his fingers laced together and resting in his lap.

"I don't know. What do you think? Should I report it to the police?"

"No." He shook his head, his voice hardly more than a purr. "I mean, I hate to sound selfish, but that sort of thing isn't going to make Simon look very good in the newspapers. People will ask what his aides can be up to if people are trying to kill them with bombs."

"I suppose you're right. But if I see that guy again, then I think I'll have to, Howard. After all, I can't turn myself into a target just to save the boss a little embarrassment."

The message had gotten through. Possibly Faircliff had put two and two together himself and given out the word that he wasn't going to allow his son-in-law to be struck off just to please Mr. Diederich, but the implied threat hadn't hurt any either. In the two months since New Hampshire there had been no repetition.

Which still, of course, left Austen with the same problem he had had to begin with. It didn't seem to be enough to have safeguarded his own life—if, in fact, he had even done that much, because Howard Diederich was still exactly where he had been before.

One of these dark nights Howard was going to do something that would destroy everything. He wouldn't get to keep on playing outside the rules forever—sometime or other, somebody would catch him at it.

And then Simon Faircliff, and God only knew who or what else, would come crashing down like the weight of the world.

But Howard Diederich was not an insoluble problem. It was simply a question of means. And there were always means. Perhaps now, having seen his son-in-law come staggering in after a near-fatal automobile crash—and perhaps having figured something out—Faircliff had learned his lesson and decided to rein Howard in. There were signs of that.

By mid-May the polls were making it pretty clear that it was going to be Faircliff against Burgess in November, and Faircliff brought his two top lieutenants over to his San Francisco apartment, a tiny two-bedroom affair he maintained only to satisfy the residency requirements of the California election laws, and the three of them spent an evening kicking around various approaches to the problem of the senator from Connecticut.

Howard knew exactly what he thought should be done. "We've had good success with it before," he said, abstractedly feeling around with one finger in the cuff of his right trouser leg. "We put people into his organization, Frank here digs until he finds the inevitable skeletons in the family closet, we create a few additional scandals of our own, if need be. We burrow from within. Frank is very good at that kind of thing."

But Frank wasn't nodding his agreement. Frank was scowling at his ginger ale as if it were so much carbonated hemlock.

"Well, Frank? What do you say? Come on, Frank—what do you say?"

"I'll tell you what I say, Simon. I say that if you start up with Clayton Burgess like that it's going to cost you the election. I say if we don't stop fucking around that way we're going to blow it—that's what I say."

Simon Faircliff regarded his son-in-law and chief thug with the expression of a man trying to overlook a calculated insult. "Perhaps you'd care to expand on that?" He raised his eyebrows and smiled patiently; children must be allowed their moment of attention, apparently.

"Yes, I wish you would," Howard echoed, also smiling. He leaned forward, having forgotten all about the interesting contents of his trouser cuff.

But for a long few seconds, Austen simply continued to stare sulkily at the ice in his glass. "All right," he said finally. "I think it's necessary for us to grow up and face a few facts. Certain things are possible in local races that you can't get away with in a national election. And you can't run against Clayton Burgess by pretending that he's just some creep who got into public office as an alternative to stealing hubcaps. I've made the man the object of very close study for several years now—it's not as if none of us saw this one coming, you know—and there's nothing, absolutely nothing, that we can use against him. In 1964 he got a parking ticket while he and his wife were having an ice cream cone at the Carvel's in Bridgeport, and that is it. Believe me, Burgess is so clean he hurts your eyes."

"Very well, then, throw a little dirt on him," said Diederich softly.

In that one moment, Austen came close to something very ugly. He could feel it, a cold sensation that seemed to knot itself tight in the exact center of his chest. When he could bring himself to answer, he didn't even look at Howard. It was as if he were alone in the room with Faircliff, as if it had been Faircliff who forced him to explain the obvious.

"You don't get to do that kind of thing anymore, chief. Between now and November, every move we make is going to be all over all three networks, and if we screw up—or somebody tumbles to one of Howard's bright ideas here— we're going to get to watch it on television that very night."

"My God—it sounds like Frank's been favored with a religious conversion."

"Howard . . ."

"All right, Howard. We don't need any of that." Simon Faircliff rose out of his chair. He seemed to fill the room, and, as always, the effect was to cut everyone off while they waited for him to have his say. Even Howard lapsed into a studied quiescence.

"I think Frank is right," he said, thrusting his hands deep into the pockets of his green and tan tweed jacket as his eyes searched angrily over the living room carpet. "If the campaign is anything other than completely disinterested and aboveboard, I'm not sure the voters would ever forgive us. It's the best way, under the circumstances, and Frank's seen it clearly, I think. This time, we don't really have any choice."

The meeting broke up just a few minutes after nine that evening, and Austen, who found himself without any motive for going back to the room he was renting at the Glover Residence Hotel on Stockton Street—after all, what was he supposed to do there all by himself, stare at the ceiling?—simply walked. For some reason he had missed dinner, so he had a vague idea that perhaps he would stop in at one of the Hofbrau houses south of Union Square and then, when he had fortified the inner man, find an all-night movie and let himself be lulled to sleep by *The Texas Chainsaw Massacre* or something. He didn't have any better ideas.

At that time of night, as usual, everything south of Post had the appearance of that species of harmless depravity that was always the tourist's chief impression of life in San Francisco. People were ready to sell you anything—silver jewelry, pornographic novels, the future, your name engraved on the edge of a Lincoln-head penny, anything you wanted. Every door was open—you could take a steam bath or watch naked girls dance or have your trousers pressed, or any combination of the above—and the streets pulsed with the music from bars and pool halls and the huge portable radios a few adolescent blacks carried around pressed against the sides of their heads, and whores of all five sexes paced back and forth with tiny, dancelike steps on nearly every corner, trying to catch your eye or win your heart or just get you to slow down.

Somehow Austen found himself down on Market Street—force of habit, he imagined—and looked up to discover a light from one of the windows above the "Faircliff for President" sign. He supposed it was probably the cleaning lady, but he thought he just might go up and visit his office for a couple of minutes and have a look. It would be a chance to say a couple of words to somebody; even a "Hello, how are you?" from the sixty-year-old Mexican woman who did the floors would be better than nothing. He unlocked the front door and walked across the dark lobby to the elevator. But there was just the light burning in an empty room.

The office had a WATS line, so he wouldn't be costing anybody any money, but after all it was well after midnight in Washington; Dottie was probably fast asleep and, in any case, wouldn't appreciate a phone call from her faithful Frank—those days, apparently, were gone.

But it would be all right. Everything would still be fine if Simon could just shake himself free of Howard Diederich's influence and be everything that he could be. Clayton Burgess was a good man, one of the best, but Simon had a capacity for greatness, and that was something more. He could be one of the outstanding presidents of modern times if he would simply allow himself to follow his own nature. And perhaps now he was beginning to do just that. The private happiness of two little people seemed a small enough sacrifice to make for such an end, so he would stick with Simon Faircliff and be glad of the chance.

And Dottie . . . Well, perhaps finally Dottie could be brought to understand that her husband's motives weren't so entirely contemptible as she imagined. Not every exile lasted forever.

At that moment in the apartment on Miller Place, a very different sort of destiny was shaping itself.

When the party broke up, Howard Diederich left first. He waited in the shadow of a doorway while Austen stepped out onto the sidewalk and started his solitary wanderings down from Nob Hill, and, when at last that unhappy figure was out of sight, he crossed back to the other side of the street and returned to the apartment.

"He took long enough," Diederich said, removing his coat and putting it carefully over the back of a chair. "What did you two have to say to each other?"

"He advises me to get rid of you, or at least prune you back enough to keep you from getting us into trouble. He thinks you're dangerous. Are you?"

Diederich's only answer was a bored sigh as he sank back into the sofa cushions. The expression on his face was one of simple annoyance, as if he suspected that someone was about to ask him to exert himself.

"Simon, do you think I could impose on you for a cup of tea? It was cold out there, and my feet are like ice."

For a long moment Faircliff hardly seemed to move at all. It was as if he were making up his mind about something. Then, very slowly, his right hand closed itself into a loose fist.

"You know, Howard, I'd hate to think you had anything to do with that 'accident' of Frank's back in New Hampshire. I'd hate to think that was anything more than just what it seemed. If I thought that, I'd . . ."

"You'd what, Simon?" No one ever looked less intimidated than Howard Diederich as he rested the point of his chin against his right palm. His very stillness was an act of defiance. "Just exactly what would you do?"

"Just be advised. Nothing is to happen to my son-in-law."

"What would ever happen to Frank, Simon?" Diederich asked, smiling. "Could I have that cup of tea now?"

A few minutes later, Simon Faircliff came back from the kitchen with a single teacup balanced in his huge hand. He set it down on the coffee table in front of his guest and resumed his own seat. Diederich picked up the cup and took a tentative sip.

"I couldn't remember whether you used sugar—is it all right?"

"It's fine." Diederich smiled thinly and then took another sip. "But we *are* going to have to do something about Frank. I suggest you fire him."

"That's precisely what we can't do. Howard, do you honestly think he'd just recede tamely into the background? Don't kid yourself. You give him a reason to go after you and may God help you. May God help us both. No, as long as he works for us, we can keep some control over him." Faircliff shrugged his shoulders, as if resigning himself to the inevitable. "After all, he still thinks he's on my side. He's worried that you'll estrange me from my higher self."

"All right. But you realize, of course, that that commits us to following this Mr. Clean campaign strategy of his; we can hardly do anything else with him around."

"Well, I think he's right about that anyway, Howard. He usually is right about things like that. We bagged the nomination following his advice; we don't want to ignore him now and have it cost us the election."

That seemed to settle the question. Howard Diederich merely nodded as if it were a matter of indifference to him. He had finished his tea but continued to hold the cup, with his fingers wrapped around the outside as if to crush it.

"Have you considered your choices for after the election? You'll have to give him something, you know, and it'll have to be something important enough to keep him from feeling he's being shunted aside. And, God knows, if you make him chief of staff he'll tie you up so tight you won't be able to breathe. Have you thought about that, Simon?"

"No, I can't say I have." Faircliff showed his teeth in a stiff little grin the voters would never have understood. "But I'll bet you've done that for me, haven't you, Howard. Tell me, what *am* I going to do with my right arm?"

Howard Diederich actually laughed. It wasn't much of a laugh—just a kind of low gurgle—but it was quite genuine.

"You're going to make him director of Central Intelligence."

"You're kidding."

"No, I'm not. It's perfect." He set the teacup down again with the air of a man who is clearing away trifles before he announces some great truth. "The CIA is supposed to be more-or-less nonpartisan—that'll keep him out of your hair politically. He has a conspiratorial turn of mind—let his attentions be directed outward, toward the Russians and the Chinese and away from us. He can worry about the rest of the world, and we can stop worrying about him. It's perfect."

"But, like you said, it's supposed to be nonpartisan. They'll never go for it."

Howard Diederich, if he didn't laugh, at least smiled. "They'll go for it," he said. "Kennedy made his brother attorney general; Carter gave the CIA to his roommate from Annapolis. Hell, Casey was Reagan's campaign manager. We're the majority party, remember? Make it understood that you want someone in there upon whom you can rely absolutely, that you'll take direct responsibility for his actions in office. They'll make a fuss, but so what? You'll be a brand-new president—they won't turn the nomination back."

"Wonderful." Faircliff studied Howard Diederich's face as if looking for some suggestion of a trap. Then he knitted his fingers together tightly enough to make his knuckles white and rested them against his lips, like a man praying. Except that he wasn't.

"Come on, Simon, trust me. I've never steered you wrong. Didn't I lay that Kyauktada business out for you? We've done all right so far."

"And I suppose you also know just what we're going to do with Clayton Burgess in the meantime." Faircliff looked up again, his eyes restless, but Howard Diederich's expression was smooth and uncommunicative. Except that his eyes were open, you might have thought he was asleep.

"You leave Clayton Burgess to me."

VII

Yates had considered his problem from every possible angle, and it resolved itself into one of access. It would have been a relatively simple matter to plant a bomb in Clayton Burgess's car, or even to catch him in a crowded elevator and gun him down, but an assassination that was supposed to be indistinguishable from death by natural causes was another matter. You had to reach the man and then somehow get away undetected.

The means compounded the difficulty. As a general rule, provided there was no particular hurry, poisons were the easiest things in the world to handle. You could put the stuff in the subject's toothpaste, just around the nozzle of the tube so that only the first dose would be lethal, and you wouldn't run the risk of giving the show away by wiping out the entire family. Or you could coat the bottom of a drinking glass; since Burgess was living more or less exclusively in hotel rooms just at present, and his wife didn't always travel with him, nothing could have been easier to arrange.

But this junk had to be introduced into the bloodstream—Mr. Defoe had been explicit about that. "It doesn't require more than the merest trace, and a scratch no deeper than a paper cut will do, but it has to be absorbed through a break in the skin."

It was a clear, high-viscosity fluid, in a bottle with a nylon brush attached inside the cap; he might almost have been dealing with model airplane glue. It wouldn't be hard to manage, provided he could come up with an opportunity, but obviously he wasn't going to be able to walk up on the front-runner for the Republican presidential nomination, pull out a hypodermic needle, and give him a shot between the shoulder blades.

He had considered fixing a ring with some sort of tiny barb along the bottom. The candidate walks by, you shake his hand, and the thing is done; it was a technique the Borgias had perfected centuries ago. But there were problems with that idea, not the least of which was Yates's fear that he might accidentally stab himself, perhaps without even knowing it. How could he know? *He* didn't want to wind up the one on a morgue slab.

And then there was the fact that he had a face people tended to remember. He was no beauty queen, thank God, but he stuck in the mind. He scared people. Ordinarily he didn't care about that—in fact, he rather enjoyed it—but it was a professional liability of which Yates was perfectly aware. Mr. Defoe wouldn't be pleased if he turned up in a news photo just a couple of days before Burgess cashed in. He had had a long and gaudy career; somebody might make the connection.

"Mr. Defoe"—that was a laugh. Well, if he ever needed to know the guy's real name, he supposed he could find it out fast enough.

It was easy enough to find out that the candidate planned to be in California for the two weeks before that state's primary election, and that his people had booked a floor at the Beverly Hilton in Los Angeles for the entire period. That was reasonable; after all, the southern counties were heavily Republican, and they would decide who won or lost. Naturally he would use Los Angeles as a base.

Four days before Burgess was scheduled to arrive, Yates booked himself into a room on the sixth floor.

He spent the better part of a week simply studying the routines of the place—when and in what order the maids did the rooms, how laundry got delivered, where the service elevators were and how often they were used, how often the shifts were changed. He knew that Burgess's entourage would have the floor above his, and he was down in the lobby when the motorcade from the airport pulled in and everyone started cheering as the people's choice made his way through the crowd, pumping hands like a machine. For a moment he was sorry he had abandoned the ring idea; it would have been so simple just to push his way through and pretend he was another true believer eager to touch the hem of the master's robe.

Well, fortunately there was no hurry. "Anytime before the nominating convention," Mr. Defoe had said, and that was still a couple of months off. All the time in the world.

But it was obvious he would be at it forever if he tried to get to Burgess when he was alone. Burgess was never alone. All the major candidates had by this time been extended Secret Service protection, and besides, their aides clustered around them like flies around a rotting carcass. But if he couldn't get to Burgess, he could probably arrange a few undisturbed moments in his room.

The people at the front desk were certainly your typical surfboard Anglo-Saxons, but the language you heard in the corridors and echoing out of the laundry rooms was Spanish. And the nice thing about that was that the hotel patrons hardly seemed to notice that they were there. Who looks at a Mexican pushing a vacuum cleaner? Why should anyone look at him? He might as well be invisible.

Could he pass for a Mexican? Yates studied himself in the mirror and decided that, dark Irishman that he was, he could. A little makeup perhaps, thinly applied to the face and the backs of the hands just to be on the safe side—the corridors weren't very well lit. For the rest, all he had to do was not look like himself. He had a black wig, the same color as his own hair but cut much longer. It made him look like a fag, but he supposed he could stand that for twenty minutes or so; if anybody tried to cruise him they'd be in for a shock. A pair of heavy glasses thick enough to suggest he had undergone cataract surgery would take care of the eyes. Like the wig, they were a souvenir from his days with Air America in Vietnam, standard CIA issue. When you had them on your vision was unaffected, but nobody noticed anything about your face except the glasses. It was as much disguise as he supposed he would need.

Getting a passkey was easy. He found a room that was being done—the doors were always propped open with a rolled-up towel, but they turned the television so loud to listen to the soap operas that they couldn't hear a thing—

waited until the girl was busy doing the bathroom, and pinched the key, which no one ever bothered to take out of the lock, long enough to make an impression in a piece of wax. Fifteen seconds, start to finish.

About two-fifteen, he changed into the uniform he had stolen from a fourth-floor laundry room on his second day, donned his disguise, and slipped into the service area to steal a vacuum cleaner from the utility closet. A seven-second elevator ride had him on Burgess's floor.

Nobody stopped him; nobody even saw him. Here and there he could hear voices behind a door, but otherwise there were no signs of life. Burgess's door didn't have its "Do Not Disturb" sign out, so it was a safe bet no one was home. Yates listened anyway. There was no sound, so he knocked. There was no answer, so he went in.

It wasn't a room; it was a suite. But he supposed anybody who was within a hundred delegates of having the Republican nomination locked up could probably afford a little personal luxury. He took the vacuum cleaner into the bedroom with him, just to make it look good if anyone should happen to walk in on him, and left it outside the entrance to the bathroom.

By then he had settled on a tentative plan—after all, everybody shaves.

He had ideas, depending upon whether or not the candidate was a blade man. If he used an electric razor, then Yates would fix the protective screen somehow so that whoever drew it across his face would scratch himself, probably several times. It was, by and large, the idea he liked better. It struck him as safer.

But Senator Burgess was a blade man; he had a little Wilkinson snap-in holder. People who shaved with a blade nicked themselves all the time; the only problem was to know where to apply Mr. Defoe's magic formula so it would do the job.

He could simply dump the whole bottle into Burgess's aftershave—"Royal Lyme" yet, for people with more money than sense—but he didn't know what effect prolonged exposure to alcohol might have on the stuff. He was no chemist, and nobody had told him how this junk was supposed to work anyway.

And mightn't Burgess notice if the blade in his razor was oily? It might feel different and cause him to take a closer look. It had to go totally undetected; Mr. Defoe had been quite explicit about that.

He found his answer in the black leather shaving kit that was sitting on the marble shelf into which the sink had been built. Burgess apparently cut himself often enough to have invested fifty cents in a styptic pencil.

Yates slipped on the plastic gloves he had been carrying in his back pocket—with this stuff he didn't want to take the slightest risk of exposure—unscrewed the top of the tiny bottle, and used the built-in nylon brush to paint the solution over the entire point of the styptic pencil. The alum absorbed it quickly, so he waited a few seconds and applied it again. In no time at all the whole first inch or so was completely impregnated, and no one looking at it would have noticed a thing.

He put the pencil back into its plastic tube, closed up the bottle of solution, and took off his gloves, being careful to turn them all the way inside out as he did so. Then he dropped the bottle into one of the gloves, folded them together, and returned them to his back pocket. He picked up his vacuum cleaner and left, closing the door behind him and making sure the lock had caught. Altogether, he couldn't have been inside longer than two or three minutes.

As he dragged the vacuum cleaner back down the corridor toward the service elevator, he couldn't help but laugh. Tomorrow morning, or the next, when Burgess skinned his Adam's apple because he was in a hurry to get to a breakfast meeting of the Knights of Columbus or something . . .

He only had one regret—that he wouldn't have a chance to be there for the fun.

Immediately after breakfast on the morning of his scheduled motorcade through Anaheim, Clayton Burgess began to notice that he wasn't feeling very well. It wasn't more than a stomachache, so he had an aide go down to the hotel gift shop and pick up some Alka-Selzer. He had been living on this damned hotel food now for at least three months, and he had supposed it would catch up with him one time or another.

But by ten o'clock the Alka-Selzer hadn't helped. The pain had moved up into his chest, and he noticed he was beginning to sweat heavily. It was a warm day but perfectly dry, yet he could feel his undershirt clinging to his skin.

"You okay, boss? You look kind of pale—you want us to call this circus off?"

"I'm find, Rudy." He smiled wanly and allowed the young man to open the car door for him, glad to have a chance to sit down. It was odd, but he just couldn't seem to catch his breath. It was as if the air had thinned to nothing.

During the hour's drive to Anaheim, he seemed to feel a little better. As long as he stayed quiet, the pain in his chest wasn't more than a dull ache, hardly anything at all.

They met the local Republican congressman, a slight, ascetic-looking man called either "Melcher" or "Malchak"; Burgess had never met him before and didn't quite catch the name when they were introduced. They transferred to an old Cadillac convertible for the ride down Lincoln Avenue, so they had to sit on top of the back seat where they could be seen.

There was a good crowd. The car drove along at no more than five or six miles an hour, and it would probably take them the better part of forty-five minutes to make it through downtown. It worked in rotation—first you waved with the right hand to people on one side of the street, and then you waved with the left to people on the other. By the time they had made two blocks, Burgess was beginning to appreciate that he was in real trouble.

At first it was just that his arms seemed to weigh about two hundred pounds apiece—he had been doing this kind of nonsense for months without its ever bothering him before— and then he began to experience a strange shooting pain coming out from under his left shoulder and going all the way out to his hand.

And then the pains in his chest started in earnest. It was like there was a hand in there, squeezing.

"Get me out of here," he gasped, trying to slide down onto the rear seat before he simply fell. He could hardly talk at all now; it was absolute agony even to breathe. "Get me to a hospital. Step on it."

The people collected along the sidewalks had no idea why Senator Burgess's Cadillac suddenly shot away. They could only listen to the howl of the police sirens and speculate that something had to be very wrong.

"Maybe somebody shot him," one man said out loud to no one in particular. "Remember Kennedy? Maybe somebody got this one, too."

Nobody answered.

"I called his wife. He's out of intensive care, thank Heaven. Maybe I should fly down to LA tomorrow and visit him."

Howard Diederich merely shrugged.

"Fine—visit him. I'm sure it'll go down very well with the voters. Now that he's out of the race, it won't do you a bit of harm to be perceived as Clayton Burgess's friend."

"I am his friend," Simon Faircliff murmured, hardly able to look the other man in the face as they sat at opposite ends of the sofa in the living room of his San Francisco apartment. "We came to Washington in the same year; we used to live near one another in McLean. God, I'm glad he seems to be pulling through."

"You certainly can draw a fine distinction, Simon." The dim smile on Diederich's lips curled contemptuously and then flickered out. "He's as good as dead. If my information is correct, he'll probably never be able to walk the length of a city block again. I doubt if he'll last the year, not that it matters. But by all means go and see him. Maybe he'll decide the 'national interest' would be better served with you in the White House instead of Walter Shepherd and he'll turn his delegates loose and split the convention. You never know."

Faircliff had been listening to that voice all evening, and it was beginning to be almost more than he could bear. He looked at the glass in his hand and, discovering that it was empty, went into the kitchen to fix himself another stiff scotch and water. More than anything, he wanted to get away from Howard for a moment, away from his gloating over how easy everything had suddenly become.

In the five days since Burgess's collapse, he doubted whether he had drawn one completely sober breath. He had cut back his public appearances, and when he did go out, he avoided functions where he had to do more than just smile sweetly and wave and say what a sad thing it was for the country that his good friend had been struck down. The voters didn't seem to mind, but he was beginning to make himself sick. He kept thinking that now it really was going to

be easy. He kept thinking that Sylvia Burgess would probably be a widow within the next several months. He kept
thinking that Clay really was his friend, had been his friend
for twelve years, and then he kept thinking that he needed
another drink. It had to stop.

"What does Frank make of all this, by the way?"
Diederich asked from the living room, which was separated
from the kitchen by the width of a corridor.

Simon returned with his drink and sat down. "Why don't
you ask him?" he inquired, not very pleasantly. "He
dropped out of sight as soon as Burgess had his attack; I
haven't seen or heard from him since. He's still running the
campaign—he phones in to the office, so they tell me—but *I*
haven't heard from him. Not even on primary night. Dottie's
down in Pacific Grove with that flaky aunt of hers, but I
don't think he's been near her either."

"He was always very high on Burgess," Diederich said,
leaning a few inches forward as if straining to see something
that refused to come all the way into focus. "I wonder what
he could be up to."

"Well, he's cleared the slate quite effectively, don't you
think? Or perhaps you still don't see the pattern. Have you
got yourself so hypnotized that you can be blind to what he's
doing? Even now?"

"Boothe and Burgess—that doesn't make a pattern; that
makes a coincidence. Maybe God's got it in for politicians
whose names begin with a *B*."

"Very funny."

They said a great many other things to each other that
night—some things neither of them would be able to forget
until the ends of their lives.

Dottie had flown in from Washington the morning after
Clayton Burgess's attack. She just packed a bag, got a ticket
on the red-eye special, and landed at San Francisco International at six-twenty in the morning. Austen was there to
meet her, and they drove down the coast road toward her
aunt's. It wasn't a very happy reunion for either of them.

"I haven't heard any news since I left. Is he . . . ?"

"He's still alive," Austen said calmly, staring ahead at the
road with cold, expressionless eyes. "But just barely. They
say they won't know for another twenty-four hours whether
or not he'll make it."

"Good God . . ."

At that hour of the morning, once they got off the Bay-shore Freeway, they seemed to have the world to themselves. They didn't talk; they just drove. Up over Route 92 to Half Moon Bay, splitting the clean white fog like a knife, and then south, always within sight of the Pacific, like a great gray blanket you wanted to pull up around your shoulders to keep you warm. All that way, through a landscape of split-rail fences and black earth and fields of grass and soft yellow flowers, all blurred by the fog into something as unspecific as a dream, and they hardly noticed it; they hardly looked at it at all.

"Tell me what happened," she said finally, when they were almost to Santa Cruz and the sun had broken through and brought everything back to its usual ruthless clarity. "I just heard the one report on the news; there were hardly any details."

"He collapsed." Austen continued to look only at the road ahead; his voice was as empty as he could make it. "He was in a motorcade, and he keeled over. It was a massive heart attack; he was already unconscious when they got him to the hospital, and apparently there's so much damage that he'll never really recover. They thought for a while he might not even wake up again, but he did."

"But he won't be able to run for president."

"Oh, no," he answered, shaking his head. "He won't even be able to go back to the Senate. Even if he lives, he'll never return to public life—it's a goddamned shame."

"I'll bet it just tears you apart."

He didn't say anything for a moment. He prided himself on being a cynical man, but it hadn't occurred to him that his own wife would think so ill of him as to imagine he was glad for what had happened.

"Come on, baby," she said, slipping her hand inside his elbow. "Get out of it before you're so sucked in you don't even know which end is up. Maybe you can't stop it, but you don't have to be in on it—and you're that now, even if you turn your eyes away and pretend not to see. If you let yourself go along with it, then you take your share."

"Are we back to the conspiracy theory? Simon Faircliff as the scourge of God? You're out of your fucking mind, Dottie. I was with him when he heard the news. Somebody brought it in from one of the wire services, and I saw his face. He just isn't that good an actor."

"So maybe it isn't Daddy," she answered finally, as if, after great effort, she had reached one of the important conclusions of her life. "But it's something. One after the other—one way or another—all the obstacles are being cleared from his path. He's running in an election, so his opponents either disgrace themselves or die. He needs to be a big man in the media, so some little Asian dictator he's been hyping goes out and gets himself conveniently assassinated. My mother is cracking up—and we wouldn't want anything like that to embarrass the newly fledged congressman, oh no—so all of a sudden she dies of a stroke. It's a pattern. Somebody is going around murdering people so that my father can be president of the United States."

"Time and chance, baby. Time and chance. It's just the way things have been breaking for him."

"Sure."

"Anyway, that doesn't automatically make him a murderer."

"Maybe not directly, but he accedes to it, doesn't he? He's got eyes—he can see what's going on. Just like you can."

Great. So now it was Simon the spider king, with everybody from Edward Tilson to Clayton Burgess to poor old U Ba Sein caught in the coils of his web. He could even arrange for a suicide cadre to go in and gun down one of the world's better-protected military despots. There was just no limit to the man's power.

"You're crazy, Dottie. I may have to have you locked away for your own good."

And that was how they had parted. Naturally, they both had a lot more to say first—all the way down the coast road, about as ugly a business as you could imagine. When they reached Pacific Grove, Dottie got out of the car, slamming the door behind her, and Austen drove back to San Francisco, where that afternoon he caught a flight down to Los Angeles. He had never told her what happened on that road in New Hampshire—what would he have gained?

So he went to Los Angeles and checked in at the Beverly Hilton. He talked to the members of Burgess's staff who were still there, waiting to know whether their leader would pull through before they gave up on their great crusade and went home. He visited the hospital, went over the physicians' list until he found the name of a fellow he had known in college, and asked him.

"It's a heart attack, man—what can I tell you? A heart attack, pure and simple. It happens to people every day."

The primary came and went. Faircliff won. Burgess won—apparently a big sympathy vote. Austen barely noticed. Four days later he phoned Dottie and laid it out for her. It was a heart attack. Not a vast conspiracy, but a simple, garden-variety heart attack.

Dottie listened to what he had to say and then hung up without saying another word.

Four weeks after her husband's seizure, Sylvia Burgess was still spending most of her time reading magazines in the tiny cubicle of a waiting room on the fourth floor. But there were consolations; at least Clay had recovered enough to be moved to a private room. Intensive care, with its bare little curtained-off cots and the constant jittering of the oscilloscopes, had been a terrifying place. Now it was possible to believe that he really might not die after all.

Still, she was only allowed to visit him for half an hour at a time, and every night she was driven back to her hotel room to watch television and stare through the darkness at the shadowed ceiling and listen for the telephone to ring.

Everyone was being very nice. Simon had even flown down from San Francisco and spent the whole afternoon sitting with her while they waited for Clay to wake up from his nap. Simon really was an awfully nice person and had been so sweet; he had seemed genuinely concerned and upset.

That was right after Clay's attack. It had been awful when she thought he might really die, just like that, from one second to the next. What would there be left, how could she possibly get through the rest of her life, if Clay died? But today he seemed so much better.

"How are you, sugarplum?" he had asked, smiling and reaching out for her with his large brown hand. It was difficult to imagine him as anything except the strong, healthy, vigorous man she had loved ever since she was nineteen. "God, breakfast was awful this morning. Cream of

Wheat, if you can imagine. I haven't eaten Cream of Wheat since I reached puberty."

Their fingers laced together and she returned his smile, trying very hard not to let the tears break through. Clay hated it when she cried, but she almost couldn't believe how much she loved him at that moment.

He closed his eyes for a few seconds, and it was possible to guess the degree to which he had been ravaged over the past four weeks. He would never get all the way better, the doctors said. Even now, at this distance from his crisis, she could hardly make up her mind to believe that the life hadn't flickered out and left his dear face nothing but a mask.

But the eyes opened once more, and she could feel the warmth of his hand, and her fear rushed from her. "How are you feeling?" she asked, smiling again.

"Much better." His smile turned into a grin. He was like a small boy who was getting away with something. "Tomorrow, they've promised me, I can get out of bed and walk around a little bit—maybe even give myself a shave."

VIII

Three days later, Clayton Burgess was dead.

Austen heard the news on his car radio, in the middle of an impenetrable traffic jam on the Washington Outerbelt. It was like the resolution of a well-plotted novel where the hero, for good or evil, finally meets his fate. First there was surprise, and then, as the thing was absorbed, the feeling that it couldn't have worked out any other way. The direction of events had proceeded with all the neat simplicity of a straight line.

Sitting in his car, watching the exhaust from a thousand stalled cars drifting past his window, Austen wept for the first time in his adult life. The tears streamed down his face unnoticed as he stared through his windshield, seeing nothing, as motionless as an icon or a corpse.

Those were busy times—the nominating convention was only a few weeks away—but when he finally did make it home at night and sat in the kitchen over his sweetened tea and Stouffer's frozen lasagna, he certainly enjoyed the necessary solitude in which to think things through. Perhaps that was what Dottie had intended with her prolonged visit to Pacific Grove, although other interpretations were possible.

Somehow Clayton Burgess's death had changed things.

Austen even went so far as to draw up a letter of resignation, dated for the day after the close of the convention and effective immediately, and for close to a week he kept it in the safe in his study, taking it out a couple of times every evening to have another look at it. But finally he tore it up and flushed the pieces down the john.

We have to be practical, he kept thinking to himself. There was simply too much at stake for anyone to indulge in any sentimental gestures. Barring an act of God—and not much less than that would serve—Simon Faircliff was going to be the next president of the United States. If something was going on, then Simon was as much its victim as anyone.

But a president with a problem like that was a danger to more than just himself, and the important thing was to get him free of it. That wasn't the sort of thing that could be done from a front porch out in California. Austen wasn't going to achieve anything, probably not even his own personal salvation, by retiring to private life.

He had played the scene through in his mind a thousand times. He would simply show up one day on the doorstep in Pacific Grove—or, better yet, he would go down to the beach and encounter Dottie on one of her solitary strolls, with her arms full of driftwood. It would be just a few minutes before sundown—that was the best time, while the sky was beginning to turn to a pale gray and the tops of the waves were as red as blood—and she would look up suddenly and there he would be, as if he had materialized out of thin air.

I chucked it, he would say. *I quit this morning and flew straight out. You were right all the time.* It would be highly romantic, like the last three minutes of a Ronald Coleman movie, and it would make him feel just terrific.

Except that what the hell business did he have feeling terrific? Having walked out on something that was his responsibility—his, probably, more than anyone's—he would have to live with that knowledge for the rest of his life. And when the crash came—if there ever was a crash; if all this wasn't just some kind of sick fantasy—how would he feel about that? How would he like it when the Simon of his private moments rose up in front of him like Banquo's ghost to ask, *Where the hell were you, kid? When I needed you, where the hell were you?*

So he made up his mind to do the noble thing and stick by his job, and he knew he should have felt just no end of noble about it. Except that he also knew in his heart of hearts that he really didn't want to do anything else. So he had something to balance against his feelings of heroic self-sacrifice; he still had the luxury of wondering whether it wasn't all just a double-blind so he could continue to hang on to his precious life's work. Dottie, Dottie, Dottie—the course of true love never did run smooth.

God, he couldn't even remember the last time they had had it on together. Yes, he could . . . No, actually, he couldn't, because they had spoiled that one for each other too.

It had been right after New Hampshire, when Simon had packed him off to Washington to take a couple of days off and let his arm heal. He was to report in at the Boston headquarters bright and early Monday morning, but in the meantime he could get ten hours of sleep every night.

Dottie made a great fuss over him. The bruises on his left shoulder were a dramatic blackish blue and looked as if they had been painted on with a three-inch brush, so he was Mommy's official poor little boy. He loved every minute of it.

"Shouldn't you get a shot or something for that?" she asked as she sat beside him at the foot of their bed, after he had spent a careful three minutes removing his shirt. "Do you want me to phone Dr. Bilson? You look terrible!"

"I'm fine. The doctor in New Hampshire gave me antitetanus, penicillin, and cortisone. It was all very disagreeable, believe me."

"You must feel like hell. Would you like me to make you some chicken bouillon?"

"Not to worry, I'm still man enough to lift a fork with my good arm, and besides, I'm starving. Do you imagine that if I whimper plaintively enough you might whip up some of your veal paprika for tonight? A little of that and some—ow, dammit! You'll have to learn to be affectionate from my other side."

She had actually cried when she opened his suitcase and found the sportcoat he had been wearing when it happened. It was a tan houndstooth and showed the blood well, and there had been lots of blood.

"Now come on, honey—you get cut in the face and you always bleed a lot. It really wasn't anything very serious." But she hadn't believed him. All the rest of that afternoon and evening, her eyes followed him anxiously around the room, and that night she lay beside him with her head pressed against his good shoulder, holding him by the wrist with one hand as she slept.

He couldn't sleep very well that first night. The pain kept him awake most of the time, because the thing really did hurt like a bugger. But that didn't matter. He was very happy just to lie there and listen to her breathing.

And then, just when everything seemed to be going along so well, it all suddenly went sour.

Over dinner on his second night home he had given her a carefully edited version of his crack-up. He didn't want to make it sound any more alarming than necessary, and naturally he didn't want her to know about the man with the serpentine eyes. "So then this guy drove me to the nearest town. I sat on the front seat next to his wife, who looked like a sumo wrestler; her big worry in life seemed to be that I might get the upholstery dirty. I think Mr. Furbrick must have gotten quite a lecture on the evils of being a good Samaritan after they dropped me off."

"And the car was wrecked?"

"Oh, yes. The rental company was very nice about it, though. I rather suspect they were worried I might sue."

"You should. You could have been killed."

"Well . . ." Austen smiled and shrugged, hoping he sounded more convincing than he felt. "It's not really the sort of thing you can prove."

Dottie smiled too, in an abstracted sort of way. It was a smile meant purely for public consumption—her gaze kept wandering up to the cut on his forehead, which was still covered with a translucent plastic bandage that made him look like the Spirit of '76.

"You were lucky," she said suddenly. "Have you thought maybe somebody was trying to tell you something?" It was a joke, presumably, but he experienced a slight shudder anyway—it was a little too close to the truth. "You aren't going to be up to much of anything by Monday. Why don't you take a couple of weeks off? We could take a trip—maybe go back to Bermuda for a second honeymoon."

"Can't do it, sweetheart. I don't want your old man to get the idea he can live without me."

He knew as soon as the words were spoken that he had made a mistake. He could see it in the way Dottie's face contracted, almost as if she had felt a sudden twinge.

"He can live without you now," she answered with bland irony. "He's got Howard. Howard, I've no doubt, will answer his present needs just as well."

It escalated from there. The next morning, a Thursday, he phoned the airport and booked an afternoon flight to Boston. There wasn't any point in waiting around.

And as he sat in his empty kitchen all those months later, with his wife a continent away, he felt what he recognized as a perfectly irrational resentment, as if Dottie should have understood by osmosis that life wasn't easy for him either, that he was doing the best he could. She wasn't being fair, he thought. She had no idea of the seriousness everything had assumed. She shouldn't have stayed away.

In fact, Dottie didn't return to Washington until just before the Democratic convention in Miami. Austen was already down there. The nomination, to be sure, was in the bag, but he wanted to arrive early to make certain there were no screw ups in communications and to see whether he couldn't cut a few deals to lessen the dogfighting over one or two of the minority reports coming out of the platform committee. Also, just by the way, he didn't particularly want to play the part of the welcoming husband; she had been gone for weeks, without so much as a phone call, so she could damn well take a taxi home from the airport.

He set up shop at the Doral and once again went about the business of making sure that Faircliff's assumption of power took on the character of a destined thing.

"Who's going to get the nod for vice president?" Pete Freestone asked him the second evening of the convention. It was just a friendly probe; he wouldn't be offended by the usual flimflam.

"Bob Donovan. You got that from 'reliable sources close to the Faircliff campaign.' No names."

"Thanks, Frank." Pete grinned—his editor was going to love him when he phoned tonight. "Just between you and me, how does that sit with you?"

"Personally, I think he's a lampstand. But what the hell—he gives the ticket balance and he's pretty to look at. I only hope Faircliff doesn't catch cold anytime in the next four years."

Pete just laughed. He didn't care; as far as he was concerned, he was on vacation. Nothing, but nothing, was going to bother him in Miami.

"Oh God," he said, wincing at the recollection. "It rained almost the whole time in Denver. By the time Canby was ready to make his acceptance speech, half the delegates were back in their hotel rooms with the flu. He doesn't have a chance, does he."

"Not a chance. For one thing, nobody's ever heard of him."

"Well, I don't think anybody really wants him to have a chance. It was nasty, Frank. The Republicans were split up into more factions than the Spanish Popular Front. Burgess had it all wrapped up, and then . . ."

They were walking back from the Convention Center to Freestone's hotel, where they hoped the crowds in the dining room had thinned sufficiently to allow them to get some dinner in under two hours. It would be a close thing. It was quarter to eight, and the night was warm enough to make it more comfortable to walk with their jackets off. Little halos of light had collected around the stars, which was supposed to be the effect of the humidity.

"You know, it's a funny thing about Burgess," Pete said, kicking absentmindedly at a pebble that happened to be lying on the sidewalk. He was a good journalist, and it was impossible to tell whether his casual manner was real or some kind of setup. "I talked to the pathologist down in Los Angeles, and they found the clots all right—he said it was a miracle the guy didn't croak from the first one before they ever got him to the hospital—but you know what else he said? He said that Clayton Burgess had the cleanest set of arteries he had ever seen in a man that age. He said that in the normal course of things Burgess should have died in his nineties. He couldn't understand how somebody like that got a killer heart attack on the sunny side of fifty."

"Maybe somebody iced him—did they check?"

"Yes. It seems to have crossed their minds." And yes, it was some kind of setup. Pete was studying him out of the corner of his eye like he was something good to eat. "They spun down tissue samples until there was hardly enough of him left to bury. They went over him with a magnifying glass, looking for some kind of puncture wound, and you know what they found? Zip, that's what they found. Clean as a whistle."

"Then maybe he just had a heart attack. I suppose it actually could happen—none of us is immortal."

When all the balloons had been let down and the mainte-nance men at the Miami Civic Auditorium had swept up all the confetti and the placards and the paper cups, Frank Austen went home. There was no one to meet him at the airport, so he took a cab to Alexandria and carried his suitcase and his clothing bag up the driveway.

"I've moved your stuff into the spare bedroom next to your study," Dottie announced. Those were her first words when he found her in the backyard, sitting on a lawn chair and drinking a glass of iced tea.

"What do you want, Dottie? Should I move out? Do you want a divorce? What?"

The sun was very low on the horizon, so she had to shade her eyes with the flat of her hand when she looked up at him. Whether she had actually smiled or was just squinting at the glare was difficult to say.

"You're the one with all the plans, Frank."

"You come back after all this time and then just push me out? Is that it?"

"That's it. I live here, too, but I wouldn't let that give me any ideas." She allowed herself to sink back against the lawn chair without, it seemed, a care in the world. "We live in a building together, that's all."

"What do you want from me, Dottie?"

"Sweetie, I just want you in the spare bedroom. After that—well, you don't take up much space. I don't care what you do."

Terrific. Without another word, he went back inside to the

kitchen and made himself a ham-and-cheese sandwich for dinner. At any rate, he didn't suppose he'd be home much over the next several months anyway.

He wasn't. As he had expected, Faircliff kept him moving all over the country; he was the perpetual-motion machine, part advance man, part coordinating strategist, part Lord High Executioner. The local Democratic organizations hated to see him coming. He buried himself in his work and didn't pick his head up to look around him until the fourth of November, at eight forty-five in the evening, when he found himself wandering around among the crowds in the ballroom of the Jack Tar Hotel in San Francisco.

There were television sets everywhere—in the corridors, even in the bathrooms—and a band was playing ragtime loud enough to peel the wax out of your ears. It was hellish, with people in plastic straw hats running around everywhere and shrieking like demons. Austen decided he had a headache and went up to his room for two aspirin and a couple of minutes of quiet with the lights turned off.

He hadn't even gotten to the medicine chest when the phone rang. It was Howard Diederich. "Frank—can you come up? Simon wants a word or two."

"Sure."

The guard in front of the door to the penthouse suite let him in, and to his surprise he found Faircliff alone.

"Sit down, Frank. Did you see? CBS just threw in the towel for Canby—as of two minutes ago, we've won!"

"Congratulations, Mr. President."

Faircliff rose out of his chair, and the two men took each other's hands and grinned like idiots. At that moment Austen didn't think of his doubts—he didn't have any doubts. He didn't think that his wife was no longer his wife and that his peace of mind had been a distant memory for months. None of that mattered. They had done it. In eight years, they had pulled it off. All he knew for certain was that he loved Simon Faircliff and he was glad they had won. Nothing mattered but that.

Suddenly Faircliff's smile collapsed.

"I want you to take over the CIA, Frank," he said, sitting down again and motioning Austen toward the other chair. "I want somebody in there I can trust. I don't want to end up getting suckered by those jokers the way Kennedy was. I want to know they're telling me the truth—all of it. And there's only one way I can do that. Will you take it, Frank?"

For a moment it was impossible to speak. He had expected maybe a special assistantship, something like that, but never in his wildest dreams . . .

"Nothing will change," Faircliff went on; maybe he thought Austen was holding out for something better. At any rate, his tone became a shade more conciliatory. "I'm making Lyle Des Georges the national security chairman, but you can bet he'll know who's calling the shots in foreign policy."

"I can see confirmation problems, Mr. President. I'm a political partisan, and the CIA is supposed to be outside politics. And I've no experience—"

"Bullshit." The smile returned to Faircliff's face. "You're the sneakiest bastard I've ever met. If there's a human being on earth who was born to run a spy shop, it's you. And besides, how loud can they scream? You're a lawyer, after all. And George Bush was Republican national chairman before Ford tapped him for the job. You let me worry about that end of it. Will you do it?"

"If you want me to do it, I'll do it," he said, with a perfectly straight face. "I've always done what you wanted of me, chief."

"Good boy."

On the elevator down, Austen's mouth compressed into a bloodless line. All through the campaign they had kept him busy, letting him retain the illusion that he was still at the center of events, but it had all been emptiness. And now he was to be shuffled off to run the CIA, where he would have an impressive title and lots of money and be out of Howard's hair. If he and Diederich had been struggling over the heart and soul of Simon Faircliff, then Diederich had come away with the prize. Now he would have the president of the United States all to himself.

But, to his credit, Austen's grief was not that of the slighted courtier; the wound was to his conscience, not his pride. What he felt was guilt and fear, as if he had delivered Faircliff over into the hands of his enemies. And the poor fool didn't even know who his enemies were.

Howard Diederich had won.

Well, perhaps we would just have to see about that. One time or another, Frank Austen and Howard Diederich were going to have to settle up everything between them, and Langley, Virginia wasn't the edge of the world. Austen could imagine that there were still ways of hitting back. Who could say?—Howard might just discover that he had provided him with the means he had been seeking all along.

Part Three

Soroka

I

The new director of Central Intelligence spent his first full day on the job trying to keep from smothering down in the vaults. "Jesus, don't you guys believe in dusting?" he asked, after he had exhausted the resources of his pocket handkerchief and George Timmler had had to fetch a box of Kleenex from the basement utility closet.

"Hardly anybody comes down here," Timmler answered, standing beside his new master's desk at a kind of aloof parade rest. "We don't much encourage the writing of histories."

Timmler, who was deputy director of Intelligence—the DDI to his friends—wasn't very friendly. Perhaps he had expected to succeed the former director, whom President Faircliff had retired to a melon ranch in North Carolina, or perhaps he had expected to be canned himself and figured he had nothing to lose. Either way, he hadn't exactly rolled out the red carpet.

"Fine—then I can only assume that most incoming presidents aren't left totally in the dark right up to Inauguration Day. Your ex-boss wasn't terribly forthcoming; we were just wondering what he wanted to hide."

"He wasn't hiding anything. He didn't like your boss."

"Well, he's everybody's boss now, so I suggest we all try to make the adjustment." Austen got up from the little steel desk that was just inside the door to the main safe; he tried to stretch his arms and was immediately caught by an attack of sneezing instead. "But you're right—there's nothing here worth hiding. What happened, did Coppard burn everything the day after the election?"

He wiped his nose, and Timmler's eyes narrowed with professional disdain. "You'll learn, Mr. Austen, that there are some things around here that even the director isn't allowed to do, and one of them is destroy the conduct papers. Somebody would have shot him if he'd tried."

"Who would have shot him?"

"I would have shot him."

Judging from the look on his face, Austen was inclined to believe him. Timmler was a small, slight man, with the sort of countenance that is usually described as "birdlike," and the lines around his mouth and the thick streaks of gray through his dark brown hair didn't suggest that life had been an unending series of triumphs for him. But Austen made an educated guess that old George probably wouldn't have hesitated before burning down a renegade DCI if it had come to that. That kind of toughness had nothing to do with size.

"Good for you. And now, if you don't mind, I'd like to see the files relative to everything presently on the boil."

That was how the first two months went. As Austen prepared his massive document on the current operational posture of the CIA, he began to feel his way into the new job and discovered that he liked it. It was every bit as much a gutter game as politics, but it had something that politics lacked: a certain disinterestedness. "The cause," in this case, was not the career and fortunes of a single man, even if you could see him as the last best hope. No; here, if it was us against them, then at least *us* was big enough to include the whole country. That provided a measure of saving grace. And he liked George Timmler, who hadn't even bothered to vote since 1956.

"What does he want it for?" Timmler asked, as he sat in the chair opposite the director's desk and watched him proofing the final pages of his single-copy report. He had unfrozen enough that he would sit down now and even bring his cup of morning coffee in with him.

"Faircliff likes to know what's going on. Why? Didn't Brubaker ever request this kind of a breakdown?"

"We were lucky if Brubaker read the morning briefing book."

Austen looked up and smiled. "You won't have those problems with Faircliff. As soon as he gets this, he'll be all over us with follow-up questions. Get used to it; he's going to wring us all dry. And he loves the little details—conclusions won't be enough; he'll want the data behind them, right down to the shirt size and social security number of the agent who cleaned out that particular Kremlin wastepaper basket. You wait and see."

He closed his eyes for a moment, surprised at how much they burned, and then threw the report on his desk with a sigh. The monster was finally finished, and none too soon—Faircliff had wanted it yesterday. They were all going to have to adjust to the new volume of work.

"I don't like to see a thing like that go out of the building," Timmler said, resting his fingertips on the top sheet of the fifty-page document. "For that matter, I don't like seeing it *in* the building. Summaries like that always contain more than anyone needs to know." He allowed his thumb to ruffle the corner as if doing a quick page count, and his face contracted into a slight frown. It was touching in its way, like a man sending his only daughter out on her first date.

"Relax. This is the only copy, I typed it myself, and the carbon ribbons and backup sheets went through the shredder yesterday. I'll take it over to the White House personally; nobody's going to read it except the president, and he's not apt to leave it lying around for the amusement of the housemaids. He knows it's not a reference report; he'll commit it to memory and give it back. I've already settled it with him. Okay?"

"Okay. It's nice to know you're familiar with the drill."

He tried to smile, but Austen was figuring that perhaps it was time to straighten out who the new boss was. He held Timmler's eyes with his own, keeping his expression deliberately blank. "I'm not exactly fresh out of school, George," he began quietly, folding his hands together across his stomach as he leaned back in his chair. "Simon Faircliff may have put me in this job, but I put him in the presidency." Austen's eyes narrowed—he didn't feel at all like letting anybody off lightly. "You look up my file sometime, and you'll find that when I was in the army during the late unpleasantness I was a point man for military intelligence. Do you know what we used to say about the CIA? 'If you want to check the accuracy of a Company scoop, consult the

Saigon Yellow Pages, because that's probably where they got it.' "

Timmler didn't like it much, but he was smart enough not to say anything or even to let it show. That was another point in his favor. Austen allowed the moment of awkward silence to drag on a little longer, just to be sure. "What's eating you, George?" He unfolded his hands and laid them delicately on the edge of the desk, like a presiding judge; it was a gesture he had unconsciously copied from Faircliff. "You haven't had a Company man in this chair since the Colby purge. Or is it just me?"

"You want an answer?" The atmosphere in the room had suddenly grown noticeably more tense, as if at any moment the two men might come at each other with knives. But neither stirred, and at last Austen merely nodded his head.

"Okay—fine. Yes, it is just you. It is, and it isn't." Timmler glanced around at the ceiling, probably without seeing anything, and the lines around his mouth deepened. He was clearly a man who had been nursing a grievance for a long time. "You're just the last straw," he went on morosely. "For years now it's been people like you, the friend of a friend of a friend. You're right—since Colby, there's been no continuity of command. We can't trust you guys. Everything we produce just gets retailed so you can hit the opposition's candidate over the head with it. That's not what we're for." He sighed and looked at Austen from the other side of the desk, a weary smile on his lips. "And now we've got you, the president's son-in-law, for Christ's sake. His personal spear carrier. Now, apparently, we're just an adjunct to the Committee to Re-Elect. Well, you won't have to worry. I've put in my time and I've got my pension rights, so you can fire me and be damned. It will have been worth it."

Austen had listened with polite attention, betraying nothing, and when it was clear that Timmler had finished, his only immediate response was to nod his head once more, the way a man might who has just had a puzzling phenomenon explained to him. "Is that it? Or is there more?" He raised his eyebrows expectantly and finally smiled. "No? Good—it was beginning to sound like a replay of the confirmation hearings. Well, I hope at least it made you feel better."

"What do you want from me anyway, Austen?"

"Now we're getting down to business." He threw himself back in his chair, bracing himself against the armrests as if he expected someone to fight him for possession. "You want a nice clean nonpolitical Company; do I read you? Okay— you've got it, but it'll cost you. You'll have to stay on with me. You keep Intelligence, but you move over into the office next door. You become my right-hand man, in effect the associate director. Is it a deal?"

"I don't understand," Timmler answered after a moment, and from the look of him he really didn't. "Or maybe it's just you who doesn't understand; you're Faircliff's man. Not the president's, if you can grasp the distinction. You belong to a professional office holder—I don't want any part of that action, okay? I'll just retire."

"Like Coppard? You want to follow the boss out to pasture, is that it?"

"Right—like Coppard." Timmler nodded sharply, or perhaps he just blinked. Either way, he knew where he was now.

"Let me explain something to you, George. I didn't ask for this job. It wasn't what I expected or even particularly wanted. The president just said, 'Here, Frank,' and that was that. I'm over here to be out of the way."

"I don't believe you."

Austen merely shrugged. "You believe what you like. But it's true. 'I want somebody over there I can trust,' was the way he pitched it, but the fact of the matter is, I was beginning to make certain parties nervous. Someday, if we get to know each other better, I'll tell you all about it, but for now the only important thing is that *this* is my pasture."

He tapped on the desktop with the point of his thumb to indicate what he was talking about, and Timmler watched the operation with fascinated attention.

"You get the point? Or maybe you haven't met Howard Diederich yet."

"I haven't had that privilege, no. But I still don't grasp how all this adds up to you as the Company's sanctified redeemer."

There were volumes of urbane contempt in the way Timmler pressed the tips of his fingers together and smiled; you had the impression he had heard this particular con a hundred times—*Would I lie to you? I'm above all that.* Austen didn't blame him a bit.

"You want guarantees, right?" Austen smiled—nothing could be simpler. "Okay, then, there'll be no domestic surveillance that isn't cleared through you first. That's just number one. Number two, I'll give you a written exemption from the memoirs rule. What the hell, you can resign anytime you want to; if I start sending the boys around to ring doorbells for the man, you've got advance clearance to spill your guts about it in any media you like. And, remember, if you leave me here by myself to fuck up, and Faircliff replaces me, it's going to be Howard Diederich who nominates my successor. Believe me, you won't like that. Have we got a deal?"

After a little fencing about the details, they discovered that they had a deal. Timmler could play hard to get as much as he liked, but it was obvious that the deputy director wasn't quite as ready to write off his beloved Agency as he apparently wanted to suggest. If he was going to sell out to the likes of Frank Austen he wanted to strike the best bargain possible, which was reasonable. It wasn't even a question of personal ambition. Austen understood and sympathized.

"We'll run the war like Marshall Zhukov and Stalin," he said, taking Timmler's narrow hand in his own and giving it a slight shake. "Only don't forget which one of us is supposed to be Stalin."

It was a joke, and Timmler permitted himself to smile.

"I do mean it, George," he went on. "I'll keep my end of the deal. From time to time I'll have political work to do, but I'll keep the Agency out of it."

Austen picked up the typed pages of his report, seeming to weigh them in his hand. "In the meantime, is there anything I should add to this? Any little family secrets I should know about? It's better that I know sooner than later. Anything?"

Timmler shook his head.

"Nothing? You haven't got Hitler locked away in an icehouse somewhere? No defectors? Please, God, we're not running any whorehouses, are we?"

"No." Then Timmler stopped shaking his head and grinned. "We've got old Zinoviev—would he count? He's probably around eighty by now, and crazy as a lemming. We keep him in a nursing home in New Jersey. I guess you could call him our political prisoner emeritus."

On warm days he had liked to sit outside on the cement bench in the front yard and play chess with Mr. Whitney, who was a Negro and told stories about the forty-seven years he had been a porter on the Southern Crescent, the finest train in America. A broken hip in 1972 had ended the great adventure, but for forty-seven years it had been back and forth between New York and New Orleans; Alabama, where Mr. Whitney had been born, was just a place to wave at through the lavatory window.

But Mr. Whitney had died the year before last—his son, who ran a dry-cleaning business right there in Newark, had come to collect his things and had even taken the chess-board—and besides, it was the middle of March and too cold to sit outside at his age.

A-la-ba-ma. Noo-wark and Noo-yark. Places had such comical names in this country, like the nonsense syllables in a child's rhyme.

"Now, Mr. Eisenstein, you mustn't just sit on your bed all day. You have to help the circulation along, you know. Go have a nice walk in the recreation room until it's time for lunch."

Stupid bitch. In the recreation room the televison blared like the bullhorn in a prison yard, and the old women sat against the walls and whispered to themselves. Every so often one of them would get dizzy and collapse on the floor. *Go have a nice walk,* she whined, like a fat, butter-colored caterpillar bursting from her rayon cocoon. Stupid bitch.

They watched him all the time. The nurses, the boys who wheeled by with the meal carts, all of them. His room had bars in the window, and they watched him all the time because they were waiting for him to escape again. The fools. When he was ready, how would they stop him? They didn't even know his name.

He had papers—a social security card, an out-of-date driver's license, his passport—in an envelope in the business office. They all said he was Jacob Eisenstein, an old Jew from the death camps. That was to explain the numbers tattooed on the inside of his arm. They were good papers— the CIA could do those things as well as anyone—but they were all lies a child could have seen through. All lies.

Ten sons he had. Ten fine American sons. They would know it was all lies. *Father Georgi Fedorovich,* they would say, *we are the fine boys who claim you. We know you are not an old Jew.* He would find his sons, and together they would pay everyone back. Everyone would be made to pay.

He would have them burn down the nursing home—at night, after the doors had been locked. Everyone would die, and he would stand outside on the sidewalk and listen to the screaming and laugh. Old Mr. Eisenstein would laugh.

Eisenstein, Zinoviev—Soroka. It was all lies. *The magpie is a nest robber and a mimic.* Soroka would find his little fledglings, and then all the lies would become the truth, and everyone would be paid back. The Germans—no, they were all dead now. The Russians, the Americans, OSS, now CIA. GPU, then NKVD, now KGB. Soroka would have the last laugh.

When he was ready, how would they stop him?

One of the perquisites of high government office was that you didn't have to worry about trying to find a parking space in downtown Washington. You got driven around in a black limousine, and the one for the director of Central Intelligence had all the modern conveniences, including armor plating in the doors, a telephone in the rear seat console, and even a small safe in place of the glove compartment. But the nicest thing was that it was always waiting for you when you were ready to go home.

It was comforting to know that at that moment the thing was parked down in the FBI building's basement garage. Austen thought of it with a certain longing as he sat with a fixed smile on his face and listened to Oscar Monke describing how he was going to chew the hide off his back in strips if the president wasn't persuaded to follow the example of his predecessors in office and request from Congress a further exemption from the federal retirement provisions. Oscar Monke didn't want to retire.

"You tell Faircliff I've been in this job for a long time, and if he thinks Mr. Hoover's files were really burned in seventy-two he should think again." Monke wasn't even looking at him—in fact, his back was turned. He was standing by the big picture window behind his desk, gazing out over the lawn, his right hand clutching his left forearm just at the base of his spine. He was bluffing, but his voice was perfectly serene.

Austen continued to smile. Somehow that was the way you always reacted to Monke, even over the telephone. It was as if he were examining you under a microscope. "What exactly have you got, Mr. Director? Maybe, at the outside, a few sexual indiscretions—nobody's perfect. There's nothing more, and Faircliff knows it because he's heard it from me."

"Things can be twisted around, boy. I'm not saying I've got proof, but that business with Ted Boothe when your boss was running for his second term never smelled right. You want that going to the papers?"

Austen's smile broadened into a ratty grin. "Mr. Director, you're dating yourself. We've been through that; I checked the accident out myself. The worst you could do would be to hand us a few embarrasssing inside-page headlines, and the only tangible result would be that you'd end up making yourself an enemy in yours truly here, and I know how that game is played as well as anybody. Have you led such a blameless official life, Mr. Director? Is that how you want to spend your retirement, on the witness stand at federal court?"

The message worked its way through. Oscar Monke was standing so still his eyelids didn't even flicker; he could have been turned to stone. "I don't even know if I'm talking to the right man," he said finally. "I don't even know if you've got that kind of drag."

"I've got the drag. Count on it—Faircliff wants your ass out, but one word from me and you can stop cleaning out your locker. If you want that exemption, you might try being nice."

"What is it *you* want?"

"To start, George Timmler tells me that liaison with the Bureau almost doesn't exist, that you got pissed off at Coppard and told your people not to cooperate. Fine; Coppard was a horse's ass. But it's a new team now, and we think you should open your files to us."

"Done."

So apparently it was going to be easy. Austen drew a deep breath and decided to go for broke. "And it just may happen that once in a while you and I could do each other the odd small favor. The kind that doesn't go into any reports—not even the ones the president gets with his luncheon chat when you come calling. I would appreciate that, Mr. Director. We all have people breathing down our necks."

Oscar Monke merely nodded this time; perhaps he was afraid that Austen had come in wired. Austen rose out of his chair, the two men silently shook hands, and the meeting was over. Two minutes later a Bureau usher was holding open the door to his limousine.

So that was settled. Now there was only the White House and a quiet drink with the president. Austen smiled as he leaned back against the upholstery; he would tell Simon about their political prisoner emeritus. That would hand him a laugh.

II

There had been rumors for weeks, so when Major Serebryakov received the telegram at his sister's home in Baku ordering him to rejoin his battalion, he wasn't particularly surprised. Dounia, of course, made a great fuss, but women never understood these matters and were subject to all the terrors of the ignorant. He was the last of the family, she said; he ought to leave the military and get married to some pretty woman who was still young enough to bear him children. She begged, with tears in her pale old eyes, that he should be careful and volunteer for nothing, pleading with him that he was all she had left to live for in the world. It was very tiresome.

He packed his kit and went to the railroad station to catch his train to Saratov, making Dounia stay at home; they were both well past the age at which public farewells were seemly. He had survived Hungary and Afghanistan, he told her, so it struck him as unlikely that he would die in some little border skirmish with the Chinese.

She had made him up a basket of food. The trip was nearly two thousand kilometers, and everyone knew that the meals one got along the way weren't worth the trouble of eating. He sat by the window watching the countryside slip by, huddled up in his greatcoat because the carriage was freezing, nibbling at one of Dounia's cold *pirozhki* and trying not to regret that his leave had been cut short. It seemed so unsoldierly.

But the truth was, as he perfectly well understood, that the army had lost its charm for him. Perhaps Dounia was right and he really ought to retire, except that the two of them could hardly make a great show in the world on their combined pensions. As for marriage, for years it had been out of the question, and now he discovered he had lost interest in the idea.

He had expected to make colonel by forty, but already that honor was seven years overdue and would certainly never come now. He was a good soldier, and if there had been another war . . . But chasing after peasants in Afghanistan hardly answered, and he was without the sort of family connections that made a peacetime career possible. So it had been rotating tours along the Mongolian border and garrison duty in Poland. A life without romance. He would not be unwilling to spend what was left of his life keeping his widowed sister company on the shores of the Caspian Sea—except that there wasn't enough money.

In Saratov the railroad station was alive with uniforms, and there was barely time enough to change trains. In the officer's compartments he found himself sitting next to Semyon Kostylev, who was a lieutenant colonel and four years his junior but a good fellow nonetheless. They had done a tour together in one of the armored companies, but since his promotion Kostylev had been a staff officer and now they hardly saw one another. Serebryakov dug a bottle of vodka out of his sister's hamper, and within an hour of departure they were both pleasantly drunk. There was little enough else to do.

"So it is to be China again, Rodian Prokofyich," Kostylev said quietly, nodding with the air of someone imparting a great secret. "And this time, I hear, there is to be some action—give the little yellow devils a taste of Russian cannonfire and see how they like it. Teach them a lesson."

"Where are we to be stationed—Noyon? Eh, that was what I was afraid of. A terrible hole. In the officers' mess the cooking fires are fueled with dried yak dung, and the women all have flat noses and lice. We made a great mistake having anything to do with the Mongolians."

"Then you have been there?" Kostylev raised his eyebrows in interest. "I, never. I was in Ulan Bator, which is not so bad. They say Noyon is hardly more than an outpost. Why would they be raising such a place to division strength, I wonder."

"Is it to be a division, then? Ah, they must be interested in the oil fields; it is a straight line from there, maybe four or five hundred kilometers. You follow the river and miss the Ma-tsung Shan Mountains. It must be the oil fields."

They were almost into the Urals by then, and the snow was still heavy on the ground. There was hardly a speck of color for as far as the eye could see. It was so cold in their compartment that Serebryakov wished he had a glass of tea with a chunk of lemon in it and some sugar cubes; dinner wasn't for another three hours.

"A division, you say?" He shook his head, making a contemptuous sound rather like a low whistle. "What do you suppose they expect to do with a division? Four hundred kilometers inside the border—enough to take a few towns, perhaps—more than enough—but not enough to hold them. Not if the Chinese want them back. And they will want them back if we are heading for the oil fields. They must be crazy in Moscow."

"Well, then, perhaps it is not the oil fields after all, Rodian Prokofyich. Perhaps it is something else, eh? Like the pretty women."

But Serebryakov only frowned and wondered silently at the folly of those in command. South of Noyon there was only the Gobi, nothing but sand and rock and mountains, one of the poorest places on earth except for the oil. Except for the oil, the Chinese would not defend it against a company; even the Great Wall stopped there. But there was the oil, and it would take more than a division to hold fast. The Chinese would fight, and drive them away, and the oil would still be there in the ground when they left. Somewhere in this, there was madness.

Half a world away it looked like something else. So far the indications were fragmentary—the Chinese were very tight about that sort of thing, so it was difficult to get hard independent intelligence—but what was available so far was scary enough for Peking to break its customary silence about such matters, and the Company office there had been sending along some perfectly terrifying cables. The satellite photos confirmed it; the Russians were penetrating their Mongolian client state in force and building up along the southern border.

"They mean business, Simon. This isn't going to be some little punitive raid to teach the local goatherds not to stray over the line. They're massing for a strike against the oil fields at Chiu-ch'uan and Yü-men—that's what it looks like—and the Chinese have a heavy investment there. It would mean a war."

President Faircliff stood beside his desk, looking down at the map Austen had brought along with him from Langely. His thick fingers traced along the red thread indicating the boundary between the Mongolian People's Republic and China proper. He seemed to be feeling for a crevice, something real to mark the political abstraction. And then the hand came to rest over a blue line that indicated the Jo Shui River.

"If it came to that, could we give them any help?" he asked, although he knew the answer to his own question.

"From Korea, maybe. But we're talking about a distance of around two thousand miles, and Outer Mongolia is Russia's backyard. If they cross in strength, we couldn't deliver enough to make a difference. Not with conventional weapons."

"And if we decided on the nuclear option?"

Austen again had the impression that he had stopped breathing. It was one of those moments when you felt your mortality closing in around you like a cold shroud. He reminded himself that all of this was real, that he was the director of Central Intelligence and was being asked his opinion on a question within his official purview, and he didn't even smile.

"Mr. President, that region is mostly desert. The Russians don't have anything out there except troops and the kinds of mobile tactical weapons that usually accompany an invasion force, so it's hardly worth the candle. And I'm sure the Chinese won't be any happier having their refineries melted down by an American warhead than if the Russians just annexed them."

"Okay, Frank." Faircliff smiled and put his hand on his son-in-law's shoulder. "It was just a fugitive thought. So I assume the gist of what you're telling me is that there's no way we can intervene directly?"

"That's right. If it comes to a fight, the Chinese are on their own."

"Well, let's hope it doesn't come to that."

But over the next few days it became apparent that it probably would come to that. Langley was like a madhouse; nearly all their best sources were reporting the same conclusion—Moscow had decided on some sort of final reckoning with the Chinese. They seemed to *want* a war.

It was dreary. George brought in batches of coded cables, all pointing in the same direction. "Usually it doesn't work this neatly," he said, slumping into a chair. "When all our finks start singing us the same sad song, it generally means that we're having something planted on us. But these people are just too well placed; they couldn't all have gone bad at once."

"Are these the ones I wrote up in my famous report? You're right; they've been too reliable for too long."

Timmler nodded. "Precisely. So everybody in Russia must know about the invasion. I'm surprised we haven't read about it in *Pravda*."

"Have you checked with anybody else? Is everybody getting the same word?"

"You mean our continental allies?" There was a smile and a shake of the head, as if to say that all hope from that direction was long dead. "Don't be naive. Nobody talks to us anymore. Since we got our lovely new charter and have to clear every move through half a dozen different congressional committees, nobody trusts us with the name of their cleaning lady. I don't blame them a bit, but it's an arrangement that makes the Kremlin very happy, let me tell you. They've even stopped sharing with each other for fear some of it might leak to us."

"How very nice for Moscow."

Austen got up from behind his desk because he was beginning to feel restless. He went to the small refrigerator concealed behind a panel in the wall and fetched himself a bottle of ginger ale.

"You want one?" he asked, holding it up by the neck, but Timmler shook his head. As far as anyone knew, George never drank anything except Sanka.

"Have you checked the satellite photos from the last China flyover? What kinds of numbers are we getting from there?"

"An augmented division." Timmler shrugged his shoulders, as if to say, What did you expect? "Some air cover—they won't need much against the Chinese. Lots of ground-to-ground stuff. I don't think they're taking the whole thing very seriously; that's just a glorified raiding party they've put together for themselves."

"And this is what's got the Moscow operation all twitchy? An augmented division?" Austen frowned. "It doesn't make sense."

"I know—that's what worries me. You hear one thing, you see another. I'll always tend to believe the satellites over some disaffected bureaucrat. I just find it a little disturbing that all our Russian sources are having the same scary dream." He raised his eyebrows and pantomimed a whistle.

"So you have the impression the Russians *don't* plan to move in for keeps?" Austen asked, almost out of embarrassment. "I'll settle for a best guess."

"No, I don't. I don't know what they plan, but if they're thinking of staying they'll need to bring in more than they have so far, and there aren't any signs of that. They're not fools; it isn't Soviet policy to send Custer off to the Little Bighorn. Whatever they've got in mind, it'll be in and out. I give the whole thing three weeks, start to finish."

As Austen poured his ginger ale into a glass, he found that his hands were shaking. His throat was even dry, as if his tongue might cleave to the roof of his mouth.

Three weeks. A little spat between a couple of communist countries who probably deserved each other. It hardly seemed like a good enough reason to blow up the world.

Almost as soon as he reached the garrison town of Noyon, eighty kilometers from the Chinese border, Rodian Prokofyich Serebryakov came down with a mild case of diarrhea. He had had a delicate stomach from childhood, and something of the kind happened to him at the beginning of every stretch of foreign duty. It was the food, of course, and the fact that the local soldiers who did the kitchen work could not be persuaded to wash their hands. It was misery while it lasted, but he knew he would be back to his duties within a few days.

After the first really bad day, when he felt confident enough about the state of his bowels to risk walking around a bit, he was struck by the oddly stable atmosphere of the place; it wasn't a bit like a garrison readying itself for combat. The soldiers, even the thick-faced, imbecilic Mongolians, who could be counted on to desert at the first prospect of battle, were still being given twenty-four-hour passes and were still coming back well within the time, invariably drunk and frequently infected with the terrifying local venereal diseases against which nothing, apparently, could warn them. Even the officers paid little attention to anything except housekeeping concerns and the poor quality of the mail service. Except among the new arrivals, there weren't even any rumors of mobilization. No one expected anything to happen.

The last time Serebryakov had been in this part of the world it was summer. The temperature was above forty centigrade before noon, and twice a day there were sandstorms from which escape was, as a practical matter, impossible. You would sit in the slat-board officers' mess and watch that fine, bone-colored grit working its way across the floor in little undulating waves. It got into everything. The food, one's ears, the folds of one's underwear—life was a torment.

But it was just possible that the beginning of spring was worse. He had arrived on the fifteenth of March, and it rained the better part of each day of the week he had spent in camp. Everything seemed to be rotting, and the earth had been turned to mud with such perfect uniformity that the paths from one building to the next were covered with planks for people to walk on. In Russia, even in the dead of winter, it was at least theoretically possible to stay warm, but not here. Here you spent every moment soaked through to the skin; the very tent walls were spongy with damp. And worse, there was no distraction. There was nothing but your misery to assure you of your continued bodily existence. Dounia was right—it was time he retired.

Everything would have been supportable if he could have believed that, perhaps as soon as the rains stopped, they would move against China . . . But it was obvious that this was an army that would never see combat. It was not even intended to.

The fuel depot was clear enough evidence for anyone. Serebryakov was a tank commander; he had the hemorrhoids to prove it. And tanks do not run on Marxism and yak piss, so one of the first places he visited when his diarrhea subsided was the fuel depot.

The gasoline drums, approximately a fifteen-minute walk from the camp gate, were arranged in neat squares perhaps forty meters across, far enough away from each other so that a rocket fired into the middle of one square would not set them all off. All were in mud deep enough to cover your hand up to the wrist, and none were stacked; they would have made an easy target from the air.

Then, with the uncharming suddenness one came to expect in Mongolia, it began to rain. Serebryakov was about to begin running clumsily back to camp when something about the sound attracted his attention. The rain was coming down very hard, and it struck the gasoline drums with a decided ping. He stopped, went over to one, balanced his hands against the rim, and gave it a shake. It moved quite easily. Just to be sure, he tapped the side with his middle knuckle, going down almost to the ground. The thing was empty. A few moments of checking confirmed his suspicion—they all were empty.

All those hundreds of empty gasoline drums—just something to be seen by a satellite or a reconnaissance plane. There probably wasn't enough gasoline available to move the whole division five hundred meters.

He walked back to camp through the rain, the mud sucking at his boots with sullen obstinacy, and mentally composed the letter to his sister that he would write as soon as he reached his tent.

Beloved Dounia, I think I may be home with you by the middle of summer . . .

By April Fools' Day the policy of the United States government toward the impending Russian invasion of northwest China was fixed. And it had everybody, right up to the secretary of state, shaking like a leaf.

Harry Towers, who had been a professor of political science at the University of Michigan before President-elect Faircliff dragged him to Washington to run Foggy Bottom, was almost beside himself. "For God's sake, Frank, what does he want to do, preside over the end of the world? Can't you talk him out of this? He listens to you."

The two men had left their cars and drivers behind and were walking along a stretch of the Potomac embankment, under the nervous eyes of their bodyguards, who kept a discreet forty feet behind. It had been a cold winter and it was still hanging on, so at six-fifteen in the morning they had the place pretty much to themselves. Neither of them had been anywhere near his home in the last thirty-six hours.

"I've been all over it with him," Austen said resignedly.

"He's made up his mind. In two hours the Soviet ambassador gets called in to hear the ultimatum, and the president goes on television at noon. If the Russians cross over into China . . . Well, you know the scenario as well as I do."

"But China? Jesus!" Towers swept his fingers through his gray, thinning hair in a way that suggested he really was interested simply in keeping his head from splitting open. "Carter let them get within four hundred miles of the Straits of Hormuz, and our response was to cut off their grain shipments and boycott the fucking Olympic Games. Now they want to blow up a couple of oil refineries so the Chinese won't forget who they should be afraid of, and Faircliff proposes to start World War Three. What the hell do we care about the goddamned Chinese, Frank? Or is there something out there that I haven't been told about?"

"No, Harry—there's nothing out there but sand fleas and heavy crude. Even the Chinese could get along very well without it."

"Then he really is mad."

Austen instructed his driver to take him home. He had no more heart for the struggle; he simply wanted to get back to the familiar rooms of his own house, make himself some breakfast, and perhaps catch a few hours of sleep before he was once again called upon to bear witness to the unfolding of the final disaster.

He went upstairs and peeked through the open door of the master bedroom—where the master no longer had a bed—and saw that Dottie was still sound asleep. Why should she be anything else? It was only a few minutes after seven, her antihistamines had made her drowsy, and she hadn't the faintest idea that the world wasn't in the best of hands. Dottie was cynical about many things, but not about her father's capacity to govern. He was a bastard, but he knew what he was doing. Austen wished to God he could believe that much.

He returned to the kitchen, fixed himself a glass of orange juice and three slices of buttered toast, and took them with him into what the real estate lady had called the "family room," where he promptly fell asleep on the sofa.

"I didn't want to wake you, but they said on the radio that Daddy was going to make some sort of announcement at noon."

He opened his eyes and saw her sitting perched on the very edge of the sofa, her hand just touching his shoulder, and he understood at that moment what it was he had been looking for when he had come home.

"Right—thanks," he said thickly, smiling and trying to wake up at the same time. "I wouldn't miss it for the world. He's going to tell the country that we're very likely going to war to protect our good friends the Chinese. I'm sure everyone will be delighted."

"You don't sound as if you approve."

"I don't, sweetheart." He patted her cheek as he got up to turn on the television set. "But, you see, he doesn't listen so good anymore."

They sat down together, almost touching—it was closer than they had been to each other in perhaps five months—and waited through the last two minutes of some incomprehensible game show before NBC cut to a picture of the presidential seal and John Chancellor told them that the president of the United States was about to make an announcement that was billed by his aides as "of historic importance."

Within ten seconds, there was Simon, sitting behind the prop desk in the White House media room, resting on his elbows with his hands folded in front of him. "My fellow Americans, I wish to speak to you this afternoon on a matter of grave national—indeed, international—importance . . ."

Jesus, Austen found himself thinking, *who could have written this drivel for him?*

"At this moment, along the Chinese-Mongolian border, the Soviet Union is massing elements of its Second Army, with the intention . . ."

It was very solemn, very presidential. Probably, if you weren't familiar with the numbers, it was even very convincing. It was also scary; Faircliff was issuing an ultimatum, almost a dare. The Russians couldn't possibly understand it as anything less than a threat of nuclear war.

"We must regard the territorial integrity of China as vital to our national interest . . ."

It was then that Austen became aware that Dottie had slipped her hand inside his arm; possibly she was unaware of it herself. He let it be and hoped she wouldn't notice.

"And so now all that is left to us is to await events. I know that, until the current crisis is resolved, this country can rely on the courage and the patience—and the prayers—of all its citizens. Good afternoon, and God bless you all."

Austen got up to turn the set off. He didn't want to hear what the boys in the newsroom thought about Faircliff's little fireside chat. Above all, he didn't want to see any instant replay. The whole thing—the announcement, the presentation, the text—looked and sounded like something that ham Diederich had pulled together when no one was watching. Simon had been awful. And, besides, it was too terrifying to bear thinking about.

"Does he mean it?" Dottie asked, looking up at him from the sofa, her brown eyes large and moist with perfectly understandable fear. Probably all over the country people had that same look on their faces.

"He means it. Welcome to the Faircliff administration."

At that precise moment the telephone rang. There was a receiver on the coffee table, but it was three or four seconds before Austen could nerve himself to answer.

"Frank, is that you?" It was Timmler, of course.

"What is it, George? I'll be over in ten minutes."

"Relax—it isn't about the China thing. I just had something interesting to tell you. Are you on a safe phone?"

No, he wasn't. Only the telephone in his office was connected to the scrambler, but he wasn't sure he could wait.

"Go ahead and tell me, George. Just be cautious."

"Okay. You remember old Zinoviev—our political prisoner emeritus? His nursing home was firebombed about four this morning."

In one of the back rooms of Austen's mind a light went on. He couldn't have said why, but somehow George's news struck him as terribly important.

"Did they get him?" he asked, wondering why he was so certain it had been an assassination attempt, aimed at that one single person. After all, there could be other explanations. "George, is he dead?"

"We aren't sure, but we don't think so. We also know he couldn't have set the fire himself, but they haven't yet found a body. They're still looking."

"I'll be right there."

III

What would come to be known as the "April Fools' Crisis" was suddenly over. Within forty-eight hours satellite photos indicated that the Russian military concentration along the Chinese border was beginning to break up. *Pravda,* of course, denied that there had ever been any aggressive intent and painted the American president as an irresponsible warmonger, but the effect was simply to underline for everyone the indisputable fact that they had, indeed, backed down.

It was the Cuban missile crisis all over again. At home and abroad Simon Faircliff had become a hero, and if a few of the Western allies, and even a few members of his own government, wondered what could have possessed him to run such an enormous risk for a thousand square miles or so of remote Asian desert, their voices were drowned in the general applause. It was the beginning of Faircliff's magic popularity; he seemed to have some special knack for making things turn out right.

But long before most people's television sets had cooled down, before the country had even had time to absorb the shock of that first announcement, Frank Austen found himself with other things to worry about.

"They're sure he wasn't caught in the fire?"

George Timmler shook his head. "They're not sure, but they don't think so. They've got twenty-three bodies, and most of them have been identified. Zinoviev isn't among them."

Timmler had called from a public telephone booth and came over in his own car to pick Austen up. It had started to rain; big, soft drops were falling against his windshield, and the tires made a swishing sound against the asphalt road. None of the trees had begun to put out leaves yet, but somehow that stretch of highway still managed to seem shaded, almost gloomy.

"I want you to get a couple of men up there," Austen said finally, breaking a long silence. "The police are to be persuaded to issue a list of the victims that includes Zinoviev—I assume he was admitted under a false name. If you have to, supply them with another corpse. Then I want a complete breakdown—the nursing home's latest financial reports, insurance, background checks on eveybody, staff and patients. And I want Zinoviev, alive and undamaged. I don't care where he is—find him. Use all the manpower necessary, but find him."

Timmler only nodded from time to time, as if Austen were his wife reminding him of things to pick up at the A&P on his way home from work. He was wonderful that way, the perfect bureaucrat; you never knew whether he thought you were right or wrong, or even whether it mattered.

"Am I overreacting, George?"

"I don't know," Timmler answered evenly, never taking his eyes from the road. "Let's put it this way—I'm not sure I know where you're coming from on all this."

"That's fair enough. I'm not sure I do either."

They drove on in silence, right up to the gates of the Langley compound. There was nothing more to say.

There was a back way into his office from the underground garage. He let himself in with his key, and, even before he took off the tan trenchcoat the presidential campaign staff had given him after it was announced that he would head the CIA (*If you're going to be a spy, then you'd better look like a spy,* the card had read) he hit the red button on his desk console that summoned his secretary's voice over the intercom.

"Kay, go down and get the file on Georgi Zinoviev. Z-I-N-O-V-I-E-V. No—don't send a courier; fetch it yourself. Bring it right to me. Thanks a million."

It took her about four minutes.

To keep access down to the minimum—couriers had been discovered leafing through things, apparently just for their own amusement, on their way to and from the records room—all operational files were kept in locked metal boxes, not unlike the cardboard letter boxes you used to see sometimes in old-fashioned law offices, and possession of the necessary keys was a function of job assignment and security clearance. Austen, as director, had a key that would open any file box, but some of them even he was permitted to read only in the presence of the chief security officer, and in the main vault. And, of course, you had to sign for everything.

The Zinoviev file, however, was old business dating from the Truman era and therefore had a very low security clearance. They wouldn't let the cleaning ladies read it, but that was about the only limitation.

The introduction, written in 1955 when the case had finally been deemed unproductive and recommended for termination, wasn't very helpful:

> Subject was discovered by forward units of the American Third Army, June 9, 1944, approximately fifteen miles inland from the Normandy invasion site. He was dressed in the remnants of a German private's uniform (trousers were Wehrmacht general issue) and claimed to have been employed as part of a slave labor battalion building antitank defenses along the road leading to Rennes. Subject was in an advanced state of malnutrition and suffering from what was later diagnosed as the early stages of tuberculosis; he was assigned to medical corps for treatment.
>
> As soon as he was sufficiently restored to do so, subject notified military intelligence of his membership in Russian NKVD (rank, lieutenant colonel; confirmed through photographic evidence of his participation in 1936 trade delegation to Spain). Subject claimed to have been captured in September 1942, during the German invasion of the Ukraine.
>
> Intelligence council [cross-reference to *Minutes*, January 14, 1945] ordered subject retained for interrogation. Subject interned at Gorham Military Hospital, Phoenix, Arizona.

So far, so good—just what anyone would expect. What American intelligence knew about the NKVD in those days you could have stuck under your fingernail, and doubtless Zinoviev wasn't very eager to be repatriated. Stalin was shooting anyone suspected of collaboration, and having survived close to two years in German hands might have been taken as sufficient evidence to convict. Those people played by their own rules.

And then, of course, the natural inertia that governs all such matters had set in. At first Zinoviev was too sick for extensive questioning; later, inevitably, he got lost in the paper shuffle. People seemed to have forgotten all about him.

It wasn't until 1947 that an enterprising file clerk brought his dossier back to the surface, and a team from the newly formed CIA was sent out to Phoenix to make an assessment. They decided that the colonel might be worth talking to and brought him back with them to Washington. He was grilled at intervals of several months over the next four years.

Initial information provided by subject on NKVD (KGB) infrastructure proved reliable (confirmed by Deriabin, 1954), but testimony concerning his own career judged to be extremely suspect due to growing evidence of mental deterioration.

Well, what could you expect? It wasn't the sort of thing anyone had noticed when he was already half-dead—you don't expect a man to be perfectly in control of himself when he's been turned into a walking corpse by twenty-one months on a Nazi chain gang—but once he was restored to health and people with an interest in something besides the state of his lungs had a chance to listen, it became clear that Georgi Fedorovich Zinoviev was seriously psychotic.

For one thing, he labored under the permanent impression that he had family in the United States—sons, in fact. The number shifted around a bit at first, but eventually it settled on ten.

ZINOVIEV: Ten little red Indians (laughter). Just braves now, but someday all of them will be chiefs. All my sons, my little boys.
INTERROGATOR: Could you assist us in locating them? It would help in your resettlement.
ZINOVIEV: You wish to make provision for my old age (laughter)? No—when the time comes . . .

That was how the transcript read.

Ten little Zinovievs, all corporate lawyers and college presidents, to hear him tell it. Inquiries were made, of course, but no one was ever able to trace any of these distinguished relatives.

Subject claimed to enjoy the highest access to covert strategy planning against the United States, maintaining that as early as 1927 Stalin had planned to foment a communist revolution here, with the purpose of enveloping Europe between Russian numbers and American industrial power. On another occasion he asserted that the intention had been to establish the nucleus of a resistance movement against the emergence of an American fascist dictatorship. Neither of these reports has ever received independent confirmation.

And apparently people had checked. That kind of story probably went over very big in the late forties and early fifties, but Zinoviev had been so vague about specifics that even in the McCarthy era it was difficult to give him much credence.

Still, for a long time there were always a few ready to listen—Zinoviev was such an intriguing subject. Perhaps they kept asking themselves where he had learned to speak English with an American accent; a phonologist had reported it indistinguishable from the dialect, if there was one, of west central Oregon. Perhaps they wondered what use the NKVD would have made of such a man.

But after a while the entropy of boredom took over. The hole was declared dry, and Zinoviev was shipped off to a succession of mental hospitals; there didn't seem to be anything else to do with him. Every once in a while, as a practical joke that eventually became almost an initiation ritual, some brand-spanking-new case officer would be sent off to interview the political prisoner emeritus, primed to believe that the secrets of the Kremlin would shortly be within his grasp. It was a million laughs, and it kept Zinoviev from feeling completely neglected; that was felt to be important, too.

From the power of staff rank in the NKVD to the CIA's in-house comic legend—it must have been a hard fall. Austen locked up the file. He hadn't learned anything that threw any brilliant light on anything, but he hadn't really expected to. After a couple of minutes of staring at it as it sat on his desk, he decided to take the file back to the records room himself. That was five floors down, in a subbasement, but he had an itch to take a look at the record book and he didn't particularly want to call attention to his interest.

Sure enough, he found Kay's signature, with the time and that day's date entered beside it, and nothing else within the last five years.

As early as twelve hours ago, someone had, in all probability, tried a hit on Georgi Zinoviev, relic of another time. And the only two people who had recently discovered his existence were: (1) the director of Central Intelligence, and (2) the president of the United States.

He had no knowledge of how things were now at home, but in Comrade Stalin's day the business had had a certain elegant simplicity. People simply disappeared. They were arrested, removed quietly from their office desks or their beds, and vanished forever. Sometimes, if there was still some purpose they could be called upon to serve, they might surface again as the object of a trial, after which they were once more submerged as effectively as if they had never existed. A bullet through the base of the skull in some prison corridor, extinction, or, what was perhaps worse, the frail continuance of life in a labor camp at the edge of the Arctic Circle—no one ever knew.

The Americans, on the other hand, had no sense of style.

He had known for years—for decades, in fact—that eventually the CIA would attempt to assassinate him. He had expected, all the time he had been languishing in that hospital in Arizona, that one night one of the injections they gave him to help his breathing would contain cyanide, or that an orderly would come in while he was taking a nap, lock the door, and smother him with a pillow. Those who were in possession of dangerous or embarrassing secrets often died thus. But it had not happened. They had merely packed him off to a succession of lunatic asylums, periodically moving him from one to the other, sending strange young men to question him from time to time, perhaps from some unspecific dread of what he would or would not say. They had left him alive; he could only ascribe it to a failure of nerve, and these things did not last forever.

So he was prepared for the eventuality. He had formulated certain plans. They would discover they were not dealing with a child. He had long expected a fire in the nursing home, either this one or some other. Such a plan had exactly the mixture of indiscriminate carelessness and panic-stricken lack of resolve he would expect from the Americans. Twenty or thirty elderly innocents would perish. This he did not regret; their lives amounted to nothing, and he had witnessed the deaths of many hundreds of the young and strong—but he, the object, would escape. These were the consequences of a debilitating morality.

The bars covering his window filled a metal frame that was merely bolted into place. It had been a simple enough matter to steal a screwdriver and remove the bolts. He had filed the bolts down until almost nothing except the heads were left, replaced them, and painted them over so they gave the impression of never having been tampered with. All the rooms were painted the same color, and the cans were kept in the basement; anyone with the daring of an altered rabbit could carry off enough paint to fill an aspirin bottle. He used the torn-away end of a paper match for a brush. The whole process had taken close to three months—one had little privacy and, even with nothing to do, even less free time— and in the end all that was required was that he take the bars in his hands and pull the whole thing free. Even at his age he had strength enough left for that.

On that particular night he heard the alarm sound. The home was provided with smoke detectors and a sprinkler system, but the fire spread too quickly for these to make a difference; he supposed they had used some compound of aluminum powder and iron oxide.

He hardly knew whether he had been asleep or not, but he knew what was happening as soon as he touched his door-knob and felt the heat. In an instant the window was open and unobstructed. Fortunately, his room was on the first floor; perhaps they had always expected that eventually he would defeat the bars and hadn't wished him to hurt himself jumping from one of the upper floors. He always kept his clothes rolled up in a tight little bundle on his chair, and so he had simply to pick them up and be gone, and quietly as any thief.

For perhaps half an hour he stood on the other side of the street, watching with the rest of the crowd as the old building collapsed into a charred ruin they would not even have to bulldoze flat. When firemen began carrying out the bodies of victims, wrapped in oilcloth shrouds, he slipped away into the darkness.

He had no idea where to go. Except for one trip to the hospital, when he had been suffering too much from a kidney stone to pay very great attention to his surroundings, he had never been away from the nursing home grounds. Newark was a foreign landscape to him. He walked on until he reached a boulevard where at least there were streetlamps, and he would have less to worry about from the casual mugger who would naturally think to prey on an old man, and he stayed on that, waiting for dawn. He really was just an old man, and he was tired and his legs ached and he had no plan. It was cold, and the wind stung his face like a lash.

It was hard to make good an escape when one had no money. That would be the first task before him when the sun rose and the shops began to open; he would need money. With twenty dollars—ten, in fact—he could disappear forever. He could reach his fine boys, and they would hide him until he and they had matured their revenge.

But until then, what? How does a tired old man get twenty dollars without attracting the attention of the police? Of the muggers he was not really afraid—he was old, but he was NKVD and could deal with the violence of amateurs—but the police would deliver him back into the hands of the CIA and death.

In his trouser pocket he had thirty-five cents, hardly even enough for a cup of coffee.

At last he found a bus stop and sat down on the straight wooden bench. Perhaps he fell asleep for a while, because suddenly he was aware of the sun in his face, and he was no longer so cold, and the noise of the traffic and of human voices buzzed in his ears. Yes, it was morning now—he had been asleep. It was morning, and his mind was empty.

"You were right about the money. We found him in a Salvation Army soup kitchen on South Street. The poor old bastard must have had a rough time of it. He looked awful."

Austen, who had taken the call in his office, glanced at the correspondence his secretary was still holding in her hand. He motioned for her to put it down, and, knowing the rules, she quietly withdrew and closed the door behind her.

"How would you look at his age after three days on the bricks? Did he give you any trouble?"

"Not a peep." It was almost possible to see George's head shaking, for all that he was in a phone booth somewhere in the slums of Newark. "I guess he knew he was beaten; he seemed almost glad to see us."

"Fine. Take him out to the Fishing Bay house. Drug him if you have to, but take him yourself. The people there are expecting you, but they won't know anything about Zinoviev. Tell your boys to come in, and to keep their mouths shut."

"They already know to do that, Frank. This isn't any Brownie troop I've had chasing around with me out here."

"I know that. Tell them anyway."

He replaced the receiver and picked up a pencil that had been lying on his desk, almost breaking the eraser off with the point of his thumb. Everything had gone perfectly. They had Zinoviev back and would keep him in cold storage. Somehow or other, Timmler had seen to it that the name *Eisenstein, Jacob* appeared in all newspaper accounts and official reports of the Belmont Avenue Nursing Home fire, and the staff actually did believe he had died there; there was even a death certificate. Georgi Zinoviev, for all the practical purposes of this dark world, had ceased to exist.

But there was a feeling about the business . . . It was impossible to define, but Austen knew with a kind of wordless instinct that his problems with the old man were just beginning.

IV

The great social and diplomatic event of the following January was the visit of the Chinese Premier, Hua Yung T'an. The pretext for his journey was to thank the United States for its intervention the previous spring and to seek increased technological assistance for his industrial modernization program, but his real purpose, according to the Agency field officer in Peking, was to take the measure of the man who had risked nuclear war with the Soviet Union over a couple of drilling rigs on the fringes of the Gobi Desert. Apparently Simon Faircliff was an object of genuine curiosity.

George Timmler was curious too. Ordinarily CIA personnel, even ranking members of the central administration, didn't venture much into Washington political society. It wasn't encouraged; there was too much chance of somebody's getting, say, two and a half sheets to the wind and betraying Company secrets just to impress some broad who was falling out of her bodice as she listened to stories about his exciting life as a real live spy. Nevertheless, Austen was out of town, and Timmler wanted to know why, all at once, the two senior intelligence officers were such sought-after guests. Somebody had to go. So he rented a tuxedo and showed up.

It started out to be a pretty dull evening; he was seated next to some second deputy vice-chairman's wife who couldn't speak a word of English but kept addressing remarks to him in Mandarin. On his other side was a woman from the Swiss delegation who complained a lot about the chopsticks. It wasn't until after dinner, while he was touring the main reception room and admiring its collection of hand-painted ornamental screens, that things began to pick up. Out of nowhere appeared a spruce-looking Chinese fellow, possibly in his early sixties, decked out in a carefully tailored version of the standard light gray Mao jacket and trousers and holding out to him a small thimble-shaped vessel of enameled brass filled with a substance about the color and apparent consistency of brake fluid.

"We serve it in small quantities, Mr. Timmler. Its name in English means 'three cups and you will not make it over the mountain.' "

Timmler ventured a sip and decided it was probably some sort of heavily fortified plum brandy. He didn't experience the slightest temptation to finish it, so he simply stood there, holding the tiny cup between first finger and thumb and smiling, wondering what the head of the Hsin-Pao, China's version of the CIA and Murder Incorporated all rolled up into one, was doing so far from home.

"You surprise me, Mr. Yüan," he said finally. "I don't remember your name on the retinue list for this junket."

"That is because I am not here, Mr. Timmler. I am presently back home in Peking, taking my grandchildren on a tour of the Forbidden City. This conversation is not even taking place."

He grinned broadly, and Timmler understood at once. This was to be a little something between professional colleagues who had their own side of the street to walk. The politicians, of whatever allegiance, could damn well look out for themselves.

"A Taiwanese freighter into San Francisco—I was a deck hand—and then regular air fare to Washington, carrying an American passport that is the finest forgery I have ever seen."

"Very slick. I suppose you also knew that Director Austen would be in London this evening, and you sent the two invitations so my presence here wouldn't be too great a strain on anyone's credulity."

The Chinese spy grinned again. "Something like that. Your director is, I believe, President Faircliff's son-in-law."

"He is that," Timmler said quietly, his eyes narrowing just a trace. "He is also someone you would do well not to underestimate."

"Doubtless—that is not the point. One can imagine where his loyalties are to be found."

Timmler began to say something and then thought better of it. A year ago he wouldn't have offered any reservation, but now he wasn't sure what he made of Frank Austen, except that he wasn't stupid and he wasn't in anybody's pocket. But it wouldn't have done any good to communicate those opinions to Mr. Yüan, and Timmler contented himself with a nod.

"I simply wondered whether the Central Intelligence Agency was aware that the threatened Soviet invasion of last April was perhaps less serious than any of us imagined at the time. Indeed, I suspect that, unless they were counting on our being frightened to death, they never intended to take any directly offensive action. Would that surprise you?"

"Yes, that would surprise me. That would surprise anyone."

Yüan nodded a second time. "Yet such is what our agents tell us. Petrol, food, ammunition, spare parts—they had nowhere near enough to sustain them for even a week in hostile territory. And there were none of the—how shall I express it?—the psychological preparations for such an attack. My people tell me their garrison had rather the atmosphere of a Junior Red Brigade camping trip in poor weather; the Russians simply wanted to be on their way home. Do you understand me, Mr. Timmler? These were not men in the process of readying themselves for war."

"Yes, I understand you, Mr. Yüan. You think they were bluffing."

"Quite succinctly put, Mr. Timmler."

It was a great deal to think about. As he drove back to his home in Falls Church, where his wife would grill him about who had been there and what the dinner service was like and what the women had worn, too wise to ask why she couldn't have been allowed to come along but probably cursing him until three in the morning—*You, a spy? You never notice anything important*—George Timmler tried to remember everything Yüan Chu Lin had told him and tried to assess what it could possibly mean.

The Russian invasion force had been a paper tiger. He was prepared to take the Chinese at their word; after all, they had had a better chance for a good close look than anybody else and didn't have a motive to lie.

Suppose that, somehow, Faircliff had known the truth. You always call a bluff when you know the other player doesn't hold the cards, and calling that particular bluff had given the president enormous political and diplomatic leverage. Both the voting public and the Kremlin, in their very different ways, now thought they had a regular John Wayne on their hands. All the polls indicated that the Americans had at last found their hero, and the Russians were probably shitting in their pants lest, on the slightest provocation, this crazy cowboy would blow up the world. If he had known the truth, he had played his hand with remarkable skill.

But how the hell could he possibly have known?

Frank Austen understood him perhaps better than anyone. Austen had said that the president was not a screwball—not at all the type to take unreasonable risks, and not the least bit given to displays of adolescent heroism. The April Fools' Crisis had been completely out of character.

QED: Simon Faircliff had known more about what was happening in the Gobi Desert during those few weeks than either the Chinese or his own Central Intelligence Agency. Somehow he had developed some private source, circumventing regular channels of information. The president was in business for himself.

But if one question was answered—and that was by no means as sure as it looked; after all, the guy could still be just your basic screwball, regardless of what Austen said—an even bigger question rose up right behind it: why would the Russians have put themselves in such a position? Why does somebody assemble an army of invasion and then not invade? To wring concessions from the Chinese? Apparently not, since there had been no diplomatic activity, no ultimatum delivered in Peking. And if you don't invade, and you're not trying to shake anybody down, how can you come out of it not looking like a horse's ass? Even if Faircliff had minded his manners and stayed quietly in his own backyard, what could the Russians conceivably have had to gain?

About that, George Timmler had to admit, he hadn't a clue.

"The files say he worked for us back in the early sixties, as a pilot in 'Nam. His name is Yates, Victor Yates, and he's not a real sweet fella. I want to know where he is now, and what kind of company he's been keeping."

George Timmler pushed the photograph across his desk, and Michael Starkman, one of the two men sitting on the other side, rose out of his chair and picked it up. He looked at it for a few seconds, his unsmiling face a blank and rather brutal mask, and nodded. Then he handed it to his partner.

"Anything like a current address, Mr. Timmler?" he asked. Timmler merely shrugged.

"Nothing since the Flowering Tree Hotel in Saigon, and I suspect that's a little out of date. You have lots of contacts in the soldier-of-fortune set, Mike; you'll be able to run him to ground."

"What do you want done about him?" This time it was Earl Rutledge who spoke, but it hardly made any difference—these two were stamped out of the same press and their voices had the same lack of expression. A good agent keeps his feelings about a job to himself.

"Nothing."

"Nothing?" Rutledge lifted his eyebrows—he was merely curious.

"Nothing. This is simply someone we want to keep a string on for the time being."

"Okay."

They all rose, since the interview had obviously run its course, and Timmler was shaking the hands of first one man and then the other, when suddenly he looked inquisitively into Michael Starkman's face.

"Mike, see if you can find out where Yates's paychecks have been coming from lately. Don't push it hard enough to make yourself noticeable, but if he's been working for someone fairly steadily it might be worthwhile to know who that could be."

"Sure thing, boss." The two of them turned their broad backs and shuffled out of the room like a couple of tame bears.

But they were good men, especially Mike. He did first-class work. He was a field man—there would never be any place for him behind a desk; his mind just didn't work that way—but if you wanted something done, you gave it to Mike.

At seven-thirty the next morning, Timmler climbed into the rear compartment of the director's limousine to be driven to the airport to meet the early flight from London. He had his briefcase on the seat beside him, packed with progress reports on all current operations in case Austen should want to read them on the way back to Langley, but he had a feeling that the director would find other things to interest him first—anything related to the Zinoviev situation always lit up his board.

The past week had been the first time that Austen had been away from his office since Inauguration Day, and Timmler had been impressed, finally, by the degree to which that absence had made itself felt. Austen was probably the most powerful director of Central Intelligence since Dulles's time, and his authority rested much less on his unique relationship with the president than on the qualities that must have induced Simon Faircliff to raise him so high in the first place. He was a natural spy. It was as if the man had been born to this one task.

And Timmler liked him. He was a nice guy, and, as everyone knew, his private life hadn't been particularly easy in recent memory. So if news about a rest-home fire in New Jersey made Frank Austen's day, the associate director didn't mind being the bearer of happy tidings, even if he couldn't understand why anyone should care.

The plane arrived on time, and Timmler had barely had a chance to sit down in the passenger lounge when Austen, only the second person off, stepped into sight behind the security gate.

"London was freezing," he said, handing his baggage stubs to the driver as he took Timmler's arm and they started down the corridor. "The fucking Brits wouldn't let me in the same room with any of their Moscow product; I thought you said they were being better about that lately. They seem to be under the impression that we're just about completely blown everywhere east of the Berlin wall. Did Monke finally come through with anything on the nursing home fire?"

Timmler grinned. "Some crowd photos—our people discovered one familiar face. I brought them with me. Did you have a good flight?"

"No."

They hardly said anything more until they were both seated in the limousine and the smoked-glass partition between the front and rear seats was up. Without waiting for it to be offered to him, Austen took Timmler's briefcase from the floor, unsnapped the locks, and started sorting through the manila file folders until he came to one that contained photographs. He laid them out on his lap and went through the stack, one sheet at a time.

Finally, near the bottom, he found a face he knew. It was in three-quarter profile, as if the man had just seen the camera and was beginning to turn away, but the features were perfectly recognizable. The subject was a little under medium height and wearing a hat, the brim of which didn't quite conceal a pair of narrow, almost reptilian eyes. Along his upper lip there was a straight black moustache. Austen took a ballpoint pen out of his shirt pocket and circled the head.

"You know him?" Timmler asked, his voice an incredulous whisper.

"I know him—who the hell is he?"

"His name's Yates, and he's definitely one of the bad guys. There's a file on him back at the office; he's had a very colorful career. I don't suppose it would do me any good to ask where you could have made his acquaintance?"

"None at all."

V

"You'll never guess who came down for the state dinner, Frank, never in a million years. Sylvia Burgess. Apparently she's been hiding up in Connecticut ever since Clay died. I hadn't seen her since the funeral."

"How did she look?" Austen was only asking out of politeness; he wasn't blind, and Simon Faircliff was lit up like a Christmas tree. It was obvious the lady had lost none of her charm.

"Oh, she was fabulous. She's come back to life." Simon

grinned and leaned back in the desk chair, clasping his hands behind his head. In that posture, he only looked relaxed if you didn't know him. "When I sent her the invitation, I wasn't sure she'd come, but she did. She looked just great, Frank—I wonder whether there isn't some way we could get her down to Washington a little more often."

"That's up to you, lover boy."

They could still laugh at something like that; on the surface at least, they were still close. They could sit together like this in the Oval Office, and it was almost possible to believe that nothing had changed since those first few years when Simon Faircliff was still dazzling his new Senate colleagues and Frank Austen was his eyes and ears and, some people said, almost his other self. They had simply grown up—the same relationship, but on a vastly grander scale. It was almost possible to believe that.

"I'd like you to look this over for me," Faircliff said, his good-humored laughter breaking off abruptly. He took a thin report, encased in stiff blue covers bearing the presidential seal, from the middle drawer of his desk and tossed it to Austen. "State thinks the Russians might be prepared to take up strategic arms limitations again, and they've drawn up what they propose as a bargaining posture. Check it out—see if it squares with the Agency's assessments. I want to know what they've got going for them before we sit down with the bastards."

"Okay."

And that was the beginning of SALT IV negotiations, which were to become, for the next three years, the great and consuming labor of the Faircliff administration.

George Timmler was probably the first person in Washington to voice his mistrust.

"It sounds great, assuming we can believe our own intelligence," he said, sitting in the small dining room behind the director's office, across the starched white tablecloth from Frank Austen. He was investigating the contents of his plate, without any marked enthusiasm, delicately turning things over with the prongs of his fork. "What is this stuff anyway?"

"Greek stew, made with veal. It's one of the cook's new recipes. I take it that you don't believe our own intelligence—or is that putting it too bluntly?"

"You're sure this is veal?"

Timmler finally pushed the plate away and satisfied himself with finishing his Sanka. The expression on his face was not, however, solely traceable to his dissatisfaction with lunch.

"It's what I've been telling you for weeks," he said at last, when the waiter had cleared the table and left. "I think something's gone seriously wrong somewhere, and now the British seem to think so too. You said yourself they claimed we were blown in Russia. I think we've sprung a leak, and pretty high up if we're getting that wet."

It was an old story; Austen had heard it dozens of times in the months since the Mongolian border scare. It was rapidly becoming George Timmler's private obsession, the controlling assumption behind almost every word he spoke. But it couldn't be written off as the kind of paranoia that comes to people after too many years in this business, because it squared too well with the facts—in ways that Timmler hadn't even guessed yet.

"More than anything, it's a question of shadings," he went on, toying with his empty coffee cup. When George talked about *shadings,* he wasn't kidding; for him, the evaluation of intelligence data was the one true art form. "After all, we haven't got a man in the Politburo; the Russians aren't such blockheads as that. We just don't ever get the whole picture—a piece here, a piece there, and that's it." He looked up and smiled, as if to say, *I know you've heard all this before . . .*

"Think of it," he went on. "Why does anybody ever become a traitor to his own side? Our agents, let's face it, are most of them disappointed men—clerical workers and second assistants, that sort of thing. Nonentities. The very fact that for one reason or another they've been kept from the real centers of power and knowledge is the reason we were able to approach them in the first place. Their access is limited, so they interpret or extrapolate or, sometimes, just make things up. They're like someone trying to follow a three-dimensional chess game from underneath the table; all they can really do is listen for the clicking of the pieces being moved."

Austen, who was working his way through a small dish of bread pudding—he had found much consolation lately in desserts—set down his spoon and sighed. He was feeling the inevitable close around him. His range of options seemed to be narrowing by the second, and it frightened him. He decided to be annoyed instead.

"I'm not unfamiliar with the problem, George."

"I know. I just wonder whether you appreciate the implications for our own little difficulty. I really don't think you do."

"Try me." Austen rose from the table and pressed the wall panel that formed a camouflaged door into his office. "Bring your Sanka."

Austen had recently had an eight-foot leather sofa put in his office so he would have somewhere to take a nap when Company business kept him away from his own bed. He and Timmler sat at opposite ends now, and he waited for Timmler to drain his cup and set it aside.

"Like I said," he began. "Try me."

"All right." Timmler crossed his knees and leaned back against the sofa cushions, making the leather groan slightly. "It comes down to this. In the real world, given the nature of your sources, you don't get consistent information. *A* says one thing, *B* says another. You can't expect them to agree all the time because their perspectives are usually vastly different and they're looking at tiny pieces of something that's way beyond anything they can understand on their own. So you pick and choose; you have to sift what you get and take your best guess. That's the way it's always been."

He shrugged his shoulders, like a man who had made his peace with the world and was willing to work with what was offered. "And now, in the last nine or ten months, all those pieces have been coming together to make nice coherent wholes. It doesn't wash. Have our snitches suddenly gotten that much smarter, or are we getting diddled? I ask you— which do you think is more likely?"

"What about aerial reconnaissance? We don't get everything from snitches, you know. What about the satellite photos?"

Like the soft tip of a leaf touched by the flame, Timmler seemed to draw into himself just slightly. It was a sign that Austen had learned to look for. It meant that some raw mental nerve had felt the tread of a strange boot, that good old George had that curious little itch in the back of his neck that good analysts acquire after a long time.

"The photos are ambivalent," he said, holding his hand

level and then tilting it from side to side. "All the fallibles, all our little tattletales will say one thing, and the photos, the only really hard evidence we usually get, neither confirm nor deny.

"Take the Jakutsk chemical research facility, just as a for-instance. All we hear from our people is that the Russians are scaling down their efforts in chemical warfare. It's too unreliable, we're assured; the boys in the brass hats don't think it can be effectively targeted; that's all we've been told for months. The satellite flies by and . . . Maybe yes, maybe no. They haven't torn the place down, but there seems to be less activity—somewhat. Maybe they're staging that too. All they have to do is dummy up for a while—keep everybody indoors, disperse the rail traffic in that area for a few days. It isn't exactly as if they don't know those things are up there, you know. And they can track them as well as we can."

Austen squirmed uncomfortably in his seat. "So you think that the British are right, I take it—that we're blown?"

"Yes." As if the statement needed confirmation, Timmler nodded his head slowly and said it again. "Yes, I think we're blown."

At Fishing Bay, along Maryland's eastern shore, the Company maintained property it had purchased several years before at a probate sale after the death of an elderly woman who had once been married to J. D. Montcleath, the department store millionaire. Apparently she had made out like a bandit in the divorce settlement, because one of the smaller holdings her will divided among her various nieces and nephews was an eighty-acre estate, complete with mansion, bordered on one side by the Blackwater National Wildlife Preserve and on the other by that quiet finger of the Chesapeake.

It was a lonely spot, and none of the heirs had shown any inclination to live there, so they were willing to let it go for comparatively little money. At present, the local people were under the impression that the house was inhabited by a retired gangster who suffered from certain unspecified but debilitating diseases and lived in constant fear of assassination. Hence the presence of the barbed-wire-topped cyclone fence, the guards, and the medical technicians in their white uniforms who occasionally were seen in town loading groceries into the back of a wood-paneled station wagon.

In fact, Fishing Bay was a CIA safe house and, for the present, Georgi Fedorovich Zinoviev's private prison, where he had been held, all by himself, in close confinement ever since a few days after the Belmont Nursing Home fire.

At four o'clock on the afternoon of February fifteenth, Frank Austen and George Timmler were on their way there, driving along Highway 50, looking for the Bucktown turnoff that would eventually lead to a private road protected by a locked steel gateway. They were setting out to test a theory.

"I still don't see what Zinoviev's got to do with it," Timmler groused, jamming his cold hands into his coat pockets. They had left the limousine at Langley and taken an unmarked Company car and the heater didn't work. "We've got a security leak, and you want to go fart around with that crazy old bastard. He hasn't been near a secret in forty years, and you act like he's the hottest thing since the Golitsin catch."

Austen smiled tightly, never taking his eyes from the road. He felt strangely exhilarated, perhaps because it was the first time he had been behind the wheel of a car in months, and perhaps for other reasons as well. He had figured something out; he wasn't sure quite yet what it was, but it was something. A couple of pieces of the puzzle were beginning to fit together.

"George, if we've got a leak of the dimensions you indicate, where would it have to be? If it's in the Company, then who's turned dirty? I won't make you answer—it would have to be one or the other of us. Am I right?"

"Yes. You're right." It was clear from the tone of his voice that George had seen that as clearly as Austen. What he might make of it he kept to himself. Austen nodded, still studying the road.

"Is there anyone else who would have access to that kind of blanket information? Anyone you can think of?"

"No."

"I can think of one."

They turned off the main road into what seemed an unending forest of tall, thin, naked trees. The ground was thickly covered with leaves, grown black and matted since autumn, and here and there were visible a few patches of snow no larger than manhole covers. There was an occasional mailbox standing beside a gravel driveway that seemed to lead to nothing, but it was a lonely place.

"You remember my famous report? I thought you would. You didn't think it was very wise, putting that kind of information together in one document, and probably, as it turns out, you were right. I wasn't dumb enough to include any names because nobody needed any, but wouldn't it have been possible, if someone had an insider's familiarity with Soviet security arrangements, to read back through all that and draw some reasonably solid inferences about where we were getting our information? When they know how much we know, can't they backtrack to their own leaks?"

"Sure—we do the same thing all the time." Austen was aware that Timmler was looking at him with a kind of horrified curiosity. "What are you getting at, Frank? I thought nobody saw that report but the president."

"The story is that nobody did. And I got the one copy back three days later and put it through the shredder. But the White House is full of Xerox machines, and I can think of at least one person besides the president who could have gotten access any time he wanted it. The president trusts Howard Diederich a hell of a lot more than he trusts me, pal."

They drove the rest of the way in silence. It wasn't every day you accused the White House chief of staff of treason. Timmler would want to consider whether such a thing was really possible, or whether perhaps the director of Central Intelligence wasn't simply covering his own tracks. And knowing George, you could bet he would do his considering in the quiet of his own heart.

Austen didn't disturb him. He knew Timmler suspected that he himself might be a double agent, and he discovered with something like surprise that he hardly resented it at all. He would have thought less of George if he hadn't been suspicious. Maybe over the last thirteen months Austen had turned into a Company man in spite of everything. It was an unsettling thought.

They pulled up in front of the gate to the Fishing Bay House, and Austen got out and whispered a few words into the intercom attached to the fence post. The gate swung open.

The house was huge, and almost as empty as a barn. The heirs had taken all the carpeting and furniture and, except for the few rooms that were used on something like a regular basis, the place had been allowed to remain as the Company had found it. Your steps echoed against the hardwood floors, and every word you said came back to you from the central stairway and the great barren rooms. Austen and Timmler were greeted in the entrance hall by a precise, fiftyish-looking woman in a stark black dress that just missed looking like some sort of uniform. She didn't smile; the most she would do was nod. She ran the place and was known simply as the Den Mother.

"And how's our patient today?" Austen asked, allowing himself to smile but feeling all the time that, as far as this lady was concerned, even he didn't have any business in this burial vault of secrets.

"Just the same, Mr. Director," she said evenly. "He is questioned every day, in conformity with your instructions, but he tells us nothing. He refuses even to answer. He seems to think it's some kind of a game." Her eyes narrowed; you had the idea that Fishing Bay's guiding spirit had very clear and settled opinions about how Mr. Zinoviev might be disabused of that notion. Austen was glad again that he had given explicit orders that no form of coercion was to be used.

"We'd like to see him if we may."

"Certainly. If you'll come this way, please."

They were shown into a small, cell-like room, empty except for a couple of wooden chairs and a bare table. There was a single window that really wasn't a window at all but the other side of a one-way mirror. Through it they could see into the next room, where an old man was lying on a cot bed, his right arm thrown across his eyes to block out the light from a single bulb in the ceiling.

"You don't keep him in there all the time, do you?" Austen asked. He had never been to Fishing Bay before and found the place slightly appalling, rather like a genteel Victorian dungeon. "I'm surprised his brains haven't turned to jelly by this time."

"There's no cause for alarm. He's taken out for a walk around the grounds every morning and afternoon, accompanied by a guard, of course. And we see to it that he has plenty of company. He likes to play chess with the orderlies.

The Den Mother smiled triumphantly and withdrew as noiselessly as a black shadow. Austen waited until he heard the door click shut behind her before sitting down on one of the chairs.

"That woman gives me the creeps," he said finally. Behind him he could hear George Timmler's quiet laughter.

"She gives everybody the creeps. That's why she's here."

As if he had suddenly remembered his reason for coming, Austen stood up and went over to the window into Zinoviev's cell. It was the first time he had ever seen the old man, and he discovered that he was disappointed. Lieutenant Colonel Zinoviev had loomed so large in his imagination for so many months that he had expected something more than the frail little figure stretched out almost corpselike on the brown blanket. He couldn't have been taller than five three or four, although it was difficult to judge.

Presently Zinoviev took away his arm and revealed a pair of sunken eyes and a grim mouth and chin traced out with deep facial lines. The hair, of course, was white, and very thin across the top of his gray skull. It was impossible to imagine what he must have looked like as a young man. This was someone who had been born elderly.

"What are we doing here, Frank?" Timmler's voice was almost pleading now.

Austen turned around and smiled. "I want to know why all of a sudden somebody tried to murder that old coot. The fire was arson, remember? He's been on ice for decades. I want to know what makes him worth killing now."

They both turned back to the window. Zinoviev remained perfectly motionless; it was almost impossible to tell that he was breathing.

"He's always been worth killing," Austen said slowly. "It's just that now they know he's around to kill." For a long moment he continued to study the reclining form of the political prisoner emeritus, and then he turned away and looked at George Timmler, who obviously didn't know what he was talking about. Austen's smile had disappeared, and his face was as expressionless as a death mask.

"I'm interested in a coincidence of timing, George. You say we have a leak—practically a hemorrhage, it seems. And just when we're beginning to notice it, somebody tries to do a number on that old man. Has it occurred to you that there might be a connection?"

Timmler didn't respond, didn't even shake his head, so Austen simply went on as if he had never asked the question. "When I gave the president my report on current Company operations, I told him a story about this old guy we'd apparently been keeping in cold storage since the year one. I thought it would make him laugh, and it did. And guess who just happened to come into the room as I finished? How does Howard Diederich sound? The president thought my little story was so odd and funny that he asked me to repeat it to Howard. And I did.

"Now a question. If you were starting from stone-cold zero, and all you knew was that Georgi Fedorovich Zinoviev, under some other name, was in a nursing home somewhere in New Jersey, and you couldn't make any direct inquiries about it because the new director of the Central Intelligence Agency had thrown too big a net over the whole of the nation's security establishment and would be certain to find out if you so much as tried, how long do you think it would take you to track down our distinguished guest?"

"A couple of months," Timmler answered. Finally, it seemed, he was beginning to understand.

"That's right, a couple of months. Or about the interval of time between when Howard Diederich hears my stupid little story and when somebody makes French toast out of the old folks at home."

"My God."

George sat down, resting his forearms on his knees, and simply stared at the floor for a long moment, without so much as twitching. "So what are you going to do about it?"

"I'm going to see what we can learn from Zinoviev."

"And how will you do that, Frank? You heard the lady—he's been here for ten months, and he hasn't said a word."

"I don't care what he *says*, George. I want to know what he does. He's always trying to escape; okay, we're going to let him. Then we're going to learn what it is that he's so terribly interested in finding."

"You're nuts—you're nuttier than he is."

Austen simply raised his eyebrows as if that possibility had never occurred to him before and he was giving it careful consideration.

"Could be—but have you got a better idea?"

"No."

They rose together and started toward the door, when all at once Timmler laid his hand on Austen's sleeve, pulling him gently to a stop. "You really think it could be Diederich, Frank?" he asked. It was simply a question. "I've only met him a couple of times, but he hardly seems the type for murder. Treason, yes—maybe somebody's got something on him—but murder?"

Austen smiled benignly, with the superior knowledge of an old stager.

"Come along, George," he said. "And while we're driving back to Langley, I'll tell you a thing or two about Howard Diederich."

VI

It was decided that the best way to proceed was to take Zinoviev back to Newark, where at least he wouldn't be wandering around lost in the piney woods—what was an old man supposed to do all alone in the wilds of Maryland's eastern shore?—and it would be easier for him to convince himself that he had made a clean getaway. As Timmler put it, "Anybody can hide out in a big city, but if we set him down in the boonies and he manages to get clear, he's going to smell a rat. After all, why shouldn't we be able to track down one guy, on foot, tramping through the underbrush? He's old and he's crazy, but there's no evidence that he's stupid."

This trip, Zinoviev would have to be well funded, especially since nobody had any idea where he was going to want to run to. Of course, if somehow he managed to scratch up a phony passport and tried to get out of the country, if he just wanted to get home to Mother Russia, they would have to stop him before he had a chance to board the plane, but Austen wasn't very worried about that contingency; he had the feeling that whatever Zinoviev was looking for would be right close to home. Forty or fifty bucks would do it, as much as the average man might carry around in his billfold. Any more and, once again, he would probably decide that somebody must be pulling his leg.

"Of course, we can't even be sure he'll make a break," Austen had warned. "At his age, he may just say to hell with it. We really haven't got any idea what his state of mind might be."

"He'll make a break—give him half a chance and he'll be gone like a shot."

Well, it was Timmler's show, so at least they could hope he was right. "And we'll give him a clear path," George went on, smiling at his own cunning. "If we try to follow him too closely . . . After all, he's played these kinds of games too. He's old, but he's NKVD."

They had not killed him after all. Perhaps they had merely lost their nerve, but after ten months he was still alive. In the last analysis, the Americans simply did not seem to have the stomach for any of the obvious necessities.

"You'll be leaving in the morning, Mr. Zinoviev," she had said, that dreadful woman who reminded him so forcefully of a crow. "A new home has been found for you, where you'll have a bit more company. We've even bought you a new suit; I'll just lay it out for you here on the foot of the bed, and you can try it on in private."

They were all such fools—did they really imagine he hadn't known all along about the mirror? *And you can just try it on in private.* Did they honestly suppose he did not know they watched him every moment?

But the clothes were well enough, and after breakfast they brought him a little suitcase filled with clean linen and he was taken out to the front of the house, where they waited for the car.

"Why don't you let me take that, Mr. Zinoviev?"

So it was to be Gordon who would be his escort. Fat Gordon, whose skin was so pink and who showed such fine teeth when he smiled, who played chess so badly but who seemed to have a kind heart. Gordon ran his thick hand down the curling blond hair on the back of his neck and picked up the suitcase, putting it in the trunk of a long car that the people on the television called a "station wagon."

"And don't forget to fasten your seat belt."

No, he would not forget.

By noon they had driven through a city called "Wilmington," and Gordon decided it was time to stop for lunch. They must have made a curious sight, sitting together in the booth at the Howard Johnson's restaurant, the old man, dressed in a heavy brown business suit, and his attendant in white trousers and a heavy black sailor's jacket. Gordon talked incomprehensibly about baseball and ate a vast meal of steak and mashed potatoes, consuming several buttered rolls and even having the special dessert, a little chocolate cake called a "brownie" topped with ice cream.

Gordon was a pleasant enough man but, like so many Americans, utterly without cultivation.

All the way, he had been very careful to watch the way Gordon drove the car. He had not driven himself in over forty years, but perhaps, like riding a bicycle, it was something one did not forget. In any case, he supposed he could do well enough when the moment came.

Of course, he would never have a chance like this again. He had very carefully cultivated an impression of harmlessness. He was an old man, no problem to anyone. And, gradually, they had begun to relax.

There had been no point in attempting escape before; he hadn't even had any clear idea where he was being held, except that it was a wooded area near a body of salt water. If he had been able to get loose, where would he have gone? But this was different. Wilmington, Philadelphia . . . These names were familiar to him. If he could just get away from Gordon, take the car somehow and get away . . . And, in the end, it was far easier than he had expected.

"I gotta take a leak." Gordon had pulled into a Standard filling station and parked the car by the side of the building. He didn't need any gas; they had already stopped for that on the outskirts of New Brunswick. "How 'bout you, Mr. Zinoviev? It's still another twenty miles to Newark."

He smiled. He was an old man, with an old man's bladder, and his friend Gordon was simply being thoughtful. "Thank you, yes. As you say—it is a long way yet."

There was only a single urinal against the wall and a toilet behind a metal partition. He used the toilet, trying to be quick lest the opportunity be gone before he had had a chance to take advantage of it. As he came out, he was glad to see that Gordon was still standing in front of the urinal, fully occupied.

"I'll just be a sec, Mr. Zinoviev."

A short, sharp kick to the back of the left knee, and Gordon careened toward the wall, collapsing almost as quickly as if the leg had been cut out from under him. The cry he made lasted only a second and was barely audible. A blow on the side of the neck with both hands together—at eighty, one cannot trust absolutely to one's strength—and he fell to the floor, striking his head against the tile. He was unconscious; he would not rise again for many minutes.

Zinoviev pressed the tips of his fingers against the carotid artery. Yes, the poor fool was still alive. That was good; he would not like to have killed Gordon.

In the pockets of the sailor's jacket he found a handkerchief, some change, the keys to the station wagon. In the back pocket of the trousers was Gordon's wallet. He took everything except the handkerchief, which was soiled, not bothering to see whether there was any money in the wallet. It made little difference now, since he had committed himself.

Gordon had had to borrow the washroom keys from the attendant, and they were on a large brass hoop that now lay on the floor. He left them there, allowing the door to lock behind him. It might give him a few more minutes' head start if the attendant became curious before Gordon returned from his slumbers.

The great difficulty with the car was the steering. Everything else was reasonably straightforward—the automatic transmission even simplified things—but the very first time he touched the wheel he nearly skidded into another parked car. There had been no power steering in 1941. He had heard of it, of course, but he had never imagined it was anything like this. And, to be sure, the brakes took some adjusting to.

He got away from the main road as quickly as he could, both to give himself an opportunity to accustom himself to the car—he had no desire to learn the fine points at sixty miles an hour—and to avoid detection. There might be an alarm out on him in as short a time as half an hour, and he didn't wish to make it too easy for them. There was a highway map in the glove compartment; he would find his way easily enough.

It took him about an hour and fifteen minutes to reach the outskirts of Elizabeth.

Now the car had become a liability. It was necessary to abandon it, to proceed by some other way, on foot if necessary. He left it in the parking lot of a grocery store—possibly no one would notice it there for several hours—and started walking in a direction picked at random, carrying his suitcase and hoping to find some main artery of city traffic.

The wallet, now that he had the leisure to examine it, was found to contain forty-seven dollars—a twenty, two tens, a five, and two ones. There was also a Mastercharge card, a driver's license, a social security card, and an oil company credit card, all made out to "Gordon Winesap," and the business card of a garage in a place called "Salisbury," with the address and telephone number of "Dave's Body Shop" printed by hand on the back. The money was more than sufficient, but he would keep everything. One never knew, and he might hit upon a way to turn the credit cards to account.

By that time he had developed the outline of a plan, which consisted of little more than attempting to reach New York City. His ten fine sons had been nurtured with the expectation that they would rise in the world, and New York, he had been led to believe, was the center of almost everything in this country. Certainly New York would be the place to begin his inquiries. If he failed there, it was unlikely he could travel very much farther with his limited resources. Perhaps it was better not to think beyond that point.

In the meantime, if he was to remain safe and free, he needed to protect himself. It was already late in the afternoon, and an old man alone would be decidedly at hazard on the streets after dark.

A pistol, of course, was out of the question—where would he obtain one, and how could he have paid for it out of forty-seven dollars? Something less expensive, and less obvious, would do just as well.

He found his solution in a pharmacy on Spring Street, where for seven dollars and sixty-three cents he purchased a walking cane. It was of heavy wood, perhaps an inch and a quarter in diameter, and would serve quite nicely. The Mastercharge card was accepted without question; the woman behind the counter never even glanced at his signature.

As he stepped out onto the sidewalk again, he saw a bus approaching marked "Airport." He stepped aboard, asked about the fare, received thirty-five cents change from his dollar, and sat down. Airports, as a rule, provided excellent means of transportation—doubtless he would be able to take a taxi or another bus into New York. He leaned back against the seat, his hands folded over the top of his cane, and fell promptly asleep.

All his previous experience had been with military airfields, and nothing, not even television, could have prepared him for the sheer size of the terminal, the seemingly endless lines of passenger counters, the linoleum floors that stretched on forever. And this was merely Newark—what must Chicago or New York be like? After twenty minutes of walking in a perfectly straight line, he glided to rest on a lounge chair, exhausted.

When he found he could face the prospect, he got back on his feet and walked diagonally across the great central plaza of the terminal to a concession stand, where he purchased a Milky Way candy bar. Somewhat restored, he hunted up a bank of telephones and found the Yellow Pages for Manhattan. There was nothing more he could do today; he was simply too tired. He would find the name of a hotel, call for a reservation, and then hit upon some means of transporting himself there.

Three or four calls to places chosen at random brought him face to face with the discouraging fact that hotel rooms in New York cost a good deal more than the forty-seven dollars he carried in Gordon Winesap's wallet. Something as small as a cane he could probably manage safely on the credit card, but wouldn't a hotel wish for confirmation of his identity? He could hardly use Gordon's driver's license, since both the physical description and the photograph would be ludicrously at odds with the bearer. Perhaps, under the circumstances, it might be best if he simply spent the night where he was, sleeping in a lounge chair. He could move every few hours; no one would have reason to notice. He would merely be waiting for a late flight.

However, thanks to the ingenious decadence of American capitalism, nothing so drastically austere was called for.

Attracted by a sign that read "Anytime Banking," Zinoviev found a grid of square metal buttons and concave slots. There were step-by-step instructions: 1) Insert card, stripe down. 2) Punch in personal code number. 3) Punch in amount desired advance [Limit, $100.00].

He examined Gordon's Mastercharge card and discovered a black stripe, approximately half an inch wide, running the length of the back. As to the "personal code number," of course, he hadn't a clue. But Gordon had never struck him as a man with much of a memory for numerical sequences. Sure enough, tucked behind a loose flap of lining in the billfold, he found a small slip of paper with six digits carefully printed in ink. In any case, it was worth the attempt.

He followed the instructions and received for his trouble the return of his card and an envelope containing one hundred dollars in crisp, new bills.

He was not so extravagant as to travel to New York by taxi. The bus deposited him at Thirty-fourth Street, next to Pennsylvania Station, and he asked directions to Eighth Avenue and Fifty-second Street, the address of his hotel.

"One long block up, pal," the bus driver said, pointing back in the direction they had come from. "Then just turn right—the streets are numbered; you can't miss it. Better take a cab, though."

Zinoviev thanked him but decided to walk. It was only a few minutes after eight o'clock in the evening, his suitcase was small and light, and the walk would provide him with an opportunity to convince himself yet again that no one was following him.

He had never before set foot in New York. For all the Americans prided themselves on their wealth, the bus had driven through some slums worthy of Madrid at the height of the Civil War.

In the yellow light from the streetlamps, as he walked under the protective scaffolding around the cement shell of some incomprehensible structure that might have been destined to be anything—a parking tower, a cathedral, anything—he felt around him a faint atmosphere of indefinable menace. The people crowding the sidewalks wore expressions of hurried, self-absorbed anxiety, as if the struggle of life here had slowly bled away their souls; the noise, the traffic, the blended murmur of innumerable raised voices, the driving chatter of music from every doorway and window, the sheer deafening complexity of it was at once dreamlike and strangely threatening.

In the early days, on his foreign assignments to Berlin and Vienna and even London, he had learned to prefer reflex over analysis, to listen with his nerve endings instead of his mind. He had been good in the field, but all that had ended in the late twenties, a victim first of promotion and then of the endless decades of captivity. Was there anything now, or was it simply an old man's fretfulness? He couldn't tell.

"Awright, Gran'pa, you jes' come along."

It was almost a relief to hear the voice and feel the strong push against his shoulder as he was crowded into a narrow alleyway between two buildings. He dropped the suitcase, because it was only in the way now, and allowed himself to be guided, squeezed along unprotestingly between ashcans and piles of empty pasteboard boxes.

"Okay now. You c'n turn aroun' an' gimme you watch an' wallet."

His antagonist was a young Negro, perhaps a shade under six feet, tall and heavily built. His face was hidden in the shadow, but the point of the knife he was carrying was clearly visible. Zinoviev realized, with an amused astonishment, that he was being mugged. This was neither the police nor the CIA—merely some amateur thief with a cheap stiletto.

He allowed his hand to slip a few inches down the handle of his cane, so that he was holding the shaft rather than the crook, and smiled. He was going to enjoy this. "I have no watch," he said, allowing his voice to quaver. "And I have almost no money. Leave an old man alone."

"No, man. You gotta gimme—you gotta." The Negro made an awkward little pass with his knife, as if he meant to cut his elderly victim open from one shoulder to the other. He even laughed.

They weren't more than four or five feet apart, but the mugger would have had to step forward if he meant to do any harm. His feet were firmly planted and wide apart, so he had no plans in that direction. He was feeling safe and powerful, content for the moment merely to inspire fear.

Zinoviev reached up to his inside jacket pocket. His hand was shaking, but that was perfectly deliberate. At the same time he held his other arm straight down against his body, bending his wrist back slightly so that the cane pointed behind him. When he brought it up, he wanted it to have the necessary momentum.

Then, quite suddenly, twisting his body sideways at the same time, he drove the cane between his attacker's legs, catching him in the groin. He heard a sharp intake of breath—the blow wasn't enough to have stopped anyone, but it gave him a few seconds' purchase.

He raised the cane over his head, holding it at the bottom now with both hands, and struck out again, hitting at random at the shape in the darkness. There was the heavy sound of contact, and the cane glanced away toward the wall. He raised it again and struck again, and then again, and now, as the other man began to go down to his knees, he could see to aim.

Three, four times he brought the cane down against the black head, until there was nothing except a body stretched out on the paved floor of the alley, lying perfectly still. After that it was like beating a pillow.

The man still held his knife clutched loosely in his right hand. Zinoviev took it, folded it, and slipped it into his pocket. He also took the man's wallet, which contained close to three hundred dollars; apparently it had been a good night. In a second he was back on Eighth Avenue. No one had noticed, or if they had they hadn't thought to interfere. He picked up his suitcase again and continued on his way, wondering, indifferently, whether the man he had left behind him was alive or dead.

They had tracked him to the Forty-second Street library, where he was sitting at one of the long tables in the Reference Room, reading a large volume with a red cover. It was the best shadowing job Austen had ever seen.

"You're sure he hasn't spotted anyone?" Austen fiddled nervously with his hat. He disliked hats, but the weather had turned unexpectedly cold that morning, and besides, a hat made his reddish-brown hair harder to see.

George nodded. "We stayed well back. Most of the time we were tracking him by radio anyway."

"Where did you plant the transmitter?"

"It's embedded in one of the buttons of his coat."

That was clever; there was no doubt about it. Austen supposed there was something to be said for having access to all the latest technology. At least they knew they wouldn't lose him.

It was a Sunday morning, very overcast and gloomy. Bits of newspaper and old handbills skipped along the sidewalk, driven by a fitful northerly wind. The ice cream store across the street was closed; they couldn't be doing a very brisk business in the middle of February.

The two of them had shared a room at the Holiday Inn on Eighth Avenue, simply because that way they could stay close to Zinoviev and be ready if their agents in the street indicated that he was on the move again. Austen slept only in snatches; there was too much noise from the girlish laughter and the clatter of high-heeled shoes out on the landing, and beyond that, he couldn't seem to turn his mind off.

Zinoviev, at least, had the advantage of knowing what he was about. It was wonderful, really; after forty years in the jug, there was still a perfect clarity of purpose behind every move he made. He was looking for something, the directions to which he could think to discover in the New York Public Library.

Or someone. After forty years, could it possibly still be a person? Who could this walking museum piece possibly know after such a time, in New York or anywhere else?

"I'll shadow him myself when he comes out," Austen said suddenly; the idea had just popped into his mind. "I think this may be the end game, and I want to be in a position to call the shots directly if anything unexpected happens."

George cocked his head a little to one side, closing one eye slightly in some very attenuated version of surprise. "You sure, Frank? You sure you don't want to leave it to my thugs? Remember that monkey last night—Earl tells me he really turned the guy inside out."

"Not to worry, little mother," Austen replied, smiling again. "I'm probably safer than any of you; after all, he's never seen me before. And I'll try to stay far enough away so that Methuselah won't get a chance to club me to death. Relax, pal."

"Okay, you're the boss. Just don't underestimate him, is all. You're not even carrying a piece." He reached into his pocket and took out a small nickel-plated automatic, but Austen shook his head.

"I won't need it, George. Besides, I can summon all the help I'll need in an instant, remember?" He opened his hand and revealed a duplicate of Timmler's own walkie-talkie.

"Then you might as well get going—I just got the hand-signal from across the street. He's on his way out."

Austen got out of the car and watched it heading up the Avenue of the Americas, where George would turn into a side street so he could be there as soon as he was called. George was a good man, but he worried too much.

The walkie-talkie, which he kept in his left hand, began to vibrate slightly, an inaudible signal that someone was trying to get in touch with him. He switched on the receiver and held the thing up close to his face, so he could hear.

"Frank?" It was Timmler's voice. "Frank, it was *Who's Who*. The book he's been reading was *Who's Who*. What do you make of that?"

"Nothing," he answered, almost like a man talking to himself. "I don't know, George. See you later."

So it was a some*one* after all.

He could see Zinoviev now, coming out of the Forty-second Street door, walking down the cement steps with the aid of his cane, looking just as harmless as the thousands of other old men you saw hobbling around this city. Austen crossed over to the uptown side and began to move in the direction of Fifth Avenue. He stopped at a shop window to give Zinoviev time to develop a lead, and then followed him up toward Central Park.

Who's Who, in the New York Public Library. It rang a bell, but there would be time enough later to sort it out. Zinoviev maintained a good pace for a man his age. He clearly had no suspicion of being followed, but Austen kept about three-quarters of a block behind him and on the other side of the avenue just to be sure it stayed that way.

The wind had died down, and Zinoviev seemed to be enjoying himself as he pushed along through the crowds of Sunday strollers. After a few blocks he dropped the pretense of needing his cane and simply carried it in his hand. Wherever he was going, it obviously wasn't such a great distance that the old man entertained any thoughts of taking a taxi. So much the better.

It was in front of the window of the Doubleday bookstore that Austen remembered the night he had followed another man down Fifth Avenue, but that had been—how long?—close to six years ago. It was easier to do these things, he discovered, in broad daylight.

Because he had missed breakfast, and because his comparative youth was beginning to tell as he gained on Zinoviev, he stopped to buy a hot dog from a street vendor, paying for it with a dollar bill from his overcoat pocket. It wasn't for several seconds, as he walked along eating the hot dog and absent-mindedly fiddling with the coins that were still in his hand, that he realized the vendor had short-changed him. Apparently he must have looked preoccupied—something to take care of, since hot dog vendors weren't the only people with eyes.

They reached Central Park and Zinoviev, who had been stopped by a light, stood staring at the street sign. There was something in his gestures that suggested a certain impatience, as if he felt himself close to his goal.

All at once Austen experienced a horrible premonition.

Ten little red Indians, he had said. *Just braves now, but someday all of them will be chiefs.* The old man had told them himself, and everyone had been too dumb to listen.

Now, as Austen himself had once done, Zinoviev was following a well-worn trail to the doorway of one of America's most badly frightened worthies.

Ten little Indians, Who's Who—possibly the same volume he had looked into himself—the link with Howard Diederich. Why hadn't he seen it before?

"He's at Fifty-ninth and Fifth," Austen whispered into the walkie-talkie. "Pull up within range, George. I'm going down to Madison, and if he starts down Sixty-first be ready to grab him off. But don't touch him until you hear from me."

"Are you onto something, Frank? Are you—"

But Austen had no time to listen now. It was all coming true, like a bad dream, and he was running down Fifty-eighth Street so he could be in position. He wanted to be ready—and he knew now that it was going to happen. The ten little Indians were standing in line.

He started up Madison and was at the corner of Sixty-first when he saw Zinoviev again, coming toward him down the sidestreet, looking around at the buildings as if searching for a house number. That was exactly what he was doing.

"Can you see me, George?"

"Yes—we can see you. We're waiting just at the corner of Park. Do you want us to go for him now?"

"Not yet. I have to be absolutely sure. When you see me raise my arm, come and scoop him up."

Austen and the old man were kitty-corner from each other now, and unfortunately the traffic light broke for Austen first. He had to cross the street, right under Zinoviev's nose, and keep on going—he could hardly hang around staring open-mouthed. But he took his time, and as soon as he could be sure that Zinoviev had crossed behind him and was around the corner, he doubled back and started down the street after him. He wasn't more than twenty feet away when Zinoviev began to slow down and seemed to be curving in toward one of the brownstone houses on that side. Number sixty-seven.

He wished to hell now he had taken that damned gun of George's.

"Just keep walking, pal," he breathed, coming up directly behind his quarry. He pressed the blunt tip of his walkie-talkie into Zinoviev's back, hoping it would fool him for a couple of seconds. "Just keep going—there's nobody home to you there."

And it seemed to work, at least for three or four paces. Or maybe Zinoviev was just biding his time. Because, just as Austen began to feel they were safely clear and started to signal George to move in, the old man spun and caught him on the arm with his cane.

The blow took him just on the elbow. He hadn't known such exquisite pain was possible; all the way up to his neck he felt as if every nerve in his arm were being twisted and wrung like a washcloth. The whole arm was in agony and at the same time just so much dead weight. He couldn't have moved it for worlds.

The next one was to the side of the face, on the cheekbone. Then, almost simultaneously, a thrust to the pit of the stomach. He could watch the pavement coming up at him and know, simply as a fact without any inherent interest, that he was falling.

Well, fine. He would just lie down there on the sidewalk for a while and take a short snooze. His head was buzzing like a beehive, and he just wanted a little peace and quiet anyway. A little peace and . . .

"Are you okay, Frank? We got him—he's in the car. Come on, let's get out of here. Zinoviev's fine—he's in the car, and we've got the leg irons on him. Come *on,* Frank. You're bleeding all over the curb."

VII

"He's out of town. Hell, he's out of the country, in the Bahamas, nursing his tan, and he won't be back until Tuesday night. Why's it so important, after all these years?"

Austen didn't answer immediately. Sitting in his room at the Eighth Avenue Holiday Inn, holding an icepack to the side of his head, he found it awkward and uncomfortable to talk on the telephone. In the few seconds before George Timmler had come screeching to the rescue, practically running him over as the car crowded up onto the sidewalk, old Zinoviev had worked him over good. He seemed to hurt everywhere, and it had been necessary to call in a doctor to stitch up a wide gash in his scalp.

"Look, Marty, don't ask for answers that would only embarrass you. I want to know his flight number, and I expect you to get it for me. And then I expect you to forget that you even know my name."

There was a brief silence, during which Marty Eilberg was doubtless trying to decide whom he was more afraid of— Frank Austen, behind whom loomed the powerful and dreaded figure of Simon Faircliff, or his employer, Chester Storey.

"I'll have to phone you in a few minutes," he said finally. "I'll have to go to my office to check."

"No—I'll phone you back, Marty. At . . ." Austen checked his watch, holding the receiver to his ear with his shoulder, "seven-fifteen. That gives you forty-five minutes, plenty of time. You be there when I call." He hung up and grinned at Timmler, who was sitting in a chair on the other side of the room. "How was I, George? Do you think I'll ever make a real hood?"

"You're an idiot; you ought to be in a hospital bed. Who the hell is this guy, anyway?"

The icepack was so cold that it was beginning to bother Austen more than the bruise on his cheekbone, which had swelled the whole left side of his face and might, so the doctor had warned, be sitting right on top of a fracture. The doctor had also thought he belonged in a hospital, but for the moment there was simply too much to do.

"Marty Eilberg used to work on Faircliff's senatorial staff, and after he got fired I arranged for him to get a job with Chester Storey, the man whose house Zinoviev was headed for when we picked him up—when *you* picked him up. Just then I needed picking up myself." He grinned a second time, but it didn't make his bruise feel any better, so he stopped. "Anyway he'll deliver, and when Storey arrives at Kennedy I want you to have somebody there to snag him the minute he steps off the plane. I don't want him to have a chance to talk to anybody."

"Fine. You want to tell me what this is all about?"

"Not particularly."

At nine-thirty Tuesday night, Michael Starkman and Earl Rutledge were standing just outside the security station at the entrance to the Eastern Airlines passenger gates at Kennedy Airport. They waited there because the metal detector at the security station would have revealed that they were both armed, and although they were also provided with dummy FBI credentials, it was no part of their orders to attract that kind of attention. The subject of the evening's exercise was supposed to simply disappear, without a trace or a murmur.

Both men appeared stoically calm, perhaps even a trifle bored—this sort of thing was nothing new to either of them—but between them stood a third man whose manner, if anyone in that busy, crowded place had taken the trouble to look, might have revealed a certain disquiet of mind. Marty Eilberg, who had been hustled out of his New York apartment, wasn't at all used to such treatment. He had the distinct impression that these friends of Frank Austen's were not nice people.

"Just finger your boss for us when he comes through," they had said. "Leave the rest to us and do as you're told, and you won't have a thing in the world to worry about."

Sure.

The announced arrival of Flight 277 from the Bahamas was an event none of them seemed to notice. The mob of people who began streaming through looked browned and happy and slightly uncomfortable in their heavy clothing, as if they remained unconvinced that Long Island in February wasn't just as balmy and tropical as Nassau. Among them, in the second wave, was a man in a charcoal-gray overcoat, his pudgy hands gripping the handle of a briefcase and no hat on his head, across the top of which just a few strands of hair were visible. It was Chester Storey.

"That's him," Eilberg whispered hoarsely, making a furtive attempt at raising his arm to point, as if afraid someone might see.

"Fine," the man standing to his right said, not even moving his eyes. "You did that just fine. Earl, why don't you escort our friend here back to the car while I deal with Mr. Storey."

The other man nodded and led Eilberg away, like a keeper with a tame imbecile. Starkman waited a few seconds longer and then walked up to the man in the charcoal overcoat. He put his hands into his own overcoat pockets, stepped in front of him, and smiled.

"Mr. Storey, if you'd come with me, please," he said, taking his right hand out of his pocket and holding up a badge case that he kept open with his thumb. Storey stopped dead in his tracks, staring at the shiny gold badge as if he had never seen anything like it in his life.

"What's this all about?" he asked finally, swallowing hard.

"Everything will be explained at the proper time, Mr. Storey. Now if you'd just come with me, there's a car waiting."

"What about my luggage?" Chester Storey glanced around as if looking for a way to run. But he wouldn't make any kind of scene at all. Michael Starkman knew the type.

"We'll have someone see about the luggage, Mr. Storey. Just come along now."

The car parked in front of the terminal was a dark blue Buick, about as nondescript a vehicle as it was possible to imagine. Eilberg and Earl Rutledge were sitting in the back, and Eilberg was staring out through the rear window, his eyes large with dread. Starkman opened the front door on the passenger side and took Storey's arm to keep him from bumping his head as he climbed inside. He went around the front and got in himself, locking all four doors behind him with a switch located next to the steering column. None of the doors except the driver's had a handle on the inside. During the trip into Manhattan, no one said a word.

Frank Austen and George Timmler were there to meet them when the Buick pulled into a basement garage on West Forty-eighth Street. Timmler rang down the steel curtain that closed off the only entrance. Starkman got out from behind the wheel, went around and opened the door for Chester Storey, and escorted him over to where Austen was standing, beside a closed van with ambulance markings on the side.

"Good evening, 'Bernard.' It's been a long time." Austen smiled and watched Starkman, who was standing directly behind his prisoner, jam a hypodermic needle into Storey's arm. Storey turned around to see what had happened and then slipped quietly to the floor.

"Put him in the van."

Starkman nodded. Austen walked over to the Buick and climbed into the seat recently vacated by Chester Storey. He leaned over the backrest, supporting himself on his right elbow—the one he could still bend—and looked at Marty Eilberg.

"My friend here is going to sit with you for about an hour," he said quietly, motioning with his head toward Rutledge. "Then he's going to let you go. Tomorrow, if anybody asks where Mr. Storey is, you tell them he called and said he had to go out to California on business and would probably be away for a couple of weeks. If they ask where in California, you tell them he didn't mention it. If it turns out that we're able to return Mr. Storey, I guarantee you there won't be any problem about your role in this."

"*If* you return him?" Eilberg's hands, which were pressed down against his lap, writhed like something in its death agony.

"Whatever happens isn't going to be your problem, Marty. Just keep your mouth shut and stick to your story about the phone call. And don't cross me on this, because if you do, nobody's going to know what you're talking about. Nobody will ever have heard of Chester Storey. You understand, Marty? Nobody has to take a fall, but if anybody does it's going to be yourself."

Marty Eilberg nodded stiffly, as if the joints of his neck had somehow rusted together, and Austen got out of the car.

Five minutes later, with Timmler behind the wheel, they were making their precarious way toward the Holland Tunnel and the road south. There were just the two of them in the van's front compartment; Michael Starkman was in the rear with his patient, who was strapped to a cot and could be expected to remain unconscious for several more hours.

"Have you got Zinoviev in his old room?" Austen asked. He had a splitting headache—the same one he had had for two days now—and the lights from the oncoming traffic weren't helping any. But he was forcing himself to go over every step of what had happened, and what was going to happen. He didn't want to overlook anything or do anything careless; it was too important this time.

All my sons, my little boys. And the old man had gone straight to the brownstone on East Sixty-first Street, as if he had expected to be welcomed with open arms. He had looked up the address in *Who's Who,* so he had known the name, and no one had told Zinoviev a new name in forty years.

How old could Storey have been when Zinoviev dropped

out of circulation? Twenty? Twenty-one? And yet Zinoviev had known his name, had known that he would find it in the lists of the great and powerful. *Just braves now, but someday all of them will be chiefs*.

Timmler nodded. Yes, the colonel was back home.

"Then when we get back to Fishing Bay put Storey next door, where he'll have that one-way window. Leave him in there for at least an hour after he wakes up and starts moving around. I want him to have a good look at Zinoviev. Then he's to be put in another room, the smaller the better, where he'll be all by himself. He's to be fed, and that's it. No one is to say so much as a word to him, or even look him in the eyes. I want him to feel nice and isolated, and I want him to have plenty of time to think, particularly about Zinoviev. Then maybe, when he's had about five days of that, he'll be ready to tell us what the fuck's going on."

It didn't take five days. After only four it was judged that they didn't dare leave him in isolation any longer, and Austen was sent for. Timmler had remained behind at Fishing Bay to keep an eye on things, and he was waiting on the veranda of the main house when Austen drove up.

"We did it just the way you laid it out," he said, waiting with his hands thrust deep into his trouser pockets while an attendant took Austen's coat. "He hasn't eaten since the day before yesterday; he doesn't even move. He just lies there on his bed, staring at the wall. This morning I got worried and had a doctor go look at him, and the verdict is that he's withdrawn into a deep depression. You'll have to be the one to decide what to do with him now."

"Is there any chance they can snap him out of it?"

"Oh, sure. Doc says it'll just take a shot of amphetamine and he'll be good as new—for a while. Once the stuff wears off, though, there are no guarantees."

They were walking down a cement stairway to the basement, where the detention cells were, and Timmler took a key out of his pocket to unlock the door at the bottom. Beyond that door, the haunted house took on the more prosaic aspect of something between a hospital and a prison.

"What happened before he went into his slide? Did he just withdraw, or did he give any indication of what was bothering him?"

"You should have been here." Timmler laughed in a way

that suggested the very farthest thing from amusement. "Just as a precaution, we had his room wired, and about twenty minutes after he came around from the shot we gave him in New York he started screaming like he'd just seen the devil. He was scared to death. We moved him to another cell, and he settled down a bit, but all the rest of that morning you could stand outside his door and listen to him sobbing. And then nothing. He just turned his face to the wall. We haven't had a sound out of him since."

"Hasn't he said anything?" They were almost to the cell door, and Austen stopped and put his hand on Timmler's elbow.

"One word—*soroka*. He said that several times. We don't know what it means either."

"Get the doctor. Let's bring our friend back to life and see how he likes it."

VIII

Chester Storey sat on the edge of the bed, wiping his nose. His eyes were red and watery, and he was sagging badly as he leaned forward, bracing his left arm against his knee, but he was awake and coherent, which by itself was a considerable improvement. They had even gotten him to eat something. He was as ready as he would ever be.

Austen and Timmler were standing against the opposite wall. There were only the three of them in the room, which made it crowded enough. Storey regarded them with an expression of mournful apology. "How much do you know?" he asked finally.

Austen merely shrugged. "Enough to have committed a federal crime in bringing you here. Enough to guarantee you'll never leave this building alive if you can't be induced to tell me the rest."

"Then you might as well just kill me now, because I'm a dead man if I say a word. Diederich will see to that." He balled his hand into a fist and began beating it weakly against his thigh, all the time shaking with huge, gulping sobs. Austen took a glass of water from the small table next to him, holding it out with the tips of his fingers.

"Take a drink and compose yourself," he said quietly.

"Tell me the truth, and I'll see to it you won't have to worry about Diederich. I don't care anything at all about you; your safety lies in your unimportance."

"Diederich will kill you."

"He's already tried—or don't you remember?"

The grin on Austen's face was perfectly demonic—an effect that was heightened by the huge black bruise sitting over his left cheekbone—and Storey's eyes grew wide and blank. For a moment he even forgot to cry.

"I'll do what I can for you," Austen continued, suddenly as mirthless as an undertaker. "I won't make any guarantees beyond simply your life, because I won't know what's involved until you tell me. But you have to choose sides now; it's either me or Diederich, and I'm the one currently in possession. You think about it. We'll talk again this evening."

"Do you suppose he'll go for it?" Timmler asked as they trudged back up the stairs to the main house. It was like coming up out of a grave.

"Sure he'll go for it. He's the head of one of the largest banks in the country, so he must have some sense of how the world works. And after all, we're the only game in town."

They were at dinner, just finishing their coffee, when an attendant stood respectfully on the edge of the carpet of the small, elegant wood-paneled room where their table had been laid.

"He's asked to speak to you, sir," he said, as soon as Austen glanced in his direction. He looked as if he expected the director to pitch something at him and was just getting ready to duck.

"Very well. Put him in a larger room, one where we can all sit down, and make sure he's had something to eat."

"He's had his dinner, sir, just an hour ago."

"Fine."

When they went downstairs again, they found Storey seated on a small wooden chair, staring at the tape recorder that had been set up on a table against one wall. There was an attendant with him, standing next to the door, trying to look like he was in the room alone.

"You can leave us now," Timmler said flatly. He closed the door behind him after checking the corridor to make sure no one was there to listen. It seemed a reasonable precaution. Then, apparently as an afterthought, he stepped over to the table and snapped on the tape recorder. All the while, Storey watched him through narrow, suspicious eyes.

"I've been thinking it over, like you recommended," he said at last, several seconds after both Austen and Timmler had taken their seats. "I had a nice life once, but I suppose that's all finished now. I stopped caring about which side I was on a long time ago; I only wanted to hang on to my nice life. After all, I'd built it. It was mine. At least, it was mine before Howard Diederich found me. Then I guess it reverted to him."

"Why don't you begin at the beginning."

He looked up at Austen, and there was a sudden flash of anger in his face, a kind of tightening around the nose and mouth. Then it was gone, and his gaze dropped back down to his hands.

"It isn't that easy. You'll see that—the beginning is hard to find. I just wanted you to understand how tangled up things got. I'm not like Diederich. I'm not a patriot, so there's no betrayal either way. Or maybe it's betrayal in both directions. I don't know. I don't really care anymore—can you understand that?"

"No." Austen shook his head and smiled. "Not until you explain it."

"Begin at the beginning?" The question was punctuated by a short syllable of voiceless laughter, as if Storey believed himself to be dealing with the impossible demands of a child.

"Sure, or you can tell me about *soroka*. You could start there."

At the sound of the word, Chester Storey drew himself up. It seemed to work like the amphetamine, to bring him back to life.

"*Soroka*," he said, rather in the manner of someone delivering a lecture, or perhaps a warning, "is the Russian word for 'magpie,' a bird notorious as a nest-robber and a mimic. It was his little joke, although it wasn't until years later that any of us understood. It was what we called him; it was the only Russian word we were allowed to pronounce."

Austen and Timmler looked at each other in frank astonishment. So *Soroka* was a proper noun, apparently the code name Zinoviev had used at some time in the past. Well, that was something.

But that past had to have been over forty years ago. And

where? In Russia? *It was the only Russian word we were allowed to pronounce.*

"Are you trying to tell me that the old man recruited you?"

"Nyet."

And then he laughed once more, slapping his thigh with the flat of his hand. He laughed until the tears rolled down his face and Austen began to consider seriously whether they oughtn't send for the doctor again; it wouldn't do for Storey to start coming unraveled on them.

Just as suddenly as it had started, the laughter stopped. "As you see," Storey said calmly, "there's one other word I remember."

The truth. At long last, they were poised near the edge of something very like the truth.

Ten little red Indians. After all, it wasn't the Girl Scouts Zinoviev had been working for when the Wehrmacht had snagged him on their way to Stalingrad.

"Mr. Storey, I can only conclude from what you've been saying that you've been guilty of espionage at some time or another, and that Zinoviev—Soroka—was your trainer, or perhaps your control. Let me ask you again. Is that so? Have you ever been—are you now—a Soviet agent?"

"I suppose I must be," Storey answered in a tired voice as he pressed his fingertips against his closed eyelids. "That was the way it started out, at least. I don't know what I am now."

"Tell us about it. Start anywhere you like."

It was an odd thing, but all at once Chester Storey looked like a man from whom a great weight had been lifted.

"I suppose the beginning is as good a place as any," he said at last, leaning back in the chair, sitting with his hands curled in his lap and his eyes closed, as if he were trying to see some object in his memory. "I was six or seven—more likely seven, but I'm only guessing. My parents had a farm; I can remember the farm, but I have trouble with them. I think my mother had blond hair, but I can't even be sure of that. It was in the summer; I remember that it was very hot when the officer from the GPU came. He came in a long car; I'd never seen anything like it. And he brought a couple of soldiers with him."

"Was that in Russia?" It was a stupid question—where

else could it have been? But the whole business was so incredible that Austen found himself wanting to confirm every detail, simply to convince himself that any of it could possibly be true.

"Yes." Storey nodded solemnly. "In the Urals. My parents were *kulaks,* although I had never heard that word, wouldn't hear it until years after they were dead. Little private farmers—'enemies of the state,' I was told later. In a few years they would be liquidated by the millions, all over Russia. Maybe my parents were the beginnings of that, or maybe there was some other reason. There's no way I'll ever know.

"Anyway, I can see them arguing with the GPU officer. I remember standing next to my mother, with the wind gathering her skirts around me, and looking up at him as he and my father talked angrily—I remember he had long, slender nostrils. And then one of the soldiers took me over to their car and the officer went into the barn with my parents. I heard two shots, just muffled little pops, and then the officer came out and we all drove away. I never saw my parents again.

"I suppose I was just young enough to have avoided ideological contamination, so they let me live. I was sent to a state orphanage near Berezniki; I was probably there for about six months. I can't remember anything about the place except the iron bedsteads; they were all painted white, and the paint had chipped off so that the iron showed through in an irregular pattern that for some reason reminded me of the backs of snakes. I was terrified to go to sleep at night in case the bed should suddenly fill up with stinging vipers and I'd be trapped there with them in the dark. It was a silly idea, but what is it impossible to believe at that age?

"And after that, I was sent to the school in Leningrad.

"That was the first time I met Soroka, only he wasn't old then. He came and picked me up at the orphanage and we traveled the whole way back to Leningrad together, just the two of us, all by ourselves in a railway compartment. It must have been over a thousand miles. We talked and played chess together—he taught me the game—and he had a big picnic basket that never seemed to get any emptier. He'd give me puzzles to work and nonsense poems to learn—I suppose he was testing me—and if I did well he'd give me an orange to eat as a reward. I'd never even seen an orange before. To this day I love oranges. And I loved Soroka; why shouldn't I have? He was like a father, and fathers were in short supply just then. All the boys in the school loved him."

"When was all this?" Timmler asked. He was sitting with his arms folded across his chest, hardly even moving to breathe. He looked bored, but that meant nothing.

"Nineteen twenty-nine or thirty."

"And you're quite sure this Soroka is the same person you saw here four days ago? There's no chance you could be mistaken? People change."

Chester Storey merely shook his head.

"You're sure?"

"I'm sure. I saw the man every day of my life until I was seventeen. I could hardly be wrong about a thing like that."

"Tell me about the school."

Storey looked at Austen with something that could almost have been interpreted as gratitude. "The school—how can I tell you about the school?" he asked slowly, seeming to savor the recollection. "It was in the country, outside Leningrad, on an estate that had once belonged to the Czarina Elizabeth. She must have been a wonderful woman—I wish I could have known her.

"The house was a palace, all made of pink stone, and the gardens and lawns went on forever. It was a place built to keep people amused and comfortable, and altogether, with the staff, there couldn't have been more than a hundred of us. We had it all to ourselves.

"My mother had taught me how to read, and I had wanted to go to the village school but it was too far away. Those were hard times, and in the orphanage they were only interested in keeping us alive, I suppose. But Soroka wanted us to learn everything—games, music, mathematics, dirty jokes, anything and everything. And we all learned English; everything was subordinated to that. 'Forget about Russia,' he used to tell us. 'Speak nothing but English and learn to think of yourselves as Americans.' We read American history and the comics, and we played baseball in the summer.

"At night, in winter, we'd watch movies. I've probably seen *Little Caesar* a dozen times, and all the Shirley Temple movies. Soroka used to say you could learn everything there was to know about American life from Shirley Temple.

"They did a good job on us—maybe too good. We really

were in America on that estate. We forgot Russia; we forgot how to be Russians. Over and over again they told us that our final duty was to the motherland, but I think most of us forgot that too. America was to be simply a continuation of life at the school, and our loyalty was to that, and to Soroka—at least, mine was. Apparently it was different with Diederich. I don't know."

"Is that where you met Diederich, at the school?"

"Oh, yes." Storey smiled wearily and shrugged, as if he wondered that anyone could ask such a simple-minded question. "He was there; he wasn't 'Howard Diederich' yet, but he was there. We had different names; every six months or so they'd change them, perhaps so we would forget that we were ever anything except that temporary identity. We'd take the names of movie stars and gangsters—when I was thirteen I got to be Thomas Edison; at fourteen I was Clark Gable and Al Capone. I didn't become 'Chester Storey' until I was about sixteen, my last year. By then we were split up into smaller groups for special coaching in regional dialects and, I think, to keep us from finding out too much about any of the others so there would be a limit to what we could betray if we got caught. In the end, we were told, there were only going to be ten of us, and each of us was to operate in ignorance of the others."

Timmler still sat with his arms folded, like a man who needed to be convinced. "Were there any others whose current identities you remember?"

"No." Chester Storey shook his head. "No, just Howard—he's supposed to be from eastern Arizona, I believe, and we were the only two of that group to survive the cut. I've wondered sometimes what happened to the others, but those were the kinds of questions you never asked."

"What was the object of this . . ." Timmler waved the fingers of one hand as if he were trying to summon the right word. ". . . this impersonation? I take it you were supposed to come to the United States—what then?"

Storey's eyes were wide with theatrical, contemptuous wonder.

"Isn't it obvious? We were meticulously trained. Identities had been created for us. We were all handpicked for the qualities of success. There wasn't a single one of us, we were told, with an IQ of less than a hundred seventy. We were to infiltrate American society and rise inevitably to the top, with a little help now and then. After that, just wait. One day, after we had long since had our hands on the levers of power, Russia would need us and we'd be ready."

IX

One thing about the Russians—they had patience. An operation of that kind, mounted over a period of several decades, and for such limited ends, required a continuity of purpose of which no Western nation would have been capable. In its way, in its sheer selflessness—for who among its planners could have expected to be alive to see it come to completion?—it was awesome.

And it wasn't as if they expected to take the joint over. The idea had been simply to have a few reliable people in positions of authority when the crisis arrived. There was no consensus about what form that crisis would take.

"We heard so many different versions," Storey went on, smoking a cigarette and stirring a cup of the tea Austen had ordered sent down after the interrogation had passed its second hour. They all had some, and there was even a little plate of cookies; it was turning into something of a social occasion.

"You have to remember that back then forward-thinking Russians looked to America the way, a hundred years before, they had looked to France. There was a positive mania for anything American—America was democratic, America was progressive, every new wrinkle in art or technology or social thought seemed to come from America. I don't know whether it's true or not, but Soroka used to tell us about how Lenin saw a screening of *Birth of a Nation* and was so impressed that he offered D. W. Griffith any money to come over and build the Russian film industry. Needless to say, Griffith turned him down, but Eisenstein was sent to Hollywood to see what he could learn. For the first few years after the civil war, things like that happened all the time.

"And is it so surprising? Europe was exhausted after 1918, but America just seemed to be waking up. Trying to get some sort of handle on the future there seemed the only thing to do.

"Even Soroka didn't have a clear idea what would happen

to us. We'd get one story one time, another the next. I don't think it really mattered to him very much. I think his obsession was really just with the country. He spent some part of his youth here, he told us once. His father had emigrated in 1912 to escape being drafted into the czar's army and, as soon as he could after the revolution, Soroka went back. But he was infected with the disease, and America remained a kind of beacon for him, a ruling passion to be somehow connected with the mystic religion of Marxism-Leninism—because Soroka was always a model communist.

"Anyway, at first one of the more popular theories was that the collapse of Western capitalism would begin here, because America was the most advanced and active of the capitalist countries. And when the whole rotten structure was ready to cave in, we would be there to give it the necessary extra little push. And to make sure, of course, that the resulting socialist state saw where its true interests lay and made the proper alliances. Europe would be caught in the middle between us.

"I don't know what made him abandon that line—or whether he ever did. But after 1934, when it was obvious that Germany was getting ready for another war in the East—you see, Soroka *had* read *Mein Kampf*—Soroka managed to convince Stalin that America was likely to go fascist and that we would be useful as a fifth column within the military-industrial complex. He didn't call it that, of course; I think his phrase was the 'war-mongering capitalist establishment,' but it amounted to the same thing. I imagine he thought the conflict wouldn't come until sometime in the late fifties. Or maybe he just didn't care. I always had the impression that Soroka was uncomfortable talking about the purposes of his little project; for him, I think, the thing was an end in itself.

"As it happened, we didn't arrive until about a year before the outbreak of the war in Europe. I was in my senior year at Harvard on Pearl Harbor Day; I enlisted in the navy the next morning and was with the Pacific Fleet in time for the Battle of Midway. You have to remember that we were trained to have all the reflexes of good American boys; it seemed the most natural thing in the world to do. I'm sure most of the others reacted in much the same way. I wonder how many of the original ten can still be alive."

He stared down at his cup as if he expected the answer to

be revealed to him there—except, of course, that the tea had been made with bags and was as clear as amber.

"When did they contact you again?"

"*They* never did," he answered, smiling thinly. "It was Diederich, but not for years. By then I thought everyone had forgotten all about me, that I was safe. By then I hardly even remembered that I had ever been anyone except Chester Storey. The face grows to fit the mask, don't you know." It didn't seem to be a very happy reflection.

"No, I didn't hear from Diederich until the summer of 1968. I had just married my second wife—I was the happiest man in the world for a while—and one day my secretary brought me a note that had been sent around to the office by special messenger: *I've made a one o'clock reservation for us at Le Lavandou on Sixty-first Street, so it'll be close to home—your treat. Magpie.*

"I felt as if someone had walked over my grave. I didn't have the faintest idea who it could be after all that time—thirty years. It was the most uncomfortable morning I've ever spent in my life.

"At first I didn't recognize him; after all, what had we been but boys in Russia? But he brought me up to date fast enough. He wanted money. He had gotten involved in politics, and Simon Faircliff needed a war chest. I was invited to make a large anonymous donation.

" 'I have high hopes for this one,' he said. 'I think we might be able to ride him right into the White House.' And that's just exactly what he did. Well, I wish Simon Faircliff joy of his chief of staff."

"Was that all he wanted, just money?" Austen strained forward in his chair, as if he expected Chester Storey to whisper the answer into his ear.

"No." Storey shook his head sadly. "At first, yes. I could simply make a withdrawal from my account and mail it, wrapped up in brown paper, to a post office box in Los Angeles. Can you imagine that, tens of thousands of dollars shipped parcel post? Over the years, I think I've probably made delivery on something like three quarters of a million.

"But after a while, especially after Faircliff announced for the Senate, Diederich wanted other things as well—confidential bank records, investment profiles, information about corporate accounts. I was his pipeline into the New York financial world, and from there, I expect, into the business community at large. And I had to do a lot of very nasty things sometimes to dig up everything he wanted to know. Over the years, I got so I hated him like poison."

"What was in the package you delivered to me?"

"Savings account passbooks, about twenty of them. He'd sent me the forms, even the deposit slips—all duly signed, of course, but under half a dozen different names—and I was supposed to pay into them. He said it was his moving expenses; he was coming out from California, and he said he needed the money to get his operation going in Washington."

"Did he ever approach you directly after that first time, or was it always through an intermediary?"

"It was always someone else. Sometimes I wouldn't hear from him for months at a time, and then I'd get word to meet some stranger; it was almost never the same person twice until the last few years."

Austen reached into his inside coat pocket and pulled out a slim manila envelope, from which he extracted a photograph. It showed four men, obviously part of a crowd, badly illuminated by an overhead street-lamp. The man in the center, around whose head a circle had been drawn in heavy ballpoint, had a strong, cruel face with eyes that were merely thin dark lines. He had a straight black moustache. Austen handed the photograph to Chester Storey.

"Was this ever one of the men sent to you?"

"Yes." Storey's eyes widened in recognition and fear as he held the picture up to the light. "Recently it hasn't been anyone else. Who is he?"

Austen took the photograph back, slipped it into the envelope again, and returned it to his pocket without answering. "I want to know more about how they thought they were going to get away with it," he said. "I mean, how do you just drop a seventeen-year-old kid down in the middle of the United States and expect him to find his independent way to fame and fortune? Explain that to me."

"Does it need explaining?" Storey asked, a faintly contemptuous smile on his lips. "Obviously they did get away with it."

"Then explain it to me anyway. How did they work it?"

But instead of troubling to reply, Storey took the pack of Camel Filters from his shirt pocket, shook one out, lit it with a paper match from the book that was lying next to his teacup, and, after casually blowing it out with a puff of cigarette smoke, dropped the match on the linoleum floor. It was a wonderfully tranquil operation; it communicated an easiness of mind that, under the circumstances, was almost as extraordinary as it was insulting.

After giving him just time to draw another breath, Austen sprang from his chair and struck his prisoner on the right side of the face, hard enough to throw him back into his chair and send the cigarette flying. It bounced against the wall with a little shower of sparks.

"I asked you a question," he said, pulling Storey toward him by the shirtfront, his voice hoarse with barely suppressed rage. "And I want an answer—now. How did they get you into the country? What kind of help did you get? Did they just turn you loose, or what?"

"It's more complicated than that." More startled than hurt, Storey nursed his jaw without any visible show of resentment, as if he could sympathize with the director's impatience. He was merely waiting for Austen to sit down.

"Soroka always told us that after a point we could expect some help," he went on. "He said we would have to look out for ourselves for the first ten or fifteen years, but that then, when our efforts could be coordinated, and the end of the war would make it easier for Russia to establish a more effective diplomatic presence in the United States, then they'd help us along. It never happened, of course. For thirty years, until I got that note from Diederich, I never got a word or a kopek.

"I'm not complaining, you understand; I was glad. A lot of things got lost in the war, and I suppose I hoped that we had too, that they had simply forgotten us. I don't know, maybe they had. Maybe the only one who remembered was Diederich. Anyway, for thirty years I was on my own."

"But they must have set you up—initially, at least."

"Oh yes." Chester Storey nodded in agreement, eager, apparently, to confirm the basic truth. "They did do that. They would have had to, wouldn't they?" He looked down at his hand, as if suddenly ashamed.

"How did they do it?" Austen's voice was beginning to drop once again to a menacing quietness. "How was it managed—I want to know, damn you."

Once again the pack of cigarettes appeared, and once again the ritual was enacted, except the composure was gone. Now Chester Storey was a man whose nerves needed settling.

"Didn't I tell you that the magpie was a nest robber?" he asked, laughing quietly and mirthlessly as he looked at the extinguished match in his hand, seeming to have lost any recollection of what it was.

"Soroka did his research very well. Each of us had been assigned an identity we could assume when the moment came, someone we could crowd out of the nest, whose life we could take over and start living as if it were our own. In my case, there really was a Chester Storey growing up in a little town in Texas. I had read all about him.

"In a country the size of the United States, there must be thousands of gifted boys at any given moment. Soroka merely selected ten, the ten who corresponded to his needs. He had their careers followed right through childhood—the music lessons, the sports, the teachers, the dental records, everything.

"He needed boys who fulfilled certain criteria. They had to be brilliant, marked for early success. They had to come from small families—an only child was best, but you couldn't always have that—so the relatives wouldn't cause any unnecessary complications. And, finally, they had to be accepted by a college hundreds of miles away from their homes so they would have a reason for not coming back. Poor Chester—the real one—he signed his death warrant the day he filled out those application forms for Harvard.

"Walter and Ida Storey had moved to Texas from Missouri in 1923, after Walter quarreled with his father over an inheritance. He seems to have been the type who quarreled with people pretty regularly; in any case, he maintained no contact with the rest of his family, so they hardly even knew young Chester was alive. Walter worked as a teller in the Weatherford National Trust until Roosevelt closed the banks in thirty-three, and then he set up as a feed grain broker. The Storeys kept to themselves. Ida apparently regarded herself as 'quality' and didn't encourage her son to make too many friends among his schoolfellows. It was the sort of setup that Soroka was looking for.

"There was a younger sister—that was the one snag. But she was only about twelve when Chester left home.

"As for physical resemblance, it wasn't considered vitally

important. We didn't have to be identical twins. The same
eye and hair color, the same general height and body type, a
certain coincidence of feature. People change between seventeen and forty; it was considered enough.

"It couldn't have been too difficult a problem for Soroka.
After all, he had hundreds of boys in the United States and
hundreds more in Russia to choose from. He only needed
ten matches. He felt that if the operation went beyond that
number it would prove unwieldy and too open to detection.

"So it came down to ten. Ten of us, preparing ourselves to
step into the lives of ten of them. We knew their relatives
and their friends, the names of all the streets in the towns
where they grew up, everything that could be learned about
them."

"How was the switch made?"

Storey paused for a moment, saw that his cigarette had
burned down almost to the filter, and stubbed it out. It took
on the quality of a meditative ritual, like counting the beads
of a rosary.

"You have to remember," he continued finally, "you have
to bear in mind that I had never been told anything beyond
the fact that after a certain date I would be expected to be
Chester Storey—not merely to masquerade as him, to to *be*
him."

"How was the switch made?"

"It was easy." This man who had become Chester Storey
but who might have been anyone, glared at Austen with
perfect if restrained hatred, as if goaded almost beyond
endurance. His eyes seemed to say, *You will have it all,
won't you.*

"On the fifth of September, 1938, Chester Storey boarded
the train in Fort Worth. I watched him from the window as
he kissed his parents goodbye. He was going off to join that
year's freshman class at Harvard."

He stopped for a moment and wiped his forehead with the
heel of his hand. It was an odd gesture, implying God only
knew what obscure spiritual suffering, as if he were attempting to wipe away some ineradicable mental wound. He was
no longer telling the story to anyone except himself; Timmler and Austen might as well not even have been in the room.
This was no longer a confession. It was an act of penance.

"We waited until he had entered his compartment; he had
a sleeper, and we knew the number. His trunk was stored in

the baggage car, and we knew that too. We waited until a few minutes before the train was to stop again, in Dallas.

"I had been brought into the country from Mexico by two men who had come with me all the way from Leningrad. We had been together for days, but they hardly ever spoke to me. It was like living with a pair of animated blocks of wood.

"Just as the people who were getting off began to collect their things from the overhead racks, the three of us went back to Chester Storey's compartment. One of them tapped lightly on the door and, when it was opened, pushed his way inside, covering the boy's mouth with his hand. He was a huge man; there was hardly any struggle at all.

"They held him down and gave him some sort of injection, just at the base of the neck. In a few seconds he stopped struggling. He wasn't dead, but he wasn't human anymore either. He simply stared ahead of him, blankly, seeing nothing. There was no will there, nothing but a nervous system that would obey any impulse from the outside, incapable of action on its own. He sat across from me, one of the men holding him upright; I've never seen anybody who looked like that in my life.

"When we reached Dallas, they led him off the train. No one seemed to notice. When the porter came to turn down the bed at night, he never even looked at me; I was just the kid who was sleeping there that night, so I must have been the kid who came aboard at Fort Worth. That was my first lesson in how easy it was going to be.

"As for Chester Storey, he ceased to exist—or, rather, he became myself. The boy who was led away by the men who had brought me had already lost any idea that he was anybody at all. So I guess the name, and the identity, could come to me as easily as to anyone else.

"About three weeks after I got to Harvard, I received a telegram saying that my 'parents' and my 'sister' had been killed in an automobile accident. How that was achieved, I couldn't say. I don't imagine it would have been too difficult to stage. Naturally, I didn't return for the funeral. What they made of that back in Weatherford I haven't any idea, and it no longer mattered what they thought.

"For a couple of years after that I kept a check on the Fort Worth newspapers, just to see whether there was ever any news from Weatherford, and every so often I would read one of the names I had memorized—so-and-so, who had been

Chester Storey's intimate friend, had drowned in a fishing accident, or so-and-so, who had been Chester Storey's godfather, had died after a sudden illness. Someone, I could only assume, was cleaning house.

"They needn't have bothered. In all the years since, I've never been near the place again."

When Frank Austen and George Timmler went back up the stairs from the detention cells, it was already close to three in the morning. As much to get away from a strange feeling of unreality as to escape any possibility of being overheard, they went outside and started walking down the gravel driveway toward the main gate; it was a direction as good as any.

"Did you believe him?" Timmler asked, breaking the silence.

"Yes. No one would make up a story like that. He knows that we'll kill him if he lies to us, and too much of it can be checked."

Austen stared straight ahead, his hands in his overcoat pockets. He gave the impression of being at a great distance from himself, like someone watching his own dream.

"Then we have our hands full," Timmler answered, kicking faintly at the gravel as he walked along. "Jesus. The White House chief of staff is a goddam Russian agent. They've put somebody in right under the president's nose."

He was startled by the short, bitter bark of laughter that cut through the quiet like a beam of light, stopping just as suddenly as it had begun. He looked at Austen as if he expected to witness some terrible transformation, but there was nothing. Only a faint smile.

Part Four

The Seal of Confession

I

Within the first twenty-four hours after listening to Storey's recital, Austen made a series of decisions the weight of which he was to feel for the remainder of his life. From the first moment the character of his predicament was uncomfortably clear.

"We can't make a move now," he said flatly, as if it were the most obvious fact in the world. "We have no idea what the Soviets have in mind, no idea at all, and if we spook them now we risk tempting them into something rash. Who knows what kind of edge they might imagine they have over us? Or really have?"

"I think they've got in mind to con us into your boss's precious treaty. I think they mean to blow our brains out."

Austen glanced at Timmler, who was walking beside him, still scuffing his shoes on the gravel driveway, and nodded. "I think you're probably right."

But of course they couldn't be sure. And so the first order of business had to be an attempt to discover just how badly the American intelligence establishment, that servant and dupe of their Constitutionally sanctioned masters, had been hoodwinked.

"I keep thinking that it's been over a year now," Austen said glumly. "I keep thinking about all those daily briefing papers we've sent over to the White House, all those little chats I've had with the president over drinks and lunch.

Everything we know about everything that's happening in the wide world . . . We must be blown nearly everywhere. And all the garbage they've been able to feed us—all this time, they've known exactly how to get us to believe just about anything they want."

They walked on in silence for a few minutes, the only sound the grating of their footfalls on the driveway.

"What will it take, George? That's your line of country, not mine. Would it be possible to backtrack through all that muck and figure out where we really are? Can you pin down what they've been trying to hide from us? Is that possible at all?"

"It's possible," Timmler answered, pursing his lips as he considered the mechanics of the problem; he was in his chosen element now. "They've got what they have to think is an unimpeachable source. Maybe we can turn that around on them.

"The really hard part is going to be replenishing our networks inside Moscow. The others can wait, I suppose; they'll have to. But we've got to have access to some information we can trust, if only for comparative purposes so we can have something to check our conclusions against. Now that we know what's going on, I can go through the old reports and make some fairly solid guesses about what the Russians have been up to, but it isn't possible to do every-thing by indirection. What it comes down to is that we need some new snitches."

"Fine. And maybe this time I'll just keep my big mouth shut and they can remain our little secret."

"Don't blame yourself," Timmler said quietly, putting his hand on Austen's arm for a moment. "It's our duty to provide the president with intelligence; that's what we're there for. This isn't your fault."

"Isn't it?"

Austen stopped for a moment and stood looking off into the impenetrable darkness. The muscles in his face were working slightly, as if twisting under the strain. Even in the dark it was possible to see that the man was in torment.

"Isn't it?" he repeated, almost to himself. "This president wouldn't even be there if it weren't for me—that's my accomplishment. Howard Diederich's patron might still be just another senator with big ideas if I hadn't worked quite so hard to further his rise in the world."

Timmler waited; finally, they started slowly down the driveway again. "Of course, we'll have to be generous and feed them one every once in a while."

"Who?"

"Diederich—the Russians." Timmler looked down at the ground and scraped the sole of his shoe over the gravel yet once more, as if this were the most impersonal topic in the world. "We'll have to give them a little offering every so often. That way they won't be looking for the rest of our new sources; they'll think they've already got them all."

"The poor little bastards; it'll be like feeding live mice to an alligator."

"From now on this is a rough game, Frank. If we're going to keep the whole thing from sliding away from us, we won't have any choice."

"I know that."

They had reached the main gate by then. A sentry was on duty with a rifle slung over his shoulder and a Doberman pinscher about the size of a small horse pacing along at his side. The sentry recognized them and brought the first two fingers of his right hand up to his eyebrow in a kind of informal, embarrassed salute, as if he didn't know what else to do. But the Doberman snarled, showing its teeth and snapping at the air. It seemed like a good idea to start back toward the house.

"Then we can begin tapping on the walls, but it'll take time." Timmler glanced at the director, raising his eyebrows as if to say, *What did you expect, miracles?* "If we could use a regular team for the analysis . . . But I'll have to do all that myself; we can't risk bringing anyone else into this. And we'll have to be careful about everything, including the amount of computer time we log. It wouldn't do even for people in our own shop to get the idea that anything special was up; we're not gossip-proof, and we don't want any rumors reaching the outside world.

"And then we'll have to figure out a way to pad the budget; extra agents have to be paid, and Diederich might be looking for something like that to show up in the accounts. Altogether, it's a problem. But not an insoluble one—it can be done."

"But not quickly?"

"No."

As they walked along, Austen kept his eyes to the ground

as if he were trying to measure the length of every stride. All at once he stopped and stood examining the caps of his shoes, the muscles in his jaw still working as regularly as the ticking of a clock.

"Then order a car in the morning and drive Storey back to New York," he said, never lifting his eyes. "We don't dare do anything else. If he disappears, Diederich is going to begin wondering what happened to him. This is the first direction he'll think to look for an answer."

"Is that safe? You know how these jokers are—they start in with the confessions and they can't stop. He's likely to go straight to Diederich and spill his guts; he's scared enough to do almost anything."

"I don't think so. He knows his only chance is with us, so he might even be useful. Anyway, what choice do we have?"

It was only a few minutes before dawn. The eastern sky was beginning to change from slate gray to pearl, and it was already possible to make out the shapes of trees as they stirred uneasily in the first of the land breezes. Somehow, at that time of the morning, you always had the impression that there couldn't possibly be anything left to live for, that within the next hour it would probably start to rain, that the coming day would last into infinity. The two men continued on, each seemingly unconscious of the other's existence, until once more they had stepped into the penumbra of light from the mansion windows.

"I wish I were more of a social butterfly," Austen said suddenly. It was just possible to imagine he was joking until you saw his face. "I've got to find a way to slow down this fucking treaty. It would be easier if my contacts were a little less obviously official, but I've never been a great one for the cocktail party circuit."

"Don't worry. Whenever some big negotiation is going on, the DCI is always in great demand. You'll have plenty of opportunities to sell your boss down the river."

"You think so?"

Austen smiled wanly. The bruise on his face had darkened into an angry black crescent reaching from the left eye to the angle of his jaw. He seemed beaten and weary, and when he reached up to cover Timmler's shoulder with his hand there was something in the gesture that spoke of an infinite, ineradicable self-contempt.

"Nobody can live like this forever, George." The words were little more than a whisper. "How long do you think it'll take you to get us back to square one?"

"With a few breaks, maybe by the next election."

"Well, at least we'll have plenty of time to learn how to walk on broken glass."

"You know, Frank, this job has aged you."

The president stared into Austen's face, his massive hands resting on his knees as he leaned forward in his chair. He seemed to mean it. Austen merely smiled.

"It's all those sleepless nights I put in worrying about whether or not you're going to blow up the world."

It was one of those weird moments—fortunately rare—when he was somehow drawn dangerously near to confessing the truth. He could feel himself preparing to speak the words and found it necessary simply to sit quietly and say nothing, waiting for the impulse to pass away. Sometimes he almost believed that Faircliff was waiting for him to speak, that he knew what he was about to say and was listening for it. It was possible, in that instant, to believe that he had somehow guessed the extent of his lieutenant's defection.

But that was probably just Austen's imagination, nothing more than the voice of his troubled conscience.

"But you really do look bad. I don't think you've had a vacation since we assumed office, have you? Why don't you take a couple of weeks off and go lie in the sun somewhere?"

"Our lease is almost up, remember? After your reelection."

They were sitting—at least, the president was sitting—in the main room of Hemlock Lodge. It was seven-fifteen on a Saturday morning, late in April of the fourth year of the Faircliff administration, and the six months remaining until November had become the central fact of life.

It had gotten to be almost a regular occurrence. Austen was summoned to Camp David for the weekend, on about two hours' notice and without a word of explanation. The chief simply wanted to talk, and he strolled down before breakfast with a draft version of the new strategic arms limitations treaty tucked under his arm. It was resting on the coffee table now, almost unnoticed. There was no reason to look at it; Austen had already read it so many times that he was in a fair way of knowing it by heart.

"So what do you think?" Faircliff asked, apparently having forgotten all about how tired his son-in-law looked. "In another couple of weeks all the technical language will have been worked out, and the goddamned thing should be ready for inking by the middle of next month. What now?"

Austen smiled cautiously, wondering whether Faircliff really wanted his opinion or was asking merely for form's sake, or for some underhanded reason that would only become clear later. He really was tired. For as long as he could remember, it seemed, his life had been about nothing but lies.

"Who are you asking—the director of Central Intelligence, or the political hack?"

"I'm surprised you bother to draw the distinction."

"Oh, I try to."

"Then give me both answers."

"All right."

Standing in front of the unlit fireplace, with the cold downdraft on the backs of his legs, Austen looked through the front windows, wondering whether there wasn't something symbolic in the fact that he was always assigned to this same cabin when he had to spend the night. Hemlock backed right up against the woods, about two hundred yards from Aspen, farther up the mountain where the president stayed. So he was always away by himself, but always directly under the president's eyes.

"I think it's a good treaty," he began, idly sliding his fingers into the pockets of his tan cardigan. "I'm surprised, frankly, that the Russians would be willing to give away that much; they must need to save the money pretty badly. We're not likely to get a better deal in the foreseeable future—go ahead and sign it."

"And what does the political hack say?"

Faircliff sat frowning, his arms folded across his chest, as quiet as a stone idol. For nearly twelve years Austen had been watching people quail in front of that look; it meant that Faircliff didn't like the advice he was getting, that his instincts had been rubbed the wrong way, like the fur on a cat's back. At this precise moment, however, the effect was strangely reassuring. The translation read, *That's what everybody says, but they don't say how—or when. I've heard from all my pollsters and all the little creeps who hang around the West Wing, and how the hell am I supposed to trust those clowns? Tell me what I should do, Frank.* And it was possible to believe that he meant it.

"Pretty much the same thing." Austen smiled again. "Around the first week in July would be a good time—close enough to the election to give you a boost but not close enough to come across as too blatantly political. Try to look presidential, like the fourth of November is the furthest thing from your mind. And you don't want any comparison with the Carter fiasco, so stay away from Vienna."

"The Soviets want to sign in Moscow."

"Fine. The weather should be lovely."

"And you think July?"

Austen nodded. "It'll mean ratification will have to wait for the new Senate, and the voters will be spared all that nasty, divisive partisanship—it's so demoralizing. Besides, after the election is safer."

"I wasn't aware we had a problem there, Frank." Faircliff cocked his head a little to one side, as if wondering whether he should take offense.

"Come on, Chief. Maybe they don't bay all night outside your bedroom window, but if I had a dollar for every time I've been approached by somebody who wanted help to put the skids under this treaty of yours I'd be able to retire. Of course we've got a problem, Simon; do you really want a public thrashing-out of the details of this treaty while you've got an election to fight?

"You know how it is." Austen shrugged his shoulders, staring at the pinewood floor. "We lost some ground in the off-year races—the party in power always does—and even our own people would be grateful for not having to explain why they voted for a deal with the Russians. Any deal. You'll win in November, but it's better if you win big, so there isn't any reason not to play it cautious. You'll still have four more years to be president in, and every incumbent's power begins to trickle away the minute everybody knows he's never going to run again. You want to start with as many of those suckers in your debt as you can manage."

Without moving so much as an eyelash, Faircliff managed to communicate that the force of the argument had made itself felt. Then he sighed deeply and sagged back into his chair.

"I don't know why everybody wants to make things so tough on me," he said slowly; one had the sense of a real grievance. "It's a good treaty; and you'd think from what you read in the newspapers that I was inviting the Russians to occupy New Jersey or something. We've had a very bad press with this one, Frank; it's almost like someone's been out there poisoning the wells on us."

There was a hard, suspicious look in his eye, an accusation directed not so much at Austen as at the world in general. Austen merely shook his head.

"If you've got leaks, Simon, don't ask me to plug them. I run the CIA, remember? It would be the biggest mistake you ever made to involve the Agency in domestic surveillance—people still remember Nixon and all that. Don't cut your own throat just because you think some donkey's been telling tales out of school."

The dark cloud was dispelled, and Faircliff smiled. He almost looked relieved.

"Let's go up to my place and get something to eat," he said finally, rising out of his chair as if propelled from behind. Once on his feet he resumed an almost Oriental calm, giving the impression that this man was simply too dignified and too massive to be capable of any sudden movement—something you might have believed if you had never seen him when he was in a hurry.

He was very spruce this morning in a pair of light gray trousers and a tweed jacket, his carefully combed gray hair looking about ten minutes away from the barber. Among the things for which it was possible to admire him were that he had never dyed his hair or yielded to the temptation to wander around Camp David in one of those silly dark blue windbreakers with the Presidential seal emblazoned just over the left tit.

Austen wondered whether all this elegance was traceable to the upcoming election or to the fact that six months ago Sylvia Burgess had moved back to Washington.

Faircliff clapped his hand over Austen's shoulder, and they walked out onto the porch and started up the trail to Aspen Lodge. Austen felt rather like a dog being taken out on a leash.

"I wonder how the voters would feel if I got married again."

"Is that purely an academic question, or have you finally worn the poor woman down?"

Simon Faircliff laughed and released his grip, and as

always on such occasions, Austen stepped circumspectly out of range; when the president was in one of his backslapping moods, he could be lethal.

"It's just possible she might see the light before long. Clay was a fine man, a hard act to follow, but—"

"But Clay suffers under the immense disadvantage of being dead."

"You have a terrible, cynical way of putting the truth, Frank; I think it's one of the main reasons I've always liked you so much."

The following morning, when the director of Central Intelligence came down from the mountain, George Timmler was there to meet his helicopter. It was a very pretty day at Langley, and the suction from the copter blades made the grass out by the little Company airport ripple like a green sea. All George noticed were the swirls of dust and the contracted expression on Frank Austen's face.

"Well? What did he have to say for himself?"

"He wants to go to Moscow." The tightness had gone out of everything except Austen's eyes, which looked anxious and weary as he took his briefcase from the pilot. "George, are you sure now that it's the treaty?"

"Yes—just about."

"Then we've got until after the election. He'll wait that long before he submits it to the Senate. Can you have everything in place by November?"

"He could just lose, you know. We could arrange something that would blow it for him; that might be the simplest way."

"No." Austen shook his head. "First of all, I don't think we could get away with it—he's too popular. I don't think anything short of the economic collapse of the West would serve. Besides, even if we pulled it off he wouldn't exactly be carted out with the next morning's garbage, you know; losing incumbents become lame ducks, but they're still incumbents. I don't want to risk giving Howard Diederich *et alii* those last nine weeks with advance warning. No, we'll wait until after the election, when they'll think they've got all the time in the world, and then we'll make our play."

II

"You could always just move back in, you know." She stood a little way from him, hunched purposefully over the stovetop as she whipped up a batch of scrambled eggs. She seemed almost ashamed, as if what she said amounted to a confession of unpardonable weakness. "We could try it out for those couple of days; I get lonely too."

So maybe it was about to end, he thought to himself. After better than three years, their estrangement seemed at last to be crumbling under the pressure of its own weight. There had been lapses before, when whatever principle she thought she was defending seemed perhaps less important, but maybe now she was really ready to give it up. In that respect she was a closed book to him, so he would probably never get to know why.

But perhaps that was what it had been about all this time, this hiatus in their marriage that had always refused to amount to a total rupture. There could be love and, at the same time, contempt—or bitterness, or disappointment, or anger, or whatever it had been—the two could exist side by side, seeming to cancel each other out, paralyzing everything. And now, apparently, for some reason hidden from him, love was once more in the ascendancy.

"All right, then," he said, trying not to sound as if he were making a great point of it. "I'll invite him."

And that was how their tenuous reconciliation began, because Pete Freestone was coming to Washington to interview the president and Frank Austen wanted to put him up for his stay. So small a thing as that, and suddenly Dottie seemed willing to be his wife again.

When he got home from work that night and went into the spare bedroom he had been using for the last three years, he found that the closets had been cleaned out and his shaving things taken out of the bathroom. Everything he needed, including his wife, was in the master suite waiting for him.

"Don't say anything," she said as he came in and sat down on the edge of the bed. "Let's not either one of us say anything at all."

It was the first time they had made love since before Clayton Burgess's death, and they were a little awkward at it. They were like people just beginning to get to know each other; perhaps that was what they really were.

Anyway, by the time Pete Freestone arrived in the first week of July, they could at least swing a fair imitation of the world's happiest married couple.

The four fifty-five from San Francisco apparently had had a tail wind, because Pete was about five minutes early as he rounded the causeway into the terminal, a small suitcase in his right hand and a clothing bag slung over his shoulder. He saw Austen behind the barrier, opened his mouth in something that, at that distance, was probably intended to be taken for a delighted grin, and put down the suitcase for a moment so he could have an arm free to wave. He was wearing a light gray suit that did a lot for him and, on closer inspection, seemed to have lost about fifteen pounds.

On the other side of the barrier, Austen took the suitcase and they walked out together to where his limousine was taking up about a block of the curb.

"Jesus—is that yours?"

"It goes with the job."

Austen's driver came out from behind the wheel and took the suitcase and the bag and opened the door for them.

"Home, Jimmie." Austen pressed the button that raised the smoked-glass partition, turned to his friend, and smiled a lopsided, slightly embarrassed smile. "I love saying that. When are you getting married?"

"How did you know I was getting married?"

"I'm a spy, remember? Look at you—*somebody's* been seeing to your wardrobe lately. Besides, everyone I know is getting married."

"Yeah, well . . ."

And then Pete Freestone, the veteran journalist, blushed deeply and muttered something about a girl he had met at Weight Watchers. He seemed eager to change the subject, and there would be plenty of time later. Austen decided to give him a break.

"So what brings you?" he asked, ignoring the stupid obviousness of the question. "Is the *Chronicle* planning to burn us over this treaty, or what?"

"Why, is that a suggestion?"

The expression on Pete's face was perfectly serious for a moment, and then he grinned—it had been a joke. Austen found he was able to breathe again.

"No, I'm on leave from the paper. I've got a contract for a book, of all things." Pete's eyes turned into perfect circles. "I'm getting a thirty-grand advance to write Simon Faircliff's biography in time for the election, so he's invited me for lunch and a three-hour interview."

"Not bad. But watch out for the pecan pie."

The next afternoon the two men sat outside on the flagstone terrace behind Austen's house in Alexandria, drinking iced tea. They were in their shirtsleeves, and the only sounds besides their own voices were the chirping of the birds and the drone from the odd speedboat passing on the river. Pete was talking about his book, which, with his usual enthusiasm, he expected would make him both rich and famous.

"I started out thinking I could knock the thing off in four or five months," he said, crouching forward in his chair. "I mean, hell, I've been interviewing and studying Simon Faircliff for the last fifteen years. And the public career is easy. It's the private man I'm having trouble with."

"Well, I don't think you'll get very far with that on Monday. He'll talk your ear off about this trip to Russia—that's what he wants to put across right now."

"Then you don't suppose I could . . . ?" He used the tip of his thumb to gesture back toward the house, where Dottie was in the kitchen making dinner. Austen shook his head.

"She won't even talk to me about him, pal—you know all about that."

"I didn't really think . . . Well . . ."

"Not a chance. Sorry."

Pete shrugged his shoulders in an embarrassed apology and then stared down at the ground for several seconds, as if he couldn't think of anything more to say. "I went up to Oroville," he said finally, making what seemed like a conscious effort to pick up the thread again. "They've got a kind of museum full of stuff about his childhood. They're very proud of him. I've never known a politician who could resist something like that, yet Faircliff hasn't been near the place in forty-five years. Don't you think that's odd?"

Now it was Austen's turn to shrug. "I was born in Scottsbluff, Nebraska, and I've never been back either. Some people just aren't real big on hometowns, Pete. But I've never heard him mention it, one way or the other."

"I think I'll ask him about it."

"Go ahead." Austen smiled, wondering whether the smile looked as uncomfortable as it felt. "But you'll probably end up listening to an analysis of the state of Soviet missile deployment instead. That's the obsession of the hour."

"Yeah . . ." Pete looked as if he hadn't heard a syllable, and then suddenly he snapped back into focus. "You know, I was up there for about three weeks, talking to people and looking the place over, and a spooky thing happened. I discovered that I was being shadowed."

They sat looking at one another for a moment, during which the outside temperature seemed to drop about fifteen degrees. The smile on Austen's face never wavered.

"Can you describe any of them?" he asked, just before the silence began to verge on the ludicrously awkward. "I doubt whether any of our people could have been shadowing you without my knowing about it—why the hell would they? But I can check it if you like."

"Okay—I got a picture of one of them."

Pete reached back to his trouser-pocket for his billfold, from which he extracted a two-by-three color photograph of a man turning away to cross an intersection in the opposite direction. The man looked annoyed, and like the sort it might be dangerous to annoy too much. The head was in profile, but the one visible eye was no more than a slit. The moustache was dark and perfectly straight.

"Sorry." Austen shook his head, tucking the picture into the pocket of his shirt. "I've never seen this article before."

Dear Frank,

It's very hot in Moscow and you can't get a decent meal anywhere, not even here in our own embassy. These people don't seem to have ever heard of air conditioning—you were smart not to come.

I am writing this and sending it out via diplomatic satchel because the Russians have got so many bugs installed in this building that I'm sure they can hear the scratching of my pen—under the circumstances, using the telephone or even a coder is just a waste of time.

Van Deman says that his private sources of information are afraid to talk to him anymore. Apparently there have been some arrests lately, and rumor has it that the KGB is about to crack down on a good chunk of our network here. I pass the message on for your evaluation.

Give my love to Dottie.

Simon

A courier brought the letter to Austen's front door just as he was about to sit down to breakfast. He read it quickly, put it in his jacket pocket, and went back into the kitchen.

He would worry about it later.

Even from the hall he could hear Dottie humming to herself. They had gone to a movie the night before to see a revival of *Song of the South*, which Austen remembered ever so faintly from his childhood, and the sound that was coming from in front of the refrigerator consisted of disjointed fragments of "Zip-ah-dee-doo-dah," rendered, as usual, about a quarter-tone sharp.

The honeymoon had outlasted Pete Freestone's visit by nearly two weeks. They were still sleeping together and had made love last night almost as soon as they got back inside the door, so it was possible to flatter oneself that the lady's good mood was perhaps not exclusively traceable to Walt Disney.

The whole business had the tentative quality of a casual, on-again-off-again affair, something that might jell for them or might not. But it was better than nothing, Austen figured. It was better than he had been doing for a long time.

"Who was that?" Dottie asked as he resumed his seat. She was holding a pitcher of orange juice that clashed oddly with her floor-length peach bathrobe; still, she looked so pretty and young at that moment that Austen experienced a decided twinge.

"Just business— a note from your father. He says Moscow's too hot and the food is lousy. He sends his love." He smiled, perhaps a little uncertainly, as if she had caught him out in something, but she hardly seemed to notice.

"I don't know," she said finally, as if to the orange juice. "You think I'm too hard on him too, don't you."

"I don't know either, sweetheart. We're none of us perfect men; maybe we have it coming."

"But you don't think he's a monster."

"No."

"And you think I'm wrong because I can't love him?"

"Yes, and it isn't that you can't love him. You do love him, or you wouldn't worry about it so much."

"Maybe." She set the orange juice down on the kitchen table and began drifting back toward the refrigerator—for what, she probably couldn't have said herself, since everything was already out. "Maybe you're right. All that with my mother, I don't suppose there's anything to it."

"I don't suppose so, no."

What else could he have said? And how the hell was he supposed to know? She had been trying so hard lately to see things from his point of view, perhaps so that she could finally just break down and forgive him and they could both have a little peace and happiness. But it wasn't destined to work out that way—he knew it, even if she didn't. There wasn't a thing in the world he could do but just keep on lying.

"Have your breakfast before it gets cold," she said.

Half an hour later he saw the limousine pull into his driveway. George Timmler was in the back.

"Take a look at this." Austen extracted the note from his pocket and passed it over. "I suppose they felt that if our ambassador had heard about it, it must have filtered down to us too. I wonder whether this isn't some kind of probe."

As they slipped along through the quiet residential streets. he could look out and watch children trudging along the sidewalk on their way to school. For the trouble of opening his window a crack, he could have heard their voices. The sight of them made him feel as if his whole world had lost contact with ordinary reality.

"It's true, though."

"I know it's true." He glanced around at Timmler with momentary annoyance. "But look who they've picked up— Karsakov, Razumihin, Florinsky, Demidov. All old names, all compromised already. I wouldn't be surprised if they planned to roll up every stick of our old network as soon as the treaty is ratified, just to show us who's the new boss."

Turning back to the window, he saw that they had already left the children far behind them. For some reason this fact depressed him. "The point is they haven't touched any of our new people. I think they're testing us; if we don't seem worried enough, they might conclude we're on to them."

Timmler seemed to weigh this for a moment, and then, as

if making the greatest concession in the world, he nodded. "It's possible we could tip them by overreacting," he said finally. "They could be looking for that, too."

"Then maybe we ought to do nothing." Austen took the note from Timmler's unresisting fingers and put it back in his pocket. "I'll wait until he gets back, and then I'll act the part of the worried liar and tell him everything's fine. Maybe he'll just assume I'm trying to make myself look good while I cover my bureaucratic butt."

"That might be best. When's he due?"

"In a week. He signs day after tomorrow, and then there are stops in Bonn, Paris, Brussels, and London so the allies won't feel neglected. I'll talk to him then."

"They wheeled me around like a fucking tourist—I must have seen a million of those Fabergé Easter eggs. And Lenin's tomb, of course. Personally, I think it's a wax dummy in there; the guy's been dead for sixty years." It was strange, but Simon Faircliff seemed to find the idea deeply unsettling. His eyes took on a glazed look, and the lines around his mouth seemed to deepen. Of course, it was only his second day back from Europe; he hadn't even gotten over his jet lag yet.

"No, it's Lenin." Austen stretched his legs out in front of him; the sofas in the Oval Office were so low that every time he sat down on one of them he seemed to be looking out at the world from over the tops of his knees. "They've got him rigged up with spigots, and they change the formaldehyde every month."

Faircliff's face wrinkled with distaste. "Jesus—is that what you get for being a hero? I think I'd rather just be buried, if you don't mind."

"I'll make a note of it."

The president smiled—it was a big joke—and pushed the half-lens reading glasses he had taken to wearing lately a little further back on his nose. He really did look tired. The coffee table between the two men was covered with briefing books and papers.

"But you don't think we're in bad shape over there?" he asked, glancing up at his son-in-law and lieutenant whom he was supposed to love and trust. "You say yourself they've got four of our people, and Van Deman makes it sound like that might be just the beginning."

"Look, Simon, Van Deman's a nice guy, but he doesn't know what he's talking about." The director of Central Intelligence held out the palms of his hands as if to say, *He's old-line Foggy Bottom—what can you expect . . . ?* "Do you know what the life expectancy of one of our Russian agents is? About five years, if he happens to be very, very good. Those people have never heard of due process, Chief; they bug your phone and toss your apartment as a matter of routine. I think the KGB is just seeing what they can make out of a few arrests."

"Okay, Frank, you're the spy."

You're the spy. The expression on his face was curiously benevolent, as if he could see right through you, knew that you were lying, and was prepared to forgive you that and all your other weaknesses and sins. And Austen, who carried the lie in his heart—what did the words matter, if the intention was to deceive?—was properly humbled.

"So what else did the lords of the Kremlin have to say to you?" he asked, discovering that he could still meet Faircliff's steady, penetrating gaze with a fair approximation of unconcern. "I don't suppose there were any offers to sell us Cuba."

One had the impression of a grief that was almost physical, as if what you saw was the soul. And then he smiled again, the way anyone might at a child's bad joke. "My God, Frank. Those people want to grab the whole wide world."

About a week before Labor Day, Austen managed to get his desk clear enough to permit him a weekend off. It was a sufficiently rare event to warrant certain preparations.

"I got tickets. High government service doesn't count for anything anymore; I had to pay a scalper eighty bucks for the two of them. We can go up to New York and have a time of it."

Dottie picked up the tickets from where they were lying on her writing desk and read the name of the play.

"I've never heard of this; it's probably a turkey."

"Probably. It's been running for a year and a half."

So they packed a suitcase, threw it in the back of the family car, and set out on Interstate 95 shortly before lunch that Friday morning.

He had booked into the Regency, which he discovered was just around the corner from Sixty-first Street. There wasn't anything he could do about it, however, and the lobby was full of tycoon types, so probably no one would think it strange that the director of Central Intelligence, escorting the daughter of the president of the United States, should check in there. No one would have any reason to look any further than that.

Besides, Austen had followed his usual practice and made all his arrangements under another name. It was absolutely essential, particularly when he went anywhere with Dottie, simply to keep from being mobbed by reporters. Mr. and Mrs. Austen's pictures appeared infrequently enough in the press that with a little luck they might be able to last the weekend without anyone's recognizing them.

So everyone's secrets were probably safe enough.

It was only about four in the afternoon by the time they had gotten settled in and unpacked. Austen picked up the phone and made a dinner reservation at Le Périgord for the decidedly uncontinental hour of six, and after that there was nothing left to do except sit around and watch Dottie preening herself for her big evening on the town. He decided he could probably have found worse ways to kill a couple of hours.

She sat on a velvet-covered stool in front of the vanity table with nothing on but a pair of pink satin panties as she did up her hair in preparation for taking a shower. Austen crouched behind her, reaching around to cup her breasts in his hands as he kissed her on the shoulder.

"Come on, Frank, we'll never make the restaurant," she said, in that tone of voice that was almost as much an invitation as a rebuff.

"I am coming on, can't you tell?" He let his lips work their way up to the hollow of her throat. "Besides, I'd rather make you anyway."

And they still arrived at their table before the maître d'hôtel even noticed they were late.

It was a lovely and frighteningly expensive meal. Austen ordered a bottle of champagne that alone cost over fifty dollars. The service was swift and unobtrusive, and the food was wonderful. For dessert they had strawberries about the size of a clenched fist. And through it all they sat with their knees pressed together like a couple of guiltily overheated teenagers.

But Dottie had been right—the show was a turkey. Nobody could have made sense of the plot, which seemed to be some sort of parody of Snow White and the Seven Dwarfs, set in Civil War Atlanta. There was even a dance number representing Sherman's march to the sea.

"This is awful."

"I know."

"Then don't you think we can get out of here?" Austen glanced around nervously, hoping for evidence of a mass defection. It seemed, however, that everyone was enjoying themselves immensely. "They've got to have an intermission pretty soon. We could make a break for it."

"Not at forty dollars a ticket. But I will let you go out to the lobby and buy me a lemonade."

So they stuck it out to the bitter end, which didn't come until quarter to eleven. They caught a cab on Eighth Avenue.

"Listen, you go ahead and get ready for bed." He was still holding the door key, smiling like a man with a guilty conscience. "I'll just take a little walk. I'll be back in a while."

Dottie simply stood there for a moment. Then, very quietly, she sank down onto the corner of the bed. She stared at him first with surprise and then with a kind of resigned understanding.

"I just thought . . . I don't know—I suppose it was silly of me."

"It's the job, sweetheart. It's nothing you have to worry about. I'll only be about forty minutes."

They both were aware of the inadequacy of the explanation—she hated this job. It was nasty and unsharable; it was the obstacle that stood between them. And because he knew what it was that had really brought him all this way—and knew that she didn't—he felt all the more a traitor.

"And I suppose I was just the decoy? All along?"

"I've got to go."

"So go," she answered quietly, her eyes devoid of expression. "No one is stopping you."

It was the old unspoken argument again. Neither of them said another word for the five or ten seconds that he remained in the room, but the silence was almost deafening. She just continued to stare at him, and his face assumed the stony expressionlessness that over the years had become his only line of defense. Finally he slipped the key into his jacket pocket and left, closing the door quietly behind him.

Silence had become the condition of his life. And nothing was ever done for one purpose alone. He was stupid to have expected her to understand.

There were no suspicious types in the lobby, and no one seemed to be following him as he followed the dark sidewalk up Park Avenue. But just to be on the safe side, he cut to the left, turning up to Madison, where he caught a cab.

"Metropolitan Museum."

The driver looked at him quizzically through the rearview mirror. It seemed on the tip of his tongue to say that the museum had been closed for hours, but then he thought better of it, nodded, and popped the gearshift into drive. They traveled the nineteen blocks in silence.

He waited for the cab to leave, standing out of range of the floodlights that washed the museum's façade and steps in pale yellow, and then started walking down Fifth, keeping the Park on his right side. When he got to Seventy-ninth Street he turned right, entering the park, and walked about half a block. Then he turned suddenly and took off into the underbrush, heading south at a dead run.

He had gone perhaps fifty or sixty yards when he stopped to conceal himself behind a tree and to listen. There was nothing. He waited another couple of minutes, just to be sure, and then went on. No one had followed him.

At the Conservatory Pond, where the smooth, oily water reflected the lights from the apartment buildings along Fifth, he found a dark alcove and sat down on a bench beside the bronze statue of Alice in Wonderland. After about two minutes another man stepped out from the surrounding woods and joined him. It was Chester Storey.

"What kept you?" he asked in a hoarse whisper. "I've been here for three quarters of an hour—I was scared to death. This is a hell of a meeting place in the dead of night."

"Beggars can't be choosers. Now what was so important that it couldn't be transmitted through Eilberg?" For about a second, Austen regarded the man with something close to real hatred. Chester Storey had ruined his weekend. If he went back to the hotel tonight and found the door bolted against him, he would know who to blame.

Storey didn't seem to notice; perhaps it was too dark. He

reached into his inside pocket and pulled out a sheet of notepaper folded in half and handed it to Austen.

"I got that in the mail four days ago, and a phone call from Diederich the same night. I'm sorry for the delay, but I wasn't sure what to do with it."

"With what? What is it?"

"A list of names. Eight names." In the darkness Chester Storey shrugged as if denying any responsibility, except it was a little late for that. "Eight names, with the names of a city and a state in brackets after each one. I assume the cities are all birthplaces; my name is fifth on the list, and that's what it is there."

"You're number five? And there are *eight* names? Have you ever heard of any of the others?"

"I know three of them by reputation. They're all very successful, wealthy men. I've never met any of them."

"And the list is from Diederich?"

"He didn't say so. I think not—the postmark is New York City."

"And what were your instructions from Diederich?"

"I was to discover the whereabouts of each one of them and approach the ones who had money, asking for a contribution—anonymous cash donations to the Faircliff Reelection Committee—except that I don't suppose anyone on the committee will ever see a nickel of it. I wasn't to accept less than half a million from any of them, and that was just for starters.

"Don't you see?" Storey went on, his voice rising to a tense whisper and his right hand opening and closing with nerveless, machinelike regularity. "I looked up the three I knew—I couldn't find anything about any of the others—and they were all born in 1921, and they all attended Ivy League universities. Don't you see? Eight men born in remote little towns in the Southwest and West. I'll bet every one of them lost his parents within a month after leaving for college. Dammit—they're Soroka's magpies."

"And Diederich would make the ninth."

"Yes. I don't know who could have been the tenth. Maybe there wasn't one, or maybe he's dead."

"Get out of here, Chester," Austen said quietly. "Go on, get lost."

Storey didn't respond for a few seconds—it was as if he had been stunned—and then he nodded two or three times, got up from the bench, and retreated back into the darkness. For some time Austen could hear the crackling of twigs, and then the sound of a man's shoes on an asphalt walkway. And then nothing.

He couldn't really blame Storey, who after all was merely doing what he had to to save his own neck—and who had brought him information that, sometime or other, he would need if there was ever to be an end to this mess. But it could have waited. How much could you have on your conscience at once?

For a long moment Austen continued to sit where he was, under the unseeing eyes of the Mad Hatter, thinking about the eight men whose names appeared on the list he still held in his hand, thinking of what was bound to happen to them now. It wasn't a very pleasant reflection.

On the way back to his hotel, under a streetlamp on Seventieth Street, he took the slip of paper from his pocket and looked at it.

Harold C. Anson (Centralia, Washington); Richard R. Crutwell (Sparks, Nevada); Chester A Storey (Weatherford, Texas) . . .

And then, on the next line, *Edward H. Tilson (Crescent City, California).*

"My God," he heard himself saying, whether out loud or not he couldn't have guessed. So that had been the poor bastard's guilty secret, the thing that had put him in Salvarini's claws. Had Salvarini known it all, or just some little part, some pale reflection of the truth? It wouldn't have had to be very much—not that there was much chance of anyone ever finding out now.

And one wondered what grotesque impulse had prompted Diederich to leave that name on the list. What was it supposed to be—a private joke? Perhaps a warning?

How could it have happened that Tilson could have found himself delivered into the hands of a man like Salvarini? Could it really have been just a favor? Could he really have been that stupid and careless? That was Mrs. Tilson's version, but poor Edward would have had to tell her something; there weren't any guarantees that it would have been the truth. In fact, considering what the truth in this case was, that might have been the last thing he would think to tell her.

And there was always the other possibility. Perhaps Diederich, with his usual foresight and indirection, had simply hit upon Salvarini as a means of removing an obstacle. And if so, then Austen had been in it even before he had known there was something to be in. He too had played his part.

III

Pete Freestone had risen quickly within his profession, largely because of the thoroughness of his research—he just didn't like to let a story go until he had all the answers. His presidential biography had been in the bookstores for three days already, and he still hadn't finished with the subject. So when the *Chronicle* asked him to do a condensation for their Sunday supplement, with particular attention to Faircliff's California roots, he jumped at the chance to take a couple of days off from a very dull election season and go back to Oroville and turn over a few more rocks.

Because there was still the inaccessibility of the private man—the widower with one daughter who is married to one of his principal lieutenants doesn't make very exciting copy. Of course, everybody knew that Dottie Faircliff Austen didn't get along very well with her father; she was hardly ever seen at social or political functions, even when Frank was there. But you couldn't very well turn that into high domestic drama unless you happened to be writing a gossip column.

And Faircliff himself hadn't been terribly helpful. His weaknesses as a father hadn't come up in their interview— somehow you couldn't ask; after all, the man was the president of the United States—but he had had little enough else to say, even about less irritated areas of his private life.

"Your parents—they died while you were in college?"

"Yes, a motoring accident."

"What were they like?"

"My father owned the hardware store in town, and my mother was very musical—taught piano and played the organ in the Methodist Church."

"Well, could you tell me a little bit more about what kind of people they were? How do you remember them?"

Faircliff had smiled, as if he were talking to an idiot, and started fiddling nervously with his left thumbnail. "They were good, solid people," he had answered after a few seconds of consideration. "Everyone liked them. It's . . . It's difficult to describe without making them sound like Mr. and Mrs. Mainstreet America."

It was all so wooden, like answers committed to memory. What was the circumference of the earth? Twenty-four thousand nine hundred miles. What was your father like? He owned a hardware store. What kind of an answer was that?

Mr. and Mrs. Mainstreet America. Well, there were one or two other versions of that truth.

"That woman led Ray Faircliff a life a dog wouldn't have touched. She used to hide up in her bedroom, sometimes for a month at a stretch. I saw her burst into tears once in front of the meat counter at the A&P, for no reason under the sun. She did that all the time. Oh, she was a trial, believe me."

That was what one heard from Miss Jessie Faircliff, an eighty-two-year-old second cousin of the president's who had lived in Oroville her entire life. Of course, she wasn't someone upon whose unsupported word you wanted to put your total trust; she had the odd habit of constantly plucking at the hem of her dress while she sat in her front parlor talking to you, apparently on the theory that the real reason you were there was to have a chance to look at her legs. And she seemed to bear the whole family a grudge based on the fact that she had never been invited to the White House. But Pete Freestone had heard similar stories from others who remembered the Faircliffs, so there must have been some truth there somewhere.

So perhaps there were perfectly good reasons why Simon Faircliff was reluctant to discuss his parents. Perhaps he simply wished that they, like his daughter, be cloaked in a decent privacy. Perhaps, under the circumstances, his evasions were nothing more than filial piety.

Anyway, what the hell. It wouldn't hurt to have another look, and it was better than listening to campaign speeches. He packed his bag and took off.

"Now you promise me you won't break your diet? No pizza and beer lunches? You'll take the time to go to a real restaurant and have a chef's salad and a glass of iced tea?"

He promised. Sheila was the most wonderful woman he had ever known. Just a chubby little brunette who wore too much makeup over her acne scars, but they kept each other on the straight and narrow. And she really loved him. It was a new experience. She meant the end of going home to an empty apartment, of living just any which way because there wasn't a soul on earth to take an interest.

So after Freestone checked into the Skyhawk Motel, the first thing he did was down three of his Melozets reducing wafers to help him get through the afternoon in a state of grace.

The second thing he did was visit the converted firehouse that had become the Simon A. Faircliff Museum.

God only knew what refurbishing that structure had cost the city fathers in unpaved roads and unbought baseball uniforms for the high school. Oroville didn't seem like the sort of town that had a lot of civic-minded millionaires in residence. It had been a labor of love, obviously; the paint was so new it almost hurt your eyes.

Maybe they would even make some money out of it, if the level of tourism it seemed to attract didn't fall through the floor as soon as the election was over. Certainly there were plenty of folks out that day sporting "Faircliff for President" buttons on the lapels of their down-filled hunting jackets. The whole town, in fact, was filled with people who wanted to be in the great man's hometown when he swept into another term.

Around the walls in a series of glass cases there were photographs, a birth certificate bearing a two-inch-long footprint, artifacts from the Faircliff home—taken out of storage and donated to the city after his reelection to the Senate—campaign posters and buttons, yellowed newspaper clippings, a high school football trophy, and three pages of a handwritten essay for third-period English, dated December 3, 1936, on "The Allegory of *The Scarlet Letter*," in ink that had faded to a pale brown.

Freestone had been here several times, always trying to connect these fragments from an almost unimaginable past with the man whose present greatness had made them worth the trouble of preserving and who now seemed to preside over the destiny of the world. As always, he found himself unable to bridge the gap.

Perhaps there was no conservation of character. Perhaps Simon Faircliff's only link with the youth enshrined here like some genteel butterfly collection was the fact that it had once been his own. But if so it had long since passed into someone else's possession—in this case, the child did not seem father to the man.

The one thing that marked his presence was a letter on White House stationery, displayed as the final exhibit in the collection. There was the Simon Faircliff of popular myth— the firm, pointed, almost disturbingly forceful hand.

Outside, the sunlight was already beginning to grow pale. Listening to the local news on his car radio that morning, he had heard they were predicting a frost that night, and Freestone discovered that he was able to believe it. He turned up the collar of his raincoat and started walking back toward his motel, wondering where he would have dinner.

About a mile outside of town, there was an honest-to-God steakhouse, the sort of place that didn't make you push your tray through a line, where there were white linen tablecloths and no sawdust on the floor. You could even get a drink before dinner, but Freestone decided to abstain because even a simple bourbon and branch water had a hundred calories and he thought he would prefer a pat of butter on his baked potato.

It was a nice place, and he would have liked it even better if it hadn't been for the goon in the brown suit who was sitting about four tables away, over by the door where he could watch every move you made.

He wasn't sure when he had picked up a tail, and he wasn't sure whether this was one of the boys from his last trip; it was possible, but there wasn't any way Freestone could be dogmatic about it. Last time, except for the clown whose picture he had snapped while walking back to his car from the museum, he had never had more than glimpses.

But this guy was on his case. Normally a tail tries to blend in with the wallpaper—a good one is a master of indirection; you just don't see him—but this guy, with his bald head and his odd, simian nostrils, was so obvious he might as well have worn a sign around his neck.

That all this attention had something to do with Simon Faircliff he just had to accept as a fact. No one was without his flaws, even the president, and Freestone had long entertained the suspicion that his and the nation's hero wasn't always so terribly scrupulous in some of his political practices. There was no evading the fact that every one of Faircliff's election campaigns had coincided with a rash of funny business—cars found with the distributor heads missing just before the start of a motorcade, elevators that suddenly jammed between floors so that the candidate was two and a half hours late for a press conference, contributors who suddenly developed cold feet and backed out of their pledges, sabotaged television transmissions—not a speck of which anyone had ever succeeded in pinning on the man himself. But there was still something . . .

Hell, Freestone had been followed before; it was the sort of thing that happened to political reporters. Not all the time, but often enough. Our elected officials were frequently the nervous type, and it wasn't just the Mafia and the CIA that kept pavement artists on the payroll. The question with which you learned to concern yourself was, what made them think it was worth their trouble?

"Would you like some dessert?" The waitress smiled—she was probably all of about nineteen and working very hard to please—and her large brown innocent eyes widened even more as she stood beside his chair, poised and expectant, as if her every chance of happiness depended on the answer.

"No, thank you, I don't think so." Freestone smiled too and shook his head as he reached into the back pocket of his trousers for his billfold. He extracted his American Express card and set it down on the table. "If you could just bring me the bill, please?"

A kind of relieved cheerfulness spread over the waitress's face, suggesting he had said just the right thing—maybe desserts were a problem for her too—and she picked up the card and flounced away.

It was only as he was signing the credit slip that the obviousness of the thing dawned on him.

He sat staring down at his signature for what felt like an eternity but probably wasn't more than three or four seconds, wondering how it could have escaped him so long. Of course—the handwriting.

How much does something like that change between sixteen and sixty? A little, certainly, but not so much that a strong resemblance can't be traced. Not so much that you wouldn't recognize at once that both samples belonged to the same person.

He probably had ten or fifteen samples of Simon Faircliff's distinctive penmanship at home in his files. The great man liked to send little handwritten notes; he understood as well as anybody the political value of that kind of small attention. Pete Freestone knew that autograph as well as his own. He would have recognized it anywhere.

And the essay, those three closely covered pages of schoolboy ingenuity, was not in the same hand. It wasn't even close.

"That's our latest acquisition," said the sniffy old retired librarian who had insisted upon showing him through on his first visit. She seemed to regard Simon Faircliff's young life as her own personal property, and she was pleased as punch about it. "Miss Garfield left that to us in her will—ninety-two she was when she passed away. Imagine."

"Oh?" Freestone had raised his eyebrows in polite interest. "Who was Miss Garfield?"

"*Only* the first high school teacher in Butte Country with a full-fledged bachelor's degree in literature," the librarian answered with a certain asperity—how could he not have known a thing like that? "A graduate of Occidental College in Los Angeles she was, and President Faircliff's teacher, for both French and sophomore and junior English. She'd kept that essay all these years. *She* knew he'd be a great man one of these days."

Pete Freestone tore out his copy of the credit slip, stuffed it and the card back into his billfold, and handed the rest of the form to the waitress. As he sat finishing his coffee and trying to recover from the shock, he watched the gentleman seated by the exit, wondering whether he could have any idea at all what he had been sent out to protect.

There were all sorts of perfectly reasonable explanations. The young Simon Faircliff might simply have bought himself a term paper; the practice probably hadn't been invented by the present generation. Except that everyone remembered him as the smartest, best-organized kid they had ever met, and wouldn't Miss Garfield have been familiar with young Simon's scrawl? No—it wouldn't wash.

Or maybe his handwriting had changed. That was supposed to happen sometimes after people suffered some sort of neurological crisis. Except that there was no record that anything of the kind had ever happened to Simon Faircliff. But after all he was a public figure, and public figures had been known to be less than perfectly candid about their medical histories. It wasn't inevitable that the boy who had written that essay and the man who sat in the Oval Office weren't the same person.

By the next morning he had almost convinced himself that his imagination had run away with him. He would go have another look that afternoon, and doubtless he would discover that the two scripts weren't as different as he had allowed himself to suppose.

There was a coffee shop about five blocks from his motel where it was possible to get a cup of vanilla yogurt, a slice of dry toast, a glass of tomato juice, and a cup of black coffee without anyone's sneering at him. He had discovered it the first morning of his previous trip and had gone there for breakfast as a fixed routine for the whole three weeks. At seven A.M. it was a pleasant quarter-mile in each direction, and he had read somewhere that you lost weight faster if you made a point of walking as much as possible.

It was late in October, and true to the weatherman's promise, there had been a frost the night before. The grass, where it was still darkened by the shadows of surrounding buildings, was covered with a white film of ice. The sidewalks along that particular street were lined with maple trees that had long since gone bare; here and there on the pavement you could still discover the outlines their leaves had left, looking absurdly like the footprints of giant frogs.

Like most people who had grown up in big cities, Pete Freestone tended to take rather a romantic view of rural life—rural, in his mind, being anyplace with a population of less than a quarter-million souls. As a consequence he enjoyed Oroville, even to the point of entertaining certain harmless fantasies about editing the local rag so he could spend the rest of his life writing stories about church rummage sales and the opening of the trout season.

There was a vacant lot about midway on his walk between the coffee shop and the motel, simply a bare patch of ground where the grass grew as high as your knees, right in the middle of what must have been by local standards the heart of the business district. Perhaps there had been something there once and it had been torn down. Anyway, the land was empty, without so much as a "For Sale" sign in evidence. Freestone was just passing it, amusing himself with visions of a clean, safe, uncomplicated pastoral existence, when he heard a car gunning its motor behind him.

He turned around to look and, for one horrible instant, thought he was dead already. The thing was coming directly at him, a late-model Chevy, dark blue, and the man behind the wheel was the man whose picture he had taken, the man with the narrow eyes and the straight black moustache. There seemed plenty of time to notice all these things—and no time at all to get away.

He watched the car coming, watched it gathering speed, and glanced down at the edge of the sidewalk, just at the point where the Chevy would come up after him. If he ran, it would simply change direction a little and nail him anyway. There was nowhere to run.

Except that just there the sidewalk sloped down to make a driveway entrance. It was worth a try.

With a sudden twist of his body, Freestone threw himself down and started to roll back the way he had come. If he had kept to his feet, he would never have made it—as it was, the car missed him by no more than a couple of inches. He was close enough to hear the whizzing of the tires just beside his head.

The car swept up and onto the vacant lot, made a sharp turn, and shot back to the street, grazing the corner of a parked truck. In an instant it was gone, leaving nothing but the track of its path over the grass and the sounds of squealing tires and crushed metal that still rang in your ears like echoes.

Freestone picked himself up from the ground, saw that he had cut open his thumb, and wrapped it up in his handkerchief. His suit was muddy and torn open under the left armhole, but personally, he was alive. There seemed to be little enough to complain about in that.

The driveway entrance had saved his life. Those couple of inches had kept Pete Freestone alive. Because that son-of-a-bitch had been trying to murder him.

All the way back to his motel room he kept glancing over his shoulder, expecting the dark blue Chevy to come back and pin him to the side of a building. He found that he had a tendency to stumble; it was simply that his nerves had been stretched so tight that he kept putting his feet down too soon. An attempt on his life was a new experience—he wasn't used to it.

He sat down on the edge of his bed and tried to think. He had to pull himself together, to decide what he should do.

These people, whoever they were, couldn't have any idea what he had hit upon; the mere fact of his presence in this place at this time seemed to be enough. Somehow he had tipped them that he was less than satisfied with the official version of Simon Faircliff's youth, and that was all the excuse they needed.

And he had only talked to two people about it—Frank Austen and, indirectly, Faircliff himself.

Could Frank have set the dogs on him? Frank doubtless had done some pretty raw things in his time, and no one had ever questioned his loyalty to his president, but Frank was also a friend. It was hard to believe that he would do something like this—try to have him murdered, for Christ's sake—on so little provocation, without so much as a warning. The guy was a hard ass, but he wasn't a monster.

And he wasn't stupid, either. Frank had seen the photograph. It was perfectly possible he had been lying when he had said the face meant nothing to him, but if that goon with the slits for eyes was one of Frank's people he would never have sent him to finish off his good friend Pete Freestone, even assuming he thought to solve his problem that way. You don't do that when you know your man's been spotted.

So that left Simon Faircliff, his excellency the president of the United States.

"I wonder that you didn't go home to Oroville to practice law, Mr. President."

Faircliff had smiled tightly and shaken his head.

"I fell in love with San Francisco. Besides, I had a job offer."

"And you've never been back?"

"No, I guess not."

"Not even to campaign? I wonder why that is. Didn't you have any curiosity about the place?"

"Curiosity? No, I guess . . ."

Dear God, how he had squirmed in those few minutes. If the president was protecting some guilty secret—and it would have to be a beaut if he was ready to kill people, just like that, simply as a precaution—

Freestone realized that, for the first time in his life, he was simply out of his league. Whom could he contact? Someone had to be told, in case he never made it back to his typewriter, but who? Frank Austen? Frank was Simon Faircliff's man.

On the other hand . . .

Freestone had seen Austen's face when he heard about Ted Boothe—they had been together that night. Frank wasn't that good an actor; no, he hadn't had a hand in that. And Frank had smelled something, too, both with Boothe and with Clayton Burgess. From what one heard, Faircliff was now sleeping with Burgess's widow.

There just weren't any other options. Frank Austen had been his friend for a long time, and that might go a little way toward making the difference.

Freestone looked through the drawers of his motel room writing table until he found the inevitable packet of stationery, extracted a sheet of paper and an envelope, and sat down. In less than a minute he had finished, and he folded the paper into thirds and put it into the envelope. They would have stamps downstairs; he would drop his note in the lobby mailbox as he left. It was time for him to try and get home.

It was odd. All his life he had been telling himself that he ate out of nerves. And finally here he was, feeling like the biggest target in the shooting gallery, and he could hardly swallow his own spit. Maybe he was finally learning.

IV

Frank Austen was just about to leave for the airport when he came down the stairs from his bedroom and found that morning's mail scattered over the tiled floor of the entranceway. He gathered up the two magazines and the advertising circulars and set them on a table where Dottie would find them and took the handful of letters into the kitchen. Most of them were bills, and there were a few that he could tell from the size and shape were probably dinner invitations, an impression the embassy stamps on the envelope flaps tended to confirm.

There was one, however, with no return address, merely an Oroville, California, postmark. Austen tore it open and read it, and then went over to the refrigerator for a bottle of ginger ale, stuffing the letter into his jacket pocket. He wasn't surprised; he had decided some time ago that very probably nothing would ever surprise him again.

When he had finished his drink, he went back upstairs to his study and got George Timmler on the scrambler phone. "Meet me at the gate, George. I've got something I want to show you."

Then he went back to his bedroom—the room next to his study; the honeymoon was over—to finish packing his bag. He found Dottie waiting for him.

She was dressed in a plain charcoal-gray suit that contrived to be at once stylish and severe, set off by nothing except a thin gold necklace he had given her for their second anniversary. She sat on the corner of the bed, her handbag on the floor beside her, as if she had just stopped for a moment before going out.

"I could still come with you if you like," she said. Her eyes kept flickering down to the carpet, suggesting a certain embarrassment. "He was your friend. I could be ready in just a couple of minutes."

Austen smiled, perhaps a trifle sadly, and shook his head. "No, sweetheart. I have business on this trip. Things you're better off not having anything to do with. But I appreciate the thought."

"Frank, what happened to us? I . . ." She left the sentence unfinished as her eyes filled up with tears. Austen reached out his hand. After a moment, when he saw she wasn't going to take it, he let it fall back to his side.

"It's as if some curse hangs over us," she went on, when she had regained her composure. "We're like the House of Atreus; we just keep tearing each other to pieces. This 'business,' it has to do with Pete's death, doesn't it."

"Yes."

"And somehow it's all connected, isn't it." She looked up at him, and there was anger in her eyes; the tears had all dried up. "I'm not an idiot, Frank—I've known for a long time that there was something going on between you and Daddy that you were keeping a secret. You and he, you're still the same on the surface, but you've turned against him, haven't you. And now this with Pete . . ."

"Don't ask me about things like that, sweetheart," he said quietly, almost pleading with her. "I can't tell you anything. Sometimes that's the worst part of it—not being able to tell you."

Perhaps it was only what he wanted to believe, but for a moment, as she looked into his face, he could imagine that she might really understand. It was because he loved her that he told her nothing—at least, that was part of the reason. Suddenly she sprang up, and he took her in his arms as she shook with weeping.

"Pete . . ."

"I know—he was a nice guy," he murmured, touching her hair lightly with his fingertips. "But it'll be all right. Someday it'll be all right. The funeral is tomorrow morning; I'll be back Monday afternoon. I'll call."

He was lying. He didn't think it would ever be all right—not anything, ever. But he could feel her nodding into the shoulder of his coat, like a child who doesn't understand the words but responds to the tone of your voice, not caring for the truth of anything. They stood together like that for a long time.

There were still ten or twelve minutes before boarding, and Austen was sitting in the VIP lounge at Dulles airport moodily tearing a flight schedule into long, thin strips when George Timmler dropped into the seat next to him. For several seconds they seemed to pay no attention to one another and then Austen reached into his pocket and took out a piece of paper folded into thirds. He handed it to his associate director.

> Dear Frank,
>
> Our friend Snake Eyes tried to run me down with a car about twenty minutes ago. They've got a Faircliff museum here—take a look at the kid's handwriting and see if it squares with the man's. I don't know what it all means, but these jokers are planning to walk away with all the marbles.
>
> Pete

"Then you were right," Timmler said quietly, refolding the paper and returning it. "It was murder."

"Of course it was murder—did they think we were morons?"

Austen glanced impatiently around the lounge as if prepared to argue the subject with anyone who had the temerity to disagree. The only other passenger, an aging actress whom he remembered having been in love with when he was eleven, seemed to be asleep in her furs, and the ground personnel continued to smoke and stare at their shoelaces in heartless unconcern.

"Of course it was murder," he repeated, somewhat more calmly. "They seem to be under the impression that they can run the whole human race off into ravines and nobody will notice.

"I want you to find this guy Yates; we cancel his ticket *right now*. And then I want you to send somebody up to Oroville to find out what Pete was talking about. If he discovers any convincing evidence that Faircliff is one of our magpies, he should photograph it and send it home. Just photographs, not the genuine article—it's probably safer where it is. But let's get Yates first."

Timmler sat with his hands in his pockets, the lines of his face looking as if they had been carved with a chisel. He wasn't happy. "Frank, consider what's at risk here. The election is less than a week away. This isn't the time to get mad."

"I'm not mad." The director of Central Intelligence presented an expressionless, unreadable face as his hands continued the careful work of tearing the airline's flight schedule into uniform shreds. "But we get him now."

"Look, Frank, I know this guy Freestone was your friend—"

"We get him *now*. Austen gripped George Timmler's wrist and pulled him around to command his absolute attention, as if he were ready to break the bones over one more word.

"We've let this jellybean run loose for years now, just because we didn't dare do anything about him. Well, now we dare. I'm going to kill Mr. Yates; I'm reserving that satisfaction for myself. You find him."

They found him. It wasn't even that difficult. Yates was at home in his apartment in Santa Barbara. He hadn't stirred out of doors all afternoon. He had even contrived to be alone.

The building in which he lived was just a two-story row that pushed its way up the side of a hill. There was a walkway, and on the other side another line of apartments, the mirror image of the first. Yates rented the second floor of the last unit, so his front window commanded a view of the entire complex. There was a swimming pool down at the bottom, and a parking lot and another line of apartments that faced the street. From a strategic point of view, he was very well served.

Austen and Timmler were sitting in a car about a block and a half away, and Timmler's men were fanned out all over the area. No one was going to go sneaking out through any back doors.

"We've checked out everyone in the complex," Timmler said blandly. "None of them are hostiles, so he won't have any help available. But just in case, we've got snipers covering both ends of the walkway."

"What about the neighbors? The last thing we need is to start a gunfight in the middle of a crowd."

Timmler could only laugh. "Come on, Frank. What kind of show do you think we're running here? It'll never come to that. Besides, it's Sunday afternoon; the place is practically deserted."

There was a slight pause, and then Timmler took a sheet of paper from his inside overcoat pocket. "By the way, we've got the results on that list of Storey's. Four of the eight are dead, but everything we've dug up about them is consistent with the assumption that they were Soroka's plants. They were all born in the same year, they all attended the right universities, and their parents all died before Christmas of 1938."

"And four of them are dead?"

"Yes." Timmler unfolded the sheet of paper and held it up to the light, squinting. "Anson and Van Ghent were both killed in World War Two, Gardner died in a boating accident in 1957, and—but, of course, you know about Tilson."

"Right," Austen nodded, his face an expressionless mask. "I know all about Tilson."

"What do you want to do about the survivors?" Timmler asked, pretending not to notice. "Do we pick them up?"

"We pick them up. What else can we do with them?"

"Storey too?"

"Storey too. Come on, George—let's get this over with."

They got out of the car and walked up to the apartment complex's parking lot, where a man in a pair of white painter's coveralls was already propping his ladder up against the side of Yates's building. He carried a small gas cannister in his hand and, coiled like a length of garden hose, about twenty feet of rubber tubing. As soon as he saw Timmler, he scaled the ladder up to the roof and started making his way toward the rear, climbing awkwardly from one unit to the next since each rose three or four feet above the other like a giant staircase up the hill.

Timmler pointed after him and smiled, his expression exhibiting all the quiet professional pride of a master craftsman.. "That cannister is full of thiopental. He'll run the tube down the vent from Yates's kitchen fan; in about ten minutes our friend should be fast asleep, but we can't let him alone too long or he'll stop breathing altogether. You did say you wanted him alive, didn't you?"

"I thought it would be nice, yes."

When the man in the coveralls appeared again, Timmler touched Austen on the elbow and they started up the walkway. They took their time and stopped in front of the stairwell to Yates's apartment.

"This is the part I like the least," Timmler said, reaching into his overcoat pocket. "Here, you'd better take this."

In the palm of his hand he held what looked like the same small, nickel-plated automatic he had had in New York. The barrel, however, had been extended about an inch by the addition of a silencer. This time Austen took it; it was the first time he had carried a weapon since Vietnam.

At the top of the stairwell Timmler felt a hand on his shoulder.

"I'll go first, George." Austen smiled rather thinly. "If he's still awake in there, I wouldn't want you getting killed doing something you didn't approve of."

If he had any brains at all, Yates would have his door dead-bolted. So you didn't bother with keys or lockpicks; you just kicked the thing down. Fortunately the stairwell was very narrow; Austen braced himself against the side wall and let go. The heel of his shoe landed just beside the doorknob, and the door opened as easily as blowing the head off a glass of beer.

He went in low and rolled for cover behind the kitchen table, all in the prescribed fashion, the gun in his hand, but no one shot at him. He waited for a few minutes, just listening, but there wasn't a sound except for the soft tinkling of a radio in the kitchen, so he got up.

"I feel like an idiot," he said.

They found Yates stretched out over the foot of his bed, face down. Apparently he had just had time to find himself somewhere soft to fall.

The first thing Timmler did was throw open all the windows, all through the apartment, and in a few minutes the sickly smell of the gas was almost gone. It was about half an hour before Yates came around. They left him to do that for himself; nobody rushed him.

Yates's first conscious act was to roll over on his side and throw up, spilling the contents of his stomach, which looked like tomato soup and smelled like hell, all over the floor. Timmler, considerate soul, went into the bathroom and brought him out a glass of water, and within thirty or forty seconds Yates was awake enough to take it, and to appreciate that he was no longer alone in the room.

"Just to put your mind at rest," Timmler began, clamping his hands over his left knee as he sat on the dresser, "we've got this place blanketed. There's no way you're leaving here alive unless Mr. Austen and I take you out on the end of a leash. If you feel lucky, however, you're welcome to try something; I'm sure Mr. Austen would feel obliged for the opportunity to blow your brains out all over the wallpaper."

Yates looked down at the mess he had made on the floor, perhaps considering how much messier the place would get if he acquired a couple of drainage holes through the back of his skull, and brought his hands up to rest inoffensively in his lap. He sat there, staring at Austen, his narrow eyes glittering with recognition and hatred.

Austen merely smiled. "That fat newspaperman you chopped was a friend of mine, sport," he said quietly, the muzzle of the automatic lined up on Yates's larynx. "I suppose it's childish, but I tend to resent things like that. Diederich should have known better."

The allusion did not pass unnoticed. Yates reached up to touch the end of his moustache with his little finger, and then his face seemed to split open. It was the most unpleasant grin Austen had ever seen. "So you figured that out—good for you."

Until the last second he hadn't known he would do anything of the kind—God knows, he hadn't planned it—but suddenly Austen was on his feet, the automatic still firmly clenched in his right hand, and in less time than it takes to draw a breath he had seized Yates by the throat with his left hand, dragged him off the bed and into a pool of his own vomit, and beat his head against the floor as hard as he could.

"You bastard," he heard himself shouting. "You fucking maniac, I'll break your face for you! You goddamn slit-eyed cold-blooded shit!"

It wasn't a very smart thing to do, and if Yates hadn't still been pretty groggy Austen would probably never have gotten away with it alive. But such considerations were the furthest thing from his mind. In that one instant, all he wanted to do with the rest of the day was pound the son-of-a-bitch into strawberry jam.

But it didn't last long. He stopped as soon as he realized that Yates wasn't fighting back anymore—there wasn't any fun in killing a man who wasn't fighting back. It had been one of the absolutely necessary actions of his life; he had felt for a moment as if something inside his chest were beginning to tear apart under the strain.

When he felt the pressure of Timmler's grip on his shoulder, he allowed himself to be pulled away.

"He's okay; he's just out cold again," Timmler said finally from where he was crouched over Yates's body, checking the pulse in his carotid artery.

Austen allowed himself a few minutes to calm down before he spoke. "I want a full confession." Timmler had turned around to look at him the way someone might look at a particularly terrible traffic accident, but Austen no longer worried about what Timmler or anyone else thought. He was beyond that. "I don't care how you get it, but get it. I want the tapes, and I want a signed transcript. And then you plug a hole with this guy—he just disappears. We can't afford to leave him alive."

"You don't want to do it yourself?" There was nothing in Timmler's eyes; it had been just a question. Austen shook his head.

"You're the boss."

"That's right—I'm the boss."

And in that sullen mood they waited for Yates to come around again.

After a while Yates brought his hands up to the sides of his head and, when he perceived that it wasn't likely to come rolling off any time soon, managed to drag himself up into a sitting position.

"I hope they kill you, Austen," he said, looking like he meant it. "I hope Diederich wastes every one of you pinko pricks."

Austen and Timmler looked at each other in perfect astonishment. This wasn't a development they had expected.

"What was that? You want to run that past us one more time, Yates?"

"You planning to plead ignorance, Austen?" Yates sat resting his elbows on his knees, showing his teeth like a devil. "You want to tell me you were just an unwitting tool? You guys are all alike."

They let him talk. It was an odd, contradictory monologue, implying that perhaps Yates hadn't spent much time thinking out the reasons for what he was doing, but the thrust of it was clear enough. They were all in it together, in some vast conspiracy of the left that seemed to include everyone who had ever stood in Simon Faircliff's way. One grasped, as one listened, the really wonderful skill with which Howard Diederich had chosen his angel of destruction.

"And so that was your job—to stop them?"

"Yes." Yates nodded. He didn't regret anything; it was his proudest boast.

"And Clayton Burgess—was he part of it?"

"Yes. Of course."

"And Ted Boothe? You killed them both?"

"Yes."

"Oh, boy."

Austen got up and went over to the chest of drawers, hunting around until he found a clean shirt. While he got it out, he saw that Timmler was already preparing an injection of the tranquilizer that was going to render Yates about as ferocious as a week-old puppy.

"Here," he said, throwing the shirt to its owner. "We want you to be presentable. And maybe, when you get to where you're going, Mr. Timmler here will be kind enough to explain to you just how badly you've been suckered."

V

"You can cut the head off a snake, but the folk wisdom is that it'll keep on wriggling until sundown. It'd probably be a mistake to assume that just because we've got Yates his boys will all run for cover, so watch yourself."

Those had been Mr. Austen's instructions, and Michael Starkman wasn't a boy to disobey instructions—not on a deal like this.

Starkman was from Providence, Rhode Island; he had never been to California before. Since joining the Company he had traveled a good bit; he had worked in Europe for eight years, in Africa for a while, and for two years in the Near East, based in Lebanon, before being posted to Langley, where he had spent the past five years. But for some reason he had never been west of the Mississippi and, like a lot of Easterners, had formed the vague impression that California was all palm trees and sandy beaches and traffic jams. Oroville wasn't like anything he had expected.

This wasn't any great roaring metropolis. Nobody wore one-way sunglasses and white shoes, and the music played over the public address systems in the department stores and diners was more likely to be country-western than hot acid rock. This was like a lot of other places he had seen, places too big to be called towns and too small to be cities, places that were scattered over New England like salt on a pretzel. This was like home.

And the hometown was going half-screwy over the hometown boy who had made good, because tomorrow their very own Simon Faircliff would be reelected to the presidency of the United States, and he wasn't going to do it by halves either. No, the good citizens of Oroville were expecting their one-time compatriot, whom almost none of them had ever seen except on the evening news, to come down on his Republican rival like a brick wall.

So the hometown boy who had never come home was a presence you felt everywhere. He was the local nature god, he was the prophet with honor, he was Big Brother all rolled into one. His face was everywhere—there were probably five or six thousand campaign posters in the downtown area alone—his name was on everybody's lips and all over the front page of every newspaper, his words and deeds were treasured up like the legends of the heroes of Troy. And tomorrow night, after the election returns were in, it would probably surprise nobody if the local GOP chairman were dragged through the city streets in chains.

Starkman had been on the Company payroll long enough to realize that it was best just to stick to what your superiors told you and never, never ask unnecessary questions. But it didn't take a Nobel laureate to figure out that Mr. Austen had decided there was something very wrong about his father-in-law, employer, and president, and that he was getting ready to do something drastic by way of a remedy.

"I don't have to draw you a picture of what will happen to you if you ever breathe a word of this to a living soul, now do I?" Austen had asked.

Starkman had glanced at Mr. Timmler, who half-raised one eyebrow and half-smiled as if to say, *Don't kid yourself, Mike—he means every word of it,* and that had been enough. He had shaken his head and answered up like a good boy, "No, sir, you don't have to."

"Good." The director's face hardly seemed to grow less rigidly mistrustful, but under the circumstances one supposed he could be forgiven. "You'll have to be told more than I feel right about telling anyone, but you need to know what you're looking for and have some idea of the stakes. Believe me, it sounds like such a small thing, but nothing you'll ever do again in your life will be as important as this."

Austen had shown him a piece of notepaper with a short handwritten letter scrawled across it, signed "Pete." Starkman read it, handed it back, and waited. There had to be more.

"Pete Freestone was a friend of mine. He was murdered five days ago. The implications of what he says are pretty obvious. What I want from you is something that will prove, one way or the other, whether the man who uses that name today is really Simon Faircliff."

So that was that. Starkman had been flown up to a private airfield just outside Chico and then had rented a car to take him the twenty-some-odd miles to Oroville, where he was absolutely on his own. He had been provided with a fake driver's license and credit cards to rent the car, but the license and the rental agreement were both burned, according to instructions, as soon as he could find a private place to do it, and the credit cards were cut into pieces and scattered over about five miles of roadway. He had five hundred dollars in cash and no identity whatsoever. No one was taking any chances.

He spent most of Monday morning just touring the sidewalks, making sure that his presence in town was of interest to not a living soul—after all, wouldn't it be uncomfortable to think he had been expected—and it was after lunchtime before he got around to visiting the Faircliff "museum."

Naturally, the day before the election, there were plenty of people around. Nothing would have been more impossible than hiding his activities, so he decided he wouldn't try.

"Would anybody mind if I took some pictures?" he asked one of the elderly ladies who sat behind a table covered with green felt and collected admission and sold little printed guides. He picked up three copies and laid a ten-dollar bill beside the rest. "I've come all the way from Spokane to be here for the big day tomorrow, and I want to be able to remember everything."

He smiled his best boyish smile, but the old bag just blinked at him as if somebody were shining a light in her eyes. Then she looked down at the ten dollars and seemed to catch on.

"No flashbulbs," she said, counting out his change. "We don't allow any flashbulbs." It sounded like something intended to be chiseled into stone.

"No, no—no flashbulbs." He tried to smile again, and this time it seemed to work better. "Perhaps you ladies would allow me to . . . ?"

His camera was a Minox-C with certain custom modifications, and he pulled it out of his pocket and took a group portrait. He couldn't have made himself any more popular if he had brought cookies and Jack Daniels.

There were thirty-six exposures on his film roll, so he allowed himself plenty of opportunities to look like a tourist, taking pictures of the potted palms and the doors and the "No Smoking" signs and only getting to the contents of the glass cases when everyone had grown sufficiently used to his presence to have forgotten all about him.

He didn't need a flash; the film was ultra light sensitive, intended precisely for photographing documents. He took at least two exposures of everything that looked interesting, including all three pages of the celebrated essay, and then left, waving goodbye to the moneychangers in the temple.

"Pete" had been right. The handwriting was different.

Now all he had to do was get the film back to Langley and he was home free.

He was walking in the general direction of his motel, where he thought he might just get in his car and drive away, when he spotted a familiar face from one of the less comfortable periods of his life—the seven months he had been stationed in Zaïre, keeping track of the civil war there.

The guy's name had been Krebs or Krall, something like that. He would turn up every once in a while in Kinshasa, where he had hired out as a mercenary, and there were some gaudy stories in circulation about how he treated the problem of defections from his native army.

The word was that if anyone wasn't there for morning inspection, he would take out the man's whole platoon and run him to earth. If they didn't catch him, then they could draw lots among themselves to see who would take his place for punishment, so you could bet they always caught him. When they did, Krall—he was pretty sure it was Krall— would put ropes over the tops of a couple of good, stout trees and have his men pull them down until they were bent over like a pair of croquet hoops. The deserter would have a leg tied to the top of each tree by a short rope, and then the other ropes would be cut. The trees would snap back up like metal springs, and the poor bastard would be torn in half. Krall was the sort of person destined to make a lasting impression.

Exotic hobbies aside, he was a striking fellow, close to six three, very solid-looking, and very blond, even to the eyebrows. You might have thought he was an ex-Nazi, except that he was about twenty years too young. He probably would have enjoyed being a Nazi.

They had known each other distantly, the way people in roughly the same line of work do—not well, or even personally, but by report and by sight. For present purposes it was enough.

Apparently it was enough on both sides. Krall was leaning against a car, and when his eyes met Starkman's he bent down to say something through the window. Starkman ducked into a sidestreet, but not quickly enough to avoid being seen—and to see that Krall was coming after him.

Well, that settled that. He couldn't very well go back to his motel—except, perhaps, just to pick up his car—because if these people were on their toes they would find his room and have it staked out within forty-five minutes. And he couldn't try to leave town because there was only the main road in and out, and they could bottle that up easily enough. While he still had his camera full of exposed film in his pocket, he simply couldn't afford the risk.

These slobs couldn't have any idea what they were here protecting. The president of the United States is a changeling—nobody was stupid enough to trust a thug like Krall with that kind of secret. But once they got their hands on that film, they would know. And their bosses would know how close Austen was to pulling the chain on them. We couldn't have that.

So he had to get rid of the camera—send it back to Austen so he could put his jigsaw puzzle together and do whatever it was that he had to do then—and after that he could feel at liberty to worry about parochial interests like his own personal survival.

But before he could even do that, he had to get rid of Krall.

He had, he figured, no more than about a two- or three-block lead, probably not even that much. Krall would be on foot and probably alone—that was the way he would want it—but there was probably a car full of his friends cruising the streets. The plan would have to be to keep the main show inside and not let himself be seen until he was ready.

Starkman ducked into the first doorway that proved handy and found himself in a bait and tackle shop, which was a lucky break. He was packing a .32 revolver, but he figured the easiest way in the world of getting himself picked up by the police—and hence picked off by Krall and his friends; jails were too damned accessible—was to start shooting. Guns were too noisy. He would have to find something else.

What he found was a hunting knife with a seven-inch blade. It was the sort of thing that could be trusted to do a reasonably efficient job even on a lump of muscle like Krall, and it only cost fourteen ninety-five.

"Has this place got a back door?"

The man behind the counter looked at him a little strangely; then he said, sure, through the back—right where you'd expect it to be, mister. Outside, Starkman found himself in a small parking lot blocked on two sides by buildings. There was no one around.

He took the knife and cut away all the top part of the scabbard, leaving only what covered the blade. The idea was that if he wore the thing inside his waistband, where it wouldn't be seen, he wouldn't accidentally slice open a kidney but the knife would come out clean when he was ready to use it. The gun was in a holster up against his backbone, where he hoped it would stay.

And now for Krall.

It took him close to twenty minutes to find the goon—like cops, the heavies were never there when you wanted them. Starkman waited in the shadow of a florist shop's awning for half an hour before he saw his man. He showed himself, trying not to be too obvious about it, crossing the street almost under Krall's nose. Then it was just follow the leader.

Buildings with elevators were hard to come by in a town that size—hell, they had all the land in the world—but he finally tracked down a Ramada Inn. After that it was largely a question of timing. Krall had to be allowed to catch up a little and had to be lulled into believing that nobody had noticed him, but it wouldn't do for him to get close enough to do anything. There weren't any guarantees that *he* would have any inhibitions about the use of firearms.

So it was five blocks of tag—working the streetlights, trying to stay with the crowds of shoppers, keeping anything and anyone between himself and his tail while he made his way.

The Inn's lobby was reasonably quiet; why shouldn't it be at a few minutes before three in the afternoon? The coffee shop cashier was reading a movie magazine, and the newsstand seemed to be unoccupied. Starkman picked the elevator most completely out of the front desk's line of sight. It was a four-flight ride to the top.

And there he waited. Krall would hang around, watching the floor indicator, trying to figure out where his quarry was getting off, and then he would follow right along. He would be impatient by then—and maybe just a little annoyed. Like a lot of big men, he would be thinking about all the terrible things he was going to do to the lousy creep when he got his hands on him.

The lousy creep smiled, stepped into a vacant car, and stood there with his finger on the stop button. He even allowed himself to take out the hunting knife, balancing it carefully in his hand.

When he heard the little bell ping, prophesying Krall's arrival, he took his finger from the button, allowing the doors to snap closed, and turned off the power switch.

It was possible to imagine the little drama that was being rehearsed out in the hallway. Krall was looking around, seeing nothing but a double line of closed doors. By now he would be aware that he had made a mistake, that he didn't even know whether Starkman was registered here, that he should have checked at the desk, that what he should do now was go back down to the lobby and do that, and maybe wait around down there for Starkman to show himself again. He would be thinking that perhaps he had better call in his friends—that, yes, he was wasting his time up here.

Through the wall Starkman could hear the elevator button snapping back and forth under Krall's impatient thumb. As if that weren't enough, the light on his own control board kept flickering on and off. Our boy was in a hurry, and people in a hurry got careless, especially when they could probably tear a telephone book in half; that kind of strength could lead you to forget that you might have something to worry about from your puny fellow mortals. It was time to let him have his ride.

Starkman crowded into the corner in front, away from the door, where he figured he could keep out of sight the longest, and turned the power back on.

The elevator doors moved with almost insulting lethargy. But as soon as they were open even a little, Krall started forcing himself in sideways. The stupid jerk, before he noticed that he didn't have the place all to himself he was almost all the way inside. And then, when it finally hit him, he didn't even move. He seemed to be struck dumb with astonishment.

But Starkman didn't wait. As fast as he could, and with as much force behind it as he could muster, he straight-armed the knife into Krall's chest. He could feel the jolt as it deflected off a rib, but that didn't stop it; the blade buried itself right up to the hilt.

By every principle of anatomy, it should have been sticking right through Krall's heart, coming out the other side with any luck. Krall was dead, but some men didn't figure that out as fast as others. Krall might be the type who needed a moment or two before the message made its way upstairs: you're dead. So Starkman stepped back out of the way, leaving the knife just where it was. More than one corpse had had time to kill someone before it did the decent thing and crumpled to the floor.

Krall didn't look dead—merely surprised. It was a couple of seconds before he even seemed to notice the knife. Then he reached up, wrapped his thick fingers around the handle—well, good; then no one would have to be concerned about prints—and seemed to want to pull it out. It didn't come easily. The more he pulled at it, the more blood started welling down the front of his shirt. It was a painful thing to see; he seemed to be opening himself up like a tin can.

Quite suddenly, the message got through: you're dead. Krall simply fell forward, leaving Starkman to dodge out of the way. He fell on the butt end of the knife; there was a little groan, and then with terrible, writhing slowness he turned over on his side. Starkman put a finger against the carotid artery and thought perhaps he felt the last flutter of a heartbeat; then there was nothing. Krall's face was a mask of astonishment. His pale blue eyes were still open, and his hard features seemed tensed with expectation. He was dead, and it was the biggest surprise in the world.

Starkman turned off the power again. This wasn't a little bundle he wanted carried down to the lobby right away, where everybody could look at it. Somebody would come along soon enough, notice the open door, and start screaming bloody murder, because that was just exactly what they would find. But that might not be for five or ten more minutes, and by then Starkman planned to be long gone.

He had a package to get into the mails, and he would have the whole mob after him now, no holds barred. They would know they had something to scramble for.

It was going to be an interesting several hours.

VI

Frank Austen examined the photographs with painstaking care, even the ones that seemed to have nothing to do with his problem. After all, a man had died delivering this roll of film.

There was no doubt left—the writing on the high school essay bore no resemblance at all to that of the mature Simon Faircliff. This kid would have grown up to be somebody else entirely.

But the real clincher was the birth certificate.

"I did a blowup—see?" Timmler held up an eight-by-ten enlargement of the right footprint of Ray and Esther Faircliff's baby boy. "That's what you call an ironclad case. Your prints don't change."

"No, they don't. It's very convincing."

Tracing along the outside edge of the heel with the point of his pencil, Austen seemed to be confirming for himself the conclusive nature of this new evidence, as if the lines and whorls of his father-in-law's footprints were just naturally the sorts of things he would have committed to memory. More probably, however, he was only remotely conscious of the thing before his eyes.

"The point, though, is not to do any more convincing than necessary," he said quietly, giving the impression that he was merely thinking out loud. "There aren't any permanent secrets; someday somebody will put this thing together, whether we like it or not. With any luck, it might not be until we're all dead or too old to care—that would be better for everybody—but for now, for the foreseeable future, we've got to keep it as dark as we can. Most of us have got to believe in something; this little piece of news would tear the country into shreds."

It was dark outside; it had been dark for hours. The yard that stretched out beneath George Timmler's office window was covered with long yellowish smears from the searchlights up on the roof. Austen got up from his chair and looked out, trying to see the perimeter wire, but of course that was impossible. It was impossible to see anything clearly; it was that kind of world.

"I wonder how they happened to miss them," he said suddenly.

"Miss what?"

"The essay, and particularly the birth certificate. Certainly they've had plenty of time to remove all traces of the real Simon Faircliff; I just wonder how these two little items managed to be overlooked."

"It can happen." Timmler stirred uneasily in his seat, uncrossing his legs. Perhaps he had been asking himself the same question. "Maybe they didn't even know about the essay; things like that can lay around in somebody's bottom drawer for decades and then suddenly float to the surface. The birth certificate—well, maybe they didn't think it was worth the risk. After all, a forgery might be noticed, and an outright theft might really get people to wondering. And what if they got caught? Besides, suspicions would have to have reached a very dangerous level indeed before anybody was going to have the temerity to ask the president for a copy of his right footprint. Probably they thought it would be safer just to leave things as they were."

"I suppose that's probably it. Actually, that's the best advice for us too—just leave things as they are. We've got our proof. Let's just hope we never have to use it."

"What about the vice president? We'll have to tell him."

"Bob Donovan? That tower of strength? Will we?" Austen turned around and smiled. "Yes, I suppose we will—but not until it's all over. Do you think it'll ever be all over, George?"

"I don't know, boss. What do you think?"

"I don't know either."

They had been at it since before dawn that morning, and during working hours it had been necessary to maintain the fiction that they were busy with the normal Company workload, so perhaps they were beginning to get a trifle punchy. They had come so far—through two and a half years of lies and treachery and fear, months and months of knowing that the slightest error could mean the end of everything, literally everything—and they were alive and undetected. Of course it would be all over. In a few more days they would be either safe or in prison or dead, but in any case it would be over.

For perhaps an hour now there had been nothing left to do, nothing to decide, but for both of them, it seemed, it was impossible to go home.

George Timmler sat limply in one corner of his office sofa, his hands folded in his lap, his eyes on nothing. But it wasn't merely that he was tired.

"Did you tell Rutledge about Mike?" Austen asked, with all the delicacy one might have employed questioning a bereaved father about how he had broken the news to his surviving children. Timmler shook his head without even looking up.

"No, I thought it would be better if he didn't know until

after he gets back. Those two were pretty thick, you know. It wouldn't do for Earl to lose his temper."

"Are they on their way?"

"You know they are, Frank. Schneider, Ross, Rutledge, and Dexter—they've all been on their way for hours."

"That's right, I did know that." Austen smiled again, but with what seemed an enormous effort. "Sorry."

And they really were, all of them, on their way. At almost that precise moment Earl Rutledge was arriving at the Houston airport on the nine-forty-seven flight from Atlanta.

Before joining the Company twelve years before as one of George Timmler's protégés, Rutledge had worked as an undercover agent for the Bureau of Narcotics, and the odd mixture of secrecy and display he had learned in that job had become deeply ingrained in his character. He was a tall, uncouth, ferocious-looking man with the sort of deep-set, baggy eyes that made you believe that he really could have been a drug dealer. For all that he was a temperance Baptist and the faithful husband of his childhood sweetheart, he looked like nothing in the world so much as a sadistic, degenerate gangster. The Company had taken him out of his embroidered Levi leisure suits and his gold chains—he always wore a coat and tie now—but no one was going to mistake him for the fellow in the toothpaste ads.

So, recognizing the uselessness of striving for anonymity, he had chosen to emphasize his disquieting appearance, wearing his hair long and ragged and affecting the shiny three-piece suits and crocodile shoes of the prosperous hoodlum. A blind man could see him coming at five hundred yards, and he tended to scare the starch out of people.

At the same time, however, he almost never traveled anywhere under his own name and was probably the best man in the federal service at shaking a tail. His neighbors in Falls Church all believed that he was the regional sales manager for a firm of motorcycle-parts suppliers. He was, in other words, precisely the man for the job at hand—a job about which he had been told next to nothing.

"The guy's an investor," Mr. Timmler had informed him. "Oil, natural gas—there's a lot of money there, so he'll expect you to be nice to him."

"Am I supposed to be nice to him, Mr. Timmler?"

"No. You're supposed to present yourself and tell him

that a Mr. Storey sent you and that he's supposed to come along. If he gives you any static about it, you drag him out by the hair. Bring him back to Atlanta by plane and then rent a van and drive him up to Fishing Bay. It would be nice if he arrived there in no condition to give any clear account of the trip—we're not running a travel bureau."

"Fine."

Well, Rutledge didn't really mind if Mr. Timmler didn't confide in him. He had learned that it's when they do tell you a lot that you have something to worry about, for the simple reason that you're supposed to be all inspired to die trying if need be. Rutledge didn't particularly want to die trying. But this seemed to be a nice, straightforward snatch job; a change from shadowing Russian diplomats around Washington just to keep them on their toes, which was beginning to make him feel like a tour conductor.

He got his canvas suitcase away from the luggage people and took a bus into town, figuring he'd charge a cab ride to his expense account and pocket the difference. He had a family to think of.

Tycoons liked to be inaccessible; it was supposed to be one of the advantages of having all that money. But nobody was inaccessible to Mr. Timmler, who had supplied Rutledge with J. D. Guthrey's unlisted home telephone number—one of them. The guy seemed to have about four.

Old J. D.—for "Jethroe Dwaine"; you could hardly blame him for falling back on his initials—was an early riser, so if you put in a call to his study phone at about six-thirty in the morning you stood a good chance of his being the only person awake in the house.

Rutledge was an early riser, too. When you had three kids, and one of them was still under five, you just lost the habit of sleeping in. Bright and early, after he had taken his shower and carefully shaved his heavily pitted face, he sat down on the only chair in his hotel room and placed his call. The voice that answered was a rich baritone, the voice of someone with little experience of fear or defeat.

"Hello?"

"Mr. Guthrey?" Earl Rutledge automatically straightened up in his chair; it was the sort of reflex the born bosses of this world seemed to call up automatically as part of what the rest of us owed them. "Is this Mr. J. D. Guthrey?"

"Yes, of course it is; if you have the number you know that. Now who is this?"

That was fine. Mr. Guthrey wanted to start shoving right away. Rutledge grinned to himself, feeling better already. "This is someone from Mr. Storey," he answered curtly. "Mr. Storey—got that? This is someone you'd better find time in your busy day to see."

There was a short silence, perhaps no longer than three or four seconds, during which you could almost hear the wind in the phone lines. Mr. Guthrey must have been holding his breath.

"Come to my office this morning about eleven."

"Sorry." Rutledge shook his head and frowned, as if the man were there in the room with him. "That's out."

He looked at the map of the downtown area that he had picked up in the hotel lobby the night before. There ought to be somewhere . . . "Tell you what," he went on. "They got a place here they call 'Tranquility Park,' just a couple of blocks from your building; that ought to suit you. Meet me there about quarter after one. Look for a man reading the Atlanta *Citizen-Journal*."

"I've got an important lunch date this afternoon. I—"

"Break it."

Rutledge replaced the receiver in its cradle and looked at his watch. It was only a few seconds after six-forty; he had hours and hours ahead of him with no demands at all on his time. He would go down and open the coffee shop for breakfast, and then maybe when the stores opened at nine he would go see whether he couldn't find something to give his wife for their sixteenth anniversary.

Thin-blooded Southern boy that he was, Rutledge hated cold weather. Washington was bad enough, but three years ago he had spent part of the winter working a stakeout in Vermont and damn near died. Even with gloves on, his hands sometimes got so stiff he couldn't unzip his fly to take a leak. The experience had almost made him wish he were still down in Florida, busting cocaine smugglers. He had told Mr. Timmler that if he'd wanted to freeze to death he would have joined the Mounties, and—so far—no one had ever again suggested that the Company might have a use for him above the snow line.

So he was reasonably miserable waiting on a park bench in

the raw Gulf wind, although, quite frankly, he was willing to concede that it was his own damn fault. His wife had warned him that he would need his heavy overcoat, but he had thought, oh no, Texas . . .

Guthrey was already ten minutes late, and if he didn't turn up in another ten Rutledge was going to stumble over to his dazzling fifteen-story office building and, in Mr. Timmler's phrase, "drag him out by the hair."

As a means of taking his mind off his own physical discomfort, he tried to interest himself in the paper he had bought during his layover in Atlanta to serve as a means of identification. Three days after a presidential election there was lots of news, but since most of the articles, at least on that page, had to do with strictly local races, Rutledge quickly found that his attention was wandering; he really didn't much care who was the new Cobb County supervisor.

He looked at his watch for perhaps the twentieth time in as many minutes and decided, reluctantly, that good old J. D. wasn't going to show up. For this kind of appointment people were either there on the tick or not there at all. You didn't come breezing in late with some story about how you had lost track of the hour. Fine. If that was the way Guthrey wanted to play it, then he'd get his way. Mr. Timmler had recommended a minimum of fuss, but the orders had been to reel the guy in.

Rutledge got up from his bench, a little stiff in the knees—good old Mike, the lucky bastard, was out there in sunny California; it didn't seem likely he'd be much worried about the cold—refolded his newspaper along the original creases, and stuffed it into a trash barrel. It was a five-block walk to the corner of Rusk and Capitol, where Mr. Guthrey sat behind his big mahogany desk and played with his millions; maybe he just needed to be reminded that in the real world when the mountain came to Mohammed it usually fell down on him with a thud.

He hadn't gotten more than a block and a half when a few fugitive words, the broken pieces of a radio news broadcast that had drifted through the open doorway of a Baskin-Robbins ice cream store, stopped him dead in his shoes.

"Guthrey . . . noted financier . . . suicide . . . survived by . . ." And then, before Rutledge had even made it over the threshold, the stupid bastard of an announcer was reading the weather.

"What was that all about?" he asked the woman behind the counter, a white-haired grandmotherly type whose skin was gathered in pouches all over her face. "Did Guthrey take himself off?"

But the only answer he got was a shrug of the shoulders and an annoyed, "Who listens?" That sort of thing, apparently, had become so much a matter of course that it slipped below the level of conscious life.

He kept going, with a certain urgency now, until he came to the site of the Guthrey financial empire and stepped in through the revolving door. The atmosphere alone would have told him everything he needed to know; the place was like an undiscovered tomb.

But there was a security guard. There was always a security guard; nobody was ever that dead. Rutledge stepped up to him in as oblique a manner as he could contrive and tried on a rueful smile.

"Say—are they still doing business up there or what?" he asked in a general, conversational tone of voice. He wouldn't want anybody to get the idea he was prying.

The guard shook his head. "Not much." He raised his eyes as if to indicate all the floors and floors of empty offices above him. "Everybody was pretty upset. I guess they all went home. J. D. was pretty popular, you know."

J. D. Wonderful—when you were dead everybody was your intimate friend.

"Why do you suppose he did it?"

"Who knows?"

"No . . . no . . . I understand . . . no, it couldn't be helped . . . no, you come back in, Earl—we'll check it out through regular channels. Goodbye."

George Timmler replaced the receiver of his office telephone and sighed. It had been a bad day all round.

"He says they found Guthrey in his car at the end of his driveway. He's supposed to have shot himself with a .38 police special; his wife told the cops that he kept it in his glove compartment. They're buying it as a straight suicide."

Austen nodded heavily. "That makes all four. A hit-and-run, a mugging, and now a pair of suicides. I feel kind of bad about Storey; we promised we'd protect him."

"There aren't any guarantees in this business, Frank. Storey wasn't born yesterday. He knew that."

Yes, Austen knew that too. And he didn't suppose that Chester Storey, if he had had any time to consider the question while a couple of Yates's goons were hanging him from a coat hook in his own bedroom clothes closet, would have thought to complain that the Central Intelligence Agency hadn't kept up its end of the bargain. He wondered what a man did think about while he was being garroted with a half-inch-wide leather belt.

"I'd say that Diederich made a clean sweep," he said, leaning against the narrow edge of Timmler's desk. "I'd say he's been characteristically thorough and imaginative."

"Wonderful—but why?" Timmler was sitting with his chair tilted so far back that only his toes were in contact with the floor. He was an old hand, and murder was hardly something that was new to his experience of the world. Still, he looked as if he had been knocked right off his feet by the sheer senseless brutality of this last day of coordinated extermination. "What did he think he had to gain?"

"I think what worried him was what he might have to lose. After all, the election is over. He didn't need those guys anymore; from this point on they were nothing more than a dangerous liability. And he's known at least since they killed Starkman that we were on to him. I think he was just cleaning house." And then all at once Austen laughed. It wasn't a very pleasant laugh. "But let's not get too outraged, George. Maybe he's done us a favor."

"What the hell are you talking about?" Timmler thrust himself forward, bringing the front legs of his chair down with a snap. "What's that supposed to mean, Frank?"

Austen could only smile. "What were we supposed to do with them, George?" he asked finally. "Put them on scout's honor not to tell a soul, and then pack them off home as soon as the dust had settled? Remember, the Russians knew those four names just as well as we did—Tidyman, Guthrey, Finch, Storey. They're all in the KGB files. Could we have afforded to let any of them run around loose? Even Storey? Like I said—maybe Diederich's done us a favor. Now the blood can be on his hands instead of ours."

After her husband's death, Sylvia Burgess had never sold the vast Norman house in McLean, Virginia, where they had lived ever since his first term in Congress. For a while she had stayed holed up in their much smaller residence in Connecticut—presumably nursing her grief for a man who, by every account, was everything any woman could want—and then she had traveled, mostly within Europe. Finally, when she had begun to feel the pressing attractions of Simon Faircliff's wooing, she had moved back to McLean.

In recent months there had been several important parties at the Burgess mansion. Simon seemed to prefer it to the White House for his less grandiose entertainments, and the fact that Sylvia was the hostess of record made it easier for him to mingle with people. Also, probably, it was his indirect way of making everyone understand that his relationship with the beautiful widow Burgess was on a special footing.

Frank Austen had been inside as a guest three or four times.

The house was on about seven acres of wooded land, well back from the road, and this evening there would be no one home except Sylvia Burgess. The president would be calling about nine, and on occasions like this not even the Secret Service was allowed near the place. For Austen's purposes, the arrangement was perfect.

George Timmler let him off about a quarter-mile from the gate. They would meet again at the same spot after Austen had phoned from the house. If he didn't phone, then George was to take certain actions on his own.

"Good luck," Timmler said, smiling tensely. "Don't get arrested for burglary."

"I'll try not to."

When the car had driven off, Austen started on his way along the well-paved but lightly traveled road that threaded its way through this little island of rural opulence. Within a mile of him lived five or six of the richest men in Washington, and that was saying something. As soon as he got to the Burgess property line, he threw his heavy coat across the barbed wire that topped the eight-foot fence and scrambled over. He didn't want to be seen going through the gate.

It had rained earlier in the day, and the grass was wet. Austen clutched his briefcase and walked along like someone only half-awake. He didn't seem to notice anything; he hardly seemed to be alive inside his own skin. The burden under which he almost visibly labored appeared to have ground all normal human sensibility out of him.

After a while he looked up and saw the lights of Sylvia

Burgess's house, and an expression of pain briefly crossed his face.

"Why, Frank—I didn't hear your car."

She was standing in the doorway, wearing a black-and-white evening dress. Even in her late forties, with her black hair heavily streaked with silver, she was a beautiful woman. She smiled, surprised, gracious, wondering at the meaning of this intrusion.

"I walked. Are you going to invite me in?"

She smiled again and stepped back to allow him to pass.

"I'll be expecting guests soon, Frank. Is something the matter?"

"One guest," he corrected, brushing aside the question. "And the president won't be here for another two hours. That's what I wanted to talk to you about."

VII

"It isn't true—it couldn't be. You're lying, Frank."

She was standing in the middle of her living room, her fists tightly clenched, shaking so badly that Frank Austen was half afraid she might simply fall down. She had just listened to a tape recording of Yates's confession, detailing how—and for whom—he had murdered her husband. It was the crowning piece of evidence.

"It's true, right enough." He allowed himself to sag into a chair, resting his forehead in the palm of his hand. He felt the full weight of the last several days at that moment, and what he wouldn't have given for a few hours of dreamless sleep probably wasn't worth having.

"You know the whole story now, Sylvia. You're one of only five people outside the Soviet Union who have any idea that any of this is happening, and two of them are on the wrong side. Have you bothered to ask yourself why I've gone to the trouble of telling you all this?"

"You're a monster, Frank," she said, holding her arms across her breast as if the room had suddenly turned cold.

"Am I?" He smiled sadly and sank back even deeper into his chair. "I suppose I must be by now. Is that what it takes to realize that beside this trouble the lives of people like us don't really count for very much? Your husband was a fine man. Perhaps by rights he should have been elected president, and instead Messrs. Diederich and Faircliff sent some creep out to murder him. But believe me, that's the least of anybody's problems right now. You've got to understand what's at risk."

"Then go ahead and murder me too." Her fists were still clenched, and her whole body was rigid with defiance. It was at once ludicrous and heroic.

"Come on, Sylvia, think about what you're saying. Suppose I do that, and suppose I wait here beside your dead body until Simon comes and knocks on the front door. I've got a Smith & Wesson .357 in my briefcase, with drilled points. That's a very efficient killing machine—I can send him to hell as he stands wiping his shoes on your welcome mat. But what happens then? What happens to the country while everybody tries to figure out why the director of Central Intelligence has personally snuffed the president of the United States?"

"Is that what you're afraid of? Getting caught?" The expression in her eyes turned from simple anger into something like contempt, but Austen only shook his head.

"You're right if you think I want to save myself," he said finally. "And my motives are at least partly as selfish as you suspect—I'm human, after all. But you and I don't matter very much. If I have to, if there isn't any other way, I'll sit quietly in my cell and keep my mouth shut while they decide how high they want to hang me, but the secret won't depend just on my silence. Somebody will figure out the truth, or some version of it. And is anybody ever going to be able to govern again once Simon Faircliff has been exposed?"

"These things never stay secrets. You said that yourself."

"No, they don't." He nodded in agreement, glad that at last they were talking like people with a common set of purposes—that was something. "But being fair to Simon Faircliff doesn't matter either. What do you think, Sylvia? How much grief do you imagine people can take all at once? All I'm trying to do is buy a little time for us, for all of us. Think—what would your husband have wanted done?"

And there they were, the widow and the spy, beyond vengeance or love or even the fear of death; they were excluded from the luxury of such personal considerations. They no longer had that privilege.

"I don't know, Frank." She sat down on the corner of the loveseat, her feet drawn under her, making her look surprisingly young and vulnerable. "I still can't believe that any of this is true."

"Believe this—and not as a threat, merely as a practical consideration—if I didn't imagine I could convince you that I'm doing what has to be done, you'd already be dead."

She was surprised and perhaps frightened for just a moment, and then the sense of what he had said impressed itself upon her and she waited for him to continue. Austen opened his briefcase and took out what appeared to be an ordinary pocket-size transistor radio, tossing it onto the seat cushion next to her.

"When he comes, you take that little gizmo and retire to your bedroom. You'll be able to hear every word we say down here, and when I'm finished I'll just leave. I won't lay a glove on you, I give you my word. Then, if you want to, you can call the cops and they can probably arrest me before I've left the property. Okay?"

Austen checked his watch. It was eight thirty-two. "Is he ever early?"

"Sometimes—not very often." She smiled to herself for a moment, and then, as if at some chilling recollection, the smile died away. "More often he's late."

"Well, we can't play the possibilities tonight."

His briefcase was lying open on the floor. The .357 was wrapped in a towel, and beside it was a portable tape recorder in a black leather carrying case. There were a few other things as well.

Austen rose and took two small listening devices no larger than poker chips out of his pocket, removed the paper from their adhesive backings, and stuck them both under the octagonal table. There was a portable bar in one corner of the room, and he picked up one of the glasses clustered together on a tray and covered the bottom with a white powder from a small aluminum capsule of the type that might once have held a roll of camera film. He left the glass standing by itself and went back to his briefcase to take out the gun. It was a massive, ugly thing, impossible to conceal. Austen hardly seemed to know what to do with it.

"You'll really kill him?" she asked. "You owe him everything; he loves you as if you were his own son."

"Have you got any ice?"

"What?"

"Ice." He glanced impatiently around the room.

"Yes—all you need. Why?"

"You don't want to know."

She went into the kitchen and came back a few moments later with a silver bucket, full to the brim. It had been a kind of test; Austen had made a point of knowing the location of every phone in the house and had followed along behind her, listening beside the pantry door for the grinding of a dial, but there had been nothing. She had, in fact, come back. There had been no slamming of a side door as she ran for a neighbor's house, so perhaps she really was ready at last to wait and see.

She gave him the bucket, and he placed it on top of the bar and watched her wiping her hands on the skirt of her dress, as if she had lost all interest in how she looked or how much the thing might cost to dry-clean. So simple an action—and yet a woman's way of declaring a state of emergency.

"Don't forget this," he said, picking up the transistor radio from where she had left it on the loveseat. She nodded and put it in a hidden pocket of her skirt. "All you have to do is turn it on."

"All right."

Neither of them made a move to sit down, so they stood there together in the center of the room for the next twenty minutes, until they heard the sound of the presidential limousine grinding over the gravel driveway.

"What'll he do about his driver?" Austen asked, his hand tightening on the butt of the .357.

"Nothing. The car will let him out in front of the house and then go. He phones when he's ready to leave." She lowered her eyes to the floor. The tacit admission that she was Simon Faircliff's mistress was apparently more than she could face.

Austen glanced away, giving her a moment in which to compose herself. "When he rings the bell, answer it. Let him in and close the door behind him. After that, your part in this business is over."

"It'll never be over—for either of us."

Austen didn't reply. He changed the cassette and hit the record button on the portable tape recorder in his briefcase and closed the lid. There was nothing left to do.

A visitor would walk straight through the entrance hall into the living room, which was at right angles. So there was no problem about remaining concealed; all you had to do was stand in the middle of the carpet and wait.

When the doorbell chimed, they both started.

It was perhaps the longest moment of Frank Austen's life as he listened to the door being opened, to the murmur of voices, and finally, to the sound of the door closing. And it took every fiber of resolve he had to step out into the entranceway and point his huge weapon at Simon Faircliff's chest.

The great man, to give him his due, never even blinked. He just looked at the revolver, and looked at Sylvia Burgess, and smiled.

"Good evening, Frank," he said.

Even after Sylvia Burgess had gone upstairs the two men stood where they were in the entranceway, so still they hardly seemed to be breathing.

"May I take my coat off?" Faircliff asked finally, bringing his fingers up to touch the surface of his lapels.

"No, you may not. Just come into the living room and sit down, and keep your hands out where I can see them."

Faircliff laughed quietly, as if the melodrama of the situation amused him—or, perhaps, to imply his embarrassment over this newly discovered streak of shabby heroics in his trusted lieutenant—and started forward, his arms slightly raised, seeming to mock Austen's caution.

"Would you like to tell me what this is all about?" He sat on the loveseat, exactly the spot Sylvia Burgess had occupied, his fingers laced together in his lap.

"You know what it's about, Simon. The old man didn't die in that nursing home fire of yours. We've still got him, and we know the whole story." Austen checked his watch. It was twelve minutes after nine. "Diederich will have been arrested by now. It's all over."

There was a short, stunned silence, and then the president of the United States merely raised his eyebrows as if to say, *Well, what do you know?*

"And what are you going to do, now that it's all over?" A faint smile played on Faircliff's lips as he spoke. "What's the plan, Frank? Are you going to drag me onto the Senate floor so they can impeach my ass? I'd love to see that show."

"No, Chief. I'm just going to kill you. And tomorrow I'll acquaint the new president with the Soviet Union's real strategic posture, and he can do what he likes with your precious treaty."

For a moment—in fairness it must be said, only a moment—someone might have imagined that Simon Faircliff was afraid. But it passed off quickly enough, leaving no trace. Another, lesser man might have needed some sort of prop, a cigarette perhaps, something to steady his hand and give him a chance to show his indifference, but not Faircliff.

"*Et tu, Brute?*" The smile was allowed to become fixed, and he shook his head slowly. "No, I haven't any right to be surprised. You would have been the one to figure out our little intrigue. Howard always told me it would be you. It looks like I've been harboring a viper in my bosom."

"Are you trying to make me feel bad, Simon? Okay, I feel bad, but that doesn't change anything."

"Yes, I believe you do," he said, the smile dissolving into a sad, knowing kindness.

And it had its effect. Austen sat down, simply because he had to, and the huge revolver rested flat on his knee. He looked at Faircliff, who had betrayed every claim to loyalty—his own numbered among them—and he felt like Judas Iscariot.

"Goddamn you, you bastard. I ought to blow you away one piece at a time. I . . ."

But he found it impossible to go on. His voice was choked with a strange compound of emotions, ranging all the way from hatred to a kind of aggrieved tenderness for this man who had somehow assumed a father's right to plague his conscience and his love. Perhaps at that moment Faircliff could have risen from his seat, walked the three or four steps that separated them, and taken the gun from his hand. And perhaps he knew as much.

In any case, he never moved.

"Don't think too badly of me, Frank. It's the easiest thing in the world to lose control over your own life. It happens all the time."

The hands that had been lying knitted together in his lap came apart, with the palms up, as if weighing out the good and the evil that had become the sum of his experience and finding them more or less equal. It was a curious, caressing gesture, as if the apology—or explanation, or whatever it was—was being rendered more for Austen's sake than for his own.

"I just wanted to be president," he went on, his open hands slowly curling into fists. "It was something I had to have, or I couldn't be everything I had inside me. I don't know whether I wanted it for them, or for this country, or just for myself—or maybe even trying to say it like that, or to explain it at all, makes it into a lie by assuming it can be simplified into something like wanting. But you've got to believe me, Frank, that I really thought I could do good things. Probably that was where I went wrong, where Howard always had the advantage over me. He understood exactly what he was doing."

"What was he doing? Where was it all leading, Simon?"

Slowly, in such subtle increments that there seemed to be no real change at all, Faircliff's expression altered until he seemed almost stricken. His face seemed to grow thick, as if it had become a mere mask of lifeless, unfeeling flesh. And then, all at once, he touched his forehead with the back of his hand and held it there for a few seconds, and the impression was dispelled. He even managed his peculiar sad smile again.

"You know what the wonderful thing about democratic government is, Frank?—maybe all governments; I wouldn't know. They limit the men who lead them so that treason becomes almost impossible. Maybe that's the secret of their survival.

"It could never be just me and Howard, up there putting the fix in; every move we made was the common property of dozens of good, patriotic public servants, any one of whom would have screamed his goddamned lungs out if he thought his president was betraying the national interest. The truly corrupt man is rarer than you would imagine. We discovered we were watched every minute, that everything we did had to seem to make perfect sense, had to seem to be part of a grand plan we had worked out with State and Defense and the NSC—our hands were tied. It's astonishing, isn't it? The Russians plant two of their men in the Oval Office, and they're helpless. Well, they were going to change all that."

Frank Austen shifted uneasily in his chair, wondering whether he dared to listen to the confirmation of his own worst fears.

"The treaty—they wanted a first-strike capacity?"

Faircliff nodded. "Very good, Frank; you were always a quick study. That's what they wanted. And eventually, within a few years, they would have gotten it. They had it all worked out, just what I was supposed to do for them in my second term, how I was to use all that wonderful new power to implement the goddamned thing. In another two, maybe three years, you would have been standing there nearly naked.

"I don't know whether they would have been prepared to use it—to go for broke like that. They would have sustained some damage in a nuclear war, but perhaps not more than they could have lived with. Or maybe they just wanted it for blackmail. I don't know."

He shook his head, and that haunted look that Austen had seen only two or three other times returned to his eyes. "You've got to believe me, Frank. I never wanted it to come to anything like this. I'm almost glad . . ."

"Get real," Austen murmured, his voice low but brutally cold as he leaned forward, the .357 righting itself in his hand. "Don't go soft on me now. You made this particular mess all by yourself, Simon, with just a little help from poor suckers like me. Don't try to hang it all on them or us or anybody else."

Faircliff seemed by turns surprised, and then wounded, and then defiantly angry, almost proud—almost arrogant. Austen was left to wonder why he had spoken, why it had seemed so important to him that in the last few minutes of his life Faircliff should not seem to be broken by regret. Did it really matter if this man, to whom he had given what seemed like his whole adult life, if Simon Faircliff went not gently into that good night? Yes, it really did.

"Good—you're right." Faircliff let his hands fall cupped over his knees, and he grinned, almost demonically. "I did, didn't I. And I almost pulled it off, too."

"Yes—you almost did."

"Did I? I wonder." His eyes narrowed, and he tilted his head to one side. "How long have you known, Frank?"

Austen's face looked as if it had turned to wood; even his eyes seemed lifeless. He seemed to have lost forever the power of independent movement. "Not quite two and a half years."

"Jesus."

"You did a lot of damage when you turned that report of mine over to your friends. We had to repair the leaks."

"I have to hand it to you, Frank; you played it very well."

"Thanks." Austen looked down at the gun he had been holding so long it seemed to have become an extension of his arm, to be roused a few seconds later by the sound of Simon Faircliff politely clearing his throat. Apparently he wasn't the only one who had decided it was time to get to the point.

"Okay—what happens now?" There was a smile on Faircliff's face, as if he were determined to take the matter with a good grace.

"Now you have a choice."

Austen rose out of his chair, surprised at the stiffness of his knees. He must have been holding himself rigid as a board, never even realizing it. He crossed over to the portable bar, set down the revolver, and dropped a couple of ice cubes in the glass he had prepared earlier. The stuff was supposed to work faster if it was in a cold solution. There were half a dozen bottles of mixer on a shelf underneath. He took a bitter lemon—Simon's favorite, what the hell—pried off the cap, and poured it into the glass.

"You have a choice," he repeated, picking up the revolver again as he carried the glass over to the table in front of the loveseat. "You can have a drink, and that will be the end of that, or you can force me to shoot you. Either way, you're dead. What you get to choose is what happens after you die, and I suppose you're bright enough to figure out the consequences either way."

Faircliff regarded the glass with distaste—it would have been unfair to characterize the reaction as fear—and the palms of his hands slid down his thighs, as if he were trying to wipe them off. "I assume the idea is that it should look like a natural death; even at the last you're thinking of my public image, aren't you, Frank?" He raised his eyes to his son-in-law's face; the expression in them was not friendly. At last he allowed himself to point to the glass. "What have you got in there?"

"You'll have a stroke," Austen replied. "There's a mild sedative mixed in, so you won't even be awake when it happens. It's the latest wrinkle; it's undetectable, and you'll never feel a thing."

"And I suppose if I force you to use that gun of yours you'll make it as nasty as you can manage. Am I right?" His eyes retained their mixture of hostility and comtempt.

Austen shook his head. "I wasn't trying to insult you,

Simon; it never entered my mind that you'd be very intimidated by the idea of physical pain."

"Well, thanks for that anyway."

Quite unexpectedly, Faircliff smiled again. It was a nice smile, the sort that said, *Don't worry about it, pal. I understand it isn't anything personal.* "How long does it take?"

"I haven't any idea—not more than a few minutes."

"A stroke, you say?" The smile seemed to have taken up permanent residence; now he was afraid. "A nice old-fashioned cerebral hemorrhage—how delightful."

"That's right, Mr. President. Just like the one you arranged for your late wife." Austen had been surprised by the sound of his own voice. In that first moment he would have given much for the words to have been left unsaid—Simon Faircliff went almost white. Around the nose and mouth, he looked like he was dead already.

"How did you find out about that?" he asked, the words coming slowly and after a long silence.

"Just a lucky guess." Austen hardened himself to go on, loathing himself, sick of the very air he breathed. "Why not? You killed Boothe, and Burgess. We got Yates too, you know, and he sang for us like Pavarotti. You killed Pete Freestone, or maybe he was such an unimportant little schmuck that Howard Diederich had him taken off without even bothering to mention it to you. You tried to kill Zinoviev—you even tried to kill me once. Why not your wife? Why should I believe that anyone dies from natural causes around you? What happened, Simon? Did she hear something she wasn't supposed to, or did you just get tired of her?"

Simon Faircliff looked like a sick man. Tiny beads of sweat were beginning to break out on his forehead, and his hands, for the first time, were shaking—at least, they would have been shaking if he had dared to lift them from where they rested on his thighs. In a matter of twenty or thirty seconds, it seemed, his flesh had accepted the fact of its own mortality.

"Does Dottie have any idea?" It was the first time he had mentioned his daughter, and his eyes, no longer defiant or humorous or forgivingly ironic, were large and moist with a terrible anguish.

"No."

In the moment that passed, perhaps they both understood the solid reality of the lie and the reason for it. Or perhaps it was nothing more than imagination—or guilt, or wishful thinking—that made Austen somehow feel that Faircliff now regarded himself as having passed into his son-in-law's debt.

"Well, I suppose I can be grateful for that." He drew a deep breath and let it out, exactly as if he expected it to be his last. "I won't look for excuses. Everything you say is perfectly true—except about you, Frank. Howard didn't tell me until it was too late. Maybe he was jealous; anyway, he's always hated you. But Mildred? No, I wasn't tired of her. I did what I had to."

He closed his eyes for a moment, whether to see something more clearly or to blot it out there was no way of knowing, but when he opened them again he was once more in control of himself.

"I don't know—maybe it's impossible to live with someone for next to nineteen years and keep a secret like that from them. She found out. Not everything, but enough. Don't ask me how; she just found out. She confronted me with it one day—'You're not who you say you are. You're somebody else.' I thought my blood was turning to ice water. And she wouldn't leave it alone; she went over it and over it, crying and carrying on until I thought she'd drive herself mad. She didn't leave me any choice at all."

"So you killed her."

"So I killed her. Howard provided the means—Howard could always be counted on to provide the means—and I killed her." Faircliff nodded. "And now that you've had your full pound of flesh, you've got to promise me something, Frank. I want your word that Dottie will never know."

"She'll never hear it from me."

But Faircliff seemed to have lost interest. Instead he was looking at the glass as if he were trying to face that down too. With no warning, he picked it up, brought it to his lips, and drained off about three quarters in what seemed like a single swallow. He put the glass back on the table with a smack.

"You see?" he said, his eyes blazing. "I can keep my part of the bargain, even if you never asked it. Oh God! I think I can feel it already."

"I don't suppose so, Simon. It'll take a little longer than that."

"You're probably right." He managed a weary smile. "You'll have to forgive me; I've never poisoned myself before."

After a few seconds he grew calmer. Austen wondered whether perhaps that wasn't the effect of the sedative.

"You know where I grew up, Frank?" he said at last, leaning back against the cushions of the loveseat. And then he laughed softly. "Neither do I. In some home for 'the children of enemies of the state.' I haven't the faintest idea where it was, and I can't remember having lived anywhere before that. Maybe my folks were killed in the revolution. Anyway, when that guy came to bring me to Leningrad, I thought they were going to kill me too. 'This is it,' I thought. 'Now it'll be my turn.' Not a bad guess for a little kid, right?"

And he laughed again. By now he was visibly sagging; he seemed to be using his arms to keep himself braced up. Austen rose from his chair, leaving the revolver behind him on the seat—no one would need it anymore—and knelt down beside him as, slowly, he began to slip sideways. He lifted Faircliff's feet from the floor, helping him to lie down.

"You won't leave me alone, will you, Frank?"

"No. I'm right here."

Twenty minutes later, when Sylvia Burgess came down from her bedroom, she found him still kneeling there, holding Simon Faircliff's dead hand in his own.

"I couldn't hear anything anymore. The radio . . . My God, I couldn't believe . . . It's all true; it's . . . I thought . . ."

But Austen didn't answer.

VIII

It had begun raining about two-fifteen that afternoon. Sitting in his study, Austen could hear the steady drumming on the roof, and his big picture window simply swam, distorting the world outside like a mirror in the fun house.

Four months had passed since President Faircliff's funeral. He was buried in Arlington Cemetery, about a hundred feet from the Kennedy gravesite, and that Tuesday morning had turned out to be the last of the fine weather. It had seemed to rain every day that winter.

But at least it had been a nice morning for the procession.

Austen had walked with his wife behind the gun carriage bearing the president's body. The sun was shining and there was no wind; the three miles of the march route had been almost a pleasure. Dottie had hung on his arm the entire distance, and the world, which had seen her over live satellite broadcast, had been suitably impressed with the calm, almost Roman dignity of her bearing. When the show was over, he had driven her to the airfield at Langley, where she boarded a Company plane to take her to California. That had been the price of her performance. He hadn't seen her since.

Everyone has a limit, and Dottie, on the night of her father's death, had apparently reached hers. Austen hardly felt himself to be in a position to criticize.

Sylvia Burgess had known just what she was supposed to do. She had waited fifteen minutes to give Austen a chance to get away unseen, and then she phoned the duty officer at the White House to tell him that Simon had been taken with some kind of seizure and appeared to be dead. Austen made it back to the road, where George Timmler picked him up and brought him home. He had to be there when the inevitable telephone call came.

He still carried his briefcase—with the things it contained, it was hardly the sort of item he wanted to leave lying around in Sylvia Burgess's front room—and he put it on the desk in his study and went into his bedroom to stretch out on the bed. He was so tired his teeth ached. It was close to eleven; Dottie was downstairs watching the tail end of a Richard Widmark movie on television.

He wasn't even aware that he had closed his eyes when the phone jolted him awake. According to his alarm clock, the time was eleven-fourteen. It was Bruce Wilders, the assistant chief of staff and one of Diederich's boys.

"Frank? Can you come over here right away? We've got a problem, and I can't raise Howard anywhere."

"What is it? What's going on?"

"Is this a secure line, Frank?" You could almost see Wilders glancing nervously over his shoulder; he was probably a lot more worried about the *Post* than about foreign spies.

"Just tell me what the problem is Bruce," Austen snapped.

"I don't know how to break it to you, Frank. The chief's dead."

There was a long pause. Austen counted off the seconds on his watch, wondering what the normal lag time for paralyzed surprise could be. He settled on six. "What happened?"

"He just died. He was over at that Burgess woman's place, and he died. We don't know anything more about it than that. I don't know what to do—I can't get hold of Howard."

"The first thing you do, stupid, is get him back into his own bed at the White House. Send a car and a couple of people you can trust to keep their mouths shut and fetch him home. I don't want my wife reading in the papers how her father died *in flagrante*. Where's the vice president?"

"He's home in Minnesota, Frank. We didn't know this was going to happen."

"You're a horse's ass, Bruce."

He hung up the phone and went into the hallway. There was a band of light showing under Dottie's bedroom door.

It was a purely nervous reaction—for days now he had had very little sleep, and the strain, of course, was somehow always worse at the end. And less than an hour and a half ago he had murdered the president of the United States. Suddenly he found he had to put an arm against the wall to keep from falling over. For a moment his whole body felt as if it weighed about four hundred pounds. The backs of his hands were tingling.

But what oppressed him most was the almost irresistible desire to run downstairs, get in the car, and drive away. Dottie had to be told, but he would have given several fingers from either hand not to be the one to tell her.

"Come on," he whispered to himself. "Don't crack up on me now."

The distance was about fifteen feet. Austen paced it off, keeping careful track of the number of steps, and pushed open the bedroom door. Dottie was seated at her vanity table, brushing out her hair for the night.

"Something I can do for you?" she asked. Austen went

over and sat down on the corner of the bed; they weren't more than four or five feet apart. He laced his fingers together and rested the points of his elbows on his knees. "I got a call a couple of minutes ago. It was from Bruce Wilders at the White House."

"Well?" She was twisted around, peering into his face. After eight years of marriage, she knew her husband well enough to see that something was very wrong; you could read that knowledge in her eyes. "Well?" she repeated. "What's the matter, Frank?"

"He says your father died a few minutes ago. I'm sorry, Dottie."

It was impossible to predict how people were going to react to that kind of news, and in this case the situation was grotesquely complicated. Anything was possible.

Other things would come later, but in that moment Dottie's face contracted with grief, the lines around her mouth deepening, and her eyes filled with very real tears. It was painful to witness. Her shoulders hunched forward in a way suggestive of an almost physical suffering.

"I'm sorry." Austen put his hand out and, as she grasped it, pulled her toward himself. In a moment they were sitting with their arms around each other, and both of them were crying.

"I have to go in," he murmured finally. "I can't take you with me—I wish I could. Will you be okay by yourself for a while? Would you like me to call someone? I'm sorry, sweetheart."

"No." She shook her head, as if trying to drive the tears from her eyes. "No, really. I'll be fine. I understand—you go ahead."

"You're sure?"

"I'm sure. You go ahead."

She was making it so easy for him; he felt like a perfect monster. All he could think of on the drive into Washington was the fact that he was guilty of murder, that he had betrayed both father and daughter, that he had killed every possibility of trust. The walls between himself and his wife were too thick to be torn down now, and they were entirely of his own design and construction. Reasons hadn't the slightest importance; that was just the way things were.

Naturally, everything at the White House was in a perfect

turmoil. Austen arrived just in time to watch his father-in-law's corpse being carried up to the East Wing bedrooms in a blanket.

Bruce Wilders was practically in tears, but one gradually realized that this was more because his real boss wasn't there to tell him what to do than because he was concerned for either the country or Simon Faircliff.

He's Howard's pet monkey, not mine, Simon had said once, shaking his head in amused resignation. *I'm sure Howard finds a use for him.*

"I don't understand what's happened to Howard," Wilders kept saying. He was a slight, natty little man, with tortoise-shell glasses and short blond hair that he kept carefully combed, but the strain of the last hour was doing bad things to him. For starters, he was sweating so much that he seemed to find it necessary to keep his handkerchief ready in his hand every minute. "I just don't understand—it's like he's dropped off the face of the earth."

"Forget about Howard. Howard's going to be out of a job when the new president finds his feet." The idea seemed to hit Wilders like a clenched fist. He blinked a couple of times and then felt compelled to wipe his face all over again.

At quarter to two they were notified that Air Force One was about to take off from Minneapolis. Donovan had already been administered the oath of office by his father, who was a retired federal appeals court judge, and everyone who was anyone—and who cared about their position in the new scheme of things—would be at Andrews Air Force Base to meet him when he touched down in Washington.

By two-fifteen, the executive offices were almost up to full staff. Austen wandered into one of the little rooms where people took their coffee breaks and found Jerry Gorman sitting with his hands wrapped around a cup of hot soup. From the expression on his face, he was another one who was considering the bleak prospects of his career in the federal service. They were alone, so Austen closed the door behind himself. The sound of the lock clicking shut made Gorman look up.

"Frank? Why isn't Howard here? I can't figure it—nobody can reach him."

"Does that bother you, Jerry? You don't have to be chained to Howard Diederich, you know."

In the moment of silence that followed, Jerry seemed to come to a complete new understanding of himself. You could read it in his face; he saw a chance to survive.

"What should I do, Frank?"

"What you should do is remember that you're the appointments secretary. What you should do is make sure that I'm the first person who sees the new president tomorrow morning. The very first person. If that happens, then things can go on very happily for you. Am I making myself clear, Jerry?"

"Very clear. Are you going to wait around here for Donovan to arrive?"

"No. I'm going home."

But what he did was go over to the living quarters in the East Wing. There was only a single Marine guard on the president's bedroom door.

Within five hours of his death Simon Faircliff seemed to have been completely forgotten. Between now and the moment after Bob Donovan returned to Washington and the official announcement was made, Simon Faircliff would be consigned to that limbo inhabited by the merely mortal. He was stretched out on the bed, still wearing his dark blue pinstripe suit, and his hands were folded together over his belt buckle. No one had even thought to close his eyes, so his son-in-law performed that service for him.

Strangely, it was only with Faircliff that Austen could experience any peace of mind. He drew up a chair and sat down, studying the dead face and realizing that probably for as long as he lived he would be nothing more than an attenuated version of this man whom he had loved and served and, finally, murdered. The bond of loyalty remained unsevered; there simply wasn't a thing in the world he could do about it.

It was ridiculous—the dead were dead—but he came away from that room with the distinct feeling that he had been forgiven.

No hard feelings. I, at least, understand. You couldn't have done anything else.

He found Dottie sitting in the chair in his study. His briefcase was lying open. The revolver, like some nasty little animal taking its ease, was nestled on the towel in which Austen had so carefully wrapped it, and the tape recorder was out on the desk. He could see that the spools in the cassette were still turning; she hadn't even thought to turn the thing off.

Yes, of course—he should have foreseen that this would happen. It would be part of the judgment on him.

Austen hit the stop button and rewound the cassette. For a long moment, the only sound was the insectlike humming of the machine.

"It'll have to be played once more," he said finally. "The new president will have to hear it, and then maybe we can bury the secret forever. I hope so. It would have been better if you'd never known about any of this."

But she merely stared at him, her brown eyes large and uncomprehending, the expression on her face a mixture of confusion, fear, and distaste. He might have been a man from Mars or a cave dweller; clearly she had lost all sense of him as a human being like herself.

He reached out his hand, trying to touch her on the shoulder, but she shrank away from him with so frank and automatic a revulsion that he drew back almost at once.

"I did what I had to, Dottie. You'll see finally—I just didn't have any choice."

"No?" Her voice had the exhausted quality associated with prolonged physical suffering; she sounded as if she hadn't uttered a syllable in days. "You imagine not?"

For a long time Austen remained standing and his wife sat in his chair, her arms drawn about her shoulders, her gaze fixed on nothing at all, as if she were still alone in the room. Finally she rose and left. A few seconds later he heard the bedroom door slam shut, and he knew it would be a serious mistake to go after her.

There was no sense in going to bed. He had to be at the White House at the crack of dawn, and besides, how would it be possible to sleep? So he sat in his study chair for the rest of the night, trying to figure out just exactly where along the line things could have gone so drastically wrong.

Around five in the morning he went into his bathroom to take a shower and shave. When he had finished dressing and gone downstairs to get some breakfast, he found Dottie sitting at the kitchen table, apparently waiting for him. She was wearing the same charcoal-gray suit she had worn the day he left for California and Pete Freestone's funeral. It was difficult to believe that was only a little over a week ago.

"I'll stay until after the funeral," she said. "I don't want to make trouble for anyone, so I'll do what's required, but I want you to see to it that I'm in California by that night."

Austen nodded. "If it's what you want."

"I don't see that what I *want* has anything to do with it."

He sat down in the chair opposite. Dottie looked very haggard. The pouches under her eyes were heavy and dark, and her temples seemed to have shrunken in a single night. "I'm not passing judgment," she went on, seemingly as calm as if she were discussing a misfortune in the lives of strangers. She held a set of car keys in her hand and was absentmindedly using the flat edge of one of them to scrape the polish from her left thumbnail. Somehow it was a cruel thing to watch. "You and Daddy always had your own rules; I gather he didn't hold it against you. Maybe you really didn't have a choice. I just don't see that there's any chance we can continue living together after this."

"There's a lot you don't understand. There's . . ."

When he saw the way she was looking at him, the words seemed to die in his throat. He couldn't even remember what they were supposed to have been. She was right, of course—words, reasons, anything he could say now meant nothing.

"You knew," she said finally, as if it were something she had only just discovered. "You knew. You've known for years, and you never said a word to me. You let me go on . . . You let us . . ."

"Yes."

"Was it that important?"

Implied in the question was the assumption that it couldn't have been—that nothing could have been.

"Yes. It was that important."

"Damn you, Frank." Slowly her hands curled into fists until the knuckles turned white. The keys must have been cutting her palm, but she didn't seem to notice. "Goddamn you, Frank. You've done it for both of us."

After a minute or two, he got up from the table and went outside. The sun was up, and already the men from the Secret Service were sitting in a pair of light gray government cars parked along the curb. They must have been there most of the night.

And that was the end of it.

*   *   *

That night she slept in her aunt's house in Pacific Grove. Austen didn't find it at all difficult to imagine that he might never see her again.

But for that first terrible day at least, there were still plenty of things to keep a growing boy from brooding too much on his domestic troubles. For one thing, the new president of the United States had to be told that his predecessor in office had been a Russian agent. It took some explaining—that sort of thing isn't easily come to terms with—but after some documentary preparation, a playing of the tape that had convinced Dottie convinced Bob Donovan as well.

He sat staring at Austen from the other side of Simon Faircliff's desk—he had only been back in town for four hours and hardly even knew where the men's room was yet—and it was obvious that the first thought in his mind was how his own position was affected by this appalling disclosure. It was Donovan's great weakness that he could never see beyond his own political self-interest.

"It's hard to believe," he said, running a hand through his curly silver-and-black hair. His eyes glittered nervously. "It's goddamn near impossible to believe."

"Nevertheless, it's true."

Donovan's handsome face split into a lopsided, willfully charming smile, reminding you why Simon had always referred to him as "the matinee idol."

"I don't know why I don't just have you arrested. Your precious Simon Faircliff may or may not have been a traitor, but in case it might have slipped your mind, you've just confessed to having assassinated him."

"He was never a traitor. He was a deep-cover agent but still technically a Soviet citizen. You can't betray a country that isn't your own."

The new president didn't seem to much appreciate having the distinction drawn for him, but to hell with what he might or might not appreciate. Austen allowed himself to slouch contemptuously back in his chair. Donovan was such a lightweight he probably had to wear special shoes to keep from floating away.

"You know, Bob, I never thought you were very bright, but I would have given you credit for enough simple animal cunning to know not to foul your own nest. What do you think this is, some crummy little night-court case? *You're* the president now, remember? Just how do you plan to stay the president if it gets noised about that Simon was a Russian agent?"

"Are you threatening me, Frank?"

Austen would have laughed out loud if this donkey hadn't been sitting in Simon Faircliff's chair.

"No, I'm not threatening anyone." Austen shook his head. "I'm just reminding you of the facts of life. If the way Simon died comes out, then it'll become impossible to keep his secret, and it won't be a matter of my exposing him to save my own hide; people are going to ask questions about a thing like that, and what I figured out somebody else can figure out. And then, pal, the institution of the presidency—and just by the way, your own personal standing; remember, it was Simon who raised you to glory—is going to be so compromised that you might as well just go home to Minnesota."

Donovan leaned forward, resting his slender hands on the edge of the desk, and frowned. "So what happens now?"

"So now you kill the treaty." Austen reached into his briefcase and pulled out a thick black briefing book. "There's our true strategic position with respect to Russia," he went on, dropping the briefing book heavily on the desk. "You read that and you'll know where we are and where they are, and then you kill the treaty. And then we can all sleep safe in our beds."

"And what about Simon?"

"What about him?" He stared at the man behind Simon Faircliff's desk as if the individual words of his question made no sense. "We bury him. And we bury his nasty little secret with him."

"Yes, but Howard . . . "

"Howard Diederich will put in a few selected public appearances—carefully supervised and up to his hairline in Thorazine if need be—and then, in about another week, he'll be found dead in his bathtub with his wrists slashed."

"Oh, God . . ." Donovan closed his eyes and turned his head away as if he could see the thing happening right in front of him.

"You asked, didn't you?" Austen's face was an impassive, brutal mask, and his voice harsh and unsympathetic. The fact was that he found he had used up his store of compassion. There just wasn't any left for Bob Donovan's moral qualms. "You'll have to learn to live with it. I'll just keep hold of the evidence myself," he went on, picking up the tape recording and returning it to his briefcase. "No one but George Timmler and I will know where it's hidden. You bear that in mind, pal; don't get any bright flashes about raids on the vaults at Langley, because it won't be there. In two or three months I'll resign. I'd go now, but some smart investigative reporter might wonder why I'm being purged. You'll appoint George Timmler my successor. He doesn't care anything about politics, and he'll do a good job for you."

"You could stay, Frank, if you wanted to. You know that. The whole country is in your debt. . . ."

"Don't be corny." Austen's face shriveled with distaste; five minutes before, the clown had been threatening to have him thrown in jail. "You'll be glad to see the back of me, and you know it—I don't even blame you. Besides, I was Faircliff's man. I lost my taste for all these games a long time ago."

In the car, on the way back to Langley, he described to George the deal he had cut.

"How are your contacts with the Army Medical Corps, George? I think it might be the better part of valor if we saw to it that somebody took a print of Faircliff's right foot when they do the autopsy. I'd feel a lot better having that little item in the National Archives, just in case."

"No sweat." Timmler nodded, continuing to look straight ahead. "Are you really going to take a walk, Frank?"

"Yes. You'll get your precious Company back in the hands of the career spooks, George. That ought to make you happy."

"Yeah, well . . . What'll you do?"

"I don't know." Austen shrugged as if the matter had never crossed his mind, which, in fact, it hadn't. "Maybe I'll hang out my shingle and practice divorce law in Beverly Hills. Maybe some fool will make me president of a dog food company. Who gives a shit?"

They rode along in silence for a while, past the bleak autumn landscape—the gray buildings, the bare limbs of the cherry trees. It wasn't even ten o'clock in the morning, and already the day seemed advanced in hopeless senility.

"Do you feel like paying a sick call?" Timmler asked

finally. "Howard Diederich—we've got him at a safe house in Bethesda. He wants to see you, and he says he'll make it worth your while."

"Oh, God . . ."

Earl Rutledge opened the door for them. He was in his shirtsleeves, although the temperature outside was only in the middle forties. Once Austen got past the door, he could understand why—the house was like an oven.

It was cooler in the basement, where Howard Diederich occupied a corner of the floor, trussed up with a special set of padded chains that wouldn't leave any marks. His arms went around his thighs, and his hands were sticking out between his shins just above the ankles. After fourteen hours it was probably a fairly uncomfortable position.

"Unlock him," Austen told the man who was sitting at the foot of the stairs with a shotgun across his knees.

"Rutledge has got the key," he answered, without moving.

"Then go upstairs and get the key from Rutledge."

Two minutes later Diederich was able to stretch his legs out at full length, and after the circulation returned to his feet he got up and walked around a little.

"Thanks, Austen—mighty white of you." He smiled one of his curious, exhausted smiles and then bent over and let his arms dangle in an effort to touch his toes. He was about four inches short. After several seconds he straightened up again, his face pink from the blood that had rushed to his head and his mocking smile still in place.

Austen glanced at the man with the shotgun, who took the hint and returned back upstairs.

"I take it that Simon's already dead," Diederich said tonelessly as soon as they were alone. All during their conversation, he kept shifting his weight from one leg to the other, which might have been nerves or simply a reaction to his hours of sitting on the floor.

Austen nodded. "Since last night."

"Who did it?"

"I did it."

Diederich's eyes widened slightly. "Well, I'm sure he appreciated all the personal attention. And you've told Donovan?"

Austen nodded a second time.

"And he didn't wet his pants and send for the FBI?"

"As you see, I'm here."

"Yes, you are, Frank," Diederich answered, his smile having finally disappeared. "Yes, you certainly are."

"What was it you wanted, Howard?"

"A deal—a chance to save my life."

"It's a bit late for that."

"And besides, I haven't got anything to deal with. Am I right?"

The two men stood at opposite sides of the basement, in the dull yellow light from a single naked bulb, and Austen was suddenly struck by how little triumph the moment afforded him. He simply wanted to get away, as if from the scene of some personal humiliation. Toward Howard Diederich he felt nothing, nothing at all. It was like looking at a photograph of some stranger's corpse.

"Then I take it you didn't summon me here for any practical purpose."

"No." Diederich shook his head, and the trace of a smile returned to his lips. "I just wanted you to see me like this. So that when those two goons upstairs kill me, it won't be just like canceling a stamp for you. You always had such a tender conscience, Frank—I just wanted you to remember me."

Austen didn't wait to hear any more. He turned on his heel and went back upstairs.

When the national shockwaves had subsided a little and Austen could walk onto his front lawn without stumbling over an army of reporters, he turned his duties over to George Timmler and submitted his resignation. They didn't really need him at Langley—George had been running things for all practical purposes since President Faircliff's death—and his heart wasn't in it.

He really didn't have any idea what he would do with the rest of his life—it hardly seemed to matter. Simon was dead. Dottie was on the other side of the continent, and even further than that in the ways that counted. After Howard Diederich's "suicide" there weren't even any enemies left anymore. Like old Zinoviev, who was still a prisoner at Fishing Bay—who would die there, certainly—he had become a captive by outliving the past in which he had had a place.

It was like being dead.

For a solid month after his retirement he sat in his study at home, watching the rain on the picture window, wondering whether there would ever come a point when whatever makes these decisions in a random universe would decide that he had done penance enough. He ate peanut butter sandwiches and drank tea, and once in a while he would go to a movie, where no one would recognize him and he could sit in the dark and watch fantasies about a full-color world in which the actions of people's lives were bounded by dramatic convention and the four straight lines of the projection screen.

But mostly he just stared through his window, thinking of those ten boys. All that bright promise, to end up in unmarked graves, God only knew where, to have even their murders taken from them—because what else is it when a total stranger takes over your life and goes on living it in your place? And their parents, and all the rest. Dottie's mother, and Mike Starkman, and Pete, and Ted Boothe and his wife, and Clayton Burgess, and . . . probably no one would ever know exactly how many more. All that death—and for not a goddamned thing.

Soroka had been mad, out of his mind. It had taken a madman to conceive of a thing like that. And he would die, someday, down in the cellars of the house at Fishing Bay, forgotten and alone. Maybe there was some kind of justice in that, but Austen found it hard to experience any sense of it.

"*Facilis descensus averno,*" the picture said. True enough. "I don't think we really need anything but the truth," Dottie had told him once. Bingo again.

And the truth was that Frank Austen needed his wife, needed her so badly that sometimes he thought he might just die of that alone. But standing in the wreckage of his life, he was still, in point of fact, alive—alive enough to know his own emptiness. *I am in despair; therefore I am.* And Dottie was alive too. Unlike so many others, they had at least survived.

"I'm tired of being dead."

At first he didn't recognize the voice. And then, with a disagreeable shock, he realized that it was his own.

"I'm tired of being dead," he repeated, just to be on the safe side.

So what the hell. He had been sitting around and feeling

bad for four solid months; the worst she could do was slam the door in his face. She would probably do just that, but that wouldn't kill either one of them. *I don't think we really need anything but the truth.* It was possible that after all this time she might be ready at least to listen.

He went into his bedroom to throw a couple of shirts and some underwear into a suitcase. He would phone; there would probably be a plane out to California that night. It was worth a try.

Suspense, Intrigue & International Danger

These novels of espionage and excitement-filled tension will guarantee you the best in high-voltage reading pleasure.

THE PRESIDENT'S MAN
by Nicholas Guild 46008/$3.50
THE BRINK by N.J. Crisp 45605/$3.50
RED OMEGA by John Kruse 44670/$3.50
SCHISM by Bill Granger 45274/$3.50
THE HASTINGS CONSPIRACY
by Alfred Coppel 47508/$3.50
FREE FLIGHT by Douglas Terman 42735/$2.95
FIRST STRIKE by Douglas Terman 45051/$3.50
CATCH A FALLING SPY by Len Deighton
44259/$2.75

POCKET BOOKS